Deadly Mixture

Pine County book 8

Dean L. Hovey

Print ISBNs
Amazon Print 9780228619086
LSI Print 9780228619093
B&N Print 9780228619109

BWL Publishing Inc.

Books we love to write ...
Authors around the world.

http://bwlpublishing.ca

Acknowledgements

As always, the assistance of many people made this a much better book. Julie does the initial review and corrects my medical diagnoses, terminology, and improves the characters, making sure they've stayed true to their roots as established in the earlier Pine County mysteries.

Frannie Brozo and Deanna Wilson urged me to forge ahead with this story when I stalled. If not for their encouragement, the rough manuscript might've been relegated to the electronic equivalent of a dusty shelf. Deanna Wilson urged me to create a new deputy and her unique life experiences added depth to the new C.J. Jensen character. She also contributed Bailey the basset hound and suggested some of the dog's colorful antics. As usual, she made sure the cop stuff is right. I tapped Kinsley Wilson for perspective on teen dialogue and slang. Her assistance added texture and realism to the teen characters and made their conversations age and time appropriate. Mike Westfall proofed and offered thoughts about the overall plot, character interactions, and dialogue. Natalie Lund and Anne Flagge proofread and offered input. My friends at BWL Publishing again came through for me. Jude Pittman, thanks for your suggestions and support. Michelle Lee again designed an interesting and engaging cover.

This book is a work of fiction. The plot, characters, and locations are products of the author's imagination. Any resemblance to actual events, people, or places is unintended. Any real locations are used fictionally.

Dedication

To Sue Kotowski

"It is nothing but you and the cows and the sirens. You are seeing more violence, and you never know where your backup is coming from." -Sgt. Brenton Davidson, Ross County (Ohio) Sheriff's Department

Chapter 1

Tammi Wagner stepped into the halo of light cast by the gas lantern. "Thanks for waiting, jerks."

Dylan Johnson's response was a sneer. "We weren't sure you were coming."

Ted Palmquist followed Tammi and closed the door. He wrapped his arms around himself and shivered, the autumn chill penetrating his un-lined jacket. "I wish we could start a fire in the stove."

"Yeah. Everyone in the county would know we're here then, dumbass," Dylan muttered in disgust.

Tammi dropped her book bag against the wall and sat on the floor cross-legged. "So, what are you holding?" She accepted the marijuana joint Dylan and Brady Werther had been sharing and inhaled deeply.

Dylan pulled a small glass container from his pocket and shook it in front of Tammi. "We did it. We made our own meth."

She blew out the smoke she'd held in her lungs and took a couple deep breaths before asking, "So, how is it?"

Brady opened his mouth to speak but was cut off by Dylan. "It's great. It's the best rush ever. Better than the stuff we were buying." Brady drew a toke and scowled.

Dylan spilled a few crystals from the vial onto a cigarette paper while Brady passed the last of the joint back to Tammi. "Here, try it." She eyed the crystals suspiciously while she inhaled the marijuana smoke.

Ted watched the activity without being invited to join. He went to a small sink and worked the lever on a hand pump until a trickle of water spilled out. He leaned down and drank directly from the spout.

After Tammi blew out the smoke, she took the cigarette paper from Dylan's hand and examined it skeptically. "This isn't powdery, like we usually get."

Dylan tapped the vial. "This is pure."

"It's really good?" she asked.

"Great!" Dylan exclaimed.

Brady shrugged.

Tammi poured the crystals into a glass pipe and held a butane lighter under the bulb. When smoke filled the glass, she inhaled.

Choking, she jumped up and ran to the sink, pumping frantically. When the water finally flowed, she drew water into her mouth and then spit it into the sink. "God, the water tastes almost as bad as the meth." She rubbed her tongue with her finger and then pumped more water. "Yuk!"

Brady started to giggle, and soon Dylan also had the giggles. When Tammi returned to the table, Ted sat down beside her. "You getting a rush?"

Tammi held out her shaking hand. "Yeah."

"What's so funny, Brady?" Ted asked.

Brady controlled his laughter long enough to explain, "No one else has tried the meth. We were afraid."

Tammi looked between them nervously. "That's not funny. Tell me you're kidding."

Dylan and Brady broke into unrestrained giggles again. The high from the marijuana made everything funny.

"We found an internet recipe for fish tank meth. It's a cold recipe and the crystals grow on a string inside a bucket." He paused. "We were afraid to try it."

"This sucks, big time," Tammi said. "I spent all afternoon trying to keep my mother's boyfriend from pawing me. Then, you guys feed me your latest experiment."

"Hey, none of us have a great life," Brady replied. "You should try living with ten people in a two-bedroom house some time. There is no such thing as a private phone call."

A few minutes later, Tammi held her hand to her chest. "You guys, this isn't funny. My heart is pounding. I think you made a bad batch." Her voice was tinged with fear.

Dylan reached across the corner of the table and put a hand on her breast. "It feels fine to me."

Tammi batted his hand away, crossing her arms across her chest. "This is not funny!"

Dylan slid next to her and pulled her close. Previous sampling of commercial meth had produced euphoria, lowered inhibitions, and a rising libido. "I've got just the thing to make you feel better." He tried to kiss her, but she pushed him away.

"I can't breathe, I gotta go outside." She staggered to the door while Dylan and Brady laughed.

Ted followed her out the door and found her retching against the siding while the first snowflakes of autumn drifted to the ground around her. He knelt down and put an arm over her shoulders. "You okay?" he asked.

Tears stained her face and spittle dribbled down her chin. She gasped for breath. "Those idiots poisoned me," she said in short gasps.

Gathering all her willpower, Tammi rose from the ground and stumbled inside with Ted close behind. Dylan and Brady watched in amusement as Tammi dug through her school bag. When she withdrew a revolver, they jumped up and raised their hands.

Dylan was the first to react. "Take it easy. You'll be alright in a couple hours."

Tammi's breath came in short gasps as she pointed the gun at Dylan with shaking hands. "You poisoned me."

Ted and Brady edged toward the door. Dylan grabbed Tammi's wrist and wrestled for control of the gun. The deafening gunshot filled the small shack, the flash blinding them.

Chapter 2

April 2021

Ted Palmquist stumbled home at midnight. The nausea had been almost unbearable throughout the day. Smoking marijuana eased it during the evening, but now waves of nausea coursed through his body with a vengeance. Ted stripped to his boxers, leaving his dirty jeans and t-shirt on the bedroom floor. As he crawled under the sheet, sweat bathed his body. He closed his eyes briefly only to have bile rise in his throat. He rushed to the bathroom.

He retched violently, then stared at the bloody spittle dribbling down his chest and floated atop the water in the toilet. "God! I think I threw up a chunk of lung," he moaned. He rolled against the wall in an effort to regain enough strength to walk back to the bedroom. A chill ran through his body, and he wrapped his arms around his knobby knees to conserve body heat.

His mother's voice jolted him. "Whatcha been drinkin'? Beer? Cheap wine?" She was wrapped in a tattered, chenille bathrobe. A cigarette dangled from her lip, the smoke curling around her face like a halo. The lines in her face were harsh, accentuated by the fluorescent light.

He closed his eyes. "Nothin'."

"I've seen drunks puking in the toilet before," she said contemptuously. She turned and walked away. Ted made sure that she was gone, then tried to stand up. Supported by the toilet tank, he tottered for a second before darkness swept over him. His muscles turned to gelatin as his brain shut down. His head hit the floor making the sound of a dropped melon.

Cheryl heard the noise and walked back to the bathroom. A look of disgust swept her fleshy cheeks as she looked at the boy's prostrate body. "I ain't putting you to bed. You can sleep right there. It'll be a good lesson." She was about to turn away when she noticed the blood on Ted's chest and trickling from the corner of his mouth. She shuffled across the tile floor and leaned close to Ted's face.

She tossed her cigarette into the toilet and her stomach turned. The cigarette butt lay on top of what looked like pure blood. Her voice was uncharacteristically gentle. She bent down and shook the boy's shoulder. "Ted. Wake up. What's wrong with you?" When he didn't respond, she felt for a pulse in his wrist. It was so rapid and faint she could barely feel it.

She knelt next to him, pushing the long, brown hair back from her son's face. She was shocked at how pale he looked. His ribs showed through the skin of his chest and his forehead was clammy and damp to her touch. She slid next to him onto the floor and rested on her elbow, gently touching the blood at the corner of his mouth. Her fingertip turned crimson. She noticed several bruises on the boy's arms and legs and wondered if he'd been in a fight.

* * *

The dispatcher punched the flashing button in the Pine County Emergency Services Center. "Pine County 911, how can I help you?" The display indicated the call was coming from an address in Pine City.

"My son is throwing up blood and has passed out."

"Ma'am, is he breathing?" The operator pressed the auto call number for the Sandstone hospital ambulance and typed in the caller's address. The computerized message went to all the sheriff's radios and volunteer firemen's cellphones as the radio sounded, signaling the Sandstone hospital to dispatch the ambulance.

"Umm, just barely. His heart's going so fast I can't count the pulse." Cheryl's voice was starting to quiver.

"Take it easy, ma'am. I've got an ambulance on the way. Where is he now?"

"On the bathroom floor." The operator heard Cheryl take a deep breath. "Is he...going to live?"

"I've dispatched an ambulance. They'll take care of him. Check his breathing and pulse, then come right back."

The phone clattered to the countertop, and the operator could hear Cheryl's slippers slapping on the linoleum floor, fading, and returning. "Yeah, he's breathing, but he's getting worse. Tell them to hurry." The phone clicked and Cheryl was gone before the dispatcher could tell her to stay on the phone. There was no answer when the dispatcher dialed Palmquist's phone number.

* * *

The night nurse's call rousted Bert Mlankoch, M.D., from bed. The nurse said an unconscious patient was coming by ambulance and had been vomiting blood. Bert quickly ran through the possibilities in his mind, then told the nurse to set up an endoscope. He suspected a patient with a perforated ulcer. Nothing in his twelve years as a family practitioner prepared him for Ted Palmquist.

The paramedics were standing near the emergency room desk when Dr. Mlankoch rushed in, his face tired, and his thinning brown hair sticking out at every angle. His denim shirttails were flagging outside his jeans, and his bare feet were in L.L. Bean boots. Mlankoch looked more like a tired farmer than the on-call doctor.

The local family practitioners rotated emergency room duty at the Sandstone hospital. Calls usually involved stitching minor cuts and sometimes delivering a baby if the hospital couldn't contact an obstetrician. The nearest trauma center was North Memorial Hospital about seventy-five miles away. All major car accident victims and severe trauma cases were sent to North Memorial by ambulance or were stabilized in the emergency room before being airlifted.

"How's the patient?" Mlankoch peeled off his denim jacket and threw it on the counter at the nurses' station. His hair had been roughly combed through his fingers and there was a shadow of a beard on his chin. Tina Banks, the night nurse, had given him a brief review of the situation on his cell phone as he had driven to the hospital.

Tina read from her notes as the paramedics stood by. *"The patient is shocky. Appears dehydrated. Stomach is doughy. Was vomiting blood. The paramedics started a saline I.V."*

"How old is this guy?" The doctor asked the ambulance crew as he pulled on a blue disposable gown.

The older paramedic shrugged. "Maybe late teens. It's kinda hard to tell. He's pretty thin and his gray pallor makes him look older."

Mlankoch brushed past the paramedics without further comment and entered the corridor that led to the ER examining rooms. The nurse followed close behind. Blocking one of the exam room doors was a large woman wearing a green Pine City Dragons jacket over a pink chenille robe. "Excuse me, ma'am."

Cheryl Palmquist turned and stared at Mlankoch without moving from the doorway. Her family physician was fifty and fat, in contrast to Mlankoch who was in his mid-thirties and slender. "Who are you?" The woman asked in a raspy voice. Layers of jacket and robe failed to hide the fleshy folds of her neck. Her face was leathery from smoking, and it drooped with age.

"I'm the doctor. Are you the boy's mother?" Mlankoch asked.

She nodded and backed out of the door, revealing the body lying on the exam table. The boy was thin and emaciated. EKG electrodes with red centers dotted his hairless chest. Mlankoch logged onto the room's computer monitor. He noted the irregular beeps of the EKG monitor as he scanned through Ted Palmquist's medical record. Turning away from the computer, he saw Tina Banks, the emergency room nurse, with a grim expression on her face.

Mlankoch put his stethoscope on the boy's bare chest. The patient's ribs pressed against taut skin. His arms and torso were covered with bruises and open sores. Mlankoch glanced at the nurse with eyebrows raised. He leaned over and gently palpated the patient's abdomen. "It looks like we have an abuse case," he whispered.

Tina nodded as she adjusted an EKG lead, then looked at the overhead monitor, beeping with each heartbeat.

"Call the sheriff, then have the lab draw blood for a CBC and blood gasses.

* * *

Floyd Swenson's unmarked cruiser sat hidden in a small gap in brush along a gravel road, just as it had for the four previous nights. A neighbor supplied a tip that owners of the property had been poaching deer, and the Department of Natural Resources conservation officer had requested assistance with surveillance. Floyd had been watching a darkened farmhouse for four hours. As a sergeant for Pine County, he had the option of taking or delegating jobs like this. Aside from some burglaries of seasonal cabins, Pine County crime had been slow, and Floyd had taken this job himself to get out of the office and avoid paperwork.

The radio crackled to life, jarring Floyd from thoughts about his fiancée's proposal to sell their houses and consolidate into a place nearer her flower shop. The dispatcher requested any unit to respond to an emergency call at the Sandstone hospital. Floyd looked at the darkened, quiet house and picked up the radio mic.

Announcing his unit number, he said, "I'll take the call for the hospital. Anyone available for backup?"

Floyd started the engine without turning on the lights and eased out of the roadside bushes that had hidden his car. He drove half a mile before turning on the headlights and went another mile before lighting the car's red and blue flashers. There were no other vehicles on the gravel roads from his stakeout southwest of town. He covered the distance in 12 minutes, the speedometer wavering around 128 mph once he hit blacktop five miles from the freeway.

When Floyd arrived at the hospital, the only other cars in the emergency room parking lot were an aging Ford Escort parked next to the emergency room entrance and the assorted employee cars and pickups in the back of the parking lot. Floyd parked and hurried into the carpeted lobby. A receptionist in blue scrubs sat at the reception desk talking to the nurse. Tina gestured toward the exam rooms and Floyd walked down the hall to where a large woman was blocking the door. He looked over her shoulder into the room.

Dr. Bert Mlankoch was standing at the exam table carefully cutting underwear from a young male patient while his mother, wrapped in a green jacket and pink bathrobe, stood in the doorway. Floyd's first impression was that the ashen body on the exam table was dead. The only sign of life was the slow "beep, beep, beep" of the EKG monitor next to the bed. Suddenly, the boy's chest heaved as he took a deep breath.

Cheryl Palmquist turned to look at Floyd, giving him a quizzical look after glancing at his uniform and badge. Floyd was eight inches taller, but probably weighed forty pounds less. "Who are you?"

"I'm a deputy. Are you the boy's mother?" After studying the woman's face for a moment, he recognized Cheryl Palmquist. He'd arrested her for a DWI a year or two earlier and recalled that her car was outside the Beroun bar most Friday and Saturday evenings until closing time. He knew she went home alone most evenings after the bar closed, unless she found a friend to who invited her over for the night.

"Yep," Cheryl Palmquist replied with obvious annoyance.

"What happened to him?" Floyd asked.

She turned back to the scene in the room. "He was out with his buddies drinking, then came home puking blood." Her voice was matter of fact. "I wonder if he got beat up, too."

Floyd watched as the doctor threw the last of the boy's clothing into a wastebasket marked with a biohazard symbol. Mlankoch touched a couple of the sores on the boy's limbs with a latex-gloved hand. The patient's arms and legs were covered with bruises, making Floyd wonder if it was Cheryl who'd beaten her son.

Mlankoch pinched the skin of the boy's belly and released it. The boy moaned and squirmed under the pinch but didn't regain consciousness. The skin stayed in a mound for a second after the pinch then slowly sank back.

"He's still badly dehydrated," Mlankoch commented, looking at the IV bag running fluids into the boy's arm. "Even after a liter of fluids."

Floyd leaned over the woman's shoulder. "Do you know if he was in a fight or car accident?"

Cheryl shrugged. "I was asleep when he got home."

At the sound of Floyd's voice, Mlankoch looked up and motioned for Floyd to enter the room.

"Excuse me." Floyd said, pushing past Cheryl Palmquist. He walked to Mlankoch and leaned close. "What's up?"

Mlankoch stared at the liquid dripping from the IV set. He pulled a sheet and blanket over Ted Palmquist's naked torso. The patient twisted with the stimulus of the sheet sliding over his skin.

"Not now, Tammi," the boy whispered.

"Who's Tammi?" Floyd asked.

"Beats me," the doctor replied. "He's mentioned her a couple of times."

"Do you think she had something to do with his condition?" Swenson pointed at the bruised arms and torso.

"I suspected abuse at first," the doctor whispered. "You know, with the doting mother and all. Now I'm not sure. The open sores throw me." He touched one of them with the latex-gloved finger, and then looked up at Cheryl Palmquist. "The mother shouldn't be in here. Could you escort her to the waiting room and send Tina back?"

Floyd nodded and walked to Cheryl. "Ma'am, you've got to go out to the waiting room." He gently took her fleshy arm and led her down the hallway. She offered no resistance.

Two paramedics were drinking coffee at the nurses' station. Deputy C.J. Jensen scribbled notes in a small spiral bound pad as she spoke to the nurse.

Floyd released Cheryl Palmquist's elbow. "Why don't you take a seat for a while?" He directed her to the chairs in the empty waiting area.

She looked around nervously. "Can I smoke in here? I don't see an ashtray."

Floyd shook his head. "Outside." She nodded and waddled out the door while digging a pack of Marlboros from the purse draped over her arm.

Floyd interrupted Jensen's questioning. "Excuse me. Tina, the doc wants you in the exam room." An alarm went off down the hall as the nurse stepped away. Tina's pace shifted from a walk to a trot as she rounded the corner to the hallway. Floyd followed with Deputy Jensen and the paramedics close behind.

C.J. looked at Floyd. "If you've got this covered, I'll go back on patrol."

Floyd hesitated. "Hang around for a while."

As Floyd walked toward the exam room, Tina pulled a red cart from a hallway alcove and hurried it into the room where Mlankoch was drawing liquid into a syringe. He plunged the long needle into the boy's chest over his heart. Tina pulled open a case from the top of the cart, withdrew a package, and stripped it open. She took the two orange pads and placed them on the boy's chest. Next, she removed the cardioversion paddles from a yellow plastic case. Holding them high, she pushed a button and a red light started blinking inside the case. Mlankoch started CPR on the boy's chest.

Mlankoch glanced at Floyd. "Is the mother gone?"

"She went out for a smoke." Floyd put a hand on C.J.'s shoulder. "Keep the mother in the lobby." As C.J. walked away Floyd motioned the two paramedics into the room. He closed the door, pushed his back against it, and held the handle. The paramedics moved to the corner of the room and watched the unfolding drama, ready to assist if asked.

Tina handed the defibrillator paddles to Mlankoch. The EKG trace was flat, and the machine's high-pitched alarm added an air of insanity to the scene. Mlankoch stopped CPR, took the paddles from the nurse, and held them against the boy's chest. When the red light turned green, he pulled a trigger in the handles. Electricity pulsed into the boy's chest, causing his body to convulse. Mlankoch looked up at the monitor. The EKG trace spiked off the top of the scale, then came back and remained flat. Mlankoch nodded to one of the EMTs, who started CPR. Everyone watched the flat EKG line. Tina inserted an airway into the boy's throat while the defibrillator recharged.

"Damn. What's with this kid?" Mlankoch watched the EMT compress the boy's chest rhythmically. Tina finished placing the airway and attached a ventilation bag to the plastic tube. She squeezed the bag with both hands, watching the boy's chest rise.

"Clear!" Tina announced as the defibrillator light turned green. The EMT and nurse stepped back as Mlankoch released another electrical pulse. The body's spasm was less spectacular this time. The heart monitor spiked as the charge passed, then immediately went flat again.

Mlankoch turned to the paramedic, "Jack, keep the CPR going." He compressed the boy's chest as Tina squeezed the bag, forcing oxygen into the boy's lungs after every fifth compression.

Mlankoch threw the paddles aside and pulled up the boy's eyelids. He felt the carotid artery in the boy's neck. "Damn, this shouldn't be so hard, he's just a kid." The doctor took a syringe from the cart and selected a medication. He drew up the solution and injected it into a port on the IV tubing as the light on the defibrillator console turned green.

"Stand back, Jack, I'm giving him a jolt."

The doctor positioned the defibrillator paddles on the boy's chest. "Clear!" He pulled the trigger, and the body gave a weak spasm.

Mlankoch watched as the EKG monitor spiked again only to go flat. Jack was compressing the boy's chest again. Mlankoch raised one of the boy's eyelids, finding a fully dilated pupil. He looked up at Tina as energy drained from his body. "We've lost him." He put a hand on Jack's arm. "You can stop." He looked at the clock. "Tina, the time of death is 1:23."

Mlankoch stripped off his surgical gloves and threw them into a biohazard bin. Stepping out of the treatment room he drew a deep breath and leaned against the wall, composing himself. Medical school never prepared students for delivering the news of a child's death to his parents, the most unpleasant task imaginable.

Recoiling when he felt a touch on his shoulder, Mlankoch turned to Floyd Swenson who looked equally tired. "What happened?" Floyd asked.

The doctor nodded. "I'm not sure what was going on. He crashed and we couldn't revive him."

"What do you think about his bruises?"

"I don't know what to think. He's covered with them."

Floyd looked toward the exit sign. "His mother is outside smoking. Do you think she beat him?"

"They're not from blunt force and she…doesn't seem like the type. She was in shock when he came in. I didn't see anything in her demeanor that pointed toward abuse."

"Was he ever lucid?"

"Not really. You heard him utter some unintelligible things, but I couldn't ask him a question."

"Did he say what happened before I arrived?"

The doctor shook his head. "Just ramblings and random nonsense. He mentioned Tammi a couple times. Oh, and something buried. When I asked where he'd been, he said, 'the fort.' It was nonsense, Floyd."

Their eyes met, both men tired and emotionally drained. Floyd reached out and put his hand on the doctor's arm. "You did all you could."

"It wasn't enough, Floyd. I have to tell the boy's mother he died."

Floyd followed the doctor into the waiting room. Mlankoch spoke to Ted's mother. She broke into tears and fell into a chair.

Floyd walked out of the hospital and saw the deputy leaning against the fender of her car. "C.J., the kid died. We've got to talk to his friends tomorrow."

"You sound strange, Floyd. Are you okay?"

"I'm just tired. We'll talk tomorrow."

Chapter 3

Mary stirred when Floyd crawled into bed. "What time is it?" She didn't open her eyes.

"About five." He slid his feet under the blankets and pulled the sheet up to his chin.

Mary recoiled from the cool surface of his skin. "Did you catch the poachers?"

He hesitated. "No poachers tonight."

She was sliding back into sleep. "Mmm. Too bad."

He lay in bed until five-thirty, haunted by scenes from the emergency room every time he closed his eyes. Finally conceding there'd be no sleep, he got up, made a pot of coffee, and sat down at the computer. He tried to write a report of the hospital events but gave up and played solitaire until Mary's alarm went off at six. When she walked into the living room, he was losing the twenty-second straight game.

"Did you get any sleep?" She ran a hand through her hair, now graying at the temples. She hadn't decided yet if she were vain enough to pay a hairdresser to hide it.

"Not really."

Pushing his chair back, she sat on his lap. "What happened? A night of chasing poachers doesn't usually affect you."

"We got a call about a problem at the hospital. A kid was there with bruises all over his body. Doc Mlankoch thought that maybe the boy had been beaten, so he called us in. Now he's not sure why the kid was bruised."

Mary gave Floyd a quizzical look. "He was bruised and the doctor's not sure he was beaten? Car accident?"

"His mother said no. The kid's mouth was full of sores, and he'd been vomiting blood. Looks like we'll have to wait for the autopsy to get a final answer."

"Autopsy? He died?"

Floyd nodded dumbly. "They couldn't save him. The boy had a heart attack and wouldn't come around."

Mary closed her eyes. "Oh Lord. How old was he?"

Floyd took a deep breath. "The mother said eighteen. His body was really in bad shape, dehydrated and covered with bruises and sores. The whole event was ugly."

Mary kissed Floyd on the forehead, then pushed a hand through his hair. "You want some breakfast? I was going to make oatmeal."

Floyd grimaced. "Oatmeal?"

"It keeps you regular and lowers your cholesterol." She eased off his lap and walked into the kitchen. "When's the autopsy?"

"The body is still in the hospital. They'll call the medical examiner in Duluth this morning to arrange a pickup."

The pots clattered and water ran in the kitchen. "You're having Tony do it? Why not wait for the pathologist to make his weekly trip to Sandstone instead of paying the medical examiner to do it?"

Floyd peeked around the corner. "Doc Mlankoch thinks that this is really unusual. We talked and decided it would be best to have the medical examiner look at the body. Just in case there's something more than meets the eye."

"What's Doc Mlankoch's gut say?"

Floyd paused. "Honey, this is not for the gossip mongers at the flower shop. Okay?" He waited for Mary to nod assent. She enjoyed sharing information with the people at work, but also realized some matters were not public information. "Mlankoch thinks the boy may have been poisoned."

An avid mystery reader, Mary perked up at the suggestion of deeper intrigue. "Like the arsenic eaters in the old mystery novels?"

"Something like that. Maybe something a little more modern than arsenic."

Mary measured water and oatmeal into a pot and set it on the stove. "So, what're you going to do now? I mean, is it a police matter?"

Floyd slid a chair back from the kitchen table and fingered the pepper grinder. "It may be. C.J. and I are going to try and find the kid's friends and talk to them. You know, see if he had a problem with anyone. It'll be more interesting than sitting around waiting for a poacher."

"How is C.J. working out? You'd hoped her city experience would give her a leg up over hiring a rookie."

"She's good. I hope the sheriff can figure out how to hire her permanently after Pam returns from maternity leave."

"Can he do that?"

Floyd sighed. "I'm not sure. He'll have to get the county board to give him permission to add an officer unless someone leaves or retires."

"It'd be a shame to lose her if she's as good as you say."

* * *

Picking up the radio mic, Floyd announced he was on duty before he drove out of his yard. He was barely on the road when C.J. Jensen called in as she left her home. Picking up his cell phone, he punched in C.J.'s phone number and asked her to meet him at the Willow River High School parking lot, midway between their homes.

Her cruiser was parked near the center of the empty lot when he turned off the county road.

He rolled down his window when they were side by side. "I'm talking to the Pine City principal to get a take on Ted Palmquist and his friends."

"Easy girl," C.J. said as she struggled to restrain the basset hound trying to crawl across her lap to greet Floyd. "Okay. I'm taking Bailey to doggy daycare, then I'll be on duty." Bailey was whining and straining against C.J.'s attempts to hold her back.

Floyd stepped out of his car and walked to C.J.'s passenger window. Bailey spun around and lunged against the door, banging her nose on the window and leaving a glob of saliva. C.J. rolled the window down and Floyd reached in. "What a pretty girl," he said, scratching her head and ruffling her ears. "You have such sad eyes."

"Stop it, Bailey! Ouch!" C.J. threw open her door, stepped out, and stood next to the cruiser.

"What's the matter?" Floyd asked, continuing to pet the dog.

"Bailey's tail is deadly. The more you pet her the harder she wags. It's like being beaten with a stick. I'll probably have bruised arms."

Pushing Bailey back from the door, Floyd laughed. "It can't be that bad." He stepped around the front of the car.

"It is," C.J. said, pointing to red welts on her upper arm. "I have dented walls in my apartment. The UPS man brings doggie treats, and she gets so excited that her tail dents the wall while she waits for him."

Floyd sat on C.J.'s fender. "Her name is Bailey? She seems like a sweetheart."

"A bull-headed sweetheart who's strong as an ox."

Bailey watched them through the windshield, whining and occasionally letting out a chirping bark.

"You're taking her to doggy daycare? Why not leave her home?"

"She's barely more than a puppy and not well behaved. I'd come home to mayhem if I left her loose in the apartment all day. She needs to burn off all that puppy energy with the other dogs at daycare." C.J. paused. "Do you have anything special for me today or should I just patrol?"

"Drive around the lakes. The summer folks are opening their cabins and we sometimes have some home burglaries this time of year." Floyd looked at the dog who was bouncing on the built-in police computer. "You'd better get Bailey to daycare before she destroys your car."

* * *

Floyd was asleep in a guest chair with his feet on the principal's desk at Pine City

High School when Frank Boquist showed up at 8:15. Floyd and the principal were equally startled when Boquist turned on the lights.

"Sergeant Swenson! What are you doing here?" Boquist slipped off his sport coat and hung it behind the door. He was past fifty but prided himself for staying in shape. "If you don't mind my saying so, you look like you didn't get much sleep last night." He shook Floyd's hand firmly, then sat in his well-worn desk chair.

The principal's office was adorned with the trophies and plaques that celebrated the school's past sporting glory. Boquist had a twenty-year-old family picture on his desk. Floyd thought that the desktop was too clean, the sign of a mind too focused on structure. Floyd's own desk was a mess with stacks of case files.

Floyd rubbed his bloodshot eyes while he collected his thoughts. "You lost a student. Ted Palmquist died in the emergency room early this morning."

Boquist froze. "A car accident?"

Floyd shook his head. "The cause hasn't been determined. He had a heart attack in the emergency room."

Frank Boquist got up and paced his small office. Floyd noticed the pattern worn into the carpet and guessed that pacing was a regular Boquist response to stress. "He had a heart attack? Was he involved in some strenuous activity? Was there something hereditary?"

Floyd spread his palms. "We're waiting for the medical examiner to do an autopsy on his body."

Boquist paced, running fingers through his thinning hair. "We'll need to get the counselor in. We'll have some kids having anxiety attacks when the news gets around. Can you tell me more?"

"Tell me about Ted Palmquist. Was he a good student with lots of friends?"

The principal sat in his chair. "He didn't have many friends. He was a stoner."

Floyd frowned as he pulled a notebook and pen from his shirt pocket. "What's a stoner?"

Frank smiled. "The stoners are the 'out' crowd. They go around with their jeans hanging so low their boxer shorts show. They're rumored to be into drugs, so the other kids call them stoners."

"Are they a gang?"

Boquist shook his head. "Not a gang. They're more a bunch of kids who are regularly truant and are in trouble when they're here. They're disruptive and disrespectful."

"Are they drinkers or into drugs?"

"Drinking, yes. Drugs, maybe. Tough talk. Poor grades. Big-time attitudes."

Floyd scribbled some notes. "You make it sound like you'd be happy if they dropped out."

The principal was obviously uncomfortable with the question. "I don't want any kid to drop out. These kids certainly try my patience and are disruptive. We try to engage them and manage their attitudes."

"How many are there?"

Boquist looked out the window. "It varies. Seven, maybe eight. The core group is five guys that are all seniors and two younger girls." Boquist counted them off on his fingers. "Brady Werther, Ted Palmquist, Juan Santiago, Dylan Johnson and Tyler Espe. The girls are Laura Tomlinson and Tammi Wagner. Tammi ran away a few months ago. The rumor mill says Tammi had a couple of abortions in the months before she ran away."

Floyd hesitated, trying to pull up a memory from the hospital. "Ted mentioned something about Tammi last night." He closed his eyes. "I remember investigating Tammi Wagner's disappearance last fall. I talked to Laura, and she told me Tammi ran away. When I talked to Tammi's mother, she wasn't surprised Tammi had run away, but said there was no triggering event. As I recall, Tammi's mother and her boyfriend aren't upstanding citizens. Have you dealt with them?"

Boquist stared at a row of trophies above Floyd's head. "I've only spoken to Tammi's mother on the phone. She had no interest in Tammi's truancy, poor behavior, or in her punishment."

"I take it that there has been no sign of Tammi around school since then?"

Boquist shook his head. "No, she hasn't been in class since last fall."

Floyd made a note and asked, "Do the stoners have a leader?"

"I wouldn't say there is a leader. Dylan seems to be the brains of the group. His father passed away a little over a year ago. His mother kind of fell apart and hasn't kept a tight rein on him since then. He has a car and always seems to have money. I think he provides transportation and booze to the group."

Floyd tapped his pen on the notebook. "Does Dylan act like a rich kid?" Not getting an immediate response he added, "You know the kind—his mother gives him everything except love."

Boquist shifted in his chair. "I don't think of Dylan's family being rich, although it's rumored his father had a big life insurance policy. Since Dylan's father got sick, his mother has been too depressed to deal with anything other than her own problems. She made a big deal about calling the school to tell us she's gone back to her maiden name after Art's death. I think that's symbolic of her transition to a new page in her life."

"And that new page involves her 'finding' herself at Dylan's expense."

Boquist leaned back in his chair. "None of the stoners are angels. They've all been in this office far too often. One or another is tardy or truant nearly every day. Juan Santiago's father, Ray, was a student here when I first came to the school. He was a troublemaker and was constantly fighting. At first, I thought it was because he was the only Hispanic kid in the area. After a while, I realized that he just liked to fight. Ray was big for his age, and he liked to bully the smaller kids. Juan's got the same attitude as his father, and when I call his parents in to talk about Juan's bullying, they refuse to come to the school. Ray's convinced that I have a vendetta against him and am taking it out on Juan."

"What about the others?" Floyd asked.

"Laura Tomlinson's mother is a single parent. She works the afternoon shift somewhere out of the area, and Laura spends every afternoon and evening on her own, or with the other stoners. I don't think her mother has a clue about Laura's activities.

"I've never met either of Tyler Espe's parents. They've never been to a school conference or any school event. Tyler was in the class play when he was a sophomore, and his parents didn't even attend. I don't know if he was too embarrassed to tell them, or if they just blew it off.

"Tammi Wagner's parents divorced several years ago. Tammi and her mother were living with a guy somewhere west of town." Boquist paused and leaned close. "I didn't like that situation at all, and I even tried to speak to Tammi's mother about it once. The school counselor feels the relationship between Tammi and the boyfriend seemed off. Tammi was uncomfortable talking about him. She said he put his arm over her shoulder all the time. Tammi wouldn't say anything more to me, or the counselor, about it."

Boquist leaned back and closed his eyes while he thought. "Let's see. The other one is Ted Palmquist. Ted seemed the most normal of the group, although I might be confusing his quiet demeanor with submission to authority. His mother never married and never finished high school. She wasn't concerned about Ted's truancy, but I don't think she encouraged his attendance either. She's coarse and antisocial. On the other hand, at least she showed up to talk about Ted when he was having tardiness problems. She even bought him an alarm clock to help him catch the bus.

"Brady Werther is a real gem. His grandparents are on welfare, and his parents were on welfare until they got cut off because of their drug use. He has seven or eight siblings and stepsiblings. The family lives in a rundown farmhouse west of town. His parents don't seem to care what any of the kids do, as long as dad can afford a bottle of booze. I think Brady gravitated to the stoners because they have money and booze."

When Boquist ended his recitation about the stoners Floyd said, "You asked if a car accident was involved in Ted's death. You suspected a DWI?"

Boquist shrugged. "If you check their police records, I suspect you'll find a couple underage drinking arrests and a DWI or two. Maybe even a shoplifting arrest. And, here at school we had the assault on Mr. Ferguson in his classroom last year, and the raw egg incident in the lunchroom."

Floyd had been involved in the investigation of the assault on Mr. Ferguson. Old Mr. Ferguson had ruled his classroom with an iron fist for three decades. He'd tried to slap a kid who had mouthed off and the kid had punched him before the slap connected. No charges had been filed because Ferguson had provoked it, but there had been some discussions with the boy's parents and a month's suspension from school for both Ferguson and the student. The other incident sounded intriguing. "Tell me more about the raw egg incident."

Boquist shook his head in disgust. "Someone pelted the homecoming royalty with raw eggs at the coronation in the gymnasium. No one will admit seeing anything or doing it. I'm sure the stoners were involved. It's their style to rebel against anything they consider an 'in crowd' event."

"Can I talk to them?"

Boquist shrugged. "Sure…if they decided to attend school today, and if they'll talk to you. They rebel against power and I'm sure they'll clam up as soon as they see your uniform."

Boquist summoned Mrs. Kennedy from his doorway.

* * *

Floyd sat behind the principal's desk until a mop of dark hair over a two-day growth of sparse beard peeked around the door frame. "You wanted to talk to me?"

"Yeah. Come on in." Floyd pointed to the visitor's chair he'd set facing away from the door at the corner of the desk.

The list from the principal indicated this was Dylan Johnson. The boy walked into the office with his shoulders hunched, staring at the floor, moving like the muscles in his legs wouldn't hold him up any longer. He flopped into the chair. Floyd appraised the sunken cheeks and sores on his face, wondering if this boy had the same problem as Ted

Palmquist or just some acne scars. The boy's jeans looked like they hadn't been washed in a decade and his black shirt featured a band logo with death heads, lightning bolts, and a wolf baring its fangs.

"Are you Dylan Johnson?"

The answer was a grunt.

"Did you know Ted Palmquist?"

Dylan looked up through his eyebrows without raising his head. "Maybe. Who wants to know?"

"Were you with Ted last night?"

Dylan slid further down in the chair, avoiding eye contact. "I can't remember."

"Was he sick? Throwing up?"

Dylan's eyes flickered and he sat up slightly. "Sorta. Why?"

The ringing phone jarred the boy. "Sergeant Swenson, the call's for you," Mrs. Kennedy called from her desk.

Floyd reached across the desk and picked up the receiver and heard the voice of Eddie Paulson, the St. Louis County Medical Examiner's assistant. "Floyd? You've got a new office?"

Floyd stared at Dylan as he spoke. The boy looked away. "No, just a borrowed one. What's up?"

"I picked up Palmquist's body this morning. Tony's got a couple ahead of yours to work on, but we'll get to him this afternoon. There was a note saying this was something special?"

Floyd wished that Dylan was out of the room, but he decided to use the conversation to crush Dylan's defenses. "Yeah, the ER doctor suggested Palmquist died from some kind of poisoning, probably compounded by leukemia. Could you pull some blood and start some chemical analysis before the autopsy?" Dylan sat up and stared at Floyd. His face registered a touch of fear for a brief second before the surliness returned. Floyd knew unguarded first reactions were usually the best measure of someone's true state of mind. People were harder to read after they'd had time to construct stories and mask emotions.

"I'll draw blood, but we usually pick up poison in the liver. We'll take a sample during the post-mortem and run some tests on it, too."

"Okay. I just wanted to make sure that you were fully aware of the doctor's suspicions before you started the autopsy."

"It'll take a few days to get most of the lab results. I can call you back later this afternoon with the preliminary toxicology."

"Great. I'll look forward to your call."

Floyd hung up the phone and stared at Dylan without speaking. The boy looked uncomfortable and took a swallow before speaking. "Ted's dead?"

Floyd nodded. "Last night. His mother called an ambulance and they rushed him to the emergency room. He'd been vomiting blood."

Dylan looked down and shook his head. "Wow. I mean, he was kind of quieter than usual. He and his ma had been having some trouble..." The sentence trailed off without an ending. Floyd suspected the comment was intended to mislead him.

Floyd stared at the boy's greasy hair and pimpled face. The jeans and denim jacket were stained with a variety of liquids and Floyd wondered what chemicals they might yield if tested in a lab. "Where were you last night?"

Dylan looked down, "Out."

"With Ted?"

Dylan looked up. "Are we in trouble? I mean, we didn't break any laws. We were just hanging out. We didn't do anything to Ted."

Floyd leaned forward. "Dylan, I'm trying to find out what happened to Ted, just trying to solve a mystery." Floyd let the words hang while Dylan digested them. "Did you know that Ted had leukemia?"

Dylan shook his head. "He's been sick for a while. He didn't say nothin' about leukemia."

Dylan's comments meshed with Cheryl Palmquist's answers. She didn't know Ted had health problems.

"Did you notice Ted's bruises?" Floyd asked.

Dylan dismissed the question with a shake of his head. "Him and his ma were always at it over something. He was bruised once in a while."

"Do you know that she beat him?"

Dylan thought for a second. "He never said it. But the way he talked; I kinda knew."

Floyd leaned back in the chair. "Who else was with you last night?"

Dylan stared at the floor. "Nobody."

"Ted and who else?"

Dylan didn't look up.

"Ted mentioned meeting Tammi. Was she there too?"

The question obviously jarred Dylan, who quickly recovered. "No, Tammi ran away last fall."

Floyd let silence hang, waiting for more response. When none came, he asked, "You haven't seen her since then?"

Dylan shook his head.

"Do you know where she went?"

Dylan's answer was another head shake.

"I heard a rumor she went to Minneapolis for an abortion. Is that true?"

Dylan paused before shaking his head.

When he was sure Dylan wasn't going to offer anything more, Floyd dug a business card out of his pocket and set it on the desk. "Call me if you think of anything else."

Dylan looked at the card. "Why bother? You're a cop." He flipped the card onto the floor and shuffled out the door. Floyd noticed the elastic of Dylan's boxer shorts showing above the waist of his jeans.

After Dylan's departure, Floyd walked to the school secretary's desk. She handed Floyd a hand-written list of names from the principal. She confirmed that Tyler Espe and Juan Santiago were not in school and gave Floyd their home addresses. She called Brady Werther's classroom on the speaker system and requested his presence in the office.

Floyd went back to the principal's office and called dispatch. He asked to be connected with the nearest deputy. "C.J., I've got two truants I want you to bring to school." He relayed Tyler Espe's and Juan Santiago's names and addresses.

C.J. sounded skeptical. "What's up? Do you usually bring truants back to school?"

"They may be material witnesses to a crime. I'm interviewing their buddies in the principal's office. Bring them in since they are supposed to be here anyway."

"Do you care which one I pick up first?"

"Go to the address that's closest to you."

Floyd hung up as another skinny teen showed up. Brady Werther was leaning against the office door frame. Cast in the same mold as Dylan Johnson, Brady Werther's hair was shoulder length, and he had a gold stud in his left nostril. His flannel shirt was at least four sizes too large, with large holes ripped in both knees of his dirty jeans. His hair was blond, his two-day beard was little more than fuzz.

"Take a seat." Floyd said, pointing to the chair.

Brady pulled a toothpick from his pocket and jammed it in the corner of his mouth. "Are you the school cop?"

"Does it matter?"

Brady clucked his tongue and rolled his eyes. "So, it's a bust, huh?" He didn't move from the doorway although his muscles tensed, like he was getting ready to run.

"Dylan told me his version of last night. What's your story?" Floyd leaned forward and put his elbows on the desk. Using 'the other guy's story' was sometimes an effective technique to get information from youthful criminals, especially those who weren't too bright or experienced. It only worked once on most people.

Brady jammed his hands in his pockets. "So, Dylan rats and tells you I was with them?" Brady rolled his eyes. "He was the one that's been making the buys. Ask Tyler and Ted. We just pay Dylan for what we use."

"Who's he getting it from?" Floyd tried to set the hook. "He said you knew the man."

Brady's eyes narrowed as realization swept over him. "Dylan didn't tell you shit." He turned and disappeared.

Floyd jumped up and dashed out the door. He caught Brady in the hallway and grabbed him by the sleeve. "Hang on. We've got some other things to discuss."

Brady jerked his arm away. "You tried to trick me. I ain't talking to you."

"Ted Palmquist died last night."

Brady sneered. "You're lying again, man. You can't trust anything a cop says."

"Ask Mrs. Kennedy." Floyd nodded to the office secretary, who had been watching through the windows used to supervise hallway activity. She nodded.

Brady turned back to Floyd. "How?"

"We're not sure yet. Maybe poisoning. Has Ted been sick long?"

Brady gave a snort. "We're all sick in our own way."

A short, chunky girl with raven hair walked down the hall and stopped. She looked at Brady and sized up Floyd for a fraction of a second, then wheeled around. Brady gave her a nervous look, then made a show of ignoring her.

Floyd called after her. "Are you Laura?"

The girl froze and turned her head, giving Floyd a good look at the six earrings in her pierced ear and the stud in her nose. "Me?"

"Yes, you. What's your name?"

"Why?" She turned full front, exposing the Edgefest logo on her black t-shirt. The exposed ear had a row of earrings.

Brady tilted his head back and took a deep breath. "Cut the shit, Laura. Ted died last night." He nodded toward Floyd. "The cop is trying to figure out why."

Laura looked aghast and shuddered, clasping her hands to her face. Tears welled in her eyes, and she let out a gasp. "Teddy Bear...dead?"

Brady gave a nod, then turned to Floyd. "Can I go now?"

Floyd pointed toward a door farther in the office area. "I think the counselor wants to talk to you."

Brady rolled his eyes again. "I can handle it. I don't need no shrink." He walked away.

Floyd walked to Laura who had her face buried in her hands. "Come into the office." He led the girl to the guest chair in the principal's office and motioned for Mrs. Kennedy to stand at the office door.

"Were you out with Ted last night too?" Floyd sat on the corner of the desk and looked down at Laura. She shook her head.

"Do you know where the guys went?"

When Laura looked up, her face was streaked with tears. She wiped her nose on the back of her hand before Floyd could reach for the tissue box on the credenza. He guessed her to be fourteen, maybe three years younger than Dylan and Brady. "They go around. Sometimes they cruise the loop in town. Sometimes they go out to the fort."

Floyd's interest was piqued, but he tried to act nonchalant. "Where's the fort?"

She gave Floyd a look like she realized she'd said something very wrong. Then she shrugged.

"It's some place that you're not supposed to be." Laura just looked at her feet. "Let's try another tack. What do you do at the fort, drop acid?"

Laura shook her head. Floyd walked behind the desk and sat down in the principal's chair. "It's where Ted, Dylan, Brady and Tyler go to smoke what Dylan buys, isn't it?" Laura shrugged without looking up.

"How old are you, Laura?"

"Fifteen. Why?"

"The guys are all seniors. What do your parents think about you hanging out with them?" Mrs. Kennedy shook her head rapidly and held up one finger. She mouthed the word "Mother." Laura was silent.

"Where does your mother work, Laura?"

Laura continued to stare at her feet. "The wooden match company, up in Cloquet." Though Cloquet was an hour away, it had a paper mill and a match manufacturing plant offering high pay and benefits that drew workers from all over the region.

Floyd nodded assent. "Umm. That's a long drive. Is she on day shift?"

Laura shook her head. "Naw. She doesn't have enough seniority. She rotates. Two weeks each shift."

"I suppose she isn't around much. And she probably sleeps the rest of the time. It must be hard keeping quiet all the time."

Laura looked up for the first time. "I go out with the guys. That way I don't keep her awake. She worries, but I take care of myself." She feigned bravado. Laura sniffed, and Floyd passed her the tissues. She blew her nose and stuffed the used tissue into her jeans. "What happened to Ted?"

Floyd shifted his position before he spoke. "He was very sick last night. His heart stopped and the doctor couldn't get it started. The doctor said Ted may have been poisoned."

Laura shook her head. "Ted was nice. No one would poison him."

"You called him Teddy Bear. Did all the guys call him that?" Laura's face colored and she stared at the floor. She shook her head, no.

"Was he special?" Floyd asked.

"Just a friend."

"But you like him better than the others?"

When Laura didn't answer Floyd continued. "Ted was sick and something else must have happened too. Did you know he was sick?"

Laura shrugged her shoulders. "He lost a lot of weight. He said he didn't feel good, like he was getting food poisoning all the time."

"Did you notice his bruises?"

"They happened easily. Like, he'd bump into something and the next day he'd have a bruise. It was getting worse all the time."

"Did he ever go to see a doctor?"

Laura shook her head, making her unnaturally black tresses wiggle. "Ted said his mom didn't believe in doctors."

Floyd scribbled a note to himself. "Was he in pain?"

"Naw, just sick to his stomach a lot. He was throwing up all the time. He'd throw up, then he'd fall down, and then he'd have more bruises. And he was really thirsty all the time."

"Did he take any medicine for any of it? Did anything make him feel better?"

"It kinda came and went. He said that the marijuana..." She froze in mid-sentence and regrouped. "Sometimes it got better."

Floyd tried to direct the conversation back to her verbal slip. "The medical folks experimented with marijuana to treat cancer patients with nausea from chemotherapy. Did you know that?"

Laura shook her head.

Floyd asked, "How long has Ted been sick?"

"Maybe a month or so."

The switchboard phone rang, and Mrs. Kennedy left to answer it.

"Did Ted smoke a lot of dope?"

Laura squirmed. "He smoked a joint once in a while."

"Ted said something about Tammi last night. Has Tammi been partying with the guys?"

Laura registered no surprise. "Tammi ran away last fall. I don't think Ted knew where she went."

Floyd's radio sounded emergency tones and the dispatcher's voice announced, "Deputy requests assistance. High-speed pursuit."

Chapter 4

C.J. drove to Juan Santiago's address, northeast of Pine City. The driveway turned off a gravel road, and the house was set back nearly half a mile. The hay field surrounding the house hadn't started to turn green yet even with the warmer weather. The cruiser raised a trail of dust.

The house looked empty as she drove into the yard. The drapes were open but there was no sign of activity. She parked on the concrete slab near the door and shielded her eyes to look inside the cab of a red pickup next to the house. On the truck's front seat was a Ziploc plastic bag filled with white powder. She called for a tow truck to impound the pickup until they could secure a search warrant.

Looking through the house windows, there was no sign of anyone home. She walked to the passenger side of the pickup. Shielding her eyes, she looked through the passenger window. The floor of the truck was covered with litter. In addition to the bag of powder there was a brown paper lunch bag near the passenger door, also filled with something.

C.J. walked back to the house and knocked on the storm door. The inner door was open a few inches, but there was no sound inside. She pushed a doorbell, but it was apparently broken and didn't ring.

"Hello. Anyone home?" C.J. opened the screen door and knocked on the door frame. Inside there was a small mudroom, with a few steps that rose to a kitchen. Dusty shoes and rubber barn boots lay randomly on the floor and jackets and caps hung from pegs on the left wall. There was a stairway into the basement behind a railing on the right side. The smell of fried bacon hung in the air. Someone had been home for breakfast.

C.J. stepped into the entryway and wiped her feet on the rag rug. "Sheriff's Department. Is anyone home?" Reasoning that something was wrong, she walked up the steps into the kitchen. There was a frying pan on the stove. A plate, dirty with egg yolk and crumbs, sat on the table next to a half glass of milk. C.J. held her hand over the frying pan. It was almost too hot to touch.

"Come out, Juan. I need to talk to you."

An engine roared to life outside and C.J. raced to the door just in time to see the red pickup skid to a stop after turning behind her cruiser in the driveway. In the quick maneuver, the pickup's bumper smashed C.J.'s taillight. The pickup's wheels spun on the gravel driveway, peppering the cruiser with gravel as it raced past the house. A young male driver with black hair was at the wheel.

C.J. scrambled into the car and started down the driveway. She switched the radio to the state-wide pursuit frequency and picked up the mic. "This is Pine County in pursuit of a red Ford pickup." The pickup turned right as it left the driveway. "It's northbound on County Road 6, east of Pine City. The driver may be in possession of dealer quantities of a controlled substance and collided with a police car just moments ago."

By the time C.J. turned from the driveway, a cloud of dust was drifting across the road nearly half a mile away. She accelerated hard and the gap between her cruiser and the dust cloud started to diminish. As C.J. approached an intersection, the dust cloud disappeared.

"The suspect vehicle has just turned right on County Road 117." C.J. steered the cruiser hard around the corner. Her tires chirped as she accelerated on the cracked blacktop road. The pickup wasn't visible on the rolling road, but C.J. kept up the pursuit. At the next long straight away she spotted the pickup at the bottom of a hill. Swampy ditches lapped at both sides of the road; the recent melting snow having filled every ditch to overflowing.

The speedometer showed 115 miles an hour as C.J. gained on the pickup. Backing off the accelerator, she was within three car-lengths after another mile.

The driver gave no sign of slowing. Instead, he seemed preoccupied with something inside the cab. As they crossed an intersection, the driver leaned across the seat and threw something white out of the window. C.J. made a mental note of the location. In the next mile, three more packages sailed out, the last being a brown paper bag that flew over the swampy ditch.

"Dispatch, the subject vehicle is throwing packages out of the passenger window. The first was something white at the 117 and 3 crossroads. There have been two more since then. The last was a brown paper bag."

Sergeant Floyd Swenson announced his location at the 'T' in the road. "I've got the road blocked."

The pickup flew over a rise in the road, nearly lifting the tires from the pavement. C.J. eased off the gas. The intersection was just past the rise, blind to approaching vehicles. When C.J. eased over the hill, the pickup had all four wheels locked. The driver steered for the right ditch to bypass the roadblock, then realized the ditch was filled with water and steered for the other side. He lost control and slid sideways toward the brown cruiser with its lights flashing.

The pickup driver swung the steering wheel in an effort to regain control. The truck was about fifty feet from the roadblock when the left front wheel caught a pothole. The truck flipped. It rolled twice, rust and dirt swirling around it, before slamming into the side of Floyd's cruiser. The police car shuddered but moved only inches with the impact.

Jensen reached for the mic. "Dispatch, send an ambulance and wrecker to the 'T' in County Road 117, east of Pine City. The subject vehicle just collided with Floyd's cruiser."

C.J. rolled to a stop next to the truck. It had landed against the cruiser's passenger's door, pinning it shut. Floyd staggered out of the car.

"Are you okay, Floyd?"

"Yeah, but the sheriff will be pissed that we've lost a car."

"To hell with the car. Are you sure you're okay?"

He shook himself out and rolled his shoulders. "Yeah, I'm fine. How's the pickup driver?"

Floyd climbed onto the cruiser's trunk, and then stepped onto the driver's side of the pickup to avoid wading through the ditch. He leaned down and tried to open the door, but found it jammed. Getting down on his knees, he shielded his eyes to look through the shattered window. "There's blood on the window," he reported.

C.J. was on the opposite side, trying to look through the spiderweb cracked windshield. "I can see him. He's crumpled against the dash...and he's moving."

It took the Pine City rescue squad almost twenty minutes to get to the accident. The firemen pried the driver's door open with a crowbar while trying to avoid breaking glass onto the moaning body below. The door gave way, but not without raining crystals of glass inside the cab. A fireman disappeared into the cab while his partner held the door open.

* * *

Floyd and C.J. watched as the ambulance crew readied a backboard and their first aid kits on the roadbed while the firemen worked to remove the victim from the pickup.

From inside the cab the fireman said, "Hand me a blanket and the bar." His voice sounded like he was in a cavern. Another fireman handed the blanket and a crowbar through the open door. A second later the windshield erupted into a million pieces and spilled onto the road and into the ditch as the crowbar smashed out the glass. The blanket, flecked with a layer of glass fragments, covered the swearing driver.

Three firemen knocked the last of the glass from the windshield and lifted the blanket from Juan Santiago. Juan's face was smeared with blood, and he lay in a heap glaring at them. "Where's the fucking idiot cop who parked in the middle of the road?"

C.J. glanced at Floyd who shook his head. "He smashed his pickup into my cruiser."

"Hey, that hurts!" Juan complained as the paramedic probed his arms and legs for fractures. "Shit!" he muttered again, grimacing in pain.

"Can you wiggle your fingers?" The paramedic gently held Juan's hand and watched the fingers flex. "How about your toes, will they move?"

Juan moaned and a shoe twitched. The paramedic looked to his partner. "Looks like there's no spinal cord separation, but he's got several breaks. Let's stabilize his neck with a collar, then put him on a backboard."

After five minutes Santiago was secured unhappily to a backboard with splints inflated on both legs and arms. He moaned continuously and punctuated each movement with a cry of pain. The paramedics and two of the firemen lifted the backboard onto a gurney and pushed it into the back of the ambulance. A paramedic closed the doors, and they roared off.

Floyd cornered one of the firemen loading equipment back into the truck while

C.J. took pictures of the scene. "How's he doing?"

"Both his legs are broken, and the paramedics are nervous about his neck. Nothing appeared to be life threatening unless he had some internal bleeding or throws a clot."

The tow truck, idling off to the side, now backed up to the pickup and attached a cable to the top. The winch strained and the truck rolled onto its roof. The wrecker operator reattached the cable and pulled it onto the passenger side, then up on its wheels. When the job was done, every piece of metal had a crumple or scrape on it.

C.J. pulled Floyd to the edge of the road. They watched the tow truck operator slide the pickup truck onto the flatbed. Its wheels made exaggerated loops due to the bent rims and axles. "We've got a job now. Our friend was tossing goodies out of the passenger window. There were three white packages and a brown lunch bag. Most of them didn't make it any farther than the ditch."

Floyd surveyed the damage to the side of his cruiser. The two passenger-side doors were dented, but the vehicle looked operable. Floyd motioned C.J. over to his car. "I'll have them tow my car to the shop and have it checked over. You and Sandy Maki can look for the packages the driver was throwing out after you give me your car."

C.J. bristled. "Give you my car?"

Floyd chuckled. "Get the keys to one of the other cars from the dispatcher."

* * *

Floyd sat in the hospital emergency room, waiting for news about Juan Santiago. He scribbled notes in a small spiral notebook. After wrapping up the notes, he called the dispatcher from the nurses' station. She connected him to John Sepanen, the Pine County Sheriff.

"I've got a quick update on this afternoon's chase. The kid is Juan Santiago. He was flinging packages out the window until he rolled his truck and hit my cruiser."

The sheriff sighed. "How are you?"

"I'm fine. The car's going to need some work."

"How'd C.J. do?"

"She was good. Very professional. We're lucky to have a veteran like her willing to take a job in the boonies of Pine County. I think she'll cover really well until Pam's off restricted duty. I assume you'll be able to keep them both after Pam's back on the road."

"Shouldn't be a problem. All I have to do is tell the board you're threatening to retire again, and they'll let me keep her."

"Cloquet's loss is our gain. What's her story?"

"She's a widow. Her husband was a Duluth PD captain who was killed when his car was t-boned during a pursuit."

"I remember that. His name was Jensen, right?"

"Bobby Jensen," the sheriff replied. "I met him a couple times. He was a hell of a nice guy. When I interviewed her, Charlene said she needed to hit a reset on her life. She left the Cloquet PD and told people to call her C.J. instead of Charlene. Perfect timing, too. Pam's doctor prescribed desk duty for a few weeks before the baby was born and C.J. was available."

"Do you know where Juan Santiago's parents work?"

"His father is Ray Santiago. He works at Willow River machine shop. I don't know where the mother works. She's changed jobs recently. I sent Kerm over to the machine shop about ten minutes ago to notify the father."

Floyd nodded to no one. "Did C.J. and Sandy Maki find any of the packages on the road?"

"Sandy brought in three plastic bags, C.J. is still walking the ditches looking for a brown bag."

"Drugs, I assume?" Floyd surmised.

"One bag had about fifteen one-ounce baggies that look like marijuana," Sepanen replied. "The second package had a roach clip and cigarette papers with the marijuana.

The third plastic bag contained a smaller bag filled with a grayish white powder and capsules. We packed up a sample for the Bureau of Criminal Apprehension to test. I had Sandy Maki take them to the BCA office in St. Paul."

Floyd gave a low whistle. "Our boy's in deep shit. Fifteen lids of marijuana are enough to nail him for dealing even if the powder turns out to be powdered sugar, and I assume that it isn't." He considered the evidence, then added, "We'd better get the county attorney involved."

"Is the Santiago kid lucid enough to interview? C.J. said he'd broken his legs, but beyond that, the paramedics thought his injuries weren't too bad."

"They had him in X-ray when I got here. I'll let you know more after I talk to the doctor."

* * *

Floyd was leafing through a three-year-old *Field and Stream* magazine when Ray Santiago rushed into the emergency room. Ray's beer belly hung over his belt. His shoulders were broad and his forearms meaty from years of hard work. He wore a light jacket over a denim work shirt. His jeans were spotted with oil stains from about mid-thigh down. Floyd had seen him wearing a leather apron around the milling machines and lathes in his shop.

Ray looked at Floyd. "Who are you?"

"I'm Floyd Swenson, a sergeant from the Pine County Sheriff's Department. I was at the scene when Juan crashed."

"Yeah, the guy you sent to the shop told me a cop was chasing him. Do your people routinely try to kill kids for speeding? Where is Juan anyway?" Santiago turned and pounded on the counter. "Nurse! Nurse!"

"Calm down, Mister Santiago. They've had Juan in the back since I got here. Just so you understand the situation, we didn't start this. My deputy went to your house on a truancy call and saw drugs laying on the front seat of the pickup. Juan made a run for it in a pickup and clipped her cruiser as he backed up. Did you know that Juan wasn't in school today?"

Santiago was seething. "What? This is about truancy? That's bull. I told him to quit school and make some real money working construction. He doesn't need to know the capitol of Rhode Island or how to do algebra to make a living."

The conversation was interrupted when Bert Mlankoch, M.D., walked down the hallway. He looked solemn, his green surgical scrubs splattered and smeared with blood.

Mlankoch nodded to Floyd and looked at the Hispanic features of Ray Santiago. "Are you Juan's father?" Mlankoch asked.

Santiago glared at Floyd but nodded.

"He's in tough shape, but not critical. Both his legs are broken, but there appear to be no spinal or internal injuries, so his life isn't in danger. I stitched up his cuts and put a cast on one arm, but he'll need a good surgeon to repair his broken legs. I called an ambulance to transport him to Robbinsdale. They've got a good orthopedist coming in who can repair his leg injuries." The doctor paused and glanced between Floyd and the father. "He's high on something. Do either of you know what he's on?"

Santiago shook his head. "He's got some drinking buddies and sometimes he smells like weed when he comes home."

"It's not alcohol or marijuana. We're screening now, but the drugs in his system are going to complicate anesthesia for the surgeon. The anesthesiologist may want to wait until the drugs flush out of his body before they sedate him."

Ray Santiago's eyes glistened as he choked out a few words. "Will he be all right?"

Mlankoch nodded. "He should be fine, but like I said, he's going to need surgery to repair his broken legs. Then therapy to get them working again after the bones set."

The color rose in Ray Santiago's face as the full impact of the doctor's comments hit him. He turned to Floyd and pointed a finger at his face. "This is your fault. There's no reason on God's earth to chase down a truant kid." He lowered his finger and turned to leave. Stalking toward the door he said over his shoulder, "The sheriff will hear from my lawyers."

Silence settled over the room as Floyd and the doctor stared at the door for a second. Mlankoch broke the silence. "Is that true? You were chasing him because he was a truant?"

Floyd shook his head. "I went to the high school to question him about Ted Palmquist's death, but he wasn't there. My deputy went to his house and saw felony quantities of marijuana and some other white powder in his pickup. He made a run for it and rammed her cruiser as he drove off."

"Why didn't you tell his dad about the narcotics?"

Floyd shook his head. "He needs a little while to cool off and deal with his grief. There wasn't anything I could have said now that would have consoled him. The county attorney will sort it out later."

Mlankoch nodded. "I suppose you're right."

"Did the kid ever get lucid?"

Mlankoch shook his head. "He was in a lot of pain and was talking crazy when he got here. Whatever he's on has got him pretty spaced out."

"You said he was talking crazy. What kind of things did he say?"

"Let's see. He said something about a fort and Tammi's buried treasure. It was pretty fragmented and didn't make a lot of sense. It sounded like the gibberish the Palmquist kid was mumbling before he flatlined."

Floyd pulled out a notebook. "I've got five other kids that are tied into this somehow and if I can get a crack, I might be able to pry it open. Is he still here, or have they transported him to Robbinsdale already?" Floyd made a note about the fort and Tammi's buried treasure.

"They were loading the kid for transport when I came out to speak with you and his father."

Floyd folded the notebook up and slipped it back into his pocket. "Let me try something out on you. The fort is a place where these kids hang out and smoke marijuana. I'm sure they won't tell me where it is, so I assume that it's a place they're not supposed to be. Does any of that make sense?"

Mlankoch rubbed his face and closed his eyes again. "Not really. I mean he talked about the fort in relation to someone named Tammi and something buried. Maybe they dig holes and stash their dope there. Maybe that's the buried treasure."

Floyd pulled out the pad again and scribbled more notes. "Tammi Wagner was one of the group until she ran away last fall. The kids all have the same story about her disappearance, but the guys all flinch when I mention her name. Did Juan say, 'Tammi's treasure'?"

Mlankoch shook his head. "I don't know, Floyd. I guess he may not have said treasure. I heard he'd buried something and assumed treasure. I was concentrating on assessing his condition and stabilizing him, not his raving."

Floyd closed the notebook and stuffed it into his pocket. "It's too coincidental that two friends both mention a girl who's been missing for six months." He glanced at his watch. "The Ted Palmquist post-mortem exam is this afternoon. Tony Oresek is cutting at one."

As Floyd walked to the door, Mlankoch called out, "Let me know what Tony finds out. I'm really baffled by the Palmquist kid."

* * *

Floyd radioed for C.J. to meet him at Amy's Café in Sandstone. He took a booth in the back, under a rack of porcelain Holstein cows. The knotty pine walls were covered with antiques, rustic art, and knickknacks. C.J. saw him as she walked in and signaled the waitress for a cup of coffee.

She slid into the booth. "What's up?"

Floyd waited while the waitress poured C.J.'s coffee. The waitress smiled at C.J. "You're that new cop who just moved to town. Welcome."

"Thanks. Sandstone seems like a nice town."

"Oh, it is. The people here are really nice and welcoming." The waitress took out her pad of guest checks and a pen. "Would you like to order something? Grandpa's breakfast sandwich is the special."

C.J. put up her hand. "I'm fine with just the coffee this morning, thanks." The waitress left. "Seems like a nice little town."

Floyd made sure no one was close. "You can live here the rest of your life and you'll never be considered a local. You have to be born here to fit in."

"Tell me about it. My husband and I lived in Scanlon for nearly fifteen years, and we never saw the inside of anyone's house except through a screen door."

Floyd leaned on the table. "I wanted to compliment you on how you handled yourself today."

C.J. smiled, showing crow's feet at the corners of her eyes. Floyd guessed she'd seen her fortieth birthday but hadn't reached fifty yet. "Thanks. I didn't hear much praise in my previous job."

"You seem to be a good cop." He paused again when the waitress delivered a plate of bacon, eggs, and hash browns. "I don't mean to pry, but why did you move here?"

C.J.'s smile disappeared, and her demeanor became serious. "I called in sick one day, at home nursing a migraine. My husband was a Duluth detective captain and was on duty. I'd just stepped out of the shower and was drying my hair when my phone vibrated, signaling the arrival of a new message. I picked it up and saw it was full of text messages. Before I could read the first one, the doorbell rang. I wrapped myself in a bathrobe with a terrible feeling that something was wrong. I rushed to the living room where I saw an officer's hat through the window. I knew something had happened to Bobby."

C.J. took a deep breath and expelled it slowly. Floyd could see her fighting against the swell of emotions that battered her. Inside C.J., the memories threatened to drown her, every feeling she'd been trying to bury bubbled up from the dark place she had lived all those years ago. Tears welled in her eyes, and she bit her lip, looking at the wall over Floyd's head.

Floyd reached out and gently took her hand. "We don't need to talk about this."

C.J. squeezed Floyd's hand, then took a paper napkin to wipe her eyes and blow her nose. Once composed, she went on. "When I opened that door, my sergeant and a chaplain were standing on the steps looking anxious.

"That day, my Charlene and Charlie personas ceased to exist. I was no longer recognizable. I'd gone on a few death notifications as a rookie in training. They were difficult and uncomfortable, but I was able to compartmentalize them. A homicide victim's sister sat sobbing on the couch. When she asked if her sister suffered, it cracked the facade I had built up. But nothing, Floyd, absolutely nothing had prepared me for this. It was like I was watching from above. I kept saying, 'it's just a dream, right? You guys are pulling one over on me.' And then, I sank to the floor in a heap. I think the guys picked me up and carried me to the couch. I was so deep in shock I wasn't even embarrassed about wearing only a robe."

"C.J., I'm so sorry to have opened that wound."

She waved her hand. "I need to talk about it and somehow you seem like a person who could understand."

Floyd nodded. "I lost my wife to cancer a few years ago. It was nothing unexpected, but it rocked my world. I spent a few nights at the kitchen table staring at my weapon, wondering if life was worth living."

C.J. nodded. "I never actually put the muzzle in my mouth, but Floyd, I was so close." She paused. "But it's better now. I'm coping as C.J. My other self is locked away and you're looking at the new me."

Floyd put jam on a piece of toast in silence. He took a bite and looked at her. "Is your life together? Are you ready to face the world?"

She stared into her coffee. "I think so, now. I stumbled through the days immediately after Bobby's death in a blur. The police department and Law Enforcement Memorial Association planned the funeral except for picking out the casket. I remember standing in the mortuary listening, but not hearing the features of each casket. In the end, I just pointed to the shiniest wooden one because I couldn't even bring myself to say, 'that one.'"

Floyd pushed his plate aside, reaching over and patting her on the hand, silently signaling that it was okay to continue.

C.J. stared into her coffee cup as though it held all the answers to the questions that had haunted her since that horrible day. "I stood and saluted my husband's casket, with all the other officers, as if he was a co-worker instead of the love of my life. I think compartmentalizing helped me get through the procession. I remember sitting in a chair between my parents, my father holding my hand while they presented me with Bobby's folded flag. I turned to my father and wanted to scream, 'Daddy, why can't you fix this?'"

C.J. swiped at a tear trickling down her cheek. She took a deep breath, sat up straight, and tugged at the body armor that pinched her collarbone when she slouched. "I think I lost like thirty pounds. My parents were afraid I was melting away. One day the doorbell rang, and my dad was standing there, holding Bailey. I think that dog saved my life."

Floyd nodded. "A few years ago, I came home to a half-breed reddish puppy sitting on the steps. I named her Penny. I don't know where she came from; maybe some idiot dumped her on the roadside. At any rate, she got me through the worst of the rough patches. She developed cancer and the vet put her down about a month ago. I don't think I can go through that again."

C.J. signaled for a coffee refill, then turned to Floyd. "Yeah, Bobby's death got to me like that. I haven't gone to church since the funeral. The minister's been over a couple times. We've talked, but he's struggled to explain why a loving God would let something like that happen."

Floyd waited for the coffee refills, then passed his half-eaten breakfast to the waitress. "Don't blame God, C.J. Bad things sometimes happen to good people, and I don't believe God has anything to do with that. I think God is with the minister who comes to talk to you, the co-workers and neighbors who brought frozen casseroles, and all the prayers that were said for you." Floyd paused. "When you're ready, come along to our little Lutheran church. It's mostly farm people who are the salt of the earth. They'll be happy to have you on your terms."

C.J. nodded. "I'm not ready to listen to a sermon about righteousness yet."

"Then come for Christmas or Easter, the times of renewal and rebirth."

"I'll think about it." C.J. looked at her watch. "We've been sitting here for half an hour. We need to be on the road."

Floyd put up his hand. "We're on duty. If there'd been a call, we would've responded. Besides, you needed a bit of therapy. You're broken, just like the rest of us."

"The rest of us?"

Floyd slid out of the booth and put a twenty-dollar-bill on the table. "I'm not going to speak out of school, but another of our female deputies is dealing with some issues."

C.J. glared at Floyd when he held the door for her. "Floyd, there is only one other female deputy, Pam, the new mom."

A smile flickered at the corner of Floyd's mouth. "Oops! Did I let that slip?"

* * *

Floyd contemplated Ted Palmquist's death as he drove to Duluth. The ER doctor suggested a number of possible causes, but drugs seemed to keep climbing to the top of the pile in Floyd's brain. They were no longer an urban problem, sold only on inner city street corners or in dark alleys. Drugs became a rural scourge in the nineties. Before crystal meth, the sheriff's department had mostly broken up beer busts and drinking parties at seasonal cabins and in farm fields. In the nineties, Mexican marijuana moved north, and teen parties evolved to smaller groups smoking joints behind the barn or in someone's basement when their parents were away. Marijuana was followed by amphetamines and angel dust. A later wave brought methamphetamine, cooked up in local labs, or later coming from Mexico. More addictive than opiates, meth users felt totally uninhibited, which led to an outbreak of STIs. Meth addicts swapped partners without using protection. The more he thought about Mlankoch's words, Floyd suspected the fort was a remote location where teens could quietly engage in drug use, and maybe sex, without being observed.

Floyd passed the Barnum exit on his northbound drive and thought briefly about a missing woman's body recovered on Spider Island in nearby Bear Lake. Finding her body had broken that case, bringing down a construction bribery ring and solving her disappearance and murder.

Tammi Wagner was another mystery awaiting a solution. Everyone who knew her expressed surprise when Tammi ran away months ago, but no one was shocked. Her parents were divorced, and she was splitting time between them. After the divorce she'd fallen in with a tough crowd. Something happened that pushed her out the door, but no one could identify the catalyst leading to her flight.

Then, Ted Palmquist and Juan Santiago both mentioned her within a day. Was she hiding locally? It was more likely she'd hitched a ride to Minneapolis and fallen prey to human traffickers or a pimp. Could she be hiding out with friends in the region? Or would some fisherman or hunter stumble across her decomposed body?

It was nearly one-thirty when Floyd walked into the Duluth morgue. He cut quickly through the hospital halls and opened the door to the autopsy suite. Tony Oresek and his assistant Eddie Paulson were garbed in green surgical scrubs, examining the surface of Ted Palmquist's bruised, naked body. Tony was speaking into a microphone suspended over the stainless steel autopsy table, recording observations for his written report.

"Hi Floyd. We just finished the external exam and were getting ready to cut." Tony

Oresek, the medical examiner, spoke over his shoulder, his voice muffled by the surgical mask covering his face.

"What do you think about the bruises?" Floyd pulled on a smock, then worked his way to the head of the table. Here, under the harsh lights, and with all the blood drained from the tissues, Ted Palmquist's body looked even more like that of a concentration camp survivor than it had the previous night in the emergency room. Ribs pressed prominently through the white skin of the boy's chest, and below that his abdomen bulged before sinking to the iliac crests of his pelvis, protruding like high ridges. The young body was devoid of hair.

"There's no evidence of broken bones or other physical damage. The bruises aren't deep, not like the deep tissue hematoma we'd see if he'd been beaten with a bat or heavy implement." Oresek stepped back, in thought. "I'd say the bruising is consistent with stage three leukemia. In stage three, the capillaries lose their ability to withstand even routine bumps and any greater trauma causes a nasty hematoma."

Oresek turned to the surgical cart and selected a scalpel. He made an incision from the navel to the pubis and additional incisions from each armpit to the navel. A large lopping shears crunched through the ribs as Eddie retracted the edges. Together the cuts made a large "Y" incision, exposing the internal organs. Eddie pulled the huge flap of chest tissue over the boy's face.

"Ah, this explains the bulge in the abdomen." Oresek made a few deft cuts and lifted a large, brownish-red organ from the belly and handed it to Eddie, who placed it in an overhead pan. A dial above the pan showed the weight of the liver.

"Three point two kilograms." Eddie lifted the liver back down and handed it to Oresek. Floyd noticed the organ was speckled with yellow spots.

Oresek sliced the liver open and carved a few small bits, handing them to Eddie, who dropped them into vials. Eddie took a small sample, placed it on a small flat screen, and turned a valve. Gas hissed and white vapors rose from the surface. Floyd watched as the liquid nitrogen turned the liver sample solid. After a few seconds Eddie scraped the frozen tissue off a square of stainless steel and dropped it into a microtome. He stood back as microscopically thin layers of frozen liver were sliced off. He slid a glass slide under two of the paper-thin pieces and carried them to the microscope.

Eddie adjusted the focus, then whistled as he peered through the eyepiece. "This liver looks like it came from a wino. The only other one that I've seen look this bad was from a woman who worked in a dry-cleaning shop and inhaled organic solvents every day." Eddie looked up and put his safety glasses back on. "This kid was probably poisoned over a long period of time."

"Can you tell what poison?" Floyd asked, watching the frost melt and the tissue thaw.

Oresek was already examining the other internal organs. "The liver stores most poisons, and we should be able to identify the chemical." Oresek cut other organs free and handed them to Eddie who weighed them and put samples in storage containers.

Floyd moved back to the head of the table and watched the ongoing exam. "How soon can we find out what the poison was?"

Eddie answered while Oresek concentrated. "If it's something common, we'll know in a day or two. If it's something complex or unusual, it may take a few weeks."

"Give me an update when you can."

Eddie waved as Floyd left. "Sure. I'll do some preliminary tests tomorrow."

Chapter 5

C.J. drove to the sheriff's office at the end of her shift and found Floyd at a desk in the bullpen. "Did you find out anything about your cruiser?"

Floyd looked up from a burglary report on the computer, taking a second to shift gears. "The shop says there's doorpost damage. They can repair it in a couple of days, but it can't be driven until then." He handed her a set of keys. "Take your cruiser back. I'll drive a spare."

C.J. fingered the car keys for a second, then looked up. "How's the kid that rolled the pickup?"

Floyd leaned back in his chair. "They took Santiago to North Memorial. His legs are broken. Last I heard, the anesthesiologist was waiting for the drugs to clear his system before sedating him for surgery." Floyd pushed the drawer shut and leaned back. "Would you like to do a little investigative work?"

C.J. perked up and sat down in the guest chair. "Sure! What've you got?" When she sat, the bulletproof vest under her uniform shirt pushed up at the shoulders, making her look like she was wearing an umpire's chest pad.

"There's a group of high school students who are hanging around together. I talked to two of the guys and a girl I'd like you to interview." He pulled out a notebook and flipped through the pages. "I talked to Laura Tomlinson, and I know there's more to learn there, but she wouldn't spill it to me. Maybe she'll talk to you."

C.J. pulled out a notebook and wrote the name down. "Where do I find her?"

"Talk to the Pine City High School secretary. She can call Laura out of class or can give you a home address if she's not there."

C.J. hesitated. "Ah, how can she give me their home addresses? Don't they have confidentiality rules?"

Floyd cracked a smile. "Technically, if underaged students are truant, the school is supposed to report it to us so we can track them down and deliver them to class."

She looked at the ready room clock. "Do I do this on overtime tonight, or can it wait until morning?"

"She's not going anywhere. By the way, the medical examiner speculated Ted Palmquist had leukemia and may have been poisoned over a period of time. Maybe you can get something on that. The kid who rolled the truck said something to the doctor about Tammi and a place he called the fort."

"Yeah, I heard the kid in the truck say something about that."

"I think it's a place they've been hanging out. They wouldn't talk about it, so I assume that it's someplace they shouldn't be. Maybe you can nail that down too."

C.J. wrote "the fort" then slipped the notebook into her pocket. "Sandy and I found two packets of marijuana and one of white powder. I walked the ditches for hours but couldn't find the brown bag. Any chance we could get someone with a dog to search for it?"

Floyd scribbled a name on a Post-it note, then looked through a stack of business cards until he found the phone number he wanted. "Call this guy. He's a dog handler in a Chisago County K-9 unit. He owes me a favor."

The sheriff walked into the bullpen, accompanied by a petite blonde. Floyd got up and smiled. "Pam, are you back?" He hugged the woman and turned to C.J. "This is Pam Ryan... er, Conrad. She's recently married and has a new baby. Pam, meet Charlene Jensen, our newest deputy."

Charlene stepped forward and shook Pam's hand. "Please call me C.J., Charlene Joy is what my mother called me when she was angry."

Pam laughed. "Aren't mothers wonderful? My mom wanted a grandchild, but she was mad because my baby came three weeks early."

C.J. frowned. "Why is that a problem?"

Floyd smiled and shook his head. "It has something to do with baby Luke being born less than nine months after Pam's wedding and weighing in at a whopping nine-pounds two-ounces. The baby looked like he was full term."

The sheriff put his hand on Pam's shoulder. "A good detective would surmise that Pam might've been pregnant before the wedding, which disappointed Grandma Ryan." The sheriff stepped back. "Pam is returning for limited duty. See if you can find something useful for her to do. If not, she'll have to inventory the property room."

Pam glared at the sheriff. "I'll scrub toilets before I'll inventory the property room."

The sheriff's bass voice boomed with laughter. "I guess you'd better hope Floyd has some other use for your time. It's in his hands."

They watched the sheriff retreat in silence, not wanting to start a conversation that might bring him back. C.J. turned to Pam. "You're legendary. Every time the conversation lags, Floyd tells me stories about something you've done."

Pam glared at Floyd. "Well, Sergeant Swenson, what lies have you been spreading?"

Floyd put up his hands. "Lower your hackles. I've just told C.J. about a couple of the humorous incidents we've been through."

C.J. sat on the corner of a desktop. "How are you doing with the new baby? I hear mommies have a lot of demands and little sleep."

"It was nuts the first few weeks, especially when both my mom and my mother-in-law decided to stay with us to help. Once Travis and I were alone with Luke, things smoothed out and we got a rhythm to our lives. It was really hard to drop him off at daycare, but I absolutely need some 'me time,' even if it's with you and Floyd." Pam turned to Floyd. "Do you have something I can do from the office?"

Floyd smiled and swept up a pile of folders from his desktop. "I've been avoiding these files. There are a couple of pre-sentencing requests, a drug dealer who skipped bail, a lawyer who's demanding the calibration specs and records of our breathalyzer in an attempt to get his client out of a DWI, and a guy who disappeared after missing three child support payments. That should get you started."

Pam accepted the files, then looked tentatively at the desk C.J. was sitting on. "Can I have my old desk back or do you want me somewhere else?"

C.J. jumped up like she'd been scalded. "I didn't realize I'd taken over your space. Here, take your desk. I'll move my stuff to the corner."

"I didn't mean to…"

C.J. picked up a file folder, a couple pens, and a picture. "It's yours! I've been keeping it warm for you."

Pam put the files on the desk. "Is that a picture of your kids?"

C.J. held out the picture frame. "This is Bailey, my basset hound. She's as close as I've got to a child."

Floyd glanced at C.J. "I thought she's been chewing up everything in sight."

"Yeah, she's been suffering a bit of separation anxiety since I moved. She's not adapting to her new surroundings very well."

Pam held the picture. "She's cute."

"She's also stubborn, strong as an ox, and too smart for her own good. She's been chewing up my underwear to punish me for leaving her alone."

Pam laughed. "At least I can drop Luke off at daycare when I'm on duty."

"Yeah, I'm doing doggy daycare this week. It's only slightly more expensive than a new bra and panties every damned day."

A mischievous grin spread across Floyd's face. "Maybe if you didn't leave them on the floor…"

C.J.'s head snapped around and her eyes blazed. "I do not leave my underwear on the floor." She saw Floyd's grin and exhaled. "Bailey pulls them out of the hamper. And what I do with my dirty underwear is none of your business."

Floyd put up his hands. "Hey, you were the one who brought it up."

Pam broke into laughter. "Oh guys, you don't know how much I've missed Floyd's inappropriate banter." Pam handed the picture back to C.J. "If you get in a bind, maybe you can bring Bailey in here. I'll be in the office, and I can watch her."

C.J. glanced at Floyd. "I don't think pets are allowed in the office."

Floyd shrugged. "Probably not on a routine basis, but if you're in a pinch, I don't think anyone would complain if Bailey came in for a day." Floyd glanced at the clock. "One of us needs to be patrolling."

C.J. nodded. "Nice to meet you, Pam." She set her belongings on the corner desk, then walked to the door. "I'll see you tomorrow." Floyd watched her disappear, then listened to her shoes click down the hallway.

Pam sat down at the desk and straightened the pile Floyd handed her. "What's her backstory? She's no rookie."

"She was a Cloquet city cop and has only been with our department for a couple months. With you out, she's been the only female deputy. While she's shown poise and maturity, my biggest concern is whether she had the resilience to deal with the death of her husband and moving to Pine County. It's a big change from her days with the small Cloquet police department, where her patrol area was a fraction of the size of Pine County. In Cloquet, her backup was minutes away unlike here where it can take up to an hour for someone to reach you."

Pam nodded. "And…"

"She's technically a probationary deputy for another two weeks, but she's been solid. I told the sheriff she's better than any rookie we've ever hired."

"Even me?"

Floyd smiled. "Let's face it, you were as green as grass when you showed up. You grew into the job, but it took a while for you to develop the confidence and poise C.J. has shown these past months."

"I know. I was just yanking your chain."

"Are you going to be happy sitting at a desk until you're cleared for full duty?"

Pam patted the stack of files. "As long as there's fresh coffee, an adult to talk with once in a while, and something meaningful to do, I'll be as happy as a pig in slop."

As he passed the dispatcher's cube, Floyd stuck his head in. "Call the Department of Natural Resources. They need someone else to help with the poacher surveillance. I'm going to get some sleep tonight."

Floyd drove to his home outside the town of Sturgeon Lake, near the northern Pine County line. The gravel crunched under Floyd's tires as he pulled in his driveway. Mary's car was already in the garage, and he could see her silhouette against the kitchen lights as he locked the car door. As he approached the house, a black dog approached him with its tail wagging. The dog, barely more than a puppy, showed evidence of black lab heritage. Judging from the white blaze on its chest, there was evidence of other heritage too.

"Hi pup, are you lost?" He reached down to pet the dog's head, but it cowered from his reach and rolled onto its back. "Are you a little scared? Someone been tough on you?" Floyd scratched the pup's belly then walked up the steps and into the house. The smell of frying potatoes filled the air.

"Where'd the puppy come from?"

"I don't know. She was sitting on the steps when I got home. I called Westbys, but they didn't know who she belonged to either."

Floyd removed his coat and slipped off his shoes. "I suppose the owner will show up to claim her."

Mary turned and smiled. "You talked about getting a new dog after Penny died."

Floyd shook his head. "They're a lot of bother." He sniffed the aroma. "What's the occasion? You never fry potatoes anymore.

I thought you were afraid that I was going to die of clogged arteries." He put his gun and holster on the closet shelf.

Mary set two plates on the table without looking up. "I've been craving hash browns all day, so I decided we'd live dangerously." Her body language said she was upset about something. Floyd quickly ran through the possible causes, which involved him. He couldn't think of anything he'd done, but that left the "sins of omission" category wide open. Her usual retort in similar situations, "Well, if you don't know why I'm mad," still stung.

Floyd slid behind her, wrapped his arms around her waist, and nuzzled the graying hair behind her ear. "I'll bet that you're just trying to get on my good side so that you can take advantage of me later."

She shook her head, and gently elbowed him away with apparent annoyance. "Let me get supper together. Go change." She went back to the stove and stirred a pot of green beans as he walked down the hall.

In spite of their three-year relationship, Floyd and Mary were adults who'd lived alone for years before they became an item. Floyd irritated Mary weekly, often over things he considered so trivial he was unaware there was a line, or that he'd crossed it. The last incident had been over a pair of pants with bloodstains. Instead of soaking them in cold water, he'd thrown them into the washer. Unaware of the stains, Mary ran a load of laundry, setting the stains and ruining the pants. After an evening of cold shoulder with no clue what was wrong, Mary dragged out the pants and explained the problem. Now he checked every shirt and pair of pants for stains before throwing them into the laundry hamper.

Floyd slid on a pair of jeans and went back to the kitchen as Mary piled sizzling potatoes next to a slab of fried ham. She turned back to the stove as he sat down and returned with a serving bowl of green beans. She scooped some onto the plate while hiding her face from him.

"What's the matter honey?" She stopped at the sink and hung her head while Floyd cut a bite of ham. A low sob preceded the shudder of her body. She turned and lurched out the back door before he could set down his utensils.

Floyd found her sitting on the steps, the puppy on her lap. He sat next to her, and she buried her face into his shoulder. They sat in a silent embrace until her sobs stopped. The puppy pushed between them and whimpered in confusion. When Mary stopped crying, she petted the pup gently. She whispered to the puppy. "I found a lump in my breast."

Floyd took the puppy from her arms and set it on the step. He lifted Mary's chin and stared into the reddened eyes. "When did you...?"

"I called Dr. Bergstrom's office this morning for an appointment. He sent me to Mora for a mammogram. They had me wait while the radiologist checked it." The tears welled in her eyes again and her voice cracked. "It's probably..." She buried her face in his shoulder and shuddered with sobs.

Floyd sat stunned for a moment. "So fast. How could they be sure without a biopsy? When...?" He couldn't come up with any other words.

As the shudders waned, she pulled a Kleenex from her pocket and wiped her nose. Between sniffles she responded. "They've scheduled an appointment with the surgeon for the day after tomorrow. They assume the worst and act aggressively." The puppy stuck its nose under her elbow and tried to climb back onto Mary's lap. Mary sat the puppy on a lower step before walking into the house. She almost fell over the puppy as it raced back up the steps and between her feet. Floyd steadied her and held the puppy back so they could slip through the door.

Mary sat down at the table and pushed some of the cooled potatoes onto her fork. "Dr. Bergstrom wants me to see an oncologist in Duluth tomorrow. Can you get away?"

Floyd was dumbstruck, staring out the window. "Sure. Whatever." He watched a squirrel push millet out of the bird feeder in a search for sunflower seeds. The squirrel attracted the puppy's attention, and she ran across the yard yipping at it. The squirrel chattered a warning in return. "Are they sure it's cancer? There are benign breast tumors too."

Mary pushed the potatoes around the plate as the grease congealed around them. "The radiologist was pessimistic. There's a chance it's benign, but it's slim."

Floyd took a deep breath as he considered the situation. He could pass off his duties at the sheriff's department. He thought of the people that he would have to call to set those wheels in motion. Then he said, "We'll have to call Trish and Emily to let them know what's going on."

Mary set the fork down and stared at the plate. "Let's not tell my sisters until we know more. Okay?"

"Whatever you want."

Mary slid her chair away from the table. "I want this to be done. I want my health back."

Floyd followed her and found her curled on the couch with a pillow clutched to her stomach. "Can I do anything for you?" He sat down next to her and stroked her hip gently.

She shook her head. "I want to curl up and pretend that none of this is happening. Why me? Why now?"

Floyd opened his mouth to offer comfort, then realized that he didn't have the words to offer. He let out a breath and ran his hands over her hair. He whispered, "I love you," as the tears welled in his eyes. They spooned silently on the couch, the fear and anxiety crushing both of them.

An hour later, Floyd got up and dialed the dispatcher. "Jodi, tell the sheriff I won't be in tomorrow. I'll call him later. Leave a note for C.J. Tell her she's got the ball on the Palmquist case."

Floyd returned to the living room and clicked through the television channels until he found *Pillow Talk* on the old movie channel. Doris Day was waltzing across the screen as he slipped in behind Mary on the couch. They curled together; her head rested on his arm as she grasped his strong hand between her two hands. "I'm so scared."

"Me too."

Chapter 6

C.J. read the single message on her desktop. "I've got the ball?"

She marched to the dispatcher's cube and leaned on the divider, waving the note at him. The dispatcher read the note and shrugged his shoulders. "Jodi took it last night. I have no idea what ball you've got."

C.J. walked back to the ready room and refilled her coffee mug. At the desk she pulled out the number for the K-9 sergeant from Chisago County. A woman answered the phone and C.J. heard children fighting in the background as she waited for Pat Radosovich.

Pam entered the bullpen wearing a sheriff's department uniform shirt over loose-fitting jeans. Pam waved to C.J., got her coffee mug, and popped a K-cup into the brewer. It hissed and gurgled. C.J. put her hand over the phone. "I got a strange note from Floyd," she said, waving the pink slip. Pam took the note from her as the Chisago deputy answered. "Has he ever said something like this to you?"

"Hi, I'm C.J. Jensen, from the Pine County Sheriff's Department. Floyd Swenson said you might be able to give me a hand finding a lost piece of evidence in a ditch."

Pat Radosovich burst out in laughter. "Good old Sergeant Swenson volunteered me for a job. Which county does he think I work for?"

"Umm, he said that you owed him a favor."

Radosovich let out another resounding laugh. "I think he's got that backwards. Woody and I have bailed him out a couple of times. I don't think he's ever returned the favor with anything but more work." He paused and got serious. "What, specifically, do you need?"

"We had a chase yesterday. The suspect tossed stuff out of his pickup window. We recovered two packages of marijuana and a Ziploc containing white powder, but the suspect threw another brown bag during the chase we couldn't find. It went into a stretch of ditch that's filled with water. Can the dog search anything like that?"

Radosovich paused before replying. "Maybe, maybe not. Sometimes the water helps by spreading the scent. What do you think is in the bag? More drugs probably." He answered his own question. "Can you get something that belongs to the suspect to give Woody a scent?"

C.J. thought for a second about going to the boy's house, then remembered Floyd's encounter with the father and decided against that. "I can probably get something out of the suspect's impounded pickup."

"I'll call dispatch while you do that and clear a couple hours. Call me back when you're ready to go," Radosovich said.

The sheriff caught the last part of the conversation as he made himself a cup of coffee from the coffee machine. "What's up with my favorite deputies today?"

Pam lifted the stack on her desk. "Floyd handed me all the files he's been avoiding for the last year."

Sepanen stirred creamer into his coffee. "C.J., did I overhear you talking to Deputy Radosovich?"

"The suspect threw a bag during the chase, and we couldn't find it. Floyd suggested contacting Deputy Radosovich to bring his dog here for a search. He wants me to get something that belonged to the suspect. I was planning to get something from the pickup truck to give the dog a scent."

"Try for fabric. Cotton is best. It holds a lot of scent. And put it into a clean, plastic bag."

C.J. nodded as the sheriff walked away. Pam watched the sheriff retreating and waited for the sound of his closing office door. "Be careful when the sheriff's around. He likes to throw out solutions to problems."

"That's a bad thing?" C.J. asked. She was unaccustomed to dealing with the Cloquet Police Chief, who interacted very little with his officers. Having the sheriff overhear and engage in conversation made her uneasy.

Pam shrugged. "His directions are usually rudimentary, meant for a rookie. He expects us to accept them gracefully and act on them." Pam looked down the hallway again. "We try not to have any case discussion when he's around. You can't say no to him, and he sometimes has us chasing wild geese."

"So, you change the discussion to the weather when the sheriff shows up?" C.J. asked.

"The weather, our dogs, our spouses, the lunch special at Nicoll's Café are all safe topics. Pretty much anything but our cases."

C.J. sat on the corner of Pam's desk. "Floyd never warned me about that. What else should I know?"

Pam glanced around. "This is still a boy's club and we're outsiders. It's getting better all the time, but don't be surprised by an off-color joke or inappropriate question about your personal life."

C.J. sipped her coffee. "Pam, I've been in law enforcement for nearly two decades and believe me, this is one of the classier departments. Floyd has been an absolute gentleman and the rest of the guys have all treated me with respect. I've got no complaints."

Pam smiled. "Good. You're tough and are prepared for this. I came in as a rookie from a small town and I had major culture shock. Between arresting felons and the shop talk here in the bullpen, I was overwhelmed. I think the guys had a lot of fun trying to see which of them could make me blush the deepest red."

"You weathered it."

"I got through it but told a couple of them they were out of line. They respected me for defining the boundaries. The guys are good, but Floyd's a master of letting inappropriate comments slip, like his comment about picking up your underwear so the dog doesn't chew it up."

"I shared too much information. I shouldn't have been surprised when Floyd got in his dig. He was just kidding around." C.J. finished her coffee, put the mug on her desk, and hesitated. "Floyd's a really nice guy, isn't he?"

Pam sipped her coffee and stared at C.J. over the rim of the mug. "Floyd's saved my butt, literally. He's my best friend."

"Floyd told me about the shootout at the old hotel when he fell down the stairs. He said you provided covering fire until he got on his feet and got his weapon out." C.J. paused, watching Pam's complexion turn from milky to red. "That took some balls."

"I knew he would've done the same for me." Pam stared into C.J.'s eyes. "If I can't count on you to do the same thing for me, turn in your badge and leave."

"In my twenty years as a Cloquet cop, I never fired my weapon at anything but a paper target." C.J. patted her holster. "But, if you ever need me, I'll have your back."

"And I'll have yours." Pam cracked a smile. "And that includes emergency doggy daycare."

"Are you working tomorrow? My doggie daycare woman is taking her father to the doctor."

"I'll be here. Remind me of her name."

"She's Bailey, and a sweetheart. She loves everyone." C.J. looked at the clock. "I've got to drive to the impound lot. I'll catch you later."

"Be safe."

* * *

Dylan Johnson threw Brady Werther against the metal lockers with a crash. A few students reacted to the noise with curiosity. The rest scattered. "What the fuck did you tell the cops, dude?"

98

Brady struggled against the grasp half-heartedly. "Hey, man. I didn't tell them anything."

A teacher stuck his head out of the door and glared at the two boys. Dylan quickly released his grip and pushed his face close to Brady's. "They must've busted Taco because you tipped them off."

"I heard he squealed at the emergency room."

Brady pushed off and straightened his drooping flannel shirt. "God man, you are so paranoid. It'll all be good. I heard Taco tossed the stash before the cops caught him." He made a furtive look in the direction of the door where the teacher had been. "But I think we need to worry about Laura. She'll crack."

The bell rang, signaling the start of class. The last of the other students disappeared into classrooms. "What's to crack over? She knows about the dope, but nothin' else. We're okay."

"She doesn't know about Tammi?" Brady asked as the two boys started toward their first class.

"You and I didn't tell her, and Ted wouldn't say anything."

Dylan hesitated outside a door where a teacher was starting his lecture. "Yeah, but she and Ted were sucking face. Maybe he..." Dylan said to no one as Brady disappeared around the corner.

* * *

The Pine County impound lot was just outside of Pine City, near the river. The chain link fence was topped with razor wire to discourage people from stealing catalytic converters or vandalizing impounded vehicles. Standing at the gate, C.J. grew anxious at the thought of wandering through the eerie mix of vehicles. Some had been seized from criminals while others had been abandoned. The most disturbing had spider-webbed windshields where heads had struck them or blood-soaked interiors from grisly accidents.

Deputy Maki's county cruiser drove up and parked near the open gate. Knowing there was another deputy inside the fence eased her apprehension. C.J. waved at Sandy, then walked through the gate, skirting the oily puddles in the mud. She heard the whine of a winch nearby, a tow truck lowering a vehicle in an opening two rows farther into the lot.

She quickly found Juan's pickup. Because the crushed top jammed the doors, she had to climb through the broken windshield to access the mangled cab. With one knee on the dash and the other on the seat she surveyed the contents. There were empty beer cans, hamburger wrappers, paper napkins, and ketchup packets strewn everywhere. Eventually, C.J. spotted the toe of a tennis shoe wedged under the accelerator pedal.

The tow truck rumbled past as she twisted around the steering wheel and reached down. The old canvas shoe, dirty and worn through on the sides, seemed perfect. Kneeling on the pickup's front seat, she slipped a Ziploc bag out of her pocket and put the shoe in it. She slid the bag onto the hood, then carefully climbed through the broken windshield taking care not to get scraped or tear her uniform.

She met Sandy Maki at the gate where he was making notes, a knee propped on the bumper of a battered Buick. "Hey, Sandy, it's past the end of your shift. Isn't Barb waiting for you at the apartment?"

He laughed. "Barb is probably still in bed. She's too keyed up to sleep when she gets off work from the bar. So, she sits up half the night watching television. It was better when she worked at the drugstore photo counter. She got bored with that after working a cold case with Floyd, so went back to bartending and sleeping days."

C.J. shook her head. "I still have a hard time picturing the two of you together. Would you have ever asked her for a date if she hadn't drafted you to protect her after arresting her biker boyfriend?"

"Probably not."

C.J. looked at Sandy's mud-spattered uniform and asked, "What happened to you?"

Sandy picked a small clump of dried mud off his shirt. "Floyd ditched a deer poaching surveillance assignment last night, so I picked it up. So, after a week of no activity, the poachers shoot a deer. I was first on the scene. One guy gave up, but the other one decided to run through a swamp. Didn't catch up with him for a while." He jerked his thumb over his shoulder. "We impounded their Buick."

As she approached, C.J. could smell the pungent odor of rotting swamp vegetation permeating Sandy's clothing. "Whew! You smell like you just got out of a hog wallow."

Sandy gave her a look of disdain. "Thanks, I like your perfume too." He folded the notebook and asked. "What're you doing in the impound lot?"

"I've got a Chisago County K-9 unit coming up. The dog is going to search the ditch for the bag that was thrown during yesterday's chase. The handler wanted something with scent for the dog." She waved the bag with the worn shoe.

Sandy smiled. "You'll get to wade the swampy ditches."

C.J. got a vision of wading in putrid swamp water. "Oh shit. I never thought of that. Does the department have any hip boots?"

Sandy shook his head as he climbed into his cruiser. "Not that I've ever seen. Maybe you could buy a pair at Walmart."

* * *

The dispatcher buzzed Sandy and C.J. through the security door at the sheriff's department. They wound their way past the offices and into the bullpen where Pam was studying a file. C.J. brewed herself a cup of coffee, then called the K-9 officer to confirm that she had a shoe for scent.

Pam looked up as they entered. "What happened to you, Sandy? You smell like a roadkill deer."

Sandy hung his jacket on the back of a chair. "Some of us have to work in the field and get dirty."

Radosovich's voice boomed over the phone. "I talked to my undersheriff who cleared my time with you this morning. Where do you want to meet?"

C.J.'s voice couldn't mask her enthusiasm. "Come right to the county courthouse. The ditch is east of town."

"I'll be there in half an hour. Is Swenson coming along? I haven't seen him in months."

"He's got some kind of family emergency. He won't be in today."

* * *

The puppy emerged from under the steps as Floyd and Mary stepped out of the house. It shivered in the morning cold and whimpered, looking at Mary with sad eyes.

"Oh, Floyd, she's half frozen. Get a blanket." Mary hurried down the steps.

He watched the puppy scramble from under the steps. Mary swept it into her arms. "Go on, Floyd. Get the old comforter from the closet."

Floyd grumbled as he went back in the house and retrieved the comforter, a huge puff in his arms as he navigated the steps. "You know that you'll never get rid of that dog if you do this." He handed Mary the comforter and she wrapped it around the whimpering puppy.

Mary ignored his comments. "Why don't you get her the scraps from supper, too. The potatoes would do her a world of good. Besides, we're only taking care of her until the real owner shows up."

Floyd and Mary watched the puppy wolf down the fried potatoes and then tied her to the railing with a length of baling twine. By the time they were through dealing with the puppy it was still too early to depart for Mary's doctor appointment, but she was anxious to leave. Mary was silent as they drove through the rural area around Floyd's house. She sat with her legs wrapped in a blanket on the seat of the pickup. Even though the heater was set on high, she shivered. Floyd had beads of sweat on his forehead by the time he stopped at the Moose Lake Co-op to get gas, coffee, and to shed his coat.

When he started the pickup, Mary reached over and clicked the fan speed up another notch. Floyd watched in despair. He'd been cooler in a sauna but didn't want to bring that up. As they passed the Thompson Hill exit, they saw a great expanse of fog blanketing the city of Duluth and Lake Superior.

"Spring fog again." Floyd commented. "I can't even see the Enger Tower on Skyline Drive." The tower, capped with its green beacon light, had been built high above the Duluth Harbor to greet the throngs of Scandinavians coming to a new homeland.

Mary didn't respond.

"Are you in pain?"

She didn't look up but mumbled into the blanket. "I haven't had any pain. The lump is just there."

Floyd sickened at the thought of a tumor growing in Mary's breast. *"What if it isn't treatable? What if it's benign? What if I lose her, like I did Ginny? Could I face that again?"* The thoughts raced through Floyd's head as the interstate descended into West Duluth.

Seeing only the downtown buildings overlooking the freeway through the blanket of fog, they took the 21st Avenue East Exit. Climbing the hill, they passed through the posh Mount Royal neighborhood near the University of Minnesota campus. Floyd pulled into the Mount Royal shopping center and parked in front of a small restaurant. "Let's have a cup of coffee. Your appointment isn't for another hour."

Mary shuddered in response. "You go ahead. Leave the engine on. I'll wait for you."

Floyd gently peeled the blanket out of her grip. "You're coming along. You can't sit out here looking like an abandoned puppy staring through the windshield." She released her grip on the blanket and shivered in pained resignation.

Floyd ordered a bagel and a cup of coffee. Mary ordered herbal tea. When their order came, she held the tea, cupped in her hands as if it were the only heat in the restaurant.

"I hate the Duluth fog," she said between sips, looking out the window. "The fog makes it seem so much colder. Did you notice that the grass isn't even starting to get green here? It's almost May."

Floyd was relieved that she was finally offering conversation without a direct question. "But it's so nice and cool in the summer."

Mary shivered again, spilling some tea on her hand. She set the cup down and dabbed at the spill with a paper napkin.

"There's no summer here, Floyd. Haven't you noticed that the lilacs don't even bloom here until a month before the maples turn red? Duluth slides right from late spring into early fall, skipping right over summer."

The waitress appeared from behind Mary and topped off Floyd's coffee. "I like it here." She'd apparently overheard Mary's remarks. The waitress was a woman about twenty who appeared to be a college student making a few dollars between classes. "It's fresh, and you don't have the bums, panhandlers, and animal rights protesters like on Nicollet Mall in Minneapolis. They say the cold keeps out the riff-raff."

Floyd smiled and gave her a wink. She set the coffeepot down and ripped their bill off a pad, setting it on the table next to Floyd. He handed her a ten-dollar-bill without looking at the check. "Keep the change."

As the waitress walked away, Mary leaned forward. "You just gave her a six-dollar tip."

"I know. She's a bright kid who's working her way through college." He pushed his wallet back into his pocket and checked his watch. "Do you want to go for a walk?"

Mary shook her head. "I'm just getting warm. Let me finish my tea and then we can go over to the doctor's office."

"Your appointment isn't for another half hour."

Mary stood. "Maybe they'll get me in early."

* * *

Engrossed in Floyd's interview notes, Pete Radosovich surprised Pam and C.J. when he walked into the sheriff's office area and boomed, "Who's Deputy Jensen?" He was nearly six-five, but barely thirty inches around the waist. He'd shaven a few hours earlier, yet the hint of dark whiskers showed on his face.

Setting aside Floyd's interview file, C.J. jumped up, and put out her hand. "I'm C.J."

His giant fist engulfed her small hand. "Nice to meet you."

"Would you like a cup of coffee?"

Seeing the Keurig brewer, he smiled. "I'd love a cup of coffee that hasn't been sitting on the warmer for a whole shift."

After popping a pod into the machine, C.J. nodded to a county map on the wall near the coffee pot. She pointed to a road that cut through an unpopulated woodland area. She traced a path along red lines with her finger. "This is where we chased the suspect. He threw out packages here." The symbols for swamp lined the road she'd indicated.

The coffee maker gurgled, signaling the end of the brewing cycle. Radosovich removed the cup and savored the hot brew. "Is the road blacktop or gravel?"

"The red lines are gravel roads with no shoulders. Eighteen inches off the road you're up to the fenders in swamp water and mud."

Radosovich nodded, then looked at Pam, who was watching them from her desk. "Is that what happened to you, Ryan? You drove into the ditch?"

Pam smiled. "Hi, Pete. I'm now Pam Conrad, married and just back from maternity leave. This is C.J.'s show."

Radosovich looked back at the map again. "So, your suspect threw something out the window along here, and you think it landed in the ditch." He considered the winding route from the courthouse to the area C.J. wanted to search. "I'll follow you."

C.J. hesitated. "Can your dog find something in the water?" She looked skeptical.

"He can if the evidence hasn't been there too long. The scent actually floats on the surface where the dog picks it. Wet is better than dry. When Woody's nose dries out, he can't pick up scent unless it's very fresh. Dampness makes the scent hang longer." Radosovich looked over at Pam, who had gone back to the computer. "We should bring Pam along too. I'd like to block the road at both ends so no one hits the dog if he gets excited and runs across the road."

Pam shook her head. "I'm on limited duty. I'm tied to this desk and doing nothing but clearing old reports."

C.J. gave Pam her teasing smile. "C'mon Pam. Floyd's out, and Sandy Maki's serving papers. We need help. You can sit in the car."

Pam closed the file she'd been reviewing. She cast her eyes to the ceiling briefly but was smiling, hinting at her willingness to get away from the desk. "Okay. Let's make it quick."

Chapter 7

C.J. pulled her cruiser to the side of the road just over the top of a rise. Radosovich and Pam pulled in behind her. The three of them stood by the vehicles and looked down a half-mile stretch of road. On each side was a narrow ditch filled with water. Beyond the ditch, the alder and dogwood were just starting to sprout leaf buds. A cold east wind tugged at the officers' caps and jackets.

C.J. pointed to the south side of the road. "I was following about thirty yards back, and Floyd had the road blocked ahead. I thought the paper bag was thrown out near the bottom of the hill. Sandy and I looked in the weeds but couldn't find anything. The kid tossed three other packages, none of them got to the edge of the water, but they were light. The one we're missing must've gone out a little farther off the road. Maybe the last package weighed more than the bags of drugs we recovered."

Radosovich surveyed the area while Woody offered yelps of anticipation from back the Chisago County cruiser. The dog anxiously paced the platform in the back of the car. "I want the road blocked on both ends. Pam, park down a quarter mile. C.J., you block the road at the top of the hill behind us, then you can ride with me. You said he threw the bag near the bottom?" C.J. nodded, yes. "We'll start walking the ditch halfway to the bottom and see what we find."

Pam parked diagonally on the road, lights flashing, about a quarter mile away. C.J. blocked the road behind Radosovich and came back to his car with the shoe from the suspect's pickup. She got in the front seat, immediately smelling the dog. Woody chirped yelps of excitement into her ear.

"This smells like my car when my basset hound rides with me. Does Woody live with you? I thought I heard him in the background when I called."

Radosovich drove the cruiser down the hill. "Woody's a family dog. It helps keep him socialized. He plays with my kids, so I don't have to be nervous about having him around children on the job. When we're in the cruiser, he's all business; he knows the difference."

Parking near the bottom of the hill, Radosovich pulled a short leash from the dash. Opening the rear door a crack, he attached the leash to the dog who bounded out but quickly heeled at his master's side. Pam watched in the distance.

"Give me the shoe, C.J." Taking the shoe from the evidence bag Radosovich held it out for the dog. Woody eagerly nosed it from top to bottom and end to end.

Radosovich handed the shoe back to C.J. and knelt down next to the dog, who was now quivering with anticipation. The deputy unclipped the leash and pointed to the ditch. "Find." Woody, now a brown streak, raced to the edge of the ditch, stopping at the first tall sedge and lifting his leg.

C.J. grinned. "He's got priorities."

Woody quickly moved down the ditch, the officers walking briskly to keep up with him. The dog pushed his nose through the grass along the edge of the water and worked up and down the narrow edge of the road between the gravel and water. He hesitated once but kept moving along.

C.J. pulled her collar up. "How will we know if he finds something?" She jammed her hands in the jacket pockets and hunched her shoulders.

"Just watch his tail. See how it glides back and forth with every step. If he finds a scent, his tail will go nuts and he'll bark."

They were nearing the lowest spot in the road when Woody's tail went berserk. The dog hesitated a second, then lunged ahead with his nose at the water's edge. Woody gave sharp barks of excitement. He raced ahead a few yards, then came back to the spot where he'd barked.

"It must be right here." As Radosovich spoke, the dog lunged into the water and bounded through the weeds. He pushed into the brush and started to whimper and bark. The tail moved so fast it was a blur.

"He's got it." Radosovich yelled across the ditch to the dog, "Good boy, Woody."

C.J. watched in amazement. "Have him bring it back."

Radosovich laughed. "Sorry, he's not trained to retrieve. We want evidence found, but not disturbed. You'll have to wade across."

C.J. looked at the canine officer with pleading eyes.

The Chisago deputy shook his head. "Uh uh. I'm doing you guys a favor."

Looking at the ditch, C.J. sighed. "I think it's more than crotch deep."

"Your point?"

C.J. wrinkled her forehead. "You wouldn't want me to get a bladder infection."

"Really! You're playing the sex card?"

"You're married. You get it."

"Oh, for Christ's sake." Radosovich pulled off his jacket and handed it to C.J., then unbuckled his belt. She set his belt and holster on top of his jacket. He waded into the frigid water, ankle, calf, then thigh deep.

Radosovich swore when he caught a toe on a submerged object and fell to his knees, getting wet to his armpits. He muttered a low oath as he stood up and fought through brush to reach the dog. Pulling grass aside, he exposed a soggy paper lunch bag. He took a pair of purple gloves out of his back pocket. Gloved, he lifted the bag, then peeled back the soggy paper.

"There's a revolver and a sack of pills," he said as he slid a gloved finger through the trigger guard of the revolver and lifted the gun out of the sodden paper. With his other hand, he scooped up the rest of the bag and its contents. The dog followed him as he slogged back across the ditch. "Woody, heel." The dog raced to his master's side and sat down. Radosovich handed C.J. the gun, bag, and pills, then reattached Woody's leash as water streamed from the cuffs of his pants.

The bright chrome finish of the Colt revolver dangling from C.J.'s finger sparkled in the sunlight. "The bag weighed a lot more than the packages of drugs, so it had enough momentum to fly into the brush. I hope we can pull some prints off it."

Reclaiming the soggy bag, Radosovich peeled back the paper. Inside was a Ziploc bag of pills and gray powder. "There must be half a kilo…of something." He watched C.J. inspect the gun. "I'll bet that revolver has some history. You don't throw a Colt Python out the window unless you've got a very guilty conscience. Those old Colts run about a grand at gun shows. That's not a throwaway gun."

C.J. opened the cylinder and ejected the cartridges into her palm. She looked up.

"The serial number is intact. I think you're right about the gun's history; there's one spent cartridge. That makes me very suspicious."

The dog shivered as they spoke. "I've got a dog that needs a towel. We're all done here, aren't we?" Radosovich led Woody to the trunk of his cruiser. He pulled out a child's beach towel and started to rub muddy residue from the dog's legs and belly. Woody arched his back in pleasure.

"I've got some evidence bags here if you'd like to bag that stuff," Radosovich said, and he dried his pants with a second beach towel. "Tell Swenson he owes me big time for this one."

C.J. placed the revolver and other baggies into evidence bags, then signed them. Radosovich opened the rear door for Woody, who hopped in happily, much less disturbed by being damp than was his handler. With his belt and jacket on Radosovich looked at C.J. She leaned on the top of the cruiser. "Are we good?"

He rolled his eyes. "Yeah, we're fine. But the next time we go out to wade in ditches, you'd better bring waders or a wet suit because it'll be your turn to get wet."

C.J. looked down. "I'm really sorry, but…"

"Yeah, yeah. Get in and I'll give you a ride to your car."

C.J. waved goodbye as the Chisago deputy and Woody drove away. Pam pulled alongside C.J.'s car. "It looked like you recovered a gun and a bag."

"A pistol with one spent cartridge and a bag of gray powder we'll have to get tested."

"I was surprised the dog handler waded into the ditch. Did he need to be the one to praise the dog and recover the evidence?"

"Um, I told him I'd get a bladder infection if the water was more than thigh deep."

Pam's eyes went wide. "You didn't!"

Looking sheepish, C.J. nodded.

Pam laughed. "There's no way any of our guys would've let me get by with an excuse like that."

C.J. shrugged. "It was worth a try, and I really didn't want to wade into the muck. Who knows, I might've got a UTI from the stagnant water."

Pam shifted the cruiser into gear. "I'll meet you at Tobies. The coffee and caramel rolls are on me."

"You don't need to do that."

"I haven't had a coffee with anyone but my husband since the baby was born. I need to have a cup of coffee and a roll to reacclimate myself to life outside the house."

Pam and C.J. parked their cruisers in the back row of Tobies' lot and got a table near the kitchen. With coffee and rolls ordered, Pam leaned forward. "Floyd and the sheriff only told me a bit about you. What's your story?"

C.J. shared the story of her husband's death and Pam talked about her fairy tale engagement, aided by Floyd and Mary, the wedding in her family church in the weeks before it closed, Luke's birth, her mother's irritation when she did the math and realized Pam had been pregnant at the wedding, and her loneliness and depression after the mothers went home and she was alone with the baby.

C.J. reached out and touched Pam's hand. "How are you now?"

Pam shrugged. "Getting back to work helps, but I hate dropping Luke off. He cries, then I go to the car and cry, too."

C.J. took a business card out of her pocket and wrote a number on the back of it. "Here's my cell phone number. If you ever need to talk to someone, call."

"That's nice, but I hardly know you."

"Pam, we're both going through rough patches. I've got my own separation issues, losing Bobby and moving. Having someone to talk to would be…nice."

Putting out her hand, Pam said, "Give me your cell phone." Pam programmed numbers into the phone and handed it back. "Those are my cell and home numbers. Anytime you want to talk, just call."

C.J. pulled her pecan-topped caramel roll apart and popped a piece into her mouth, then licked the dribbling caramel off her fingers. "Tell me about the deputies. I've met them all and they seem nice, but I don't really know any of them."

Pam looked around furtively. "I've worked with Floyd the most and he's like my second father. Sandy and I were hired about the same time. He's married to the woman he rescued from a biker—she used to be a stripper."

"No way! Sandy told me he's married to a bartender. His wife used to be a stripper?!"

"Barb has dozens of tattoos and she's hinted that some are unfit for polite company. She said some are hidden by her skimpy bikini. She's really nice and is trying hard to live the life of a deputy's wife, but every once in a while, her old persona slips out." Pam paused to eat some of her roll. "Kerm is great for backup. He wades fearlessly into anything."

"What about the rest of the department?" C.J. asked.

"Sergeant Tom Thompson is a great administrator, spending most of his time in the office. The other road deputies are good guys. I mean, they're serious and never hesitate to back you up, but they have little interest in making the phone calls and knocking on doors that make up the bulk of an investigation."

C.J. wiped warm caramel off her fingers. "So, you think this is a pretty good department. It sounds like you'd be happy if you spent the rest of your career here."

"I've never worked in another department, so I've got no point of reference. But I'm comfortable here. Floyd took me under his wing as soon as I arrived. He made me feel accepted and appreciated. It took the rest of the guys a while to warm up, but they treat me as an equal now. So yes, I'll probably stay with this department." Pam signaled the waitress for a coffee refill. "How about you? You were hired to cover for my maternity leave. Is staying on here an option?"

Waiting silently while the waitress topped their coffee, C.J. thought. "Patrolling a rural county is strange after being a city cop. I'm accustomed to backup being minutes away. Here, we're really on our own. It's nice to be independent, but it's also nice to know there's someone nearby if you get in trouble. On the other hand, there's variety here. Patrolling the countryside is more interesting than driving the same city streets every day. I'm getting used to this and enjoying it. So, yes, I could see myself staying around if it's an option."

Their radios announced an accident on Highway 23. C.J. stood and reached for her wallet. Pam stopped her. "Take the call. I'll pay for coffee."

"Thanks. Let's do this again. I haven't made many friends down here," C. J. said before trotting to the restaurant door.

* * *

Laura Tomlinson sat alone at the end of a long lunch table, oblivious to the hundred conversations going on around her. She picked the top bun off greasy sloppy joe filling and tore it apart, eating the pieces. Brady Werther and Tyler Espe took seats on either side of her. Dylan Johnson placed his tray across from her and sat down. Laura looked up from her lunch and fear swept over her.

"What?"

Dylan leaned his face close to Laura's while Tyler and Brady watched for the lunchroom monitor. "Are you feeling guilty?" he asked.

Laura shook her head. "Uh uh."

"Shhhhh," said Tyler. "Here comes Mrs. Gillespe. Eat." He wolfed a bite of his sloppy joe. As the monitor passed, she gave them a close look. Laura looked up with pleading eyes, but Dylan quickly stepped on her foot under the table, and she looked away.

Dylan pushed his tray to the side and leaned forward again. "What'd you tell the cops?" The words dripped with venom.

Laura's eyes grew wide with recognition. "Nothing. He wanted to know about Ted. I told him Ted had been sick. He wanted to know if Ted's mom ever beat him up. That's all." Her voice was half an octave too high, and the words came out with a pleading whine.

"What did you tell them about Tammi?" Brady asked.

"She ran away," Laura replied. "What else is there to say?"

Dylan pushed his face so close that she could smell his breath. "That better be all. If the cops come snooping around because you told them something, your ass is grass and I'm the lawnmower."

A bell rang, ending the lunch period. The boys pushed away from the table and walked out the door, leaving Laura staring at their trays and her own untouched meal. Tears formed in her eyes as she ran for the cafeteria door dragging her book bag.

At her locker, Laura jammed in books from the morning classes and tried to pry the afternoon books out. Her hands were shaking so badly that everything in the locker spilled onto the floor. She sat next to the pile, sobbing. Students rushed by and several stared, but no one stopped.

Laura arrived after the bell for her next class. Her eyes were red, and tears stained her black t-shirt. The teacher noted her late arrival and was going to make a comment when he saw the tear stains and the red eyes. "Laura, come here."

Don Cole led her out of the classroom and closed the door behind them. In the empty hallway he asked, "Laura, are you okay?"

She sniffled and nodded.

"I heard about Ted Palmquist. You were good friends, weren't you?" Mr. Cole jammed his hands in his pockets and leaned against the door to look like a friend rather than an authority figure. Laura just nodded in response.

"Have you talked to the counselor about Ted?"

Laura shook her head.

"Hang on a second." He disappeared into the classroom and gave a reading assignment to the class. "Let's walk down to the counseling office together."

"Um, Mr. Cole, I really don't want to…"

"Laura, something is wrong, and you need to talk to someone about it."

Chapter 8

Floyd and Mary sat in adjoining chairs waiting for Mary's name to be called. They paged through magazines and didn't speak. When the receptionist called Mary's name, she took Floyd's hand. "I'm not doing this alone."

In the exam room, Mary sat shivering in a paper gown while Floyd mopped nervous perspiration from his forehead. When Dr. Madsen finally arrived, they felt like they'd spent half a lifetime waiting.

Terry Madsen was reading Mary's chart as he walked into the exam room. When he looked up, he was surprised to see Floyd sitting in the corner. "Hello." He nodded to Floyd and offered his hand to Mary.

Madsen pulled a rolling stool next to the examining table and continued to read the chart. "I see from Dr. Bergstrom's notes that you have a suspicious lump. Any pain associated with it?"

Mary bit at her lower lip. "No. I feel fine."

"Hmm. When did you first notice this?" He went to a computer monitor over the corner desk and looked at the mammograms.

"I guess it was three days ago. I was showering and noticed a lump."

"Lie back on the table please." Madsen slipped on a pair of exam gloves, lifted the paper gown, and closed his eyes as he palpated Mary's breasts. Floyd observed, thinking it was like watching a blind man, using his fingers to read a topographic map.

When Madsen was done, he pulled the gown down and helped Mary sit up before slipping off the gloves. Without saying anything, he went to the computer and entered notes.

Madsen turned and rolled his stool to the exam table. "As Dr. Bergstrom noted, the lump looks suspicious." He let the words settle in for a second. "I recommend that we schedule you for a lumpectomy as soon as we can schedule it. I can have my assistant work out the details with you. I assume that you have some questions."

Tears streaked Mary's cheeks. "How sure are you that it's cancer? I mean, are you 100% sure?" She retrieved her clothes from behind the door and began dressing while still in the gown.

Madsen shook his head. "There's no 100%. But I wouldn't delay aggressively moving ahead based on the small chance we might be wrong."

Floyd hesitated to enter the conversation. When it seemed Mary had nothing else to ask, he jumped in. "What happens if it is cancer, and we do surgery tomorrow?"

Madsen turned on the stool to face Floyd while Mary slipped on her shoes and threw the paper gown in the wastebasket. "We'll discuss the likely options, a lumpectomy vs. mastectomy. We may want to remove the nearby lymph glands. Depending on what we see, we'll talk about chemo and radiation."

"But you won't know until you get inside?" As Floyd spoke, Mary pulled on her sweatshirt.

"No." Madsen replied. "The only way to know the full involvement is surgery."

Mary reached for the doorknob and Floyd stood up. "Where are you going?"

Facing him with tears flowing down her cheek. She barely choked out the word, "home." Then she pulled the door open and disappeared.

Floyd put his hand on the doctor's shoulder as he raced past. "We'll call back later." He followed Mary down the hall and through the lobby. Sobbing at the door of the pickup, she waited for him to unlock it.

Inside the truck, Floyd started the engine and pushed the knob to make sure the heater was at its highest setting. "Would you like to go to the Pickwick for lunch? It's right across the street."

She stared straight ahead and bit at her bottom lip. "I want to go home."

* * *

C.J. and Pam reviewed the contents of the bag. They logged the evidence and ran a preliminary NIK test, which indicated the gray powder was methamphetamine. Pam packaged a sample for shipment to the Minnesota BCA lab in St. Paul.

"I haven't heard much about speed or angel dust around here. The drug of choice in Cloquet seems to be beer rather than hard stuff," C.J. commented as she resealed the bag of powder and placed it in an evidence bag. She signed her name across the seal so it would be evident if the sample was tampered with in the property room.

Using a piece of clear tape, Pam lifted a partial fingerprint off the revolver. She mounted the tape on an evidence card and made a note under it. Then she removed the six cartridges from an evidence bag, letting them fall onto the tabletop.

"Hmm, one has been fired. How interesting."

C.J. watched. "I noted that when I emptied the cylinder at the scene."

Pam dusted each cartridge with a soft brush, then removed the fingerprint with clear, evidence tape.

"The prints on the cartridge cases are a lot better than the ones on the gun. We should get them into the federal AFIS system to search for a match. We should also test fire the gun and send the bullet to the BCA.

Maybe it's got a history." Pam carefully mounted the cartridge prints next to those from the gun. "You sent the serial number to check on the ownership?"

C.J. said, "Yeah, I called it in. ATF said they'd get back to me. The guy said the serial number was older but after they started buyer background checks. Those records would only tell us the name of the last person who'd purchased the gun through a dealer. If the gun was stolen or sold through a private party, there won't be a record."

The dispatcher paged C.J. to answer the phone. Punching the flashing button, she was greeted by Eddie Paulson from the medical examiner's office. "Hey C.J., the dispatcher said Floyd's out and you're in charge of the Palmquist investigation."

C.J., who'd met Eddie while working a Cloquet murder, gave a short laugh. "He dumped the investigation in my lap, but that's about all that's happened. Did you get something for us on the Ted Palmquist blood tests?"

"We got lucky. The first screening turned up generic aromatic hydrocarbons. We followed up with a more specific test and determined that the chemicals are primarily benzene and toluene."

C.J. scrambled to pull out a pen and paper, then scribbled a note. "What's an aromatic something-carbon? Do they smell good?"

Eddie laughed. "Well, yes. They do smell sweet, but they're the more toxic components of gasoline. They're most often distilled for industrial use. The aromatic refers to the benzene ring common to all chemicals in that class. The surprise is finding benzene and toluene in the victim's liver and in high concentrations."

She scrawled the words 'aromatic hydrocarbons' on the yellow pad for Pam to read, then she activated the speakerphone. "Would that kill him?"

"In high enough concentrations, yes. Based on what we saw in the boy's liver, I'd say he'd been getting a sub-lethal dose over a period of time. At lower levels, the primary risk is that benzene and toluene are carcinogens."

C.J. looked at Pam, who was equally unfamiliar with the chemicals. "Do you think someone was slowly poisoning him?"

Eddie paused. "I've never heard of anyone being poisoned with benzene. It's not really a toxin of choice for someone who wants to kill a victim quickly. It's more likely he was ingesting it accidentally. I saw a guy get into a case of denatured alcohol once when I was in the Army. The manufacturers add a hint of benzene to 'denature' the ethanol, making it undrinkable. The trouble is benzene is only a deterrent to people who are chemists. A little benzene doesn't mean squat to an alcohol addict. Hell, I've seen winos come into the morgue with their bellies full of Lysol."

C.J. set the notepad aside. "So, you think he was getting lab alcohol somewhere?"

"That's my guess. See if he had a job at the hospital or a veterinarian's office. Then have the school check their supply of denatured alcohol. I wouldn't put it past a high school kid to raid the chemistry lab."

C.J. finished her notes. "Thanks for the chemistry lesson and the leads. Anything else that's pertinent?"

"I don't know how it affects your case, but the victim was also diabetic and had spiked his blood sugar."

"Hmm." C.J. made a note. "If I understand you, the bottom line is that this is not a homicide."

"Right, it's probably not a homicide. He was just a kid with a gut full of toxic chemicals and a sugar overload. I suggest you get his friends together and make sure they're not full of benzene too. He may have been sharing his stash."

"Good point." C.J. scribbled a note. "Anything else?"

"Well, there is one thing." Eddie hesitated. "Umm. You know how we worked together on the Cloquet murders last year. Well, I thought you were pretty professional…and I have a lot of respect for your work." He hesitated again. "I was wondering if you would consider having supper with an old vet who deals with dead bodies all day?"

C.J. hesitated and stared at Pam. Her eyes grew wide, and her face flushed. She'd known Eddie for a year, and he had always been polite and professional, but it had never occurred to her that they might go on a date. "I guess that'd be okay." Pam's face got a sly smirk.

"Great!" Eddie replied a little too loudly. "Is there someplace down there where we could meet, or would you like to come up to Duluth? We have a few more restaurant choices here."

C.J. continued to stare at Pam as she answered. "Well, I guess Duluth would be better. I've sampled every restaurant in Pine County, and it'd be nice to get a change of menu options."

Eddie's voice filled with excitement. "Are you free tonight by any chance?"

C.J. turned off the speakerphone. "Tonight is okay, as long as you don't keep me out too late. I'm on day shift again tomorrow."

"No sweat. I'm no night owl either. What time can you be up here?"

C.J. looked at the large clock in the ready room, then replied. "I can take some comp time. I'll run home, let the dog out, and change. I can be in downtown Duluth at five-thirty. Where should we meet?"

"Park at the morgue. No one will bother your car." He paused. "I should be able to get the stink off me by then."

C.J. laughed out loud. "Oh good. I'd like you not to smell like a cadaver while we're in a restaurant."

Pam watched C.J., waiting for an explanation after she disconnected.

C.J. shrugged. "It's not a date. We're just colleagues getting together for supper."

Pam grinned in response. Two of her loneliest friends were going out.

* * *

The ride from Duluth to Sturgeon Lake was torturously silent for Floyd. Mary leaned against the door with her eyes closed and Floyd didn't dare speak. Upon arriving home, he parked near the door and turned off the engine. When the truck stopped, Mary's eyes popped open and she gave him a brief, sad look, before opening her door and getting out. The black fuzz ball peeked out from under the steps. Recognizing them, the puppy raced to Mary's feet, and she bent down to pick it up. A piece of twine hung from the puppy's neck. She had apparently set herself free.

"Hello puppy. No one's come looking for you yet?" She looked at Floyd. "Can you check with dispatch to see if anyone has lost a puppy?"

He shrugged. "Sure, but I don't recall anyone ever calling in a lost puppy before."

Mary set the dog at the bottom of the steps, and it tried to follow her into the kitchen. Once inside, Floyd and Mary hung their coats behind the door and Mary went into the bedroom. Floyd watched her disappear and waited a few seconds for her to return. When he heard the bedroom door close and latch, he picked up the phone and called the dispatcher.

"Helen, any messages for me?"

"Oh, Floyd. The sheriff asked a couple times if you'd called in. I don't think he had anything special—just wanted to know what was going on."

"Hmm. Is he around?" Floyd glanced at his watch and realized that he hadn't eaten lunch and it was almost two in the afternoon.

"He's at the county offices reviewing a budget request with the county board. He said he'd be back by three. Do you want me to leave him a note to call you?"

Floyd closed his eyes and decided he needed to get out of the house for a while.

"Ask him to meet me at Nicoll's in half an hour." As an afterthought he asked, "How about C.J.?"

The dispatcher's voice brightened. "She's in the ready room. I can page her."

"In a second. Has anyone reported a missing black lab mix puppy? We've had one hanging around the house for a day-and-a-half."

Papers shuffled on the dispatcher's desk as she searched her notes. "No lost puppies. We had a report of two puppies hit by a car about half a mile from your house three days ago. Sandy took it. I think he said one was dead and he took the other to the vet in Moose Lake. I don't know if it lived or not."

"Anyone claim it?"

"As I recall, Sandy thought they might have been dumped in the ditch by someone who wanted to get rid of them."

"Hmm. Typical dump and run, hoping that they'll find a home. I bet the one at our house is the sister." He thought about options for a second and then gave up. There weren't many, short of turning her over to the Humane Society or taking her to the vet to be put down. "Put C.J. on. I'll talk to her now."

The line came alive with C.J. Jensen's voice. "Floyd, I've got so much news for you." C.J. was brimming with excitement and Floyd found it refreshing. "First of all, we recovered the bag the Santiago kid threw out of the pickup. It held a gun, and the plastic bag of powder with it is methamphetamine. The gun had been fired once. We test fired it again to get a bullet for comparison examination. Samples of the chemicals and a bullet are on the way to the BCA for analysis. Both the gun and cartridge were covered with fingerprints we're running through AFIS."

"Are you planning to run the serial number past ATF to see who the original owner was?"

C.J. grinned and then nervously looked to make sure that no one was watching. "I checked the county register of concealed carry permits. The gun is registered to Harold Wagner, who lives in Pine City. He didn't answer his phone when I called about half an hour ago."

Floyd was pleased that his new deputy was forging ahead independently. "Talk to him in person. His daughter Tammi disappeared last fall. Both Ted Palmquist and Juan Santiago have mentioned her. When I questioned Dylan Johnson and Brady Werther, they both flinched when I asked about Tammi."

"That's reaching, don't you think? He bought that gun almost twelve years ago. What are the chances this has anything to do with his daughter's disappearance?"

Floyd took a breath. "Maybe it's too obvious, but maybe not. Over the years I've found very few coincidences in law enforcement."

"Okay." C.J. pushed the slips of notepaper around her desk looking for other news. "Eddie called from the ME office. Ted Palmquist was diabetic, and his liver was saturated with benzene and..." she found the note and read it back verbatim, "'aromatic hydrocarbons.' Eddie says the cause of death was chronic poisoning and Ted was probably getting denatured alcohol from a lab somewhere. According to Eddie, manufacturers put a little benzene into tax-free alcohol to keep people from drinking it. Maybe Ted didn't understand that. We should follow up with his friends too, just to make sure that they aren't suffering from the same problem."

Floyd said, "Good suggestion. Sounds like you have enough to keep busy for a while."

C.J. chuckled. "Are you coming back soon to give me a hand?"

Floyd took a deep breath. "I'm afraid I just don't know right now. Plan on pushing it along yourself for a while. At least no one is rushing us to arrest a murderer or rapist. We can take a little time to get through it."

Chapter 9

Laura Tomlinson and Wendy Ptacek sat in the tiny counseling office. After realizing Laura wasn't going to open up to her as an authority figure, Ptacek moved to Laura's side to remove the physical and subliminal barrier the desk presented. At the end of an hour, they were shoulder to shoulder, a box of tissues on Laura's lap.

"Ted was nice," Laura sniffled, pausing to wipe her nose. "I can't believe he's gone."

Wendy thought there was more underlying Laura's tears than her concern about Ted's death. "Laura, who else do you hang around with?" When fear gripped Laura, Ptacek let the question dangle, sensing she was on the right track.

"Um. A few guys and a couple girls."

Wendy put on her most non-threatening facade. "I've never seen you in the hall or at lunch with anyone, who do you hang around with?"

Laura shrugged. "Heather Benson, Mollie Ault, Dylan Johnson. They're all students here."

Dylan Johnson's name stood out from the other names. Everyone in the school administration recognized Dylan's name and knew it meant bad news.

"Do you socialize with them?" Wendy asked.

"They're, you know, just some people to hang out with." Laura shrugged repeatedly as she spoke. The girl's body language said more about her discomfort with Dylan than the words.

"Didn't you hang around with Tammi Wagner too?"

Laura nodded. "Yeah, before she ran away."

Wendy proceeded carefully. "Did anyone ever contact you when they were trying to locate her?"

"Tammi's dad called a couple of times to see if I knew where she went, but I couldn't help. She wasn't with me."

"Did the police ever ask you about Tammi?"

Laura shook her head. "Uh uh. But I didn't know anything. I heard she ran away."

The counselor reviewed what she knew about Tammi Wagner's story in her head. Tammi came from a split family. She was known to the faculty as a poor student and a party animal. When Tammi had asked about a pregnancy test, Wendy referred her to a Duluth clinic. The girl missed a few days of school after her clinic appointment and returned with an excuse slip signed by a doctor, but neither of her parents. Turning in the slip, Tammi told the counselor she'd discussed safe sex and birth control. Wendy had excused the absence, quietly accepting Tammi's version of the events, but suspecting she'd missed school after an abortion, not a discussion of safe sex. Wendy wasn't surprised to hear Tammi had run away the following fall. Like others before her, Tammi had fallen into a cycle of events that shattered young lives.

"You don't know where Tammi went?"

Laura shook her head. "She was there one day and gone the next."

"You don't think she was having problems at home, do you?"

"She was like all of us. We put up with the shit..." Laura's face flushed and hesitated for a second. "Umm...stuff we don't like. But it's probably still better than living on the streets. We get by."

"Who was Tammi's boyfriend?"

The question put Laura on edge. "She hung around with a few guys, but I don't think she was serious about anyone."

Wendy Ptacek stared at Laura's straight black hair, white face, black lipstick, and loose black clothes. Then she listened to the girl's quiet, child-like talk. Laura's persona was a strange combination, an innocent cherub in devil's clothing. "You're right, home is better than life on the streets."

Wendy paused, wondering if there was something more going on at Laura's home. Abuse drove many students out of school and away from home. "Are you safe at home, Laura?"

Laura stared at her hands. "I don't know. Mom has stupid rules."

"What kind of stupid rules?"

Laura picked at the black fingernail polish on her thumb. "Like having to be home before ten and making me pick up the floor in my room." She paused. "It's my room, why should I pick it up if I don't want to? It's not hurting anything."

Wendy Ptacek leaned back in her chair. "Don't your friends have the same rules? Ten o'clock is curfew for teens under eighteen. That's the law."

A spark of backbone emerged in Laura. "It's a stupid law. What difference does it make if I'm at a friend's house until midnight?"

Wendy smiled. "Midnight is late when you've got school the next day. If you're at a friend's house until midnight, when do you get homework done and sleep?"

"Homework is stupid." Laura scrunched her face into a pained expression. "Adults don't have homework. It's stupid. Besides, we just review it in class the next day anyway." Laura was pulling at the loose heel of her black boot with the toe of the other boot.

"That's not why you were crying in the hallway, is it?"

Laura froze and peeked at the counselor through her eyebrows. She didn't say a word, and Wendy let the silence fill the room.

"Are you afraid of something here at school? Is someone bullying you?"

Laura shook her head but didn't speak.

Wendy dealt what she hoped would be a trump card. "It's Dylan, isn't it. He's causing you trouble?"

Wrapping her arms across her chest, Laura rocked for a second before she leaned forward. Wendy reached for the wastebasket as Laura vomited.

* * *

Marge Olander gently stroked Laura's hair as the girl lay on the cot in the school nurse's office. "Feeling any better?" Wendy Ptacek, the counselor, stood in the corner.

"My stomach's still upset."

"You don't have a temperature. Do you think that you're upset because of the conversation that you were having with Mrs. Ptacek?"

Laura shrugged her shoulders.

The counselor pulled a chair from the corner and set it next to the cot. "Dylan Johnson is the problem, isn't he?" Laura didn't respond. "Has he threatened you?"

Laura's eyes darted back and forth between the two women. Her teen-aged mind raced through the possibilities. If she told them about Dylan's threat, he probably would do something unpleasant to her. If she didn't tell them, he might do something to her anyway. She was convinced that there was nothing these two could do to protect her. Laura's eyes glazed with fear, and she vomited again.

* * *

C.J. had been on the phone for several minutes when she waved Pam over and put the phone on speaker. Pam walked to C.J.'s desk and sat down. "What's up, Floyd?"

"What help can you offer C.J. without leaving the office again?"

"Again?"

"I heard about your trip to help recover the gun. You're restricted to office duty."

"All I did was sit in the car while they searched!"

"The sheriff heard about it and gave me hell for letting you slip out of the office. He expects you to be at your desk until the doctor clears you for more. Understood?"

"Got it." Pam expected him to tell her what was going on with Mary, but he ended the call.

C.J. shut down the speakerphone. "I just got handed a lot of responsibility."

"You're not a rookie and Floyd's handing you a big opportunity."

"Why wouldn't he pass this on to one of the more experienced deputies?"

"History says they'd prefer to not spend their days on the phones and interviewing people about old crimes. He's testing to see if you've got the patience to pursue an investigation."

"He said you could help."

Pam laughed. "Sure, hand me anything that can be done while chained to a desk."

"Floyd was a little irritated that you'd come out for the search."

"That's the strongest rebuke I've ever gotten."

C.J. nodded. "I had a sergeant who yelled all the time, and no one took him seriously. Floyd never raises his voice, so when he gets serious you know he's saying something important."

Pam panicked and looked at the clock. "Crap, I've got to pick up Luke from daycare. I'll see you tomorrow."

"I'll bring Bailey."

"That'll be perfect."

* * *

The final bell ended classes and streams of students rushed into the hallways. They fought their way to lockers and the Pine City High School doors. Dylan and Tyler elbowed their way viciously through the crowd to cries and epithets. Since they didn't care about school, they weren't carrying books and didn't need to retrieve homework from their lockers.

Among the first students out the front doors, Dylan and Tyler nearly bowled over a short, rotund woman who was entering the school.

Tyler looked back over his shoulder as they jogged to the parking lot. "I think that was Laura's mom. I heard Laura was in the nurse's office all afternoon. Do you think that she'll tell anybody anything?"

The boys piled into a rusty blue Mustang and Dylan coaxed the big V8 to life. It roared, spewing a huge cloud of bluish white smoke behind it. Dylan slid the transmission into gear and eased the clutch out; they rolled past the students queuing up for buses.

Tyler watched impassively as the car nudged some students who didn't yield to the rumble of the engine. "She's too afraid. Besides, she's just as deep into this as we are. She can't tell anyone without getting herself busted."

Dylan gunned the engine once they'd passed the clutch of students milling in the parking lot. "She's smoked a little dope and dropped a couple tabs of acid. She's clean beyond that."

"You're right, she doesn't know about the rest. As long as Taco, Brady, you, and me stand tough, nothing is going to happen."

Dylan drove out of the parking lot and hit the gas. The Mustang's tires chirped. "But we've got to get the stash out of Taco's house before his folks find it and call the cops."

Tyler shifted nervously in his seat and adjusted his backwards-facing cap. "I don't think we should go breaking into a buddy's house. I mean, he's one of us."

"Listen, dumbass, what else are we going to do? Should we go knock on the door and ask Taco's mom to give us the drugs?"

They drove silently as the paved streets became a gravel road. Tyler broke the quiet. "But how do we know if anybody's home?"

Dylan shook his head. "Taco's in the hospital, down in the Cities. His folks are there with him."

"But how do we KNOW that?"

Dylan reached under the car seat, pulled out a cell phone, and handed it to Tyler. "Call his house. If anyone answers, we'll go back later."

Tyler punched in the numbers and pressed the send button. After five rings he was prompted to leave a message after the beep. He pushed the end button. "No one home." He handed the phone back to Dylan.

"See, stupid. That's why we call you Doofus. If you had a brain, you might be dangerous." Dylan jammed the phone back in his pocket. He wound down a number of roads, then up the long driveway at the Santiago house. The gravel was washboard and heaved from recently thawed frost boils. The stiff suspension caused the car to rock violently.

At Santiago's home, the boys got out. Dylan went to the back door and tried the knob. "Locked." They walked furtively around the building, checking doors and windows until they located a basement window that had been left unlocked and open. The odor of musty air wafted through the opening. Dylan wrestled the window out of the frame and held it while Tyler slid through the opening. He crashed to the floor, scattering mop buckets and cleaning supplies off a shelf that gave way under his weight.

Dylan set the window on the brown grass. "Can you make any more noise?"

"I think I broke my ankle." Tyler's voice was weak. Bottles and cans skittered across the floor as he tried to get up.

"Get your ass off the floor and quit whining. You're okay. Haven't you ever twisted an ankle before?"

Tyler's voice was muffled inside. "I'll set this stupid shelf back up and meet you at the back door."

Dylan peeked around the corner of the house when he heard a car approaching. It raised a cloud of dust nearly a quarter of a mile away. He rushed back to the window. "Forget the shelf. Grab the stash and bring it out. Hurry up!"

Dylan hustled to the door and peeked around the corner of the house as the car passed without slowing. After what seemed like an eternity, he pounded his fist on the door. "C'mon! Let's go!" There was no answer. He pounded on the door again, then raced back to the basement window. He got on his knees and tried to look in, but his body obscured the only light shining into the basement.

"What are you doing?" There was no reply. Dylan contemplated going through the window, then remembered the collapsed shelf and scattered junk. He trotted back to the door and pounded again.

Finally, Tyler opened the door. His expression was one of despair. "I can't find it."

"What do you mean?" Dylan pushed past Tyler and raced down the stairs to the basement.

"It's not over the furnace vent," Tyler called after him. "I checked all over down there. I was just going to look in his room. Maybe he moved it to the dresser or something."

Dylan raced back up the stairs and pushed past Tyler. "Would you put something in your dresser that you didn't want your mother to find? C'mon, look in the closet and under the bed."

They waded into the mess of clothing scattered on the bedroom floor. They pulled out drawers, flipped the mattress, and cleared closet shelves.

Tyler watched Dylan rifle jacket pockets in the hallway closet. "Even the gun's gone. Do you think he had all the stuff in his truck when he rolled it?"

Dylan's face froze. "If he did...and the cops found it..."

Tyler pulled Dylan's sleeve. "C'mon. We gotta get outta here before somebody comes."

They raced out of the Santiago house, jumped into the car, and sped out of the yard bouncing dangerously close to the electric fences bordering the driveway. Half a dozen white face-mix steers raised their heads from the fresh grass, watching curiously as the Mustang passed.

Dylan roared away from the Santiago house through increasingly narrow roads until he turned onto a gravel township road. After following it a few miles, they turned onto a driveway with a battered "for sale" sign nailed to a wooden gate post. Tyler opened the metal gate to let the car through, then closed it behind himself after ripping down the for sale sign and throwing it into the underbrush. They followed a one-lane grassy driveway over the crest of a hill to a small hunting shack wrapped in tar paper. A metal chimney stuck through the roof. The only window was caked with dust; it hadn't been washed in a decade.

After stopping the car, Dylan removed a small duffel bag from the trunk. Tyler pulled a poorly hidden key down from the molding strip over the door and unlocked the padlock securing the building. He hung the lock on the open hasp and replaced the key over the molding.

The structure was a single room hunting shack. Mice skittered across the floor as the door opened. Tyler lit a propane lamp with a match from a box on the table, bathing the room with intense white light.

One side of the shack interior was a kitchen, with a small table and chairs, and an open cupboard with a few cups, plates, pots, and pans. A small sink with a hand pump was built into one end of the cabinets. The opposite wall sported two sets of built-in bunk beds. Stuffing from the mattresses had been scattered in every nook and cranny by the resident mice. The floor was littered with acorn shells and seed hulls.

Dylan set the duffel bag on the counter and unzipped it, pulling out a small plastic bag and a brass pipe. He filled the pipe with dry, green leaves, while Tyler watched intently. Dylan lit the pipe, inhaled deeply and held the smoke deep in his lungs. He passed the pipe to Tyler who did the same.

After a half minute, Dylan sputtered and exhaled. "I don't know what to do about the stash at Taco's. I mean, the gun was gone and everything."

Dylan took another toke on the pipe as Tyler exhaled. "If the cops have the gun..."

Dylan exhaled quickly. "The cops don't know shit about the gun. It's not hot, and it's never been used in a crime they know about. Don't worry about it."

Tyler shifted uneasily and adjusted his cap. "I just don't like it. It's too close. We've gotta do something."

Tyler started to stand, but Dylan grabbed his forearm. "We're not doing anything. We're going to sit here, smoke a joint, and mellow out. Then we'll get something to eat. Life will go on. No one's going to squeal and no one's going to dump on us. Okay?" Dylan's voice was even and carefully modulated. The strength of it reassured Tyler, as it had so many times in the past. Dylan had always been right.

A wave of paranoia swept Tyler, and he pulled his arm away. "What about Taco? If they find the stuff, he's going to take the fall. Do you think he'll take it all alone?"

Dylan took another long draw on the pipe and held it out for Tyler. While he held his breath, he contemplated Juan (Taco) Santiago. When he exhaled, the THC from the marijuana started to pulse through his bloodstream and his thoughts focused.

"Let's go to the hospital and visit Taco. Then we'll know exactly what went down." Dylan started to collect his paraphernalia and put it back into the duffel.

Tyler looked frantic. "Now? You want to visit Taco right now?"

Dylan shrugged off Tyler's question. "Sure. You got something better to do?"

Tyler threw up his arms. "We ransacked Taco's house, then we broke in here. We get wrecked on dope, drive to the Cities, and ask Taco how much the cops know about the crimes we've committed. Sounds like a perfect fucking thing to do." Tyler paced back and forth as he ranted.

"Shut up, kill the lantern, and lock the door." Dylan knocked the ashes from the pipe onto the floor. Tyler turned off the lamp. The light faded quickly as he walked out the door.

Chapter 10

Sheriff John Sepanen was drinking coffee and reading the *Minneapolis Star Tribune*. The lunch rush at Nicoll's was long past and the last remaining waitress was wiping tables and refilling ketchup containers. Floyd walked into the café. Across the street from the old courthouse, Nicoll's was one of his favorite places to hold impromptu meetings over coffee and pie. It was a quiet afternoon, and the only other patrons were a group of retired women planning a Lutheran Church rummage sale. Floyd slid into the booth across from the sheriff and popped a TUMS antacid into his mouth.

The sheriff folded the paper and signaled the waitress for another cup. "Stomach problems?"

Floyd dropped the roll of antacids into his shirt pocket. "Mary's got some stuff going on that's got me gurgling." The waitress set down a cup and poured Floyd's coffee. She topped off the sheriff's cup.

The sheriff waited until the waitress was out of earshot. "C.J. seems to be doing well."

Floyd reached for the sugar container. "She's good. I've got her checking on this thing with the high school kids. Ted

Palmquist's death is suspicious and Juan Santiago fleeing C.J. is strange. Did you hear we recovered drugs and a gun that had been thrown out during the chase?"

"I overheard C.J. talking to the BCA lab about testing the drugs and bullet."

Floyd stirred two teaspoons of sugar into his coffee. Sepanen looked at him and wondered how Floyd could maintain a weight of 145 pounds on a five-eight frame. Floyd loaded two spoons of sugar in every cup of coffee the sheriff had ever seen him drink for the twelve years Sepanen had been sheriff. Floyd's face was lined with age, but his hair showed only a touch of gray and it hadn't thinned at all.

"C.J. is sharp, John. She's sharp and has good cop sense. A little more seasoning and she'll be one of your top deputies if she's not there already." Floyd paused, his eyes misty. "She'll be ready for my sergeant's stripes when I retire."

"Big praise for a little woman," said the sheriff. He watched Floyd's face for a reaction over the rim of his cup.

Floyd leaned across the table and spoke in a low voice. "I'd take her over Tom Thompson any day of any year. She's got the schooling, experience, and common sense. That's a powerful combination in a female deputy."

Sepanen smiled. "Or in a man."

Floyd nodded his agreement. "On top of that, she's willing to do the boring detailed work. She happily makes hours of calls and tracks down people and records. Most of the deputies prefer to drive the roads. I paired her up with Pam to take on the Palmquist/Santiago case. The two of them make a good team, tracking down loose ends and doing interviews."

Floyd signaled for a refill and stirred two more spoons of sugar into the cup. The sheriff waved off his refill and reached for his coat. "I appreciate your candor."

"John, I need to talk to someone." Floyd looked away, struggling to say the words in his mind. "Mary has breast cancer."

The sheriff closed his eyes and took a deep breath. "Floyd, what can I do to help you?" He watched Floyd's face for a hint of what was to come.

Floyd looked down into the coffee cup. "We saw the oncologist in Duluth today and Mary walked out. She said that she wanted to go home..." The words choked in his throat, "...and die."

The sheriff shook his head. "You can't let her do that. She can't give up without a fight."

"I know. But how can I make her change her mind when she won't even talk about it?"

Sepanen pulled a paper napkin from the dispenser and flattened it on the table. Taking a pen from his uniform pocket, he wrote *Mary* in the middle. He then drew a number of lines radiating from Mary and wrote Floyd's name at the end of one line. At the end of the next line he wrote *sisters*. On the third he wrote *flower shop*. On the remaining lines he wrote, *minister, family doctor*, and finally, *Pam*. He spun the napkin around so Floyd could read it.

"Mary has lots of support. At each of these spokes is someone she needs and trusts. She's just like all of us. We depend on the support of others to keep things in balance. Right now, she's spinning out of control and needs to start touching each of these spokes to get the wheel back in balance."

Floyd stared at the drawing, then pushed it away. "But she won't even talk to me. How will I get these other people involved?"

Sepanen gave a sly smile. "Start by calling a friend of hers from the flower shop. Tell her what's going on and have her call Mary."

Floyd ran a hand over his face. "John, she'll have my head if I start telling people."

"It'll rip your heart out if she doesn't at least try to get some treatment. Right?" Floyd nodded. "Another thing. Call the oncologist now and *you* schedule the surgery. It's easy to cancel. She's going through a classic cycle of shock. She'll be past the denial and into anger tomorrow."

Floyd looked the sheriff in the eye. "Tomorrow?"

Sepanen took the napkin and wrote, **Tomorrow!** under the wheel drawing. He pushed it into Floyd's hand.

* * *

Floyd drove back to the courthouse and locked himself in the sheriff's personal office. He left voice messages for Mary's sisters, Dr. Bergstrom, and the Lutheran minister. The oncologist's assistant scheduled Mary's lumpectomy.

Floyd had always thought of himself as Mary's best friend. He had to think about the women at the shop to come up with Barb Watson's name. He dialed the shop and asked for Barb. She and Mary often had lunch together and Floyd knew the people he chose to eat lunch with were actually closer to him than many people who claimed to be his friends.

Barb's voice chimed in on the line, "Floyd?" She said Floyd's name as a question.

"Hi, Barb. Umm, Mary's kinda sick." He hoped that his despair didn't come through on the phone too clearly.

"I hope it isn't anything serious. She called and said she wouldn't be in today."

Suddenly, Floyd realized that he needed to let the shop know this wasn't a short-term situation. "Yeah. She's going to be gone for a while and I was wondering if you could do me a favor."

"Sure. I'll do whatever I can."

"That's great. Would you give Mary a call?" The words stuck in his throat and tears clouded his eyes. He struggled to speak without his voice cracking. "Mary's got breast cancer, Barb. I need someone to convince her to get it treated. She won't talk to me about it."

"Hang on." He could hear a door close in the background. "I'm back. Say it again please."

Floyd rolled his eyes, knowing he wouldn't be able to utter the words again without breaking down. "Barb, Mary has breast cancer." Floyd paused to compose himself. "The doctor wants to do surgery, but Mary declined. She told me she wanted to go home and die."

"Oh, Floyd! That's terrible." Barb paused, thinking. "You know, Hester Stanglund caused her to say that."

Floyd was lost. "Who's Hester Stanglund?"

"She's one of our customers. Mary and I talked a lot about it. Hester went through three rounds of breast cancer treatments, then died. We talked about her a lot because she's about the same age as we are. We shed a lot of tears. Mary said she'd rather die than go through the hell that Hester suffered the last year of her life. She was sick, lost weight, all her hair fell out, then grew back twice. When she finally slipped away, she weighed about eighty pounds. Now her husband is trying to pay off $200,000 in medical bills."

"Money is not the issue. We've got insurance."

"You're right, money isn't the issue. It's the quality of life—having dignity and choice." There was a pause, then Barb came back. "I'll give her a call. She needs the first surgery to see if things have metastasized. Hester didn't start treatment until her cancer was stage four and in her lymph nodes. I'm sure I can convince her to do that much."

"Thanks, Barb. I appreciate your help." He hung up the phone and prayed that he'd done the right thing.

Before he could think about what to do next his cell phone rang, the oncologist's office showed on the caller ID. "The hospital had a cancellation tomorrow. Can you be there at ten?"

Floyd let out a sigh. "I think so. Thanks." He hung up the phone and closed his eyes in prayer. "Dear God, please let Mary go along with this."

* * *

The drive to North Memorial Hospital in a Minneapolis suburb took Dylan and Tyler nearly two hours. They hit the last of rush hour traffic and turned the wrong way on Highway 100. The last hues of twilight lit the sky when they arrived in Juan Santiago's hospital room. The two boys were surprised to see family members crowded around Juan's bed; their plan had been to talk to him in private.

The figure covered by a white sheet hardly looked human. A plastic collar engulfed Juan's neck, tubes ran into an IV port, and a machine over the bed displayed numbers while beeping with each heartbeat. At first, Dylan didn't recognize his friend, then he saw Juan's father looking out the window across the room.

Neither Dylan nor Tyler had ever visited a hospital before. The combination of smells, intense medical personnel, and sad family members made them uneasy. Dylan edged to the foot of Juan's bed and looked toward Juan's mother and a nurse, one standing on each side of the bed. The nurse was adjusting an IV line and his mother swept back a lock of Juan's unruly hair. Three other people were talking quietly with Juan's father.

Juan's mother looked up at the two boys. "Juan, some of your friends have come to visit."

Ray Santiago turned and looked at the two boys with obvious disdain, a typical adult response to their long hair, tattered clothes, and piercings. He turned back to the window without comment.

Juan's mother was gracious. "C'mon over, guys. Juan can't sit up yet, so you have to come to the head of the bed to talk to him." She backed away so they could move closer. The nurse finished adjusting the IV and left.

Tyler's eyes darted around the room. He was uneasy about being near the teen's parents, knowing he'd just broken into their house. His anxiety was heightened by the marijuana they'd smoked on the drive. He hung back as Dylan moved to the head of the bed.

Both of Juan's legs were in traction, the metal parts looking like torture devices screwed onto Juan's legs. The arm closest to Dylan was in a cast, and the other had tape holding an IV line in place. A cord ran from an IV stand to a button in Juan's hand, a light on the box blinking as a timer ticked off seconds. The pulsing light caught Tyler's attention. He stared at it, wondering what happened when the countdown went to zero.

Dylan put a hand on Juan's shoulder. Juan's eyes swollen, nearly shut and his face was an unrecognizable mass of purple and black bruising. "How's it going, Taco?"

The counter of the blue box flashed zero, it beeped, and a green light came on. Juan lifted his left hand and pushed the button on the end of the cord. A small motor inside the box hummed, the green light went out, and the timer started another countdown.

Juan looked at Dylan. "Morphine," he explained, his voice garbled by his swollen lips. "It's on a timer."

Dylan gave a furtive look at Mrs. Santiago, then whispered to Juan, "Awesome."

Juan relaxed as the pain subsided. "It doesn't stop the pain, but I kinda don't care for a while," Juan mumbled the words through bruised lips.

"How bad does it hurt?" Dylan surveyed Juan's leg traction.

Juan shifted his shoulder position in the bed. "It's more like an ache now. But it never goes away." He tried to wet his lips with his tongue, but his tongue was swollen and dry.

Dylan watched with fascination. "How long are they gonna keep you? A couple more days?"

Juan licked his lips again and looked past Dylan. "Could I have a drink of water, Mom?"

Mrs. Santiago lifted a foam cup to Juan's lips. He sucked some water from a straw as Dylan stepped back, amazed to see his friend so helpless he couldn't drink water without help.

Mrs. Santiago leaned toward Dylan and whispered, "They think he might have to be here for a couple of weeks because he may need more surgery. Afterwards, they'll probably send him to a rehabilitation unit for a month or two of therapy."

"Months?" Dylan rolled his eyes. "That's fucked up."

Juan's mother blanched at the profanity and his father turned from the window, glaring at Dylan with disdain.

Tyler continued to stare at the morphine pump. He got excited when the light turned green again. "The light's green. Can I push the button?"

Mr. Santiago turned toward Tyler and scowled. "Drugs! Is that all you kids think about?" He shook his head and stalked out of the room, the other couple following him.

Lillian Santiago watched her husband leave, frowning. "Juan's dad is a little uptight right now."

Dylan, immune to typical adult responses to anything that teens said or did asked, "Could we talk to Taco…I mean Juan alone…just for a second?"

Mrs. Santiago looked around nervously, then picked up her purse. "I'll get a cup of coffee."

Juan grimaced in pain, pushing the button again and waiting for the expected wave of relief to sweep over him. After Mrs. Santiago left the room, Dylan leaned close to the pillow and asked, "Taco, where's the stash? We looked in your house and we couldn't find it."

"I grabbed it when the cops came. Threw it out the window…the Wisconsin Road…in the ditch." He licked his dry lips again. "So the cops wouldn't get it."

Dylan pounded his fist against the mattress. "That was a fucking dumb thing to do!"

The outburst startled Tyler and he looked toward the door. "There are people in the hallway. Put a lid on it," he hissed.

"Yeah, okay, I'm cool." Dylan looked around furtively then leaned close to Juan. "Where's the gun? We couldn't find it."

The wave of morphine swept Juan and he relaxed. "I threw it in the ditch. The meth was in the bag with the gun, too. I don't think they'll get it." Juan's eyes closed and his breathing slowed.

Dylan leaned close to Juan's ear. "Did you tell the cops anything about us?"

"No. I didn't tell them about Tammi. She's dead, but I didn't tell them."

"Shut up!" Dylan panicked and put his hand over Juan's swollen mouth to stifle any more morphine hazed conversation about Tammi.

Mr. Santiago heard the outburst and hurried back into the room. He pushed Tyler back from the foot of the bed with a sweep of his massive arm, then saw his son apparently being suffocated by Dylan.

"Lillian!" He lunged across the bed, grabbed Dylan by the arm, and threw him against the empty bed on the other side of the room. Ray Santiago checked Juan. Once he was sure Juan was breathing normally, he stalked across the room, reached down with one hand, and grabbed Dylan by the throat. Tyler watched in speechless horror as the action played out in marijuana-hazed slow motion. Dylan's eyes bugged out as he was lifted from the floor, his hands clawing at Santiago's hand as it squeezed his throat.

"What in hell were you up to, you slimy piece of shit?" Dylan gasped for air and kicked wildly with his feet. Ray Santiago's adrenaline rush narrowed his vision to Dylan's face. His other hand grabbed Dylan's crotch in a vise grip, lifting him even higher.

A nurse raced into the room as Dylan gagged and writhed in pain. He tried to reach the ground with his toes, while clawing at Ray Santiago's massive right hand. "Why did you have your hand over his mouth? Were you trying to kill him?"

The nurse rushed to Ray Santiago and placed her hands on his arm. "It's okay, Mr. Santiago. Security is coming." She pulled on Santiago's arm, trying to ease his grip. Adrenaline stopped him from hearing the nurse, and her touch increased his annoyance. He was preparing to throw Dylan to the floor when Lillian's voice pierced the room.

"Ray. Set him down!"

Ray looked at his wife and the fire faded from his eyes. He released his grip. Dylan fell to the floor gasping for breath and clutching his bruised testicles. Running feet pounded toward the room.

Ray took a deep breath and glared at Dylan. "He was smothering our son. I told you we shouldn't leave these scum in here alone with Juan."

Followed by a doctor, a bulky security guard charged into the room, surveyed the situation, then looked to the doctor for direction. The doctor stepped between Ray and Dylan. "It's under control right now." He spoke to the security officer without taking his eyes off Santiago. "Please escort these two young men down to the security office."

Lillian elbowed her way to Juan's side. The morphine was fading again, and his eyes were open. "Why did that boy have his hand over your face?" She asked as Dylan, Tyler and the guard left.

Juan blinked, seemingly unfazed by the incident. "He didn't want me to tell anyone Tammi was dead."

She looked at him, sure he was mumbling nonsense. "Okay, dear. Would you like another drink of water?"

* * *

The puppy raced from her hiding place under the steps when Floyd's car pulled into the yard. Floyd stopped short of his parking place to keep from running her over. Littering the yard were the remnants of the comforter they'd wrapped the pup in that morning.

"You've been busy today, haven't you?" He swept the puppy up and petted her, while she squirmed in his grasp. He set the dog at the bottom of the steps and beat her to the kitchen door before she could sneak inside. The house was quiet, and the kitchen lights were off.

Floyd hung his jacket on the coat tree behind the door and kicked off his shoes. Slipping silently down the hall, he pressed his ear against the bedroom door. He knew that there was going to be a confrontation, but he hoped that Mary was asleep, and the discussion could be deferred. He heard Mary's voice on the phone so retreated to the kitchen and opened a Michelob.

Floyd was watching the early weather report on the television when the bedroom door opened. Mary walked down the hall, stopped at the living room, and leaned against the corner. "You couldn't let it be, could you?" she said, looking tired and drawn. Red streaked her eyes and her body language said she was defeated.

He set the beer on a coaster and got up. She met him at the couch and let him cradle her in his arms as they stood. He gently patted her back as he nuzzled her hair. "Have you changed your mind about surgery yet?"

A shudder ran through her body. "I don't know." She pulled away and sat on the couch. "I can't..." Her words died.

He sat back in the chair and picked up the beer. "Can't what? Can't face it? Can't bear the thought of the pain?"

She shrugged. "I can't believe it's me." Tears welled in her eyes. "I can't leave with so much life left to live." She choked on the final words, "I don't want to die."

Floyd sat next to her on the couch and held her. "We have to know more. All we know now is that there's a problem. You need to have the surgery to find out how bad it is and if it's spread."

Mary shook her head. "It's too late. I can feel it, Floyd. It's already too late." She was stoic and resolved. He felt the strength and conviction in her voice.

"Do it for us, for the life we want to have together." He stroked her hair. "Please."

Turning her head to look at him, she glared at him with her hollow, dark eyes. "You've already scheduled it, haven't you?"

He nodded in embarrassment.

She gave him a resigned look. "Then I guess you've already decided. When do I go in?"

"Tomorrow at ten."

Mary sucked in a breath and nodded. "You're not wasting any time."

"The hospital had a cancellation." Mary didn't respond. "The surgeon's assistant said sooner was better than later, so I took the opening."

Mary closed her eyes and nodded.

"Would you like to go out for supper?"

"I'm not hungry."

Floyd leaned over and hugged her. "I love you."

She put her arms around him. "What if they remove my breast?"

"I'll still love you."

"Do you know how many people called this afternoon?"

"Who called besides Barb?"

"Pam called next, then Dr. Bergstrom. I was talking to the minister when you came home."

"What did the pastor say?"

"He told me we'd get past this. Then he told me to pick a date."

Floyd leaned back. "Pick a date?"

"For our wedding. He told me it was time to stop talking about it, move ahead, and make plans for our future."

"What did you say?"

"I told him I wasn't sure about the future, but he was reassuring. He told me he'd prayed, and it isn't my time yet. There are more chapters to be written in my life with you."

Floyd pulled her close. "He's a smart man."

"You're supposed to call him back."

"Why?"

Mary sniffled and pulled a tissue from a box on the end table. "He didn't say."

"I'll call him tomorrow after surgery."

"You're the one rushing us through this. Call him."

Floyd took out his cell phone and punched in the pastor's private number, assuming he'd get a recording. When the pastor answered, Floyd stepped outside and sat on the steps.

"Hi, this is Floyd Swenson." The puppy pushed her nose under Floyd's elbow and crawled onto his lap. "Mary said I should call you."

"Mary and I had a long talk and I think she's ready to move ahead with surgery. You should schedule it before she changes her mind."

"It's scheduled for tomorrow morning."

"That fast? I'm amazed." The pastor paused. "What's your plan after surgery?'

"Depending on how extensive the surgery is, she'll have to stay for a few days."

"Floyd, what's *your* plan?"

"I'll take a few days of vacation and stay with her until she's ready to…"

"Floyd, think further out. What's your plan?"

"What do you mean?"

"We don't know God's plan, but Mary's getting a reprieve. Take advantage of it."

Floyd flipped his hand. "I'm sure we'll have a rich full life."

"I rarely give unfiltered advice to people. I usually offer hints meant to make people consider my words and revise their choices. I'm not doing that now. There's a clock ticking for you and Mary. You're made vague plans for the future, without putting them on a calendar. Floyd, take out your pen, sit down with the calendar, and write your plans down, *in ink*."

Floyd chuckled. "Are you telling me to schedule a wedding?"

"Schedule the rest of your life. A wedding is a milestone, but how are you going to take advantage of the days you have together after the wedding?"

"I haven't…"

"I know your job saved your life after Ginny died. Maybe it's time to close that chapter and write another."

Floyd tipped his head back and clutched the puppy. "I…"

"Think very hard about your future. Talk to your best friend. Pray. The right answers will become clear."

"I'm getting a second chance."

"You and Mary are being given a second chance."

"What's your advice, pastor?"

"Don't miss it."

Floyd disconnected the phone and carried the puppy into the house. He set her on the kitchen floor and watched her tentatively sniff around the unfamiliar entryway.

"You let the puppy in the house?" Mary asked.

"It's time."

Floyd took the calendar down and carried it to the couch. Hearing Mary's voice, the pup raced across the living room, then whimpered when she couldn't jump high enough to get onto the couch. Mary scooped her up.

"The minister told me to put some things on the calendar." Flipping over the page, he stopped in May. "How do you feel about a May fifteenth wedding?"

"That'd be nice, but why then?"

"I'm retiring May first and that'll give me a few weeks to adjust before the wedding."

Mary sat up. "You're retiring? Really?

"How else are we going to take advantage of the time we're being given?"

"Is that what the minister told you to do?"

Floyd took a pen out of his pocket. On the first, he wrote, retirement, in large letters. "No, he told me to consider the time we're being given and figure out how to make the most of it. Retiring is the first step."

Chapter 11

C.J. stopped at Harold Wagner's apartment on her way home. He had rooms over a store in the older part of Pine City. At one time, it probably housed the owner of the downstairs business. From the back, it looked like a shabby, low rent option for someone who was one step from living in his car. C.J. climbed the rickety wooden steps running up the back of the building.

A slender man, about fifty, opened the door after her second knock. His face registered surprise at seeing a person in uniform. The surprise became fear. "Oh, God. You've found Tammi?"

C.J. didn't answer him. "Are you Harold Wagner?"

He waved her into the entryway of the tiny apartment. The door opened into a kitchen filled with the aroma of garlic and onions. A small white stove was nestled into the end of a short countertop. Dirty dishes sat in the sink. A drop-leaf Formica table and two unmatched vinyl-covered chairs, both patched with duct tape, were placed on the border between the kitchen and living room.

C.J. looked into the living room furnished with old, overstuffed chairs and a threadbare couch. A small television was tuned to *Jeopardy!*

"Yes, I'm Harold Wagner." He ushered her to the small kitchen table and pointed to a chair. "Is this about Tammi? Have you found her?"

C.J. sat down in the chair and pulled out a notebook, deciding to play ignorant about Tammi's disappearance. "I'm not familiar with Tammi's case. What happened to her?" C.J. paused and watched the anticipation melt from the man's face.

"Tammi's my daughter," he replied. "She ran away last fall. When I saw your uniform, I thought maybe you'd heard from her."

"I'm afraid I don't have news about your daughter. I'm here to ask you about a gun you purchased. Can you show it to me?"

He fell into the other chair. "Oh, the gun." His fingers brushed through his thinning gray and brown hair. "The gun disappeared a while ago. I kept it around the place for protection. I was digging through the drawer where I stored it, and it wasn't there."

C.J. scribbled notes. "You never sold it?"

Harold shook his head, "No. It just wasn't there one day. I don't know how long it's been gone. Coulda been months." The smell of burning food hit Harold and he jumped up, rescuing a pot from the stove. He stirred the contents vigorously, then set the pot on the countertop. "I don't even remember the last time I had it out," he said over his shoulder.

"Had you fired it before you put it away?" She watched him run water into a different pot and set it on a burner.

Harold returned to the table. "I don't think so. I mean, I'd gone out to the gravel pit to shoot a couple of times back when I got it. But it's been years..."

C.J. looked up from her notes. "We recovered the revolver. Did you fire it once and leave the spent cartridge in the gun?"

Harold shook his head. "No way. I had six rounds in the cylinder. Whoever took it must've shot it once."

"Anything else missing?" C.J. looked around. This was a small efficiency apartment and anything missing would stand out. Clutter filled every corner. Magazines, clothing, and unopened mail sat on the living room coffee table. Antiques that didn't seem to fit Wagner's style sat on shelves. They were all covered with dust, possibly there since the previous resident's tenure.

"I haven't noticed anything gone. I suppose that something else might be missing. But I haven't got anything that's worth much."

"Have you seen evidence that someone broke in?"

Harold shook his head.

"Who else has a key?"

"The landlord...Tammi had one too."

C.J. folded up her notebook and put it in a pocket. "Tell me more about Tammi?"

"She disappeared last fall—ran away. I was hoping you'd come to tell me she'd been found."

"Did she live with you here?" As soon as the words came out C.J. realized that it sounded very judgmental.

Harold shook his head. "She lived with her mother, my ex-wife, outside of town. But she came over and spent time with me some weekends. She slept on the couch. We'd watch TV or sometimes we'd play cribbage."

"Any chance Tammi took the gun when she left?"

Wagner fidgeted, flicking a crumb off the tabletop with his finger. "I don't know why she would. She wasn't into guns. I didn't think she even knew where I kept it."

"But she knew you had a gun, right?"

"I suppose she knew about it, but she'd never handled or shot it."

"Did the gun disappear before or after Tammi left?"

Harold's eyes drifted around the room. "I don't know. Maybe after. Yeah, I noticed it was missing last winter. That was after she ran away."

Wagner's pause led C.J. to believe he wasn't being entirely truthful. She decided to push him a little. "Have you seen it since Tammi disappeared?"

Harold didn't look her in the eye. "Maybe not."

"No word about Tammi since last fall?" C.J. asked.

"Nothing. Not a trace. I talked to a cop named Swenson. Some woman, with an Indian name, called from the Minnesota BCA and asked a bunch of questions. She thought maybe Tammi had run off to Minneapolis or Chicago. She said sometimes runaway kids call after a while." Tears started to fill his eyes. "She never called."

"I assume the sheriff's department followed up with her friends?"

Harold turned away. "Her friends weren't anything to brag about. They're stoners with green hair and piercings."

"Stoners?"

"Drug users. Tammi called them stoners."

"Do you know for sure that they were into drugs, Mr. Wagner? I mean, kids are big talkers."

Harold nodded his head. "I had to hold her one night when she had a bad trip. She was afraid to go home to her mother. We sat here the entire night while she cried and had flashbacks. Her stoner friends dumped her at the bottom of my stairs and ran. Some friends! They wouldn't even walk her upstairs to the door."

C.J. got her notebook back out. "Do you know who her friends are?"

Harold sat back and closed his eyes. "Umm, I remember Dylan. And maybe she mentioned some others."

"Dylan Johnson? Juan Santiago? Do those names sound familiar?" C.J. scribbled quickly in the notebook.

Harold shrugged. "Yeah, Dylan. I think the guy she called Taco was named Juan. I don't remember hearing last names. There was a girl named Laura, oh and Ted, too. I think she liked Ted. Maybe more, but those are the ones I heard most."

C.J.'s curiosity was piqued. "Was Tammi sick before she disappeared?"

Wagner frowned. "Sick? Like how?"

"Weight loss or sores on her skin. Did she have any symptoms like that?"

Harold's eyes had been fixed on the table. They suddenly riveted her. "Her stomach had been screwed up for a month or two. She complained about cramps and was throwing up sometimes." He shrugged his shoulders. "I figured maybe she was having her period or something. She asked me to buy tampons once and that's the only time we ever came close to discussing sex or anything."

"Mr. Wagner, a boy named Ted Palmquist died. He'd been very sick, and his autopsy showed he had some nasty chemicals in his system. The medical examiner asked us to see if his friends had been drinking denatured alcohol stolen, possibly from a lab. The alcohol was tainted with benzene."

"I don't think Tammi drank." He gave a nervous laugh. "But I didn't think she did drugs either. Before she disappeared, I talked to her about a residential treatment program, but her mother wouldn't go along with it. She didn't want the stigma of chemical dependency to show up in her daughter's records. She said that'd scar Tammi for the rest of her life."

C.J. pulled a business card out of her pocket and handed it to Wagner. "Call me if Tammi contacts you or if you think of anything else."

Harold took the card and set it on the table. "No one is looking for Tammi anymore, are they?"

"I'm new. I'll reopen the case. Okay?"

Harold nodded. "Thanks."

* * *

After a quick shower, C.J. changed into khakis and a black golf shirt. While excited about the prospect of a relaxed dinner away from the prying eyes of the county residents, she wrestled with her feelings about a date with Eddie.

"Well Jensen, what have you gotten yourself into?" she asked out loud as she drove north. "You've got butterflies like you're going on a high school date, but you're spending the evening with an old guy who works with dead bodies all day. Why did you say yes?"

She pondered the question as she passed Willow River exit. "Maybe you should just take the next exit and turn around," she mused. "Nah, it's great to take a break. Since Floyd turned this investigation over to me, I've had nothing but the investigation on my mind. I need a diversion."

Her mind drifted to her encounters with Eddie at the morgue. His face was lined with age, but his eyes sparkled mischievously. He liked to kid her. He was ex-military but chose to wear his salt-and-pepper hair in a ponytail. He wasn't particularly good looking, but his personality drew her to the inner man, the one who was kind and considerate.

Am I looking forward to a date with Eddie, or am I just using him as an escape from Pine County?" With that question in mind, C.J. met Eddie Paulson at the morgue entrance.

Eddie, wearing a leather Vikings jacket and khakis, was waiting, leaning casually on the door frame. "I was afraid you'd chicken out." His ponytail flagged when he hopped down from the platform.

C.J. laughed. "Why do you wear a ponytail? You look so straightlaced in your scrubs."

A smile spread over his face, accentuating the wrinkles at the corners of his eyes. "A legacy of war. I've had it ever since I got back from my overseas deployment. I decided to never wear someone else's haircut again. Tony asks me to keep it tucked under my hat when we're in the field or around strangers. C'mon." He led her to a red Nissan Pathfinder in the corner of the paved parking lot.

Eddie played tour guide for C.J. as he drove. "The West End of Duluth follows the St. Louis River to Duluth Harbor. Downtown Duluth is huddled along the hill that slopes down to Minnesota Point. That's where the lift bridge is built across the mouth of the harbor. London Road is on the East End of Duluth and runs along the north shore of Lake Superior. It's where a lot of the ship and mine owners built their houses in the 1800s."

From Superior Street, Eddie and C.J. got occasional glimpses of the lake between houses and buildings. They made small talk about the weather and driving on snowy roads in the winter. As Eddie turned onto London Road, he pointed to a park near the lake. "That's the Leif Erickson ship. A group of Norwegians built it and sailed across the north Atlantic to prove Erickson could have discovered North America before Columbus. Past the ship, the Duluth Garden Club maintains acres of rose gardens above the lakeshore trail."

They followed London Road until Eddie turned up the hill and turned onto Superior Street. He pulled into a parking lot next to the old stone structure that housed Fitger's Brewery. The Duluth tour and easy banter had quickly chased away any apprehension C.J. had about the evening. She found herself transported from the intense concentration of the case to a friendly evening with a genuinely nice guy.

"Are you into micro-brewery beer?" Eddie asked, pointing to the old complex that housed the downsized brewery, amid shops, an Inn, and a café. "Or would you prefer a little more class? We could go to the Pickwick for prime rib," he said, pointing to the classic stone front of the old Fitger's brewery.

In a sudden change of character C.J. said, "Let's do the brew." She slid her arm through his as they walked down the sidewalk. Eddie was surprised by the move.

He held her arm close to his side as they ambled toward the restaurant. "It's not often I take an attractive woman to dinner," he said. "Why'd you agree to go out with me? I didn't expect you to accept."

C.J. looked at him with raised eyebrows, acting surprised, as if she hadn't asked herself the same question. "Why not?" she said.

"Well, I'm nearly old enough to be your father, for one thing. Just an old Nam vet who still has nightmares."

"Your age isn't a problem for me." She smiled at Eddie with dimpled cheeks to disguise the white lie.

They located the beer pub inside a small mall. Everything was built out of rough gray stone, giving it a castle-like feeling. The knotty pine tables were heavily coated with urethane, making them look like the wood was wet. The air was filled with the luscious aroma of char-broiled steaks, and the hostess seated them at a table overlooking Lake Superior.

"This is great," C.J. said, marveling at the expanse of water that went on until it met the sky. Eddie nodded approvingly.

They ordered two of the house specialty ales.

C.J. read through the menu, and after making a choice, set her menu on the table. She watched Eddie, who was wrestling with his dinner decision. She stared at his weathered face and carefully manicured fingers. They seemed incongruent with his job as the medical examiner's assistant. It was as if she were seeing him for the first time, which was true, in a sense. Strange, she thought, how sometimes you can look at a person and not really see them.

She waited for him to look up from the menu and said, "I said yes because you're an interesting guy. Besides, the nightlife in most of Pine County is slow. They roll up the streets at five o'clock. I thought I'd come up here and take a chance." She smiled.

A lopsided smile crept over Eddie's face. "Oh, so you're just using me to get away from town? Now I feel cheap."

C.J. leaned on her elbows. "Why'd you ask me out?"

A hint of a tick twitched in his left cheek. "Are you kidding? You're pretty and smart. I thought you'd be interesting and fun. I never thought you'd accept."

C.J. smiled at Eddie's apparent low self-confidence. The waitress brought their beers, and both quickly began to sip them in embarrassed silence.

"What do you think of the ale?" Eddie said finally. He watched C.J.'s expression as she took rather tentative sips.

"Tastes like it's made of acorns dissolved in lake water," she whispered.

He nodded. "You're right. It's a little heavy on the hops. That makes it a little bitter. You can order something else if you want. You won't hurt my feelings."

C.J. waved him off. "Nah, it's okay. Maybe it'll grow on me." She took another sip and made a face as she swallowed. It obviously wasn't growing on her. "Well, tell me, what's it like working with dead bodies all day." She leaned back in the chair.

Eddie stared into his ale. "Oh, I suppose it's like working in a packing plant. You get calloused to it after a while." He sipped his beer and waved to the waitress with his menu. "Until something really bad comes in, like a kid. Then it brings back the nightmares. How about you, are you handling the new Pine County job okay?"

The waitress came and C.J. ordered a chef's salad. Eddie asked about the chicken curry but decided on London broil on homemade noodles.

"You're only having a salad?" He asked. "They have a fabulous grill with steaks and chops." He stopped suddenly, and asked, "You're not vegetarian, are you?"

C.J. shook her head. "Not at all. It's just that I haven't been getting much exercise lately. I decided to take it easy on the calories tonight."

C.J.'s mind drifted to the investigation. She turned somber, staring out the window at the lake. "I don't know if I'll get calloused about it. I mean there are real people getting hurt and killed out there. How can you walk away and shut it off? I mean, it's tough."

Eddie leaned forward. "Do you like the job?"

C.J. smiled. "Most of the time I like it. Floyd just asked me to take the lead on an investigation and that's…incredibly challenging and stimulating. My brain is working on it all the time."

"I've learned to separate what I do from the rest of my life. If I don't, it'll eat me alive." He tipped his glass toward her. "That goes for you, too. Soldiers, cops, and therapists have high suicide rates because of all the stuff they see and deal with." His voice was almost a whisper.

"You talk like you know," she said, staring into the foam on top of her beer, trying to decide if she wanted to drink any more.

Eddie's demeanor turned serious. "I spent years in a vet's hospital trying to get over the war. Now my job is my therapy and I work hard at it. When I walk out the door, I've got something else to focus on."

"Really? What?" C.J. looked relieved that the topic had changed.

"I write poetry," he said, smiling. "As soon as I'm out the door I'm composing new verses. It really helps me."

C.J.'s eyes sparkled. "Poetry. You're pulling my leg!" She searched his face for a hint of mirth. "Has your poetry been published?"

He shook his head. "I've got it in three-ring binders on the shelf. Maybe someday I'll send it in. Right now, it's just for me."

"What kind of poetry? War stuff?"

"It's mostly observations of nature and things that make me feel good."

"Show me some after dinner," she said, surprising herself with the request.

He stared at her with a look of apprehension. "Nobody else...I mean it's kind of personal."

Her eyes twinkled. "Poetry is a chick magnet. You might be missing an opportunity. I just invited myself up after dinner."

His face flushed. "I didn't clean. My place looks like a locker room."

"I doubt that. You're too organized. 'A place for everything and everything in its place,' Right?"

Dinner interrupted the discussion. As they ate, the conversation turned to the city of Duluth and Lake Superior. After dinner they walked the trail behind Fitger's in the frigid wind blowing off the lake, listening to the waves slapping the breakwater.

"How is your investigation of Ted Palmquist's death going?"

"I've been planning to interview Palmquist's friends to find out where he got the aromatic hydrocarbons in his liver." She smiled, secretly pleased to have recited the chemical name correctly. "They've been elusive."

Eddie nodded in appreciation. "Any progress at all?"

"Not yet, but we have another issue that may be connected. One of the boy's friends ran when I went to his house. He rolled his truck, but not until after he threw a couple bags of marijuana and a bag with methamphetamine and a gun out the pickup's window."

Eddie shook his head in wonderment. "We never used to see meth, crack or cocaine up here," he said. "But the last couple of years they've been showing up a lot more. We've been seeing way too many overdoses in the morgue."

C.J. started to shiver. "The strangest part of this investigation is that the gun we recovered from the ditch was purchased years ago by a man whose daughter ran away a few months ago. I talked to him just before I drove up here. It was really sad. He was hoping I was there to tell him that we'd found his daughter."

C.J. leaned close to Eddie. "Share some of your body heat. I'm freezing."

He shyly pulled her closer. "What did he say about the gun? Did his daughter take it when she ran away?"

"Wagner, the father, didn't know. He hadn't missed it until after she was gone." A cold gust of wind off the lake swept past, tugging at their jackets. C.J. slid her arm behind Eddie's back and pulled him even closer for warmth. "What was even stranger," C.J. added, "there was one spent shell in the gun."

Eddie tried to concentrate on C.J.'s comments while trying to sort his own emotions with their bodies pulled so close together. "I'll bet the kid who threw it out the window knows what happened to that one shell." They took a few more steps in silence before he added quietly. "And I'll bet it isn't good."

She looked at him curiously. "Why'd you say that?"

Eddie shook his head. "Sorry. It's just a premonition. I talk to myself. People who live alone tend to do that. Besides, it helps me if I verbalize questions, instead of rolling them around inside my head."

She nodded knowingly, thinking about the conversation with herself on the drive to Duluth. They walked silently to the Pathfinder, parked by Fitger's.

C.J. turned the heat knob up when Eddie started the engine. Cold air blew on their feet as he turned toward downtown.

"Ah…when do you have a day off? I'd like to take you to the zoo. It's one of my favorite places."

C.J. smiled. "I'd like that. I'll check the duty roster and give you a call tomorrow."

Chapter 12

Pam was making a cup of coffee when she heard toenails clicking on the hallway tile. She peeked around the corner and saw C.J. trying to restrain the basset hound dragging her down the corridor. Pam knelt to welcome the dog, giving Bailey an extra boost of energy, pulling the leash out of C.J.'s hand. The basset loped down the hallway, bowling Pam over, and licking her face.

"I'm sorry," C.J. said, picking up the leash. "Bailey is as strong as an ox. Luckily, she's friendly."

Pam recovered and got on her knees. "What a sweetheart. How old is she?"

"She's not quite two, so still a bit of a puppy."

Pam wrapped her arms around Bailey's neck and hugged her. The dog's tail made circles.

"You said you could watch her today. I hope you don't mind. If it's too much trouble, I'll call my dad."

Pam stood and retrieved her coffee mug. "I think Bailey and I will be okay together. Do I need to take her out or feed her?"

"She's housebroken, so I don't think she'll have an accident in the office, but I'm sure she'd like to take a walk around the parking lot when you take your lunch break. Just hang on tight. If she sees a rabbit or squirrel, there's no holding her back. She usually naps after her walks, so that's a strategy to keep her out of trouble."

Pam took the leash and led Bailey to her desk. C.J. handed Pam a small blanket. "Throw this under your feet and she'll sleep under your desk and not bother you for most of the day."

C.J. was typing her report about the chase and recovery of the Colt pistol when the dispatcher paged her to pick up line four.

"Deputy C.J. Jensen."

"Deputy Jensen, this is Reg Carlson from ATF. I have information on ownership of the gun you found."

"Wow, that was quick. I just phoned in the serial number yesterday afternoon, and I didn't expect to hear from you until at least next week." She scrambled to find a pen on the desktop.

Carlson went on. "Actually, it only took a couple of seconds on the computer. There's only been one recorded sale of that gun. Its original purchaser was Harold Wagner, who bought it from a licensed dealer in Mora in 2004. It's listed as a nickel-plated .357

magnum Colt Python. Wagner's address is listed as a P.O. box in Pine City."

"Perfect! That matches our concealed carry permit." C.J. scribbled Wagner's name and P.O. box number on a Post-it note, planning to add them to her report on the Wagner interview. "Thanks!"

Bailey whined and gave Pam a sad look. "Does this mean she wants to go out, C.J.?"

Sighing, C.J. nodded. "Bailey's already pushing your buttons. Yes, that means she wants to walk."

Pam hooked Bailey to the leash and led her down the hall. C.J. picked up the phone. With her fingers hovering over the keypad, she closed her eyes. *Do I call Eddie to tell him I had a great time, or would that send the wrong message? It was nice but I don't want to be more than his friend.*

* * *

Making himself a cup of coffee, Floyd watched C.J. After she hung up, he sat in her guest chair, breaking her chain of thought. "Floyd, um, sorry. My mind was..." she waved her hand to clear her thoughts.

"The Robbinsdale police had an incident at the hospital with Juan Santiago's friends last night."

She went to the counter and put a coffee pod into the brewer. It hissed as coffee dribbled into her mug. "What kind of incident?"

"Juan's father, Ray, swore out a complaint that Dylan Johnson tried to kill Juan. Ray came into the room and found Dylan trying to smother Juan in his hospital bed."

C.J. set the cup on the desk and leaned back in her desk chair, trying to digest the information. "Wow! Dylan tried to kill Juan. Why?"

Floyd leaned back in his chair and steepled his fingers as he thought and spoke. "I see a couple possible motives. Dylan might have owned the drugs Juan threw out during the chase and was trying to punish Juan for losing his stash. Or Juan knows something damning and Dylan's afraid Juan's going to spill it."

C.J. tapped a pencil on her coffee mug. "Sounds like I should go down and lean on Juan."

"I talked to the county attorney. Juan's still on narcotic pain killers. We would jeopardize a future court case if there was even a hint that we'd coerced him while he was medically impaired."

"So, I should lean on Dylan until Juan's off pain meds?"

Floyd got up and lifted his jacket from the back of the chair. "Lean on Dylan and all the others—Tyler Espe, Brady Werther and Laura Tomlinson. Maybe one of them will crack."

C.J. gulped her coffee and grabbed her jacket. She followed Floyd to the parking lot. "I caught up with Harold Wagner last night. He confirmed that he's the owner of the gun Juan threw in the ditch. He said the gun disappeared from a drawer, but he's not sure when." She kept walking, waiting for Floyd to comment. When none was forthcoming, she went on. "I also talked to Eddie Paulson last night. He thinks we should ask Juan about the spent shell."

"Add that to the list of questions for all the teens."

C.J. took a few steps then added, "Harold Wagner thought I was there to tell him we'd found Tammi. He wanted to know if we were making any progress on the investigation. Fill me in on that case."

Floyd stopped. "Harold Wagner/Tammi Wagner. I didn't make the connection before. She was a runaway. We took the report, talked to the school, and sent out a bulletin, but never got any response. The case is open but there's no ongoing investigation."

"It never went any further than that? I mean, didn't you question her friends and try to locate her?"

"As I recall, Pam talked to the parents, who are separated, a few school friends, and the school. No one had any ideas. The principal saw her as a kind of a troublemaker. He suspects she got fed up with her home life and headed for bright lights of the big city. We lose a few girls that way. Some just show up later; some never do. I'm sure you saw some of that in Cloquet."

C.J. nodded. "We didn't have many runaways in town, but we were right on the edge of the Fond du Lac Reservation. There's an epidemic of missing Native girls across all of the U.S. and Canada."

Floyd stopped next to the "police parking only" sign. "I have a contact in the Bureau of Criminal Apprehension who's dedicated her life to tracing missing children. I don't know how she handles it because it seems like there are a hundred lost for every one she finds."

"Did your BCA person investigate Tammi's disappearance?"

Floyd nodded. "Tammi was added to the list of missing and exploited children. Tammi's name, date of birth, and a picture were entered into the database. If she's arrested her name will pop up."

C.J. became frustrated. "Her friends were Dylan Johnson, Brady Werther and Tyler Espe. Did someone interview them?"

"Think about that bunch. Do you think any of them would give you the time of day...even if they could tell time?"

"Floyd, why'd you give me this case? Don't you usually handle this kind of investigation yourself?"

Floyd started walking and C.J. jogged to catch up. "Mary's having cancer surgery today."

C.J. stopped. "Cancer surgery? I didn't hear anything about it."

Floyd opened the cruiser door. "It just came up. She saw the cancer doctor yesterday and she's having surgery today. I haven't been spreading the news around." He looked at his watch. "I've got to pick her up."

* * *

Floyd and Mary arrived at the hospital early and checked in with admitting personnel, who recorded Mary's insurance information. A matronly assistant led them to a pre-surgical floor where Mary changed into a hospital gown and put her clothing in a locker. She was led to a room where Floyd sat reading a *Budget Travel* magazine. The nurse helped her into bed.

"This magazine says that Orlando is the cheapest place to visit in Florida if you skip all the Disney stuff."

Mary glared at him. "Why go to Orlando and not see Disney?"

"There's lots of other things to do there. Look at this." He held up the magazine. "Sea World, outlet shopping malls, Gatorland Zoo and the Camelot Dinner Theater are all within a few miles of Orlando. Busch

Gardens and Cape Canaveral are within a day's drive."

A man in blue surgical scrubs swept into the room, chart in hand. "Hello, I'm Eric Jackson, the nurse anesthetist assisting with your surgery today." He consulted Mary's chart. "Mary, do you have any drug allergies, or have you ever had an adverse reaction to anesthesia?"

Mary glanced nervously at Floyd as tears welled in her eyes. Floyd spoke for her. "No drug allergies, and she's never had a problem with anesthesia."

The anesthetist scribbled notes. "We'll be giving you a general anesthetic through an intravenous line today. I'd like to start the IV now, if you're ready."

Mary nodded. He pulled on a pair of gloves and reached in a cart, arranging the IV set up on a tray. Mary and Floyd watched numbly as she received a shot of lidocaine, and he inserted the IV in the back of her hand. The anesthetist attached it to the IV bag and left the room.

Floyd set the magazine aside. "You froze up for a second."

Mary nodded. "I guess it just now struck me that this was really going to happen."

Floyd reached over and squeezed her hand. "It'll all be over soon and then we'll make travel plans. Would you like to see Orlando?"

Mary nodded. "Sure."

The surgeon breezed through to see if Mary had any last-minute questions.

"What happens if I die during surgery?" She asked without apparent emotion. Floyd suppressed his shock at the abrupt question.

The surgeon had been reviewing the mammogram on a computer screen. He turned and looked at each of them with a steady, serious gaze. "You won't die during this surgery, Mary, I promise." He entered something in the computer and stood.

Mary sighed. "Even if I make it through surgery, how long will I live?"

"Mary, there's no time stamp on your chart and I'm not clairvoyant. Let's get through the surgery and have this discussion later."

Mary sighed. "Why waste everyone's time?" She stared at the ceiling.

The surgeon patted Mary on the shoulder. "We're going to take good care of you." He looked at Floyd with sympathy and left. The surgical orderly arrived, raised the side-rails, and wheeled the bed to the door.

Floyd stopped him and pecked Mary on the cheek. "It'll be okay." His voice cracked and tears filled his eyes as he watched them disappear down the hall.

Floyd leafed through two magazines, then stared out the window for a few minutes. The spring weather was blustery, and pieces of paper and plastic swirled in corners of the hospital parking lot. People walked down the streets with their coats being whipped by the gusts. He felt as lost and helpless as he had ever felt in his life. After a moment of soul searching, he had a moment of inspiration and took the elevator to the basement.

Eddie Paulson was sitting in an unmarked office reading reports. He set aside the reports when the door opened. "Hi, Floyd. What's up?"

"Mary's having surgery, and I need some help."

"Surgery?"

Floyd nodded. "She has breast cancer and she's in surgery now."

"Breast cancer is very treatable. The five-year survival rate is nearly one hundred percent if caught early."

"Can you watch the surgery?"

Eddie frowned. "I'm the medical examiner's assistant. Why would I watch surgery?"

Floyd shook his head. "What if the doctor screws up? I want someone to make sure that everything goes okay? Can you do that?"

Eddie gave a meek smile. "That's a little out of my league. Surgeons often have big egos and wouldn't appreciate a morgue technician watching for their mistakes." Eddie saw that he wasn't getting through to Floyd.

Floyd let out a deep breath and rolled his head back, staring at the ceiling. "I'm helpless here, Eddie. It's just killing me. Everything else in my life I can control, but this..."

Eddie pushed back his chair and stood next to the desk for a second, tapping a pen on the desk calendar. He finally looked up at Floyd. "What the hell, what's the worst they can do, fire me? I was looking for a job when I found this one. I'll put on scrubs."

He disappeared through a back door and returned wearing green surgical scrubs, his ponytail was under a disposable head cover and a surgical mask was tied around his neck. "You get yourself back up to the family waiting room. If anyone asks about this, it was my idea. Okay?"

Floyd nodded numbly as they walked to the elevator together.

* * *

C.J. arrived at the high school where the buses were dropping students at the curb. She parked in a spot reserved for visitors and garnering uncomfortable stares, followed the flow of students into the main entry. The hallways were noisy and crowded with clutches of students blocking the flow while they engaged in animated discussions. C.J. waded through the crowd to the principal's office and found Frank Boquist at his desk.

"Good morning, Deputy Jensen. What can I do for you?"

"Good morning. I'd like to talk to one of your students. Can I borrow your office again?"

"Um, well, sure. Give me a second to finish a couple of things. Ask Mrs. Kennedy to call the student down to the office while I wrap up."

C.J. walked to the front office desk and waved to the school secretary. "Mrs. Kennedy, I'd like to interview Tyler Espe. Could you page him to the office please?"

Mrs. Kennedy was very close to retirement, and she reminded C.J. of her own grandmother. She smiled politely at C.J. "I'll try, but the kids are just going to their homerooms now. They might not all be in the classrooms for another couple of minutes." She pulled Tyler's schedule out of a wooden box that looked like a library card catalog reject. She called Tyler's homeroom and asked him to report to the office, then held the button down, waiting for a response from the room. For a moment, all that came back was the cacophony of students' voices. A female voice finally responded, "He just arrived. I'll have him go to the office."

Frank Boquist exited his office with an armload of papers and a legal pad. "The office is all yours. Try not to leave any blood on the desk or floor."

C.J. smiled at Boquist's attempted humor. "Thanks, Mr. Boquist," she said, walking into the office to await Tyler Espe.

Tyler wheeled into the office. At the sight of C.J.'s uniform, his expression turned sour. Standing at the door, C.J. directed Tyler to the single visitor's chair. She leaned against the door after closing it.

"Where's the old cop?" Tyler asked as he fell into the chair. His hair was long and apparently unwashed. The unkempt look matched his jeans—frayed and torn at the knees. They hung so low around his hips that the elastic of his boxers showed over the waistband.

"He decided to not waste any more time talking to you."

Tyler shrugged. "His loss." He slid down in the chair with his legs spread wide.

"Tell me about Juan Santiago. Is he a good friend?"

Tyler didn't look at C.J. as he spoke. "I know Taco. Heard you guys almost killed him."

"He had dealer quantities of drugs in his possession. He's going down hard unless he squeals on someone else. Knowing him like you do, will he take the fall alone, or do you think he might implicate someone else if he was offered a deal?" C.J. walked to the far side of the desk. "Of course, if you were to

201

set the record straight before he made his statement, you could be the one with the plea deal."

Tyler scratched his crotch, watching C.J. for her reaction. "I got nothin' to say. Can I leave?"

"Ted Palmquist died from benzene poisoning," C.J. said, pausing briefly to let the information sink in. Tyler looked at her without comprehension. "The medical examiner said the benzene may have come from drinking denatured lab alcohol. Have you guys been dipping into the chem lab supplies here at school?"

Tyler shook his head. "What's denatured alcohol?"

She left Tyler's question unanswered. "You wouldn't know what happened to the spent cartridge in the gun that Juan threw out the window, would you?"

Tyler hesitated a fraction of a second too long before answering. "What gun? I don't know nothin' about Taco having a gun."

C.J. smiled. "We're running the fingerprints on the gun and the cartridges. Will any of them be yours?" She reached down and lifted Tyler's hand as if she were looking at Tyler's fingerprints on the desktop.

Tyler jerked his hand back. "I don't know what the fuck you're talking about, beeyotch." He phrased the slam so it was two syllables, then turned so that he was looking at the wall.

C.J. grabbed Tyler by the collar and lifted him from the chair. "Did you just call me a bitch!" She pulled Tyler's face within an inch of her own. The boy struggled, but C.J. surprised him and was prepared for his resistance. "I hope your prints are on the gun and on the bags of drugs we recovered from the ditch. Then I'll throw your skinny butt in jail with Bubba and you'll be his bitch."

C.J. pushed the boy back into the chair. "You're eighteen, right?" Tyler nodded dumbfoundedly. "That's great. You'll be tried and sentenced as an adult."

He sneered as C.J. walked from behind the desk. From her position at the door, C.J. added, "You were there when the Robbinsdale police arrested Dylan for attempted murder last night. They had to peel Juan's father off when he caught Dylan trying to smother Juan."

Tyler's head snapped to look at her. His face flushed. "That's so much bullshit."

"What's Dylan afraid of, Tyler? What does Dylan think Juan might tell someone? You know either Dylan or Juan could plea bargain to avoid a felony charge for distribution of a controlled substance. That would leave you as the one thrown under the legal bus."

"It's all bullshit. Dylan didn't do nothin'. I was there. It was no big deal." There was no confidence in Tyler's voice.

"Get outta here. I'm sick of your face." C.J. opened the office door. Tyler hesitated for a second, then got up to leave.

As he passed the door, C.J. laid a hand on his shoulder. "What happened to Tammi Wagner?"

Tyler pushed C.J.'s hand off his shoulder. "Go to hell." The words were spit into her face, with venom. She'd obviously hit a nerve and caught Tyler by surprise with the question. His reaction pleased her, and she suspected it would be enough to keep his mind working overtime.

Mrs. Kennedy spoke from her desk. "Did you want me to call someone else?"

C.J. thought for a moment. "Call Brady Werther, then Laura Tomlinson."

Tyler knows something about Tammi Wagner's disappearance, C.J. thought to herself.

Brady Werther had Tyler Espe's fashion sense, down to the visible elastic of his boxers. C.J. waved an apprehensive Brady to the visitor chair and closed the office door.

"Brady, I'm C.J. Jensen from the Pine County Sheriff's Department." She stepped behind the chair where Brady was sitting. "We have several bags of drugs that Juan Santiago threw out of his car when we chased him. Juan's sitting in the hospital right now, but when he gets out, we're going to charge him with possession with intent to distribute. Do you know what that means?"

Brady sat up in the chair and turned his head, trying to see C.J. "Ah, not really?" He was obviously frightened, and he followed her every move.

"It means that Juan can be convicted of a felony and as an adult. Because there were dealer quantities of drugs involved and a firearm, he's looking at three to five years in prison."

C.J. moved to the principal's chair, not saying anything, letting the silence work on Brady's emotions. Finally, she said, "Of course, if he agrees to testify against his co-conspirators, the county attorney will probably let him plead guilty to misdemeanor drug possession. The county attorney might negotiate the sentence down to supervised probation if Juan helps get convictions on other people. Would you be one of the other people that Juan might rat out?"

Brady's face was bathed in sweat, and he swallowed hard. "I don't know what you're talking about."

"Tell me about the drugs, Brady, Whose drugs were they? Yours? Dylan's? Juan's?"

"I..." He shook his head. "They'll kill me."

"Who would kill you? Juan? Dylan? Tyler? Ted's already dead. Did they kill Ted?"

Brady's complexion turned gray and one drip of sweat rolled down his temple. He stared at the floor and didn't answer.

C.J. paced, letting the pressure build. "Tell me what happened to Tammi Wagner."

Air rushed from Brady's lungs, like he'd been punched. He sucked in a deep breath then seemed to stabilize.

C.J. squatted next to Brady's chair so that their faces were inches apart. "Brady, if you know where Tammi is you've got to tell me. Her family is very worried about her. It'll be better for you and all of us."

Brady stared at the floor. "Can I have a lawyer?" he whispered.

"Sure, you can have a lawyer. Do you need one?"

"I think so."

C.J. lifted one of Brady's arms and he stood without resistance. "I'm going to handcuff you, Brady, and take you to my car." She slipped one wrist into the cuffs and reached for Brady's other hand.

"Do you have to put on the handcuffs?" Brady looked over his shoulder at C.J. with sad eyes. "I mean, like everyone on the west side of the school is going to see me get hauled off."

C.J. nodded. "It's a department regulation. We can't transport a suspect unless he is cuffed." She took Brady's other wrist and snapped it into the cuff as the secretary watched. "Is Laura Tomlinson available?"

"She's on her way."

"Is there an office where Brady can sit while I talk to her?"

Mrs. Kennedy nodded to the open door next to the assistant principal's office. "Mrs. Hinz won't be in until later."

* * *

Laura Tomlinson sat inside the principal's office looking guilty. C.J. walked in and pulled the door closed behind her. "What's going on with Tammi Wagner?"

The girl went to the guest chair and sat on her hands. "She ran away last year." Her words flowed without hesitation. C.J. thought Laura believed it was the truth.

"Do you know where she went?"

"No one knows where she went. She just disappeared." Laura's voice was confident, and she spoke without hesitation.

"She used to hang around with you guys, didn't she?"

"Sometimes."

The girl's demeanor was shifting and C.J. became less convinced of her sincerity. "She never told any of you where she was going?"

Laura shook her head. "Not really. At least she didn't tell me."

"Were you and Tammi close?"

"Sorta. We talked some."

"Did she give any warning that she was going to leave? Did she have a fight with her parents, her boyfriend, or other friends?"

"No, no, no. She just disappeared." Laura made Tammi sound like a bird that had simply flown away.

"Did any of the guys ever talk about her leaving? Did they give her a ride somewhere?"

"Nobody ever talked about her after she left. She was, like, just gone! It was no big deal. People run away."

"Who brings the drugs when you get together?"

C.J.'s sudden change in direction caught Laura by surprise. "I…uh, don't know. They're just there."

"Just where?"

"There." Laura shrugged. "Wherever we are."

C.J. sat on the desktop. "What drugs have you seen?"

Laura shifted uncomfortably. "I don't know. Maybe some grass. Sometimes a tab of acid. I saw one of the guys pop some white pills once. I never did anything but the grass."

C.J. circled the desk and squatted down next to the chair, eye-to-eye with Laura. "Any booze or beer?"

Laura wouldn't look at her, staring into her lap instead. "Sometimes the guys have clear booze in a bottle. I thought it tasted bad. It made me cough."

"Was it in a clear liquor bottle or a brown chemical bottle?"

"What difference does it make?" The girl fidgeted, picking at her black fingernail polish. "I guess it was a booze bottle. I never thought much about it. Most of the guys drank it straight out of the bottle. Ted always had to put it into a glass and diluted it with water. The other guys made fun of him because that's how Tammi drank it too. They called him a girl."

"Laura, does anyone ever get violent? Some white pills are pretty bad stuff. Meth and angel dust sometimes make people violent."

Laura fidgeted. "I don't think so... No, everyone's cool. We mostly do..." An air of recognition swept over Laura as she realized C.J. had her telling too much. She bit her lower lip. "I can't say anymore. Are we done?" She looked up at C.J. expectantly.

The deputy shook her head. "I'm afraid this is just the beginning. You're in deep trouble."

Laura's eyes filled with tears. "Oh God, don't tell my mom. She'll kill me." Then the girl sobbed and gasped as another thought came to her. "Dylan." Her eyes went wide with terror.

C.J. put her hand on Laura's shoulder. "You're afraid of Dylan?"

Laura nodded and sniffed back her tears.

"Has he ever hurt you?"

Laura dabbed at her tears with the cuff of her oversized shirt. "Not bad." She paused. "But he will if he finds out I ratted him out."

C.J. leaned close. "Do you want to go back to class?"

Laura shook her head. "Maybe the nurse's office. She'll call my mom."

Chapter 13

C.J. was leaving the nurse's office when she ran into Frank Boquist.

"Are you done with them?"

"For today. I've still got questions that are unanswered. I'm taking Brady Werther to meet with the county attorney and a public defender."

The principal grimaced. "Well, if there's any way I can help, just let me know."

"There's one thing. Do you know if any denatured alcohol is missing from the school?"

The principal smiled. "I wouldn't know denatured from natured alcohol. You need to talk to Daryl Wilcox. He teaches chemistry and orders the chemicals used in the science department labs." Boquist looked at his watch. "If you hustle, you'll be able to catch him between classes. He's in room 205."

The bell rang as C.J. approached room 205. Students poured into the halls like an approaching avalanche. She pushed her way into the room and saw a gangly, red-haired man gathering papers on his desk.

"Excuse me, are you Daryl Wilcox?"

The man looked up from his desk and his face broke into a wide smile. "Ahh, I've been busted. Was it that stop sign in Finlayson I rolled through or the time I peed behind the gas station in Wyoming?"

C.J. smiled back and offered her hand. "C.J. Jensen. I'm here to see if you're missing any denatured alcohol."

Daryl raised his eyebrows. "Denatured alcohol? That's all you want?"

Daryl was engaging and she couldn't help but smile at his attempted humor. "I don't want any. I want to know if you're missing any."

Daryl pointed toward the hall. "Come this way. We'll look." He led her down the hall. "Any particular reason you suspect we might be missing some?"

They waded through the throng of students and C.J. raised her voice to be heard over the din. "When Ted Palmquist died, the autopsy showed that his liver contained benzene. The medical examiner speculated that he might have been drinking denatured alcohol."

Daryl stopped at a locked door at the end of a long hallway and pulled a ring of keys from his pocket. He unlocked the door and turned on the light. The room was lined with shelves of brown bottles in assorted sizes. There was a chemical odor to the room that C.J. found offensive. Daryl walked toward the larger containers and lifted a one-gallon brown bottle. He swirled the contents.

"It's still here. The biology classes use it for mounting microscopic tissue samples, but I haven't ordered any for a couple of years." He set the bottle down and reached for another. "And here's the benzene." He swirled it. "It's here, too. Anything else you want to check on?"

C.J. shrugged. "It was just a hunch. Thanks for checking." She moved toward the door.

"You're not interested in the chemicals that are missing?"

C.J. froze. "Other chemicals are missing? Like what?"

Daryl pointed to a bare spot on the shelf. "We've had a bunch of stuff disappear last school year; glacial acetic acid, hydrochloric acid, lithium aluminum hydride, methylamine, trichloromethane, thionyl chloride, phosphorous, and anhydrous ammonia, to name a few."

C.J. took out a notebook and wrote the chemicals phonetically. "When did you notice they were gone?"

"I check our inventory every August, so I can order materials for the upcoming year's lab experiments. They could've disappeared any time between when we did our reduction lab experiments and August. I suspect they disappeared before school ended last spring, but I can't say that with certainty."

"Did you report any of this to the police?" C.J. scribbled notes.

"Nah. It's not a big deal. I mean, it's not like anyone could make a bomb or anything." Daryl ushered her out of the storage room and turned off the light. He locked the door as C.J. watched. "I'm sorry, but I've got to get back to my class." He walked past her and turned the corner in the now-empty hallway as a bell rang.

C.J. hustled along behind. "Can you give me a written list of those chemicals and what they're used for?"

"They're used for reductions and substitutions in our junior chemistry lab class."

C.J. asked. "But what does that mean? Can they be used to make poisons?"

Daryl stopped at the door to room 205 for a second. "They're toxic chemicals but I don't think anyone would use them for poison. Let me do some research and get back to you." Wilcox froze in thought. "I took a summer class and one of the Minneapolis teachers had a kid ask her how to make methamphetamine. She laughed it off, but immediately checked her inventory."

"Do you know how to make meth?"

Wilcox glanced into his classroom to check on his students. "In a general sense, yes. But I haven't made any, nor have I taught my students how to make it."

"Is it hard to make?"

"I don't know that it's difficult, just dangerous as hell if not done properly. That's why you hear about meth labs blowing up."

C.J. closed her notebook. "You wouldn't run that experiment in the chemistry lab?"

Wilcox laughed. "Oh, hell no. The principal gets nervous when I teach the students how to use Bunsen burners."

"Thanks! Email me a list of the missing chemicals." C.J. said, jamming a business card in his hand as he disappeared into the classroom.

* * *

The surgical suite was bustling with activity. To an untrained eye, the activity looked like chaos. In fact, it was a well-rehearsed ballet with each participant anticipating the moves and needs of the others. The nurse anesthetist sat on a stool near an EKG monitor. Two surgical nurses moved around the room as a third nurse stood at the surgeon's side. The room was cool, with the odor of antiseptic, chemicals, and body tissues mingling in the air. The surgeon made a small incision through an iodine-colored plastic drape adhered to Mary's breast as Eddie slipped into the room. He stood near the door until the surgeon was well into the surgery, then moved behind the scrub nurse and watched the surgeon compare Mary's mammogram to the incisions he was making inside her breast.

The surgeon asked for a scalpel and worked out of Eddie's sight. He dropped a small mass of red tissue onto a piece of white gauze. Eddie leaned to the side to look at the tumor. The center of the normally pink tissue was discolored and irregular.

From behind the circulating nurse Eddie said, "I'm with histology. Pass me the tissue sample. I'll set up frozen sections for you."

The surgeon looked over his shoulder. "I didn't ask for histology."

Eddie thought quickly. "The head of surgery did. This lady is married to a VIP. He wants frozen sections done in the suite."

Impatience was evident in the surgeon's voice. "The head of surgery isn't here. I don't need frozen sections."

Eddie projected indifferent confidence. "It's your choice, but it'll save a lot of time if I slice and mount them for you now. If you have to take more tissue, she'll still be open."

The surgeon looked Eddie in the eye and let out a deep breath. "Who's the VIP?"

"Commissioner Swenson from the Minnesota Department of Public Safety. The patient is his wife." Eddie was reaching, but he was sure that no one knew the commissioner by name.

The surgeon let out a sigh and looked down. "Fine. Set up sections of the tumor and lymph nodes."

Eddie smiled under the mask. He quickly went to work setting the specimens on the nitrogen jet that instantly froze the tissue. He used a microtome to slice thin layers of tissue, then mounted the thin slices on glass microscope slides and set them on the stage of the microscope. It was exactly what he did in the morgue, but the medical examiner wasn't in a hurry for results and rarely questioned Eddie's observations.

With the specimens mounted, he slid the first of the tumor slides under the microscope and adjusted the focus. He found a field of dark material under low power then clicked up to the 300X to inspect the individual cells. They were irregular and many showed necrosis from poor blood flow. Cancer. He moved the slide to view the edge of the specimen and let out a breath as he found healthy, pink tissue.

"I've got the first breast field under the scope."

The surgeon didn't look up. "What's it look like?"

"DCIS." Duct cancer in situ was the least invasive and most treatable form of tumor. "The margins of the sample are clear—you got all the affected tissue."

The surgeon walked over and looked through the scope, moving the microscope stage from side to side to examine the entire sample. Then he looked Eddie in the eye. "How about the lymph nodes?"

Eddie deftly slipped in another slide and quickly scanned the tissue under low power. "They're clear. No evidence of metastasis." He stepped back and let the surgeon look.

"Check the lymph node in the tray."

"Yes, sir."

The military response garnered a look of surprise from the surgeon, who frowned, then went back to Mary.

Eddie quickly froze and mounted the sample. "Everything's negative. Do you want to view this specimen?"

The surgeon looked up and shook his head. "That's what I expected."

Eddie took pictures of the tissue samples, saved them to Mary's patient file, and put the slides in a biohazard bag. With his intense focus on the slides completed, he registered the regular beep, beep of the heart monitor. Mary's face was sallow, and the oxygen mask covered most of her face. It was easy to be detached and analytical when staring at the microscope, but it was Mary lying on the table. He was suddenly aware this was not the autopsy suite, and the tissue wasn't from some anonymous corpse. He'd been conditioned to be clinical and detached, until remembering he was dealing with a living person who meant a great deal to his friend…and to him.

* * *

Floyd had a paper coffee cup in his hand when Eddie walked into the family waiting room. He was staring out the window and Eddie walked up and stood next to him.

Floyd looked at Eddie's reflection in the window. "Want some coffee? It's bad, but it's free." He studied Eddie's face. "I assume you've got bad news."

"What makes you say that Mr. Detective?" Eddie asked.

"You changed clothes. If you'd been happy, you'd have been here in your scrubs and been all smiles." Floyd set the cup down on the sill, then he turned and faced Eddie. "How bad is it?"

Eddie stared out the window. "I should let the surgeon explain."

Floyd set his hand on Eddie's arm. "The surgeon is going to couch his opinion in medical-ese and soften it to make it what I want to hear. I want the straight scoop, with no icing. No sugar coating."

Eddie turned to Floyd. "Act surprised when you talk to the surgeon because I could be fired or arrested for what I just did and am about to tell you."

Floyd's lips pursed to a hard line. He stared at his hands. "Okay, spill it."

"The doctor removed a small tumor. It is the least invasive form of breast cancer, and it hasn't spread to any of the surrounding tissue or lymph nodes."

Floyd stared into Eddie's eyes in a state of near shock. "Is that a medical judgment?"

Eddie nodded. "It's not bad. I've looked at a lot of cancer tissue and Mary's condition is very manageable. I'm not an oncologist, but he might not even feel the need for further treatment."

Floyd set his coffee cop on the windowsill and embraced Eddie. Unable to restrain his tears he sobbed as Eddie patted his back and smiled. "By the way, the doctor thinks you're the Minnesota Director of Public Safety."

Floyd stepped back and pulled a handkerchief from his pocket. Wiping his eyes, he said, "What?"

"I had to tell a white lie to justify testing the tissue samples in the surgical suite."

Floyd put his hand on Eddie's shoulder. "And who does he think you are?"

Eddie shrugged. "He never asked my name. As far as he knows, I'm some random histology technician dispatched by the chief of surgery. Let's hope he doesn't dig into that too deeply."

* * *

Dylan spent the night in the Hennepin County jail before his arraignment on the assault charges. The judge released Dylan on his own recognizance after he entered a not guilty plea and the public defender said he had no previous criminal record except traffic citations. The judge set a trial date for July but encouraged the attorneys to discuss a plea agreement.

Dylan's car was at the hospital. The public defender gave him enough money for a cab back to Robbinsdale. His car was where he'd left it and he drove back to Pine City, popping some meth from the glove compartment to wake him up. The night in a jail cell with two inner-city drug dealers and a car thief had been tough. He'd slept a total of two hours, and that was in ten-minute catnaps while sitting on the floor with his back against the wall.

Dylan's mother was at work when he arrived home and he was relieved. He didn't need the hassle of answering questions about where he'd spent the night. Because he was over eighteen, neither the court nor public defender contacted her. He threw his clothes on the bedroom floor and grabbed a clean t-shirt and a fresh pair of boxers from a laundry basket on his way to the shower.

Plans rushed through his head as the hot water pounded his back. He needed to hide the reserve stash and the cash. Exhaustion swept over him as the meth metabolized. He fought to stay awake as he dried off. He fell onto the bed and was asleep in seconds.

*   *   *

C.J. pulled into the driveway of Dylan's house and parked behind the Mustang. The driver's door was still open, and she shaded her eyes to look inside. A small plastic bag lay on the seat. She put on a pair of nitrile gloves and picked up the packet of white powder. Bending over, she slipped it into an evidence bag, then into her shirt pocket. She poked in the open ashtray and spotted roaches from a couple of marijuana joints among the ashes. She put them into another evidence bag and marked them.

C.J. knocked firmly on the storm door and waited for a response. The inside door was open, and she looked around the kitchen for signs of life.

"Hello! Sheriff's Department. Anybody home?" She opened the screen door and stuck her head into the kitchen. Again, there was no response.

C.J. walked into the kitchen, aware that evidence she found wouldn't be admissible in court without a legal reason for the entry. On the other hand, the drugs she'd found in the car gave her probable cause to enter. The argument didn't sound plausible even to herself. If there was evidence, she'd have to back out of the house and return with a search warrant.

The kitchen and living room were neat, furnished with newer furniture, typical of a middle-class household. A few magazines were neatly stacked on a coffee table and a basket of folded clothes sat on a chair in the corner.

"Hello! Sheriff's department! Is anyone home?" C.J. walked into the hallway that led from the living room with a sense of foreboding. She slid her hand onto the butt of her gun. In the first room she found a neatly made bed with a hand-made quilt spread on it. The closets were closed, and a bottle of moisturizer sat on the dresser. The master bathroom had towels hung over rods and toothbrushes and toothpaste set in a cup on the end of the vanity. She pushed back the shower curtain exposing sparkling clean tile and a rack holding bottles of shampoo and cream rinse.

She walked quietly down the hall to a second room and peeked around the corner. The room smelled like a gym locker. The floor was littered with dirty clothing and a wicker clothes hamper overflowed in the corner. A laundry basket of clean clothes sat on the floor next to it. A snoring heap dressed in a t-shirt and boxers slept on the unmade bed. Dylan.

C.J. kept her hand on the butt of her gun. "Dylan, wake up." The body didn't stir. She moved into the room, checking the closet and under the bed to prevent an unpleasant surprise. There was still no movement from Dylan. C.J. shook the boy's shoulder but there was still no response. Concerned about a drug overdose, she put her hand on the boy's neck and felt the strong, regular beating of his heart. She left the bedroom and quickly cleared the rest of the house. Returning to the second bedroom, she shook Dylan hard and garnered a moan in response.

"Wake up."

Dylan rolled over and struggled to open his eyes. "What?"

"You're under arrest."

Dylan's eyes fluttered. "Who the fuck are you?"

Rolling him onto his stomach, she clamped a handcuff around one wrist. The deputy pulled the second wrist behind Dylan's back without resistance.

Dylan shook his head to clear the mental haze. "Hey, cut it out. What the fuck are you doing?"

C.J. pulled Dylan's legs to the edge of the bed and rolled him over. "You have the right to remain silent. You have the right to..."

The haze refused to leave Dylan's head in the mental crash after the meth high. He struggled to see and think but neither function responded. He got to his feet with C.J.'s assistance and stumbled to the cruiser without further exchange of words. In the cruiser, Dylan lay down on the rear seat and was asleep again before they reached the end of the driveway.

* * *

Floyd was sitting in Mary's room when she was delivered from the recovery room. Her face was ashen, and tubes ran from her arm to an IV bag. The surgeon had made his visit to inform the VIP of her condition. Floyd thought it was funny to be treated as a celebrity and knew the doctor's deference was mostly bullshit. The surgeon told Floyd he wanted Mary to recover for a few days then meet with the oncologist to discuss follow-up treatment to be determined from a study of the tissue samples taken during surgery.

When Floyd had asked specifically about Mary's recovery, the surgeon was reassuring. "The cancer appeared to be localized and is a very treatable type. Your oncologist will explain it to both of you during Mary's follow-up appointment."

Floyd held Mary's hand in his and her eyes flickered open. "Hi honey, can I get you anything?"

Mary smacked her dry lips. "A little water." Her voice was hoarse and weak.

Floyd fished an ice chip from a Styrofoam cup and fed it to her with a spoon. "The nurse said only ice chips to moisten your mouth until later."

Mary's eyes closed as she swallowed, showing the pain in her throat from the endotracheal tube. "Did you tell me what the surgeon said?"

"The tumor was small and was totally removed. He said this type of cancer is very treatable."

Mary's gaze went to the ceiling. "Metastasized?"

"Localized."

Her head turned and her eyes riveted on him. "How far?"

"Not at all. The surrounding tissue and lymph nodes were clear. He removed all the cancer."

Mary glared at him. "No sugar coating."

"Really, it's all good news."

"Ask the nurse if I can have something for pain."

Floyd walked to the nurse's station and caught the eyes of a nurse marking up a chart.

"My wife wants something for pain."

The nurse set aside the chart she'd been reading and reached for Mary's chart. "Mrs. Jungers?"

Floyd nodded numbly as the nurse leafed to the pages of the doctor's directions. "He didn't order anything for pain. I'll page him."

The nurse paged the surgeon and in a few moments the phone rang. She spoke briefly and then hung up. "He gave me an order for Demerol. I'll call the pharmacy and have some here in a couple of minutes."

Floyd nodded. "Thanks. I'm a little keyed up and Mary's convinced she's dying."

The nurse typed a bit and pulled up Mary's chart. She read for a few seconds, then looked at Floyd. "Didn't the doctor tell you about the surgical results? I mean, it's not my place to advise you guys about her medical condition, but everything I see is positive."

Floyd nodded. "Her mind is made up that she's going to die."

The nurse smiled and closed the computer file. "We'll have to work on that."

Chapter 14

After booking Dylan for drug possession, C.J. drove through Pine City thinking about the chemicals missing from the high school storage room. The pharmacy sign caught her attention and she pulled into an empty parking spot a half block down. Except for two teenage girls checking out the fingernail polish display, the store was quiet. She found Harold Parks checking his inventory of over-the-counter medicine and vitamins.

The pharmacist looked up, surprised to see a uniformed officer. "How can I help you?"

C.J. offered her hand and re-introduced herself as the newest member of the sheriff's department.

Smiling, the pharmacist nodded. "Charlene Jensen! I didn't recognize you in uniform."

"I was wondering if you could help me. A number of chemicals have been stolen from the high school, and I was wondering if there was something specific the thieves were planning to use them for." She handed the list to the pharmacist. "The chemistry teacher said that they were used for reduction experiments in the chemistry lab classes."

Parks pointed to a tan book on his back shelf. "That volume lists substances the Federal Drug Enforcement Agency tracks for unusual purchases. Those reducing agents and oxidizers react with common chemicals to make controlled substances."

"Give me an example." C.J. leaned on the counter.

Harold took down the tan book and slid his reading glasses back on. "The thionyl chloride and lithium aluminum hydride can be used to modify pseudoephedrine hydrochloride to produce methamphetamine, if you know how and have the right equipment." He stopped on a page halfway through the book and turned it so C.J. could read it. "Here's the reaction."

C.J. shook her head. "Can you explain the reaction in English?"

Harold slid off the glasses. "You can turn any over-the-counter cold remedy with ephedrine or pseudoephedrine, into crystal meth, or a close cousin."

C.J.'s mind ran back to the screening test they'd run on the powder in the bag with the gun. "But...where would someone get the recipe and equipment? They'd have to be a chemist, right?"

"The recipes are available on the internet. So, anyone with a computer and

Wi-Fi can get the recipe. I assume the equipment could come from a high school chemistry lab, or a chemical supply house by mail order."

"Should I suspect the chemistry teacher?"

The pharmacist laughed. "I sincerely doubt Daryl Wilcox is your most likely suspect. He's certainly got the equipment and expertise, but he doesn't seem like the type. It doesn't take a PhD chemist to cook up meth once you've got the chemicals. There are high school dropouts and half-wits running meth labs all over the U.S. and Mexico. I think about a quarter of them blow up their labs or themselves during the process. The rest get a final product, but they sell meth with varying levels of active ingredients and contaminants. There's no quality control and their customers aren't going to call the FDA because their supplier sold them a bad batch."

"They could be killing their own customers."

Harold picked up the book and slid it back onto the shelf. "The chemicals on your list were stolen from our high school?"

"They're missing from the science lab stockroom." C.J. considered his earlier comments about cold medicines. "These chemicals aren't enough. Have you had a run on Sudafed sales lately?"

Harold typed into his computer. "We don't sell more than limited quantities in a transaction. That said, we sell lots of cold remedies during the cold and flu season." He paged down through numerous screens. "I hadn't noticed it, but the sales of pseudoephedrine containing products were pretty high this winter." He moved to a different database, typed in some information, and waited. He paged through more screens, then looked up. "Wow! I hadn't been tracking it very closely. Sales for the past eight months are almost three times higher than historical levels."

"If all those additional sales were turned into meth, just how much drug are we talking about?"

The pharmacist pulled over a calculator and punched numbers for a few minutes as he paged through the computer records. He hit the total button and looked up. "Maybe as much as two kilograms." Seeing C.J. trying to do the conversion in her head he added, "About four and a half pounds."

C.J. gave a low whistle. "Two kilos? Can you tell who's been buying all the cold meds?"

Again, his glasses came off. "Not really. I deal with the prescriptions almost exclusively. Those we track by computer. Over-the-counter cold medications are kept behind the counter. The clerks verify that the purchaser is over 18 and the quantity being purchased in that transaction is below the maximum allowed. Then, they ring up the sale and there's no record of who those medications are sold to." He scratched his chin. "We can talk to the clerks. But they'd only remember a few purchases and that would only cover what's sold during their shift and in this store. You can buy cold remedies at any grocery store, superstore, or gas station. I'm sure you can buy them on a dozen internet sites, too."

C.J. spent the afternoon going from store to store, checking Sudafed purchases. Many of the stores didn't have accessible records, but those that did reported sales significantly up from previous years. No one seemed to remember any one person buying extraordinarily large quantities of the drugs repeatedly.

* * *

When C.J. got back to the courthouse there was a message to call the medical examiner's office. She wondered if that meant Eddie was being discreet, or if he had official ME business. She looked at the clock and realized it was almost six. She dialed, planning to leave a message on the recorder.

Eddie answered the phone on the second ring. "Morgue."

"Really, Eddie? That sounds a lot more disgusting than saying, 'medical examiner's office.'"

"Hi, C.J. Realistically, it is the morgue, and more people call for that than the medical examiner. Anyone who wants the ME knows that his office is in the morgue." Eddie paused as he changed mental gears. "I assume you're returning my message about the tests on Ted Palmquist's liver."

"Oh, I thought that we had it all. There were abnormal aromatic hydrocarbon levels," she recited from memory.

"The lab says the predominant chemical is benzene, but there are traces of chlorinated hydrocarbons too, mostly trichloroethane."

"What's that mean?" C.J. scribbled a phonetic spelling in her notebook.

"You can rule out denatured alcohol. Trichloroethane is a common non-flammable cleaning solvent. Ted didn't work for a dry cleaners, did he?"

C.J. flipped through her notebook. She quickly reviewed the notes about Ted. "I can't find anything about him having a job at all. Let's assume he didn't. Where else could it come from?"

Eddie leaned back in the chair. C.J. heard the spring creaking against the pressure. "Maybe an auto shop or machinist with a degreaser tank. I don't know right off hand. Those are industrial solvents—not something you'd buy at a hardware or paint store."

"Hang on." C.J. quickly flipped to the back page of her notes. "Any chance that those chemicals would be used to reduce pseudoephedrine to crystal meth?"

Eddie chuckled. "You're doing well with your chemical pronunciation, but your organic chemistry is a little weak. The meth reaction is run in an aqueous medium...err...in water. You wouldn't use chlorinated organic solvents for that reaction." He paused. "What made you ask?"

"I checked at the high school to see if they were missing any denatured alcohol. They weren't, but they were missing a bunch of stuff like thionyl chloride. I gave the list to the pharmacist, and he told me all the stolen chemicals were what you'd need to synthesize meth. He also checked his order history and found that purchases of pseudoephedrine cold medications are way up. I checked around a little more and found out that everyone's cold medicine sales are up."

"Hmmm. Sounds like you've got your own meth lab somewhere in Pine County. Be careful if you find it. They're prone to explosions and fires." Eddie paused. "You said the gun was found in a bag with methamphetamine powder, too. You think it's tied in with Ted's death?"

"We recovered a bag of meth after chasing down one of Ted's pals."

"Hang on a second while I pull up something." C.J. heard him leafing through pages. "That's a pretty tough synthesis. It's easy to get some minor variations of pseudoephedrine, but it's very difficult to get the hydroxyl group loose from the pseudoephedrine molecule to turn it into amphetamine or methamphetamine."

"Slow down, Eddie. What does that mean?"

"If they're really doing that synthesis, you've got a pretty sharp guy using good lab equipment. This isn't happening on the back burner of a stove in an aluminum pressure cooker. If you find the chemist and the equipment, you've got the whole operation."

C.J. bristled. "What makes you think it's a guy?"

"Eighty-five percent of drug addicts are male, as are ninety-nine percent of the meth lab chemists and dealers. The boyfriends or pimps usually drag the women into it. Women, in general, are smarter than men when it comes to drugs."

C.J. smirked. "Nice recovery. Is that really true?"

"That's what I see coming across the autopsy table. It's not from FBI statistics or anything." There was a short pause as C.J. could hear Eddie closing the book. "Are we still on for the day after tomorrow?"

C.J. smiled. "Sure. You want me to swing by your place and pick you up after I drop off Bailey?"

"That'd be great! Let's plan for ten in the morning."

When C.J. hung up the phone she realized that the sheriff had been listening. She flushed, thinking that he had overheard her plans with Eddie. "Sheriff, what's up?"

The sheriff walked to her guest chair and sat down. He settled into the chair and crossed his legs. "Floyd says that you're running the Palmquist death investigation. I had a call from the *Duluth News-Tribune*, and I promised to call them back. I'd like an update."

C.J. ran through the past few days in her head. "Well, that call was from the medical examiner's office. Ted Palmquist apparently died from some toxic chemicals that had been accumulating in his body. He had some other medical problems too, diabetes and leukemia. It seems that he wasn't being treated medically for any of these things, but the chemicals were what finally killed him."

The sheriff frowned. "Was he deliberately poisoned by someone?"

C.J. took a deep breath. "Probably not. It was more of a long-term exposure to industrial chemicals than acute poisoning. The medical examiner asked if he had been working in a dry-cleaning shop, because that would've been a likely source for one of the chemicals, but I don't think the boy had a job at all."

"Meth lab?" The sheriff asked.

"No, the ME said his liver was full of aromatic hydrocarbons. They're not used in making meth."

Sepanen nodded. "So, the bottom line is that he had some chronic chemical poisoning and you're continuing to investigate the source." He stated his conclusion and started to stand up.

"Umm, there's more. Ted was on the periphery of a group called the stoners." C.J. waited for him to get resettled. "Juan Santiago was one of the guys Ted hung out with. You know about his truck crash during the chase and the damage to my cruiser. We recovered marijuana, methamphetamine, and a gun from the packages he tossed out during the chase.

"Dylan Johnson is another of the stoners. He wasn't in school, so I went to his house, found a package of what's likely meth on the front seat of his car, and a couple marijuana roaches in the ashtray. I arrested him. Some chemicals were stolen from the high school and there's been a run on cold medicine. I have two sources who said those chemicals are used to make crystal meth. I think we have a drug lab, and I suspect the bag of meth we recovered after the chase may be homemade."

The sheriff raised his eyebrows. "You've made a lot of headway. Keep me posted." He stood and started for his office.

* * *

Dylan slept most of the day in a county jail cell. Failing to wake him, two jailers struggled to change him into a regulation orange jumpsuit. When they brought supper, Dylan opened one eye and told them to fuck off. At ten o'clock that night he started to rebound from the crash and his stomach rumbled. When he opened his eyes, he was staring at the metal toilet. Graffiti littered the wall above the toilet paper roll. He realized he was in a lower bunk. He rolled out of bed to check out his cellmate and found the top bunk empty.

"Hey! What's going on?" He rattled the door and waited for a response. It took almost five minutes for a jailer to walk to the cell.

"Well, if it ain't sleeping beauty. What do you want?"

"What's going on?"

The jailer smiled. "You're under arrest and locked in a county jail cell."

Dylan looked down at the orange jumpsuit and flip flops without laces. "Where are my clothes?"

238

"Listen dipshit, you're wearing the clothes you're going to be in until you post bail or get released."

Dylan's stomach rumbled. "Bring me something to eat."

The jailer laughed. "Sorry, Sleeping Beauty, this hotel doesn't have room service. You'll get scrambled eggs and toast in the morning."

"That's bullshit."

The jailer turned and walked away. Over his shoulder he said, "Welcome to the Pine County jail."

* * *

Mary fell asleep immediately after the painkiller drip was set up. Floyd sat in her room for most of the day, watching her drift in and out of sleep. Late in the evening her eyes opened, and she looked around the room. "Can I have a drink of water?"

Floyd held a straw to her lips and Mary drank a few swallows of water.

"Is the clock right? Is it almost nine o'clock?"

"You've slept the day away. Are you feeling okay?"

Mary pushed herself up in the bed and adjusted the pillow. "I guess so. I'm not having any pain." She paused, trying to remember something. "What did the doctor say?"

Floyd bit back a flippant remark, realizing Mary had been in a drug-induced haze. "He got all the cancer. You'll be fine."

Mary looked at him skeptically. "I suppose the oncologist has to be the one to break the bad news."

"There is no bad news."

Mary's eyes closed. "I'm going to sleep. Go home and check on the puppy."

Floyd reassured himself that he'd done the right thing by pushing Mary into surgery. *Eventually, she's going to realize we've made the right choice*, he said to himself.

* * *

The puppy crawled out from under the steps and ran toward the car. Floyd had to stop in the middle of the driveway. He opened the door and swept her into his lap before driving the rest of the way to his usual parking spot.

"I bet you're hungry." He carried the pup into the house, letting her sniff around the kitchen while he rummaged for leftovers in the refrigerator. The puppy nosed around every corner of the room and tugged at the corner of a garbage bag overhanging the wastebasket.

Floyd opened three small Tupperware containers and loaded the leftovers onto an aluminum pie tin. The puppy attacked the food hungrily while Floyd petted her.

"What's this?" He probed her fur with his fingers and removed a wood tick the size of a kernel of corn. "That one's been on for a while. How many more do you have?"

As the pup finished licking the pie plate, Floyd scoured her body with his fingers and pulled off six more ticks. The puppy loved the attention and Floyd didn't think about Mary for fifteen minutes. When he was done, he shooed the pup outside and called Mary's sisters, Emily and Trish, to update them on the surgery and promising prognosis.

He opened a beer after the last phone call and stared at it before pouring it down the drain. He'd avoided drinking alone or when depressed after his wife's death, deciding both could lead down the slippery slope to alcoholism. He'd come too far to let it grab him now. After rinsing down the foam, he decided to drive to the courthouse, hoping work would provide a temporary diversion.

The pup followed him to the car, and he tried to shoo her back to the deck. She scratched at the car door as he started the engine. Retrieving a length of clothesline from the garage, Floyd tied the puppy to the railing. "Little pest. If you stay around, we'll have to get you a collar and chain."

It was after eleven o'clock when Floyd got to the courthouse. He spoke to the night dispatcher for a minute, then turned on the computer, pulling up the reports C.J. had written about the Ted Palmquist investigation. C.J.'s first report summarized the Santiago chase and arrest. Her second report said Dylan Johnson had been arrested and was in jail awaiting arraignment for possession of a controlled substance. She explained finding his car door open, the discovery of the contaminated baggy and the marijuana. A third report summarized her interviews at the school with Brady Werther and Laura Tomlinson. She'd arrested Brady, but he contacted a lawyer and had already been released to his parents.

Floyd reread the reports, then picked up the phone. He dialed the number for the county jail. Harold Pederson, the night jailer, answered the phone. "Harold, you still got the Johnson kid locked up?"

It took Pederson a moment to recognize Floyd's voice. "Uh, hi Floyd. You mean Dylan or Dave Johnson. We've got 'em both in."

"I want Dylan. Could you bring him to an interrogation room? I'd like to talk to him."

There was a pause. "Sure. He slept most of the day. I'm sure he's sitting in his cell. C'mon down."

Floyd met the jailer in the hallway outside the interrogation rooms. Harold had been a road deputy until he'd injured a knee chasing a burglar through a swamp. He was an imposing figure at well over six feet tall, but most of his muscular chest had sunk to his waist. The red hair had thinned and was salted with gray. The ring of jailhouse keys dangled from one hand.

"Dylan's in here," said Pederson, nodding toward the interrogation room. "I'll warn you, he's not happy and he's got a mouth on him like a mule skinner."

Floyd nodded and held the door for Harold as the two of them entered the small interview room. Dylan was sitting with his feet propped on the edge of the table. He had placed his chair so Floyd had to look over his feet to see the boy. The room's lighting made Dylan's face look jaundiced. Floyd walked to the side of the table. With a swing of Floyd's hand, Dylan's feet flew from the table so quickly that he nearly fell from the chair.

"What the fuck you doing, man? You can't hit me!" Dylan caught himself and stood up facing Floyd. Harold watched from the door with a smirk on his face. He'd been a deputy or jailer for thirty-two years and genuinely missed the days when they used to physically pressure people into admitting their crimes.

Floyd pointed to the table. "This is county property. You were defacing it. Sit down." Floyd's words were spoken quietly, but with unmistakable authority.

Dylan's eyes flickered with hatred as he weighed his options. He decided to stay standing. He lifted his cuffed hands and pointed to Floyd's chest. "I don't have to take shit from you. I'm innocent until…"

Dylan let out a shriek as Floyd grabbed the offending finger and jerked it back violently. Dylan pulled his hand away and shook it, making sure the finger wasn't broken. "Mother fucker. I want to see my attorney. I'm going to sue…"

Floyd leaned forward and put his palms flat on the table. "And who might that be? Do you think that he'll be in his office at eleven at night?" Floyd stood back up and pointed to the chair. "Sit down. You can call him in the morning."

Harold moved up to Floyd's shoulder and pointed to flashing red light on the camera in the top corner of the room. Dylan backed to the corner and stood there, holding his finger.

Floyd's voice was even and controlled. "Get your ass in the chair."

Dylan advanced to the chair, pulling it back with his foot rather than exposing the injured finger. He fell into the seat as if his legs had given out.

"For the record, this is an interview with Mister Dylan Johnson. It's 23:12 and I'm Sergeant Floyd Swenson. Deputy Harold Pederson is here with me." Floyd paused to compose his thoughts.

"I understand Deputy Jensen found marijuana, roaches, and a bag with white powder in your car." Floyd stood up and walked around the room with his arms crossed. He circled behind Dylan who twisted to keep him in view. "Your buddy, Juan Santiago, was arrested with a couple bags of drugs and a stolen gun. The Robbinsdale police report says you assaulted Juan in his hospital bed. The high school is missing chemicals known as precursors for formulating methamphetamine. Someone's been buying up cold medicine all over the county, and you seem to keep showing up in the center of every circle we draw. Add Ted Palmquist's death, and we've got a whole lot of mysteries that all seem to point back to you."

Dylan watched in silence as Floyd spoke. He glanced at the jailer a few times but remained aloof. When Floyd stopped talking, Dylan just sat there silently staring ahead.

Floyd sat down on the table. "We can wait until you get an attorney. But, if you're innocent, you can clear the air and get out of here. Do you have anything to say?" Dylan never looked at him.

Floyd leaned forward until his face was inches from Dylan's. "Well?"

"Fuck you, old man." Spit flew from Dylan's mouth and hit Floyd's face.

Harold anticipated Floyd's response and lunged forward, grabbing Floyd's shoulder. He jerked back as Floyd reached for Dylan. "Knock it off, Floyd. This scumbag isn't worth risking your pension." Realizing the camera was recording, Harold added. "Even if he did just spit in your face."

Floyd seethed as he pulled a handkerchief from his pocket and wiped away the spittle. His eyes were riveted on Dylan, who maintained a contemptuous grin.

After a dozen deep breaths, Floyd turned to Harold and nodded. "Take that piece of shit back to his cell."

* * *

Floyd stood on the pistol practice range, reloading the magazine with .45 caliber shells when Sandy Maki walked in. Sandy watched Floyd fire a dozen times into a silhouette target. After the last shot, Floyd set the gun on the counter. Sandy walked toward Floyd, calling his name from twenty feet away, trying not to startle him. Floyd turned and nodded to Sandy. He took off his hearing protectors and set them on the counter next to the gun. He flipped a lever, and the target silhouette rolled toward him.

Sandy glanced down and estimated there were over a hundred spent cartridges on the floor. "The jailer said you'd probably come down to the range."

Floyd examined the shredded paper representing the silhouette's chest. He unclipped it and set it on top of three other targets with similar damage.

"You've thrown a lot of lead tonight. Any particular reason?"

Floyd ejected the magazine and loaded it with another dozen shells. "I needed to blow off some steam and this seemed like a harmless way to do it." When the clip was fully loaded, Floyd slapped it back into the butt of the pistol. He slid the de-cocking lever, then slipped the pistol into his holster.

"I hear Dylan Johnson didn't want to talk to you."

Floyd grabbed a broom and swept the spent cartridges into a pile. "I nearly lost it. If Harold hadn't grabbed me, I might've killed that kid."

Sandy picked up a dustpan and held it as Floyd swept cartridges into it. "It's hard to control adrenaline when it's flowing."

When he'd finished sweeping, Floyd leaned the broom in the corner. "I can usually do it, but tonight…I just lost it."

Sandy stood awkwardly at the end of the range. "Umm, you want to talk about it?"

Floyd shook his head. He picked up the ear protectors and stowed them in a locker. "It's home stuff."

Sandy didn't know whether he was on thin ice, but he plunged ahead. "I heard Mary had surgery today. Is she doing okay?"

Floyd took a deep breath and hesitated, uncertain about sharing his personal problems with Sandy. "The surgery went fine." He picked up his jacket from the chair where he'd laid it. He carefully considered the next words, not sure if he could get them out without falling to pieces. "The surgeon thinks they got it all, but Mary's convinced she's going to die."

Floyd hurried up the stairs. Sandy followed him to the door outside of the dispatcher's cube, where Floyd hesitated. "I've gotta get some sleep. I appreciate you checking to make sure I'm okay. I suppose Harold was afraid that I'd gone to the range to do something stupid."

Sandy's sheepish smile was the answer.

Floyd nodded. "Thanks." He put on his jacket and held the door for Sandy. Struggling to find a less morbid topic, he said, "Did I tell you we have a new puppy? I think she's part black lab. Right now, she's all feet and legs. I've been waiting for the owners to show up and want her back, but I think she might be a permanent addition to the household."

Sandy walked alongside Floyd to their cruisers. "You haven't fed her, have you?"

"I gave her a tin of scraps tonight and she ate them like she was starving."

Sandy put his hand on Floyd's shoulder. "If you've fed her, you own her. You should stop at Walmart and pick up a bag of puppy chow."

"I don't think I'm ready for another dog."

Sandy laughed. "You should've thought about that before you fed her."

Chapter 15

Tyler Espe dug through the dresser drawer and found the hidden slip of paper taped inside the back corner. He carried it to the phone and dialed the number with a 612 prefix, indicating a general Minneapolis location. He didn't know specifically where the phone was located or who would answer his call, suspecting only that it was a throwaway cell phone purchased with a limited number of minutes.

Pacing the kitchen, he noticed the cluttered counter littered with dirty bowls, plates, and flatware left unwashed after previous meals. The clock on the stove was blinking, 8:23 P.M., not reset after the last power outage.

I can't believe Mom can't figure out how to set that thing. He said to himself, never thinking he could reset the clock himself, or that he should wash the dirty dishes.

The ringing stopped and a male voice said, "I'm not here. Talk." The message was followed by a series of beeps.

Tyler's mind rushed, trying to put together a meaningful message. "Umm,

Dylan's in jail. Umm, I guess that's all." He hung up the receiver and sat staring at the phone for a second, unsure about what to do next. He considered going to school, then reconsidered. He was already ten minutes late and his arrival now would only lead to drama.

Carrying the slip of paper with the phone number back to his room, he set it on top of his dresser, already covered with clutter. He then removed a lower dresser drawer and set it on the bed. Taped to the back of the drawer was a zippered plastic bag containing several hundred capsules. Tyler took out two and set them on the crumpled linens, then reattached the bag to the drawer and slid it back into the dresser.

He took a glass from the kitchen cupboard and filled it with water, popping one capsule into his mouth and washing it down. The other went into the pocket of his jeans for later. He stared at the sink, waiting for the rush to hit. The phone startled him.

"Yeah?"

"You left a message." The voice was male and unfamiliar.

"Umm, yeah. Dylan's in jail." He stopped, unsure what else to say.

The voice was impatient. "Your message said that. Where and why?"

"They busted him for drugs. He called me last night and I didn't know what to do." The meth was starting to course through his veins, and everything speeded up. "Taco's in the hospital too. They chased him and he crashed his pickup."

"Settle down. Tell me where Dylan is so I can get him a lawyer."

"Umm. Pine City. I think a county cop busted him...He got busted in Robbinsdale too, but they let him loose."

There was a pause. "Say that again."

"Umm. Robbinsdale busted him. He tried to smother Taco...to keep him from talking about Tammi."

"Jeez. He tried to kill Taco?" The voice sounded exasperated. "Who else has this number?"

"Dylan gave it to me for use in case of an emergency. I don't know. Maybe Taco has it too. Maybe Brady." Tyler's mind was racing, and he was getting frustrated with the slow conversation. He wanted to hang up, but the voice had an air of authority and he decided to stay on the line.

"Clean out everything and dump it where no one will find it. Where would that be?"

The words flew past Tyler so fast that he couldn't comprehend. "Dump what stuff?"

There was silence for a second. "Where are you?"

Tyler looked around. "In my kitchen."

"Where's that, dumb shit?" The voice was angry now.

"I'm not dumb! I had a problem and I called you. Maybe that was the stupid thing to do." Tyler slammed down the phone and stared at it, his temper boiling. What had the voice said to do? Dump the stuff. Maybe that was a good idea. His mind raced through options as he walked to the bedroom to retrieve his stash.

The phone rang again, and he ran to answer it. He had the bag of meth caps in his hand. "What?"

"Listen Tyler..." The voice was now calm and reassuring.

"How'd you get this number? I didn't leave it when I left the message." Tyler was rattled. He felt he was being violated by someone he'd never met, but who knew his name and had his phone number.

There was a discernible sigh. "Have you heard of caller ID?"

"Oh. Yeah."

"Tyler, this is very serious. I want to help, but I need to see you. Where can we meet?"

Still bitter about the earlier call. Tyler snapped, "Go fuck yourself. I don't need you. Maybe Dylan does, but I don't, and I don't trust you. I don't want to meet."

Tyler was about to hang up the phone when the voice was talking to him again. "Easy, Tyler. Are you tripping now?"

Tyler froze. Was he that transparent? "No. I'm clean. What made you think I was tripping?"

There was another sigh. "Tyler, you're going a mile a minute. Slow down and think.

We've got a problem. Dylan's in jail. You said that Taco's in the hospital. Both of them were busted with stuff on them, right?"

"Umm, yeah. Right. So what?"

"Have the cops talked to you yet?"

A wave of paranoia swept Tyler. He looked out the kitchen window as he jammed the bag of caps into his pocket. He wanted to run, then remembered the phone in his hand. "They're not here now, but they talked to me yesterday."

"Okay. The cops aren't there. But they talked to you. What did they ask? What did you tell them?"

Tyler closed his eyes. "Mostly, they wanted to know about Ted. They asked about Taco..."

The voice interrupted him. "Ted? What about Ted?"

Tyler was pissed at being interrupted. "I was telling you they mostly wanted to know about Taco and the gun. Then they wanted to know who poisoned Ted." Tyler's voice was sharp with frustration.

"Easy Tyler. Focus. Tell me more about Ted. Somebody poisoned him?"

"Well, that's the deal. They were asking us questions about Ted being poisoned, and we didn't know anything about it. I mean, he'd been sick and all. But we didn't even know he'd been poisoned."

There was a long pause. "Did they say which poison?"

Tyler peeked out of the window again. "Huh? Oh, umm...I don't think so." Tyler's paranoia was growing, and his patience was at an end. "Listen, I gotta go."

"Wait! You've got to do one more thing. Take all the chemistry lab glassware and chemicals and dump them somewhere. You're smart. You can find a place where the cops won't find them. Someplace wet would be good to get rid of the powder and pills. They'll dissolve and all that evidence will disappear. Maybe a river or a lake would be good. Definitely not your toilet or around the house. Dump them far away. Somewhere remote. Can you find a place like that? Take all the glassware and break it up. You guys should've gotten rid of the glass a long time ago. It isn't needed for the recipes you're cooking."

"Umm. Maybe I can throw the glass in an old dump or a gravel pit. But shouldn't we stash the meth somewhere we can get it back again? It's worth a lot of money."

"Don't worry about the money now. I just want it gone. And destroy this phone number. I'll call you. Make sure the cops aren't following you. Okay?"

"Sure." Tyler nearly threw the phone as he rushed for the door.

* * *

Chuck Dreyer ended the call, looked at his burner phone, unsure if he should destroy it now or hang onto it a little longer. He considered the risk of staying in Minnesota against the benefits of maintaining the pipelines he had developed. Then he weighed those risks and benefits against buying a ticket back to L.A. or San Diego and starting all over again. He had money stashed where the cops wouldn't find it, but the money flow would stop. It would take time to start a new life and business.

He picked up the phone and dialed another Minneapolis number. The call was answered by a sultry female voice. "Planck and Washburn Law Office."

"I need to talk to Glenda."

"May I tell her who is calling?"

"This is Mister White." It was a not-too-clever cover name that kept his identity hidden even from the lawyer. The name had been inspired by the white powder, which funded all his wealth.

Elevator music came on the line as he waited for the lawyer. She was expensive, but a legal wizard who took his business without hesitation, and as long as he paid her generously in cash, she didn't report it to the IRS. He hated dumping cash into legal fees for the kids, but if they felt secure the cops might not be able to peel back the layers that hid his connection to them.

"Mister White. How can I help you today?" Glenda Planck's voice belonged on a phone sex line. She had a way of purring to her male clients that made any words she spoke seem like a proposition. While he'd never heard her speak to a female client, he assumed she had an equally appealing persona for her female clientele. Or maybe she only dealt with men. He'd watched her talk to a male judge while he was sitting anonymously in the courtroom. She argued on behalf of one of his associates and White was sure the old judge was ready to invite her out to dinner by the end of her summation.

"I have a young associate named Dylan Johnson who is currently a guest in the Pine County jail. I want him out of jail as quickly as possible."

There was a pause, and he could hear a pen scribbling notes. "Pine County?"

"Right." He waited for her to make more notes. "Dylan is cocky. Please don't take offense to anything he says or does."

Glenda laughed. "I doubt that he can say or do anything I haven't dealt with before. I assume the financial arrangement will be the same as in the past? A retainer and my usual hourly rate."

"That's what I expected." He paused. "There's another complication. Another associate, Juan Santiago is hospitalized in Robbinsdale. The kids call him Taco. I understand that the police are holding him too. Can you see what can be done to get him released from custody? Please assure my friends that your services are totally covered, and their silence will be rewarded."

"I'll make that clear to them." Glenda purred.

"A courier will deliver the retainer to your office this afternoon."

"I'll call the Pine County attorney to let him know I'm representing Dylan and Juan."

Chapter 16

Floyd sat at the kitchen table with the puppy on his lap. They'd shared scrambled eggs, bacon, and toast. Floyd was gently stroking the puppy's back as he read through the paper. She lay quietly with her eyes closed.

The cell phone buzzed in his pocket, and he answered it, expecting to hear Mary. Instead, he heard the sheriff's deep bass voice. "How did the surgery go?"

"The surgery went really well." Floyd paused. "Mary is still convinced she's going to die and won't listen to anything I tell her."

"The doctor told her, right?"

"He only spoke to me after surgery. I assume he'll talk to her this morning and maybe she'll hear what he has to say. I thought I'd come in for a while and then check in with her later."

"Floyd, you have only one job and that's taking care of Mary. C.J. and Pam have things under control here. I'm sure they'll benefit from your guidance once things with Mary are settled. Until then, we've got things covered here. Understood?"

"John, I could really use the distraction…"

"It's taken me a few years to figure this out, but the department here has momentum and things continue even when you or I are gone for a few days. The other bit of wisdom I'm going to share was hard to discover and accept, but our families are more important than anything else. Anything. You come back when you can look me in the eye and tell me everything at home is under control."

"Thanks, John. I appreciate your advice." Floyd paused. "What's the sawing noise I'm hearing?"

"C.J. dropped off her damned basset hound and the damned dog is snoring under Pam's desk."

"Really?"

"Yep. That dog does two things—snore and fart."

"Pam's taking care of C.J.'s dog?"

"I guess. It's sleeping on her feet under the desk right now."

"You can hear it snoring all over the bullpen?"

"Well, I'm on the phone in my office and you can hear the snoring all over the building."

"Pam's putting up with it?"

"She seems to be, although I'm not sure how unless she's lost her sense of smell. Every time the damned dog farts, the dispatcher smells it and runs to the bullpen to see if there's a dead body."

Floyd chuckled. "Maybe I won't rush back."

* * *

Floyd ignored the sound of crunching gravel in the driveway and waited for a knock on the door. Instead, he heard a key in the lock. The door opened without a knock before he could stand.

"Hi, Floyd," said Emily, Mary's youngest sister, as she closed the door. "I thought that you didn't want another dog."

The puppy peeked from under Floyd's arm, eyeing Emily with suspicion, her tail thumping against Floyd's leg. "She's a stray your sister started feeding. We're waiting for the owner to show up."

Emily set her purse on a chair and shrugged off her coat. "I got a day off and thought I'd drive up and visit Mary. The hospital said she wasn't accepting any calls. What's going on?"

Floyd folded the newspaper and set in on the table. "The surgery went well." He stood up and took the puppy to the door and put her outside. Emily sat at the table, waiting for the rest of the story. He took a cup from the cupboard, poured coffee, and set it in front of Emily, who waited impatiently for more information.

"The cancer was localized and hasn't spread to her lymph nodes." His voice was so flat and factual it scared her.

Emily took a sip of her coffee. "She'll need chemo and radiation?"

Floyd picked up his cup and stared into it. "Probably not. We won't know until we meet with the oncologist." Floyd paused. "Before surgery she told me she wouldn't do any treatments at all, but she was convinced she was on death's doorstep back then."

"So, she's willing to have chemo or whatever?"

Floyd shrugged. "I made her have the surgery. The rest is her call and she'll know the consequences when she makes the decision." He looked up and saw tears staining Emily's cheeks.

"Then I'll make her do it! Somebody around here has to have the balls to tell her what needs to happen." Her voice was angry as she threw her coat over her arm and flew to the door. She turned to look at him, tears running down her face. "Aren't you coming along?"

He shook his head, "I think it's best if I don't get between the two of you. I'll be up in a bit."

Setting his coffee down, Floyd watched the puppy scamper between Emily's feet until it finally got stepped on. The puppy yelped and recoiled from Emily, then watched Emily's car spit gravel as it spun out of the driveway. It hit the asphalt with a squeal of burning rubber.

With Emily gone, Floyd stepped outside and whistled. The pup ran to him and crashed into his shins. Floyd scooped her up and went back inside. Sitting at the kitchen table, he stroked the pup's ears. Floyd ignored the pup's wet paws on his pants and shirt as she nipped at his fingers. "Well girl, what should we do to waste some time?"

The puppy continued to nip at Floyd's fingers. He finally rolled her over on his lap and pinned her until she stopped struggling. "Here's the deal. The sheriff officially put me on family leave until Mary's situation is resolved." He looked out the window, noting fresh green growth highlighted in the morning light. Droplets of overnight rain on the leaves sparkled like diamonds in the morning breeze.

"Mary doesn't want me at the hospital," he explained to the puppy. "The county attorney may call and chew my butt for shoving the Johnson kid. I'm not going to sit here and rot until something happens, so I think I'll do a little unofficial investigative work. How's that sound to you?" He gave the pup a vigorous belly rub and watched her ears flop as she struggled to right herself. Setting the puppy on the floor, Floyd punched a familiar ten-digit number into the phone. It rang three times before the female voice answered.

"Minnesota Bureau of Criminal Apprehension, Inspector Lone Eagle."

"Hi, Laurie. I need some help with a missing girl."

Laurie Lone Eagle had been a Pine County rookie earlier in her career. After leaving the Pine County Sheriff's Department, she earned a law degree and moved to the BCA as their expert in missing children and teens. "Hi Floyd. What's up?"

"I need help."

"You never call unless you need help." Laurie chuckled.

Laurie was right and Floyd felt guilty about only calling when he needed assistance. They hadn't been socially close, and he'd never done anything to change that. "Sorry. I'm trying to resurrect a file on a girl who disappeared from Pine City about a year ago. Her name is Tammi Wagner. Do you have a file on her?"

Floyd heard computer keys clicking. "Your new deputy, C.J. Jensen, called yesterday with the same question. I have the file up on my computer. Like I told C.J., there hasn't been any activity since the case was opened last fall. No one has reported a sighting, she hasn't been arrested, ticketed, and hasn't contacted social services or any police agency."

Floyd considered Laurie's words as he watched the puppy drag a shoe from the bedroom into the living room. "Refresh my memory. Was there any indication of abuse or parental involvement in the disappearance?"

"Hmmm. There's nothing indicated, although I interviewed the girl's mother and her boyfriend. I didn't feel good about the boyfriend. Although they didn't say anything specifically, he seemed too overwrought. It seemed like a put on. Other than that, the parents are both around, so it wasn't a parental rights kidnapping. Sounds more like a runaway. C.J. gave me more information than was originally in the file. She said there may have been some drug involvement with some teen boys up there. Let's see, Dylan Johnson, Brady Werther, Tyler Espe and Juan Santiago. She also mentioned Laura Tomlinson as an acquaintance. I haven't had time to follow up, but maybe I can run a search on them tomorrow.

Laurie paused. "C.J. mentioned that Juan said something weird about Tammi while he was with the ER doctor. I was just trying to remember the exact words. I think he spoke about her in past tense and knows more than he's saying."

"I interviewed the ER doctor while Santiago was there. He said Juan mentioned something more about Tammi." Floyd paused, trying to pull the words from his memory. "It was really cryptic, something about Tammi's buried treasure."

Laurie considered his words and saw little that she could add. "Well, let me know if there's anything I can do."

"Thanks, I think C.J.'s tracking on it pretty well." He set the phone down and stared at it for a second. C.J.'s report said something about Dylan trying to smother Juan Santiago because he was mumbling about Tammi. Obviously, Juan knew something about Tammi that Dylan didn't want revealed.

Floyd stood just as the puppy peed on the kitchen floor. He scooped her up, set her outside, grabbed the roll of paper towels, and mopped the puddle before taking his jacket off the peg and walking out the door.

The puppy met him at the bottom step. Floyd reached in his pocket for the red nylon collar he'd purchased on his way home from the hospital. After adjusting the collar and clicking in on, Floyd clipped a plastic-coated cable to the collar and steps. The puppy yelped and tugged at the cable as he walked to the county car.

* * *

Pam was sitting at her desk when C.J. walked in wearing jeans, running shoes, and a hoodie sweatshirt with a Minnesota Twins logo. Bailey walked at her side, much more relaxed than the previous morning. "You look like you're working undercover today."

C.J. smiled. They both knew it was her day off. "Yeah, I've got an undercover assignment at the Duluth Zoo. Don't tell anyone."

Pam smiled back. "Don't be too sure you're off. You've got a message from Laura Tomlinson." She pointed to a pink message slip on C.J.'s desk.

The message was simple. "Please call." There was no hint about the topic. It had been received by the dispatcher at 7:15 AM. C.J. glanced at the clock. It was nearly 8:30, and she was supposed to pick up Eddie at his apartment in Duluth at 10:00. She'd be cutting it close if she left now.

She dialed the number, and it rang eight times without an answer. C.J. noticed Pam watching her. "No one's home," she said as she hung up.

"Probably at school."

"Hmmm." She tapped the message with a pencil, as if it might change. "I should drive over and talk to her."

Pam leaned back as Bailey pushed under her desk and curled up on her feet. "Laura might have a change of heart before your next shift." Pam pulled her feet out from under the basset, who groaned. "I could talk to her, but the sheriff already read me the riot act for helping with the roadblock while the police dog searched the ditch."

C.J. took a deep breath before picking up the phone again. She hurriedly punched in ten digits and waited for a few seconds before Eddie Paulson answered.

"Hi, Eddie. Listen, I got a message from a girl I've been trying to reach. I've got to catch her while she's ready to talk. Can I meet you at noon instead of ten? I'll buy you lunch to make up for the delay."

Pam watched as C.J. nodded and made new arrangements. When C.J. finished Pam watched her hang up the phone. "Floyd always tells me to be careful."

C.J. smiled. "Are you warning me about Laura or Eddie?"

"Your life changed when you put the job before your personal life." Pam pushed herself up from the chair and walked to the coffeepot. "You'll do it a thousand more times if you allow it to happen. You already know that lots of people can't handle being a cop. Too many get divorced and others just crack." She set her stained white cup under the spigot and popped in a pod. "But it means you just graduated from being a probationary cop. You're a real Pine County deputy." Pam lifted her cup in a toast.

C.J. shook her head, but the words rang true. After becoming a widow, her previous job had eaten up as much of her time as she allowed. She'd moved to Pine County to get her life back under control, and now she was delaying a personal commitment to do an interview that wouldn't change if she did it today or next week.

"Thanks, oh wise one. Can I go now?"

"Hang on," Pam said, walking to her desk. He handed C.J. a key chain. "Here are the keys for your cruiser. Floyd asked you to leave the other car here."

* * *

Glenda Planck swept into the Pine County courthouse. She wasn't tall, only five-four in heels, but she carried an air of authority. Her hair was platinum blonde and her eyes piercing blue. She wore a white silk blouse over a calf-length black skirt. With a calfskin briefcase slung over one shoulder, she caught every eye as she followed the signs to the court administrator's office.

The man behind glass doors watched her approach. His eyes hesitated on the visitor's cleavage as she leaned over to hand him a business card.

"I'm Dylan Johnson's attorney. I want to meet with him, and I'd like to know when we can get a bail hearing."

The clerk picked up her business card and stared at the name and Minneapolis address. "Umm. He's got a public defender and there's a hearing this afternoon. Hang on." The clerk turned away and consulted a computer printout. "The hearing is at one."

Glenda gave the man her most dazzling smile. "I'm replacing his public defender. Tell me how I can get in to meet with my client before the hearing."

The clerk swallowed hard. "Umm. Hang on." He dialed a three-number extension. "Pat? Hi, this is Jeff. I've got Dylan Johnson's new lawyer up here. She wants to meet with him." There was a pause and the clerk's face darkened. "I know he met with the public defender this morning, but this is his new Minneapolis lawyer, and she wants to meet with him ASAP. Okay, I'm sending her down."

The clerk hung up the phone and pointed to the door. The smile had returned to his face as he gave directions. "Follow the hall to the right and then take the elevator to the first floor. There's a sign that directs you to the jail annex. Ask for Pat when you get to the counter. He'll take care of you."

* * *

Attorney Planck was sitting in an interview room when the jailer delivered Dylan. Glenda removed her reading glasses and looked up from her legal pad when the door opened. "Come in Dylan."

Dylan surveyed Glenda skeptically. He stepped up to the table and sat uneasily in the chair opposite Glenda. She smiled at him, then put her glasses on and continued making notes. "Who are you?"

Glenda stopped writing and leaned down to her briefcase. Her blouse billowed and Dylan leaned forward to stare at her cleavage. She straightened up and handed the boy a business card while pretending she hadn't noticed his leer.

"I'm your new lawyer. A friend from Minneapolis asked me to get you out of jail."

Dylan continued to look at her skeptically. Then he read the card. "Who hired you?"

Glenda crossed her legs and tapped her Cross pen on the tabletop. "I don't think it would be helpful for me to provide that information. In fact, I don't think either of us would recognize your benefactor's real name. He asked me to get you released from jail. He also asked me to assure you that all your legal costs will be paid, providing you don't share information with the county attorney or law enforcement agencies." She paused to see if her words were registering. "How old are you, Dylan?"

"Eighteen."

"Any criminal record as an adult?"

Dylan shook his head. "A couple of arrests when I was a kid…and some traffic tickets."

Glenda leaned forward. "You've got to be straight with me. I heard you were arrested in Robbinsdale."

Dylan waved his hand. "That's bullshit. Taco was running off at the mouth about…"

He hesitated. "You can't repeat what I tell you. Right?"

Glenda nodded. "Our conversation is privileged as long as you don't tell me you're planning a new crime."

Dylan took a deep breath. "Taco was talking about Tammi Wagner. She disappeared a while ago and he was going to say what happened to her. He was all drugged up and I couldn't get him to stop talking so I put my hand over his mouth."

Glenda made notes. "You were not trying to kill Juan. You were trying to shush him." She stated that convincingly in an effort to coach his future comments about the incident. She watched his eyes and decided her coaching wouldn't be effective unless delivered bluntly, and maybe with the aid of a baseball bat.

Dylan smiled. "I guess."

Glenda stared at Dylan intensely. "Were you or Juan involved in a crime that was related to Tammi's disappearance?"

Despite Attorney Planck's assurances, Dylan felt uneasy about revealing anything more to her. He shook his head and looked into the corner rather than meeting her eyes. "Tammi ran away, and no one is supposed to tell where she is."

Glenda immediately knew he was lying, but let it slide. She stared at her notes. "But you know where she is."

Dylan hesitated. "I guess, in a general way."

"Okay, Dylan, here's the deal. We've got a hearing at one this afternoon. The judge will ask for your plea. You'll say, 'not guilty, your honor.' I'll ask the judge to release you on your own recognizance. The county attorney will throw out some outrageous bail amount. The judge will probably refuse to release you without bail because of drugs found in your car. He'll set bail. I'll write a check to the clerk, and then you'll be free to leave."

Dylan smiled. "Cool."

Glenda narrowed her eyes and pointed the pen at him. "But here's the deal. You've got to stay clean until after trial. No drugs. No drinking. Not even a speeding ticket. Understood?"

Dylan shrugged. "I guess."

Glenda glared at him. "'I guess,' is not an acceptable answer if I'm writing a bail check for you. Try that again."

Dylan tensed and flashed back to confrontations with the school's female vice principal. He didn't take shit from women, although this lawyer had an edge he'd never experienced before. He appraised her for a moment. "Okay. I agree."

"Better. I can probably get you a plea agreement that will involve only probation. You'll have to plead guilty to something less than a felony, but you'll be able to go back to doing whatever it is you like to do." Glenda paused to make sure that Dylan was paying attention. "In return for that, you say nothing, repeat, nothing to the cops about anything. You demand to see me if anyone tries to question you. If you can manage that and not get arrested for something else, your friend in Minneapolis will make sure that you're taken care of." She pushed her business card across the table. "Don't lose this. I'm your best friend right now." Glenda packed her papers into the briefcase and stood. "Any questions?"

Dylan looked at her figure and hesitated. "Um, do you date clients?"

Glenda's eyes narrowed and her face got hard. "Dylan, I'm your lawyer. I don't even like you, but that doesn't mean I won't fight for your rights. Are we clear?"

Dylan turned red with anger, but he managed to contain himself. "Sure." As soon as she was out the door, he shook his head. "Bitch."

Chapter 17

Laura Tomlinson hurried from her classroom to the principal's office. She swept past the school secretary, and stuck her head into Frank Boquist's office, hoping C.J. would be there.

C.J. smiled at her. "Hi, Laura. You left me a message." The girl closed the door as she entered. Her hair was an even blacker shade than it had been the previous day, reflecting a hint of purple under the fluorescent lights. The rest of Laura's outfit was the same black t-shirt with the faded logo of a rock group and jeans with holes torn in the knees.

Laura looked at C.J. with surprise. "You aren't wearing a uniform. Did you get promoted?"

C.J. smiled. "No. It's my day off. I got your message and decided you were so important I changed my plans so I could talk to you." The comment obviously impressed Laura.

"Will you tell me something straight?" Laura eased onto the guest chair.

"If I can. If there's something that's related to an ongoing investigation, it'll have to remain confidential."

"Is that cop talk meaning I can talk but you can't?"

C.J. shook her head. "I can't share anything confidential that would jeopardize my investigation."

Laura cocked her head and thought. "Okay. Did someone beat up Dylan in the jail last night?"

C.J.'s eyes flickered with surprise. "I don't know. I'm off duty today and I didn't work last night. I could find out. Who do you think beat him up? Another prisoner?" C.J. ran through the arrangements at the jail. Sometimes prisoners were double bunked. They ate together and sometimes exercised together. They were supervised, but not constantly and not often when they were in their cells.

"I heard a cop beat Dylan up...when he was questioning him. He was asking about Tammi and the drugs." She watched for C.J.'s reaction.

"Where did you hear that rumor?"

Laura shifted uncomfortably. "Umm, one of the guys was in jail for a DUI last night. He overheard Dylan talking to another guy in the jail this morning."

"I'm not aware of that happening." C.J. replied. "It's against policy to beat prisoners who are being questioned. If Dylan was struck, it was probably by another prisoner or because he was assaulting someone." C.J. pulled a Post-it note from a pad on the desk and scribbled herself a note. "I'll check and get an answer for you. Okay?" After she finished the note and put it in her pocket, C.J. looked up. "Is that what you wanted?"

Laura looked at her feet. "Well, yes. But I wanted to tell you that the fort is a place out on a back road. It's a kind of hunting cabin that no one uses. Dylan knows where the key is hidden above the door. We go out there to smoke and drink. I'm always scared when we go there. It feels weird and I'm afraid that someone will catch us trespassing."

C.J. leaned over the desk. "Can you tell me exactly where it is?"

Laura didn't look up, but shook her head, "Not exactly. I mean, I couldn't give you directions there." She looked up. "But I could show you how to drive there."

* * *

C.J. and Laura drove the back roads of Pine County in C.J.'s county cruiser. The girl's memories of the route to the fort were typical for a teen who wasn't a driver, occasionally recognizing landmarks, but often backtracking to alternate roads when the countryside became unfamiliar.

After an hour of driving, Laura pointed to an open gate. Beyond it were a pair of ruts running through the underbrush. "That's it! Sometimes there is a 'for sale' sign. But the guys always take it down."

C.J. stopped abruptly and parked the car on the edge of the narrow gravel road. She turned on the yellow flashers and reported her location to the dispatcher, as best she could, uncertain of which unnamed township roads they'd been driving.

Looking at the open gate and feeling uneasy about their remote location, she tried to remember the fire number on the last mailbox they'd passed. "Um, do the guys come out here often?" She studied the ruts and noticed fresh tire tracks running through a puddle where a culvert ran under the driveway.

Laura had the door open but hesitated when she heard the apprehension in C.J.'s voice. "They come out a few times a week. Mostly at night." Laura slid out of the car and closed the door.

C.J. studied the narrow uphill driveway so thickly lined with brush she couldn't see even a few feet to either side of the rutted tracks. Cresting the hump in the driveway, C.J. realized the hill effectively hid whatever, or whoever, might be on the other side. C.J.'s instinct was to call for backup, but Laura was already walking up the driveway without hesitation. After reaching under the car seat for her pistol, C.J. slipped the gun into her jeans pocket. The rumble of a diesel engine stopped her with her hand on the door handle. A bulk-tank milk truck rolled past, stirring up a cloud on the gravel road, the driver waving as he passed. Once the dust settled, she exited the car.

C.J. followed the ruts that led up over the hill, noting the recent tire tracks indicating someone had been there since the last rain. Rusted "for sale" signs riddled with bullet holes littered the side of the driveway. Laura walked up the driveway unafraid, and C.J. had to trot to catch up with her.

As she crested the hill, C.J. grabbed Laura's shoulder. Her voice was a whisper. "Do you recognize that car?" A rusted Firebird was parked in a small meadow next to a shack. The cabin door was ajar, and an open lock hung from the hasp. C.J. instinctively reached for her holster, then patted the outline of the pistol in her pocket.

"That's Brady's Firebird." Laura answered, walking on with confidence.

"Wait!" C.J. wanted to call for backup, but Laura charged ahead fearlessly.

"Hey, Brady!" Laura pushed the door open and walked a step into the unlit cabin. C.J. followed her into the darkness while trying to get the pistol out of her tight jeans. She heard rustling noises, but it took her eyes a second to adjust to the darkness.

"Aaarrrggghhh," a male voice screamed. Before C.J. could retreat or pull the gun, Laura's body slammed into her, and they flew backwards through the door and onto the ground together. The weight of the impact pushed the air from her lungs and a sharp pain stung her back. Before she could roll free of Laura's body, C.J. was being pummeled in the face. She fought off the fists, poking at her assailant's eyes and digging her fingernails into his arms, literally fighting for her life. Eventually, the blows to her head took their toll and C.J. realized her only salvation was the pistol in her pocket.

Brady's eyes were filled with rage as adrenaline and methamphetamine coursed through his veins giving him strength and determination. With C.J.'s resistance waning, he realized she was clawing at her jeans. Reaching down, he felt her gun through the denim, and he jammed his fingers into her pocket. She rolled, putting the gun under her body. In their desperate wrestling match, he pulled C.J.'s hand away and jammed his fingers into her pocket. C.J. let out a scream and writhed as the gun discharged under her body. Gasping, she clamped her hand onto her thigh. Blood seeped between her fingers.

Laura stood a few feet away with her hands over her mouth. Pushing himself up, Brady rolled C.J. over, and ripped the small pistol free from her pocket. Rusty brown liquid was spreading over C.J.'s thigh and oozing onto the ground.

With feral eyes darting frantically, Brady got to his knees. Wheezing from the exertion, he fixed on Laura and pointed the gun at her.

"You stupid bitch! Why'd you bring a cop here?"

Backing up and holding her hands in front of her, Laura tripped over a root and fell. "No!" she wailed as she rolled to her knees and scrambled away.

Shots echoed off the trees as the gun bucked in Brady's hand. A bullet zinged over Laura's head as she scampered into the underbrush. The gun barked again and again, tearing through the leaves around Laura's body. The brush and wild raspberries clawed at her. After what seemed like a mile, she collapsed in a cold, shallow puddle.

Her heartbeat pounded in her ears and her hands ached from the raspberry scratches, but the burning in her muscles was from running, not from a bullet. She didn't know how Brady could've missed, but she was free. Listening for the sound of feet coming through the brush she asked herself, "*Where am I? Where can I go? Brady might be cruising the roads.*" Sitting up, Laura realized she didn't know where the road was. She pulled herself from the muck and slogged on, sobbing.

Having emptied the small gun at Laura, Brady didn't know if he'd hit her or not. He threw the gun into the brush and rifled through C.J.'s pockets, pulling out a few crumpled dollars, car keys, a deputy's ID, and handcuffs. Brady looked at C.J.'s unconscious body. *"Maybe later,"* he thought.

Picking up the handcuffs, Brady considered C.J.'s unmoving body. She was a cop and might become a threat if she regained consciousness. Brady roughly rolled C.J. onto her stomach, eliciting a moan of pain. Noticing that a stick had punctured her back, he pulled it out, causing her to yelp. He pulled one arm behind C.J.'s back and clipped the cuff around her wrist. He reached for her other wrist, then decided against it.

"C'mon cop. We're going to your car." Unable to pull C.J. to her feet, Brady dragged her limp body down the driveway ruts to the gravel road. At the cruiser, he pulled C.J. into a sitting position, leaning her against the passenger door with her head lolling. Breathing hard, and coursing with chemically induced energy, his mind raced. He stared at her breasts through her sweatshirt's fabric and felt aroused.

Brady reached behind her back and pulled the sweatshirt over her head. A hole, torn in the fabric, matched the bloody wound on her shoulder where she'd been impaled.

C.J. moaned as Brady pulled the sweatshirt over her face and arms. Throwing the sweatshirt into the ditch, he unsnapped the front clasp of the deputy's bra and stared at her naked breasts. Her skin was pale with shock and her breathing shallow.

Now aroused, Brady fell to his knees, kneading C.J.'s breasts and running his fingers roughly over her nipples, his hands leaving dark smudges on her pale, clammy skin. He waited for C.J. to respond but her head lolled, her nipples failing to react to his touch. Brady lifted her chin in his hand, hoping to see fear in her eyes. There was a flicker, but no recognition. When he let go, C.J.'s head fell limp against her chest.

Brady tugged at C.J.'s belt buckle and released it, then unbuttoned the snap of her jeans. Staring at her face, he waited for recognition of the impending assault to wake her. He pulled down the fly of her jeans but was unable to push his hand deeply between her legs because of her upright position.

Brady was savoring the thought of having the cop's slender body when a wave of paranoia swept over him. He imagined the sound of an approaching car as a breeze rustled the aspen leaves. He quickly lifted C.J.'s arms and wrapped the handcuffs around the door frame, clipping the other wrist in the cuffs so her arms were over her head.

He reached down and tried to slip C.J.'s jeans over her hips. They were tight and he struggled for several seconds, getting them only as far as her buttocks. Without her cooperation, it seemed like he'd never be able to get them off. He reasoned that by handcuffing her to the doorpost he'd made penetration impossible. Brady dug in her pockets to find the handcuff key, then remembered throwing her keys into the brush by the shack.

A phantom sound spooked him. He looked at C.J.'s unconscious body for a second before running back to his own car. He sped out of the driveway, passing C.J., then driving away raising a cloud of dust

* * *

C.J. had dreams and moments when she lifted her head, but the effort was too much, and she slipped back into emptiness. Throbbing pain kept her on the verge of waking. Her first conscious impression was that she was cold…deathly cold. Shivers ran over her body and wakefulness came slowly. Her shoulders and leg burned. When she opened her eyes, they wouldn't focus. Head hanging, C.J.'s eyes focused on the blue of her jeans. She could see a brown stain on her leg, but the thick mental haze kept her from connecting the pain with the bloody stain and the dark puddle on the ground.

Slowly, C.J. became aware that her torso was bare. Realizing goose bumps covered her breasts and abdomen, she pulled at her arms, unsuccessfully willing them to cover her chest. She heard a voice call her unit number, but the sound seemed to come from far away. She lifted her head to see why her arms wouldn't move and a searing pain shot through her shoulder. She cried out and then the world went dark.

Regaining consciousness some time later, she realized her hands were over her head and that there was a dull pain in her wrists. She struggled, pain shooting through her wrists as the handcuffs bit into her skin. Feeling the cold chain of the handcuffs, C.J. tried to pull herself up, but only managed to inch herself closer to the cold body of the car. Her shoulder screamed with pain.

Leaning back, the metal of the car door first felt chilling, then reassuring. Straightening up relieved the pressure on her wrists. She became aware of the sticky wetness of blood on her arms. Exertion caused a wave of nausea to sweep over her, piercing pain shooting through her right leg. She retched, spewing her stomach contents over chest and onto her jeans. The spasms of vomiting tugged at the handcuffs, pain shooting through her arms. Color left her field of vision, and everything went dark.

* * *

Floyd's cell phone buzzed as he cleaned up the puppy's latest accident.

"Floyd, Eddie Paulson here. Do you know if C.J. got tied up in something? She called to say she was running late but would be here by noon. I've tried her cell phone, texted, and left voicemails but she's not responding."

Floyd checked the clock and realized it was nearly one-thirty. "I'll have the dispatcher try to raise her and I'll get back to you."

Floyd dialed Pam's cell phone. "Do you know where C.J. is? She was supposed to meet Eddie Paulson at noon but didn't show up. She's not answering her phone or responding to text messages."

"A girl at the high school left an urgent message for C.J. I thought she was going from the school to Duluth."

"Ask the dispatcher to call her on the radio. I'll wait."

"Floyd, she didn't respond to her call sign. The last contact the dispatcher had was at ten-thirty this morning when she called ten-seven on some township road east of town."

Floyd disconnected and dialed 911.

The dispatcher was playing solitaire on her phone and was startled by Floyd's voice. "You haven't heard from C.J. for three hours?"

She looked up nervously. Floyd's voice carried an uncharacteristic edge. "It *is* her day off."

"You've tried to raise her on the radio." It was a comment, not a question.

Carol shifted uncomfortably under the questioning. "Yes, but I thought she'd taken her personal car and didn't have a radio."

"Did she say she was getting out of her car?"

"Well, yes. She had some high school girl with her too."

"Did she ever call back to say she was back in the car?"

"Well, no."

Floyd ran his hand through his hair and let out a sigh. "Give me the time and location of your last contact?"

The dispatcher swung her chair around and paged through the computer log. "Ten-thirty, on a Munch Township road, off County Road 16."

"Jesus," Floyd uttered. "Have we got anyone near there?"

"Terry is in Chengwatana Township on a domestic call and Tom Thompson is at a class in the Cities today. Do you think she's in trouble?"

"Get somebody to start a search. Put Pam on the road. Call the sheriff and the state patrol. See if you can raise Sandy Maki or Kerm Rajacich at home, too."

* * *

The dispatcher broadcast on the state-wide frequency used for pursuits and emergencies. "Pine County requesting assistance. We have a deputy who has not reported in. Her last location is an unmarked Munch Township road off Pine County 16."

With his lights and siren, Floyd sped south on Interstate 35 as the dispatcher asked for him to respond.

"Swenson." He swung the car up the Mora/Hinckley exit ramp. His stop at the top of the exit ramp was a short pause before turning east.

"Sergeant, the sheriff asked you to delay your leave."

A smile creased Floyd's face. "That's good. I'm about four minutes from the location you broadcast."

Floyd raced down the county road, checking each unmarked road for recent tracks. His mind moved at the same speed as the car. "*What happened? Did C.J. forget to call in when she left? Was she down?*" He'd given her the assignment to follow the case wherever it led. "*Was she ready for it, or not?*" He pounded the steering wheel with the heels of his hands. Maybe she was okay. Maybe he had screwed up by giving her too much. "*Heaven knows I've screwed up enough things lately,*" he thought.

Turning off the lights and siren, he turned off the county road onto the gravel township road showing several sets of tread marks. The road was barely wide enough for two cars and alder brush leaned over the watery ditch. Crossing a ridge, Floyd spotted C.J.'s unoccupied cruiser at the bottom of a hill with the passenger doors open.

"Dispatch, I'm at the location, and I've got the missing car in view. It appears to be unoccupied."

Floyd rolled to a stop and felt for his Smith & Wesson automatic as he eased the car door shut. He walked down the driver's side of C.J.'s vehicle and looked for keys in the ignition. There were none. Then he saw the bloody wrists and handcuff chain around the opposite doorpost.

"C.J., can you hear me?"

His hand on the butt of the S&W, he eased around the front to the passenger side. Tennis shoes came into view and then jeans. Seeing C.J.'s torso, his first thought was she was dead. Her chin rested on her collarbones and her face and torso were white as paraffin. There was crusted blood on the handcuffs attached over her drooping head. A puddle of blood had been absorbed by the gravel under her thigh.

"C.J." He rushed to her side, slipping the S&W back into the holster. Floyd felt for a pulse in her neck. It was faint and her skin was clammy. He struggled to lift her enough to relieve the tension on the handcuffs so he could unlock them. When the cuffs released, he held her upright as he pulled off his jacket and wrapped it around her shoulders before he slid her to the ground.

Reaching into C.J.'s car, he picked up the mic. "Officer down! Send an ambulance!"

The urgency in Floyd's voice rattled the dispatcher. She sounded the tones for the Hinckley first responders and the ambulance. "OFFICER DOWN! Munch Township off Pine County sixteen. Repeat! Officer Down!"

A dozen law enforcement officers heard the announcement they all dread: One of their peers had been struck down. A state trooper swung his cruiser through the ditch near Rush City, nearly side-swiping a semi-trailer as he rushed to render assistance. Local police from Moose Lake and deputies from three adjacent counties turned their cars toward the location.

Floyd listened to the dispatcher's broadcast. Then he added, "Dispatch, call Life Link. Have them put a helicopter up!"

The dispatcher never relayed Floyd's request to dispatch Pam and the sheriff, nor had she contacted the deputies at home. Pam heard the dispatcher urgently requesting a medical helicopter and jumped from her chair. Grabbing a bulletproof vest, she bounded down the hall while pulling it over her head. The sheriff was exiting his office when Pam nearly ran him over as they rushed toward the exit.

"Pam! You're on restricted duty," Sepanen yelled, close on her heels as they jogged out of the building.

Without losing a step, Pam yelled over her shoulder, "Like hell I am! We've got a deputy down. It's all hands on deck." She jumped into a cruiser and the tires chirped as she punched the accelerator. The car's lights were flashing before she exited the parking lot and the siren screamed as she reached Highway 61, with the sheriff's unmarked car on her bumper.

Floyd heard the wail of sirens in the distance as he assessed C.J.'s injuries. Her naked torso and her pants pulled low on her hips concerned him, but rape may have been the least of her problems at that point. Her breathing was shallow but regular as was her heartbeat. Blood oozed from her leg wound, and he noted the smear of blood on the car door, then felt for and located an injury on her back. He palpated the wound but felt slivers of wood and felt relief that it wasn't a bullet wound. Although her leg wound was the worst trauma, he knew shock and hypothermia were equally life threatening.

"C.J., can you hear me?" He rubbed her hands and clasped them between his as she lay on the gravel next to the car. Her hands were like ice, but that could be a red herring, with her body shutting down peripheral circulation to conserve the heat in her torso and brain. Again, Floyd felt the faint pulse in C.J.'s neck. It was there, but shallow and rapid. He lay on the ground next to her and pressed his torso against hers to transfer his body warmth to her. Her shallow breaths whispered in his ear as new sirens added to the wailing. One was very close.

When Pam pulled past the cars, she saw Floyd clutching C.J. to his chest. Unsure if C.J. was dead or alive, she opened her trunk and ran to them with a blanket and first-aid kit.

Floyd's voice was strained with tension as Pam spread the blanket over them. "Can you hurry that ambulance? We're losing her."

Pam tucked the blanket around C.J.'s shoulders. Floyd pulled himself away to get the blanket from his car.

Pam squatted and opened the first aid kit. She donned gloves and ripped open a gauze compress that she pressed against C.J.'s leg wound. "Hypothermia?"

Floyd tucked a second blanket under C.J.'s body. "That and shock. She's got another wound on her back. How long has she been out here?"

Pam pressed the gauze to the wound to stop the bleeding. "According to the dispatcher, about three hours."

Floyd got on his knees, pulled out a small knife and cut open the leg of C.J.'s jeans where the bloodstain seemed to be centered. He was beside himself. "How in hell could she be here that long without somebody checking on her?"

Pam lifted the gauze, the cut in the jeans exposing a long gash where the bullet had plowed through the muscle of C.J.'s thigh after the gun discharged in her pocket. Pam daubed at it with a fresh square of sterile gauze.

Putting pressure on the wound, Pam replied, "The dispatcher thought C.J. had left for Duluth in her personal car. Today is her day off."

Fire flashed in Floyd's eyes. "Carol's the dispatcher?"

Pam nodded without looking up.

"Had C.J. logged off?"

Pam shook her head. "I'm not sure. I don't think so."

Floyd rocked C.J. gently as he supported her head off the ground. He whispered in her ear. "They're coming. Hang on."

"Take it easy, Floyd," Pam said. "We'll sort it out with Carol later."

"Jesus, she's cold. Where's the ambulance?" A shiver ran over Floyd, chilled from hugging C.J.'s frigid body against his chest. A siren shut off nearby as a state trooper came into view. The sheriff led the Hinckley emergency squad down the road.

Assessing the position of C.J.'s jeans around her hips, Pam asked, "Do you think she was sexually assaulted?"

Floyd's voice was soft and professional as he watched the trooper assisting the EMT's with gear from their truck. "I hope not. Most rapists wouldn't have bothered to pull her pants back up."

Floyd peeled himself away as the first responders threw another blanket over C.J. A gray-bearded fireman, with a chief's white helmet, lifted the blankets and gently pressed a stethoscope to C.J.'s chest.

"Pulse is rapid and shallow," he said to no one in particular. He pulled the stethoscope out from under the blanket and looked at Floyd. "Any trauma?"

Floyd's voice was so soft it could barely be heard above the commotion. "Apparent gunshot wound to the right leg and an open puncture wound on her back...and tell the emergency room to check her for sexual assault, too."

The chief looked at Floyd and nodded. "Very discreet. Do you know who she is?"

"Deputy Charlene Jensen, from Pine County. Take good care of her."

The chief looked back and forth between Pam and Floyd. "Only the best, but we need that damned ambulance. She needs to get to the hospital so they can start a warm lavage to get her body temperature up. Doesn't look like she's lost enough blood to be life threatening, but she's hypothermic. Any idea how long she's been out here?"

The sheriff approached the fringe of activity. "She's been sitting here waiting for backup for about three hours."

Floyd stepped back and stood next to the sheriff. "Someone stripped off her shirt and then handcuffed her to the car. She might've been raped, too."

The sheriff turned red, and his voice filled with venom. "Heads are gonna roll."

The ambulance crested the hill, and Floyd pulled Pam back from the chaos to join him, the trooper, and the sheriff. They watched as the firemen and paramedics loaded C.J. onto a gurney and into the back of the ambulance. An approaching helicopter rumbled like a long roll of thunder as the firemen lifted C.J. into the ambulance.

A paramedic tapped Floyd on the shoulder. "We're transporting her to the county road. We'll transfer her to Life Flight there."

Floyd and Pam watched the ambulance depart while the sheriff had a heated conversation on his cell phone. Pam started to open her mouth, but Floyd put his hand on her arm, waiting for the sheriff to join them. "Somebody fucked up. C.J. called in that she was here at ten-thirty this morning. The dispatcher didn't notice C.J. hadn't cleared the scene until Floyd called after speaking to Eddie Paulson."

Pam shook her head. "I suppose the dispatcher was engrossed in a solitaire game on her phone again."

The sheriff looked at Floyd. "Is that right?"

Floyd looked away in disgust. "She's addicted to her damn smartphone."

Sepanen looked through his dark eyebrows. "Carol's the dispatcher today." His deep voice sounded like gravel.

Pam nodded. "C.J.'s friend called dispatch to check on her at one o'clock too, but it wasn't until one-thirty, when Floyd called, that Carol tried to contact C.J."

Sepanen made a sound that sounded like a growl. "How's C.J.?"

Floyd shook his head. "Probable gunshot wound in the leg, with another wound of some kind in her back. Pulse was very rapid. She's hypothermic and probably in shock. When I found her, she was naked from the waist up and her pants were around her hips." He let the final words sink in. "I told the first responders to have the ER doctor check for sexual assault."

Sepanen closed his eyes. "What a fucking mess. Have you looked around here at all?"

Floyd shook his head. "We'll do that now." He waved to a state trooper. "Hey, Harold, give us a hand sweeping for evidence." More sirens wailed in the distance as additional police units rushed to the scene.

Sepanen rubbed the back of his neck, looking at Floyd. "I guess I'll go to the hospital and be ready for the press. When you're done here, take a look at her personnel file for a next of kin."

Sepanen took Floyd by the arm and led him out of earshot. Pam and the trooper started scouring the ground around the cruiser for evidence. "Listen Floyd. I'll deal with Carol, as far as civil service will allow. But I don't want this dirty linen outside the department."

Floyd stared at the ground. "You'll fire her, like last time. That will stick until the arbitrator makes you reinstate her."

Sepanen splayed his hands. "That's all I can do."

Floyd looked up angrily. "If something happens to C.J., I can guarantee that Carol will be more than fired. I want the county attorney to bring her up on charges."

Sepanen looked skeptical. "What charges?"

"This may be negligent manslaughter. If she'd done her job, we'd have had someone out here AT LEAST two hours ago. Two hours in a hospital, rather than sitting here handcuffed to a cruiser without any clothes might mean the difference between life and death."

Sepanen grimaced. "We'll see. Okay?" He opened his eyes and paused, unsure how to change the topic. He finally just let it blurt out. "How'd Mary come out?"

Taking a deep breath, Floyd looked at the sky. "They did a lumpectomy and removed three lymph nodes. We're talking to the oncologist next to see if she needs chemo or radiation."

"That sounds excellent."

"Mary hasn't got her head around it yet."

Sepanen patted Floyd on the shoulder. "Take off whatever time you need to deal with Mary."

Floyd nodded and walked over to Pam who lifted a Minnesota Twins sweatshirt from the ditch.

Chapter 18

Glenda Planck used the courthouse restroom to call Tyler Espe's house on her cell phone. The phone rang a half dozen times, then rolled over to voicemail. She left her name, number, and a brief message for Tyler. Next, she called Brady Werther's house where the phone rang a dozen times before she ended the call. She paced for a few seconds, pondering her next task.

"Brady and Tyler, come out wherever you are. If we don't tie you up before you spill your guts to the cops, we'll be in deep shit."

Checking her watch, Glenda realized Dylan Johnson's hearing would be starting in a few minutes. She turned off her cell phone and walked to the courtroom.

The hearing went as planned. Dylan pled not guilty. The county attorney asked for a $50,000 bond. Glenda argued he wasn't a flight risk and he'd been set up on the drug charges by a county deputy who hadn't even shown up for the hearing. The judge set a $1,000 bail. After paying the bail, Glenda went with Dylan to pick up his cell phone, clothing, and other personal effects. They walked out of the courthouse together.

Glenda stopped Dylan at the bottom of the steps. "See how easy it is." She dug a pack of cigarettes out of her briefcase and lit one up. She blew out a stream of smoke. "Now, remember the deal. You have to stay out of trouble until the trial date. If you do, this will go without a hitch. You'll get probation with random drug testing, and maybe some public service. If you complete that without screwing up, your juvenile file will be sealed. The whole thing will be history."

Dylan was dazzled. "I can't believe I'm free."

"You are not free, you're out on bail." Glenda looked at her watch. "Shit! I didn't realize how late it was. Do you know where I can find Brady Werther and Tyler Espe?"

Dylan shrugged. They might be at home or at the fort."

"Do you have their cell phone numbers?"

Dylan shook his head.

Glenda didn't believe him but wasn't going to argue with him in front of the courthouse. She took another drag on her cigarette. "When you see them, have them call me." She dug two cards out of her briefcase and handed them to Dylan. "Here. Give them each a card with my number." She turned and started to walk to the parking lot.

"Hey! Wait a second!" Dylan jogged to catch up with her. "How do I get home?"

Glenda gave him a look of disgust. "Call your parents or one of your high school friends."

"Could you give me a ride?"

Glenda stopped and ground out her cigarette butt with the toe of her shoe. "I've got to visit Juan in the hospital. Then, I have tickets to the Guthrie Theater tonight. You have to find a different ride home." She walked to her powder blue Mercedes-Benz. Dylan watched her unlock the door, swing her legs in, and drive off.

* * *

With C.J. in a helicopter en route to Duluth, Floyd thanked the responding cars from Kanabec and Chisago Counties, then released them. Pam and the trooper were searching the ditches.

"This must be C.J.'s." Pam poked her gloved finger through a bloody hole in the sweatshirt she'd found in the ditch. "No footprints nearby, so it must have been thrown here." She climbed out of the ditch, her foot making a sucking sound in the mud as it pulled free.

Floyd swatted a gnat on his neck.

The state trooper, crouched in the weeds partially obscuring the driveway waved his arms around his head to keep the mosquitoes at bay. "There are fresh tire tracks here. Wide ones. The tread pattern looks like they were sixty-profile tires." He walked on further. "We can get a good tire impression in the mud here. The vehicle is definitely a car, not a pickup." He hesitated as he plucked at wood tick off his pants. "Damn! It's not bad enough with the mosquitoes, there are ticks too."

Following the tire tracks up the narrow driveway, Pam, Floyd, and the trooper, stopped at the crest where the hunting shack came into view. Floyd removed a five-cell flashlight from his belt and pulled his pistol. "No power lines and one window. See if there's a back door, Pam."

Pam eased around the back corner with her Glock drawn. The side and back walls were without windows or doors. She circled the shack, skirting around a pipe jutting through the outside wall and emptying onto the ground. She met Floyd and Harold as they pushed through the partially open door. An open lock hung on the hasp.

The cabin was dark except for light coming in the open doorway and through the dirty window. The predominant smell was mildew, with a hint of marijuana. Floyd's flashlight played around the shack, illuminating a table, chairs, and bunk beds. There was a tiny kitchen area with a propane stove. "The cabinet under the sink is open."

The dark floorboards showed scrape marks where the sagging wainscot cabinet doors had dragged across the wooden floor. Floyd pulled the door open, exposing crude plumbing, a copper pipe through the wood floor, and a 1½-inch galvanized pipe ran through the back wall. A rusty ring was fastened in the wood flooring under the sink and a single red and white capsule lay on the floor near the wall. He leaned down and focused the flashlight on the capsule, "I think someone's drug stash is under this trap door." Floyd donned a purple glove and carefully picked up the capsule by its ends, holding it up for Pam and the trooper to see.

Pam squatted down beside him and looked at the floor. "This looks like a well pit for the little hand pump. I've seen these in old farmsteads back home. The other pipe is a drain that dumps on the ground outside."

Floyd contemplated for a second. "I'm putting the capsule back. Leave everything as it is until we get a search warrant."

The trooper was the first one outside, walking the open area around the shack. He bent down to check the trampled grass near the driveway. "I've got a gun here."

Floyd shut the shack's door, and closed the hasp, but didn't secure the lock. He followed Pam across the little opening and looked at the ground where Harold Parker was squatting, swatting at the persistent flying insects. In the grass was a black pistol.

Kneeling beside the trooper, Floyd slipped a pen through the trigger guard. He carefully lifted it, taking care not to disturb any fingerprints. "C.J. carried a backup gun like this. We can run the serial number and check that easily enough." He sniffed at the barrel and looked at the open slide. "Someone fired this until it was empty. I assume the first shot hit C.J. I wonder who was shooting and what they were shooting at?"

Scanning the landscape, Floyd walked slowly through the brush where broken branches and trampled grass defined a narrow trail. "The strides are long, like somebody ran through here." He reached out and pulled the tip of a broken branch and examined the end. "Whoever ran away was being shot at. It appears this twig was clipped off by a bullet."

Floyd walked back to the area in front of the shack where Pam and the trooper were scouring the ground, finding spent shell casings in the long grass. Jared Goodman, the Pine County conservation officer, jogged up the driveway.

"Do you guys need any help?"

Floyd nodded and explained what they'd found in the hunting shack. "Jared, check for other trails leading away from the shack or along the driveway. "I'm going to follow this trail. Pam, call in for a search warrant and ask the sheriff to get the BCA to help process this crime scene."

Pam nodded. "I overheard Carol telling C.J. she had a message to meet Laura Tomlinson at the high school before she went to Duluth. Shit, maybe Laura is out here, wounded."

Floyd's eyes widened. "The dispatcher said C.J. was out here with a high school girl."

The trooper raised his eyebrows. "I wonder if she's wounded…or dead."

Pointing to the crushed grass, Floyd said, "I'll follow the trail. You guys check the immediate area for her body, then try to recreate the scene."

Gesturing to the ground, Pam said, "There are shell casings in this area. The shooter must've stood here, then threw C.J.'s pistol after firing the last shell. I think Laura must be somewhere on this side of the shack."

* * *

Emily sat in a chair next to the hospital bed while Mary explained that the tumor had been minor, hadn't spread, and they'd meet with the oncologist soon to discuss follow-up treatment.

Emily leaned back, only partially convinced she was getting the whole story. "Can I get you anything?"

Mary shook her head. "I'm fine. Floyd will be here in a bit to take me home."

"You're going to do chemo if the oncologist tells you to, aren't you?"

Mary didn't open her eyes. "It's a decision I'll make when I see the oncologist."

* * *

Floyd wound his way through the underbrush, swatting mosquitoes, and following the trail of trampled grass and bent branches. Whoever made the trail hadn't been trying to conceal the tracks. He walked slowly, listening to the hum of bugs and the rustling of the brush as it rubbed against his pants. Looking toward the sun, he realized the trail was making a slow counterclockwise loop. At the edge of a swamp, he saw the trail cut into long grass from the alder perimeter. Anyone familiar with the woods would know better than to walk straight into a swamp. Swamps quickly turn to mire and sap your energy.

After leaning against a tree for a few seconds, Floyd considered the situation, deciding to skirt the left edge of the swamp until he found the exit trail. He hadn't gone a hundred yards when he noticed a smear of mud hanging on a piece of grass. It was fresh, turning slimy when he rubbed it between his finger and thumb.

Floyd squatted and looked at the nearby foliage. A drop of muddy water slowly ran down the long blades of grass as he watched. The drop hadn't been there more than a few moments. He listened and heard rustling ahead. Reenergized, he picked up the pace. Not far ahead, a squirrel scolded something intruding on its domain.

A scrap of black fabric hung from a raspberry thorn and a drop of blood colored the next thorn on the same branch. Floyd saw staggering footprints in the fern patch ahead. He stopped and listened. Something rustled from just out of sight. The sucking sound of a foot pulling out of mud preceded the splash of someone falling and a female voice crying.

Floyd eased his hand back to the pistol, touching it, reassured by its presence. He forged ahead, avoiding the swampy patches, then placing his weight on the balls of his feet and then on the heel, minimizing the noise he made. When he felt a branch underfoot, he chose a new place to step.

The crying was nearby, and after a few steps he saw a quivering lump of black a few feet ahead.

"Laura? Is that you?"

Laura's despair over being lost quickly turned to terror. She looked in the direction of Floyd's voice, her eyes wide with fear. She pushed herself up, leaning on one arm. Her despair was so great she decided not to run even if it were Brady or Dylan there to kill her. She was relieved to see Floyd.

Pushing through the brush, Floyd knelt beside her, smiling. "It looks like the raspberries and mosquitoes have been pretty tough on you. Is anything else wrong?" The girl was lying in a heap next to the tree limb she had apparently tripped over. Her clothing was caked with mud, her black jeans and t-shirt ripped and ragged. Laura's face and arms were covered with scratches from thorns.

Laura looked down at her arms. They were muddy and myriad scratches trickled tiny rivulets of blood. She suddenly realized her t-shirt was torn open and that her bra was visible through a rip in the fabric. She clutched the shirt closed but seemed unable to answer Floyd's question.

Floyd asked, "None of the shots hit you?"

Laura looked at him as though she couldn't understand the words. "Shots?"

"Someone shot at you." Floyd offered his hand to help her get up.

Laura accepted his help, carefully holding the hole in her shirt closed as she got up from the muddy ground. She continued to clutch the shirt closed, brushing at her mud-caked jeans with her other hand. "I'm okay."

Floyd watched as Laura brushed off the swampy grime. "Who shot at you?"

"Shot at *me*?" She looked at him like he should have known that piece of information. Then Laura glanced around at their surroundings nervously. "I walked toward the sirens but couldn't get through the swamp before they were gone. Are you lost too?"

Floyd smiled. "I've been trying to find you." He nodded toward a big white pine rising above the canopy of trees. "You've gone in a circle. That big pine tree is near the hunting shack. We can walk there in a couple of minutes. Are you up to a little more walking?"

Laura nodded and started to follow, then grabbed Floyd's shirt. "OMG! Deputy Jensen was with me." Laura let go of her torn shirt and held her hands to her mouth. "Brady shot her, didn't he?"

Floyd nodded. "She's in the hospital. Do you remember what happened?"

Floyd led Laura through a narrow deer trail.

"Deputy Jensen drove me here. I told her I could find the fort. Brady was inside when we got here. He was really mad, and I think he knocked us down."

"Brady who?" Floyd continued to lead, pulling back low-hanging branches, then letting Laura bend under them before letting them swing back.

"Brady Werther."

Laura struggled to keep up with Floyd's long strides. "Oh, YUK!" She flicked a finger at a wood tick crawling up her arm. Failing to dislodge it, she pinched the tick between shaking fingers and threw it into the underbrush.

Floyd stopped at Laura's exclamation and realized she was lagging. He picked a tick off his own neck while he waited for her to catch up. When she reached his side he asked, "What happened after Brady came out of the shack and knocked you down?" He waved his arms in an effort to keep the swarming bugs at bay.

"He was yelling." Laura's response was punctuated with arm waves. "He called Deputy Jensen a bitch, then jumped on top of her when she fell down. He was beating her up and she tried to push his hands away. Then Brady reached into her pocket, and I heard this kinda popping sound. She cried out and stopped fighting."

The thought of C.J. in a physical fight with an attacker sickened Floyd. He could imagine her trying to draw her pistol and the muffled shot as the bullet ripped into her thigh. Shaking his head to clear the visions, he started down the deer trail at a slower pace.

Entering the clearing by the shack, a wave of relief swept Laura. She shuddered and her teeth started to chatter. "I'm cold." She wrapped her arms over her chest, attempting to warm herself.

Floyd put his hand on her elbow. "C'mon. My cruiser is at the end of the driveway. I've got a blanket and I'll turn the heater on."

They met Pam and Harold on the driveway. "This is Laura Tomlinson. She was with C.J. and needs to warm up."

Laura sat silently as Floyd reported finding the girl over the radio. Heat poured into the car and Floyd cracked his window open. He felt a tick crawling across his chest, and he reached under his shirt to remove it. Laura watched as he flicked it out of the window.

"I hate wood ticks," she said as another shiver ran over her body.

Floyd nodded his agreement. "My shoes are starting to melt. Can I turn the heat down a bit?"

Laura stared at the floor. "A little," she said, clutching the blanket around her shoulders and continuing to shiver.

Floyd sensed something else bothering Laura and he sat silently, waiting to see if she'd open up.

Staring at her lap and wringing her hands, Laura said, "I should've stayed to help her. Is she hurt bad?"

Floyd spoke gently. "She has a gunshot wound. I guess we'll have to see how bad it is." Floyd hesitated, then added, "You did the right thing. You couldn't have stopped Brady.

He was shooting at you. You had to save yourself."

"I don't know…I mean he might've listened to me."

"He shot at you." Floyd's voice was flat and matter of fact. "You had no choice but to run for your life."

Laura stared at him. "Brady shot at me? Are you sure? He pointed the gun at me before I ran, but I thought he shot Deputy Jensen a bunch of times."

Floyd shook his head. "She was shot once. The rest of the shots went through the brush where you ran."

The words sank in slowly. Tears welled in Laura's eyes and spilled onto her cheeks.

Floyd watched silently. "You didn't think he'd shoot at you?"

Laura dabbed the tears with the blanket as she choked off a sob. "He must've been tripping. I mean, Brady's usually nice. Not like Dylan."

Floyd fished a toothpick out of his breast pocket and poked it into his mouth. "Tripping on what?"

Laura looked at the floor. "It used to be joints, then Dylan got some acid and they dropped tabs of that for a while. We had a few bad trips, so they tried making their own meth from chemicals they stole. That was really bad and some of them got really sick from it. Now, they've got these capsules called 'white.' I think they have a source, and

311

it's secret, because they talk about it like an inside joke."

"How does white affect them?"

"No bad trips or anything. It just made them go really fast...and sometimes they'd get kinda paranoid and crazy. They get mad about stupid stuff when they're tripping."

"Are you warming up at all?"

As if on cue, Laura's body shuddered. "A little. I kinda smell like swamp from the muck. I'll probably stink up your car."

Floyd smiled. "Believe me, this isn't the worst that's happened to it." His mind shifted gears. "We should try to find Brady. What kind of car does he drive?"

"I...I'm not into cars much. It's green, some sort of sports car." She looked at Floyd, expecting him to be disappointed. "It has a shift."

Floyd picked up the radio mic. "Run a check on Brady Werther for a plate number on a green sports car." Floyd smiled at Laura to reassure her that her information was valuable.

Chapter 19

Floyd Swenson sat outside Judge Karen Albertson's courtroom awaiting a break in a trial. The county attorney's office had drafted two search warrants, one for "the fort," based on evidence at the scene of a shooting, and the second for Brady Werther's car and home. Both listed methamphetamine, other illegal drugs, drug paraphernalia, precursor chemicals, cash, firearms, drug sales records, and chemical processing equipment as targets of the search.

A murmur inside the courtroom sent him scrambling to the clerk's desk with his papers as the courtroom cleared. "They're breaking. Can I catch her for two minutes?"

The young female clerk looked at him with irritation. She was a fresh law school grad getting experience before going into practice. "Wait here. I'll see." She got up from her desk and knocked once on the judge's office door before entering.

The door flew open a second later, Judge Albertson blowing out like a November Nor'easter coming down Lake Superior. Her black robe flowed in the wind created by her speed. She gave Floyd a glare as he jumped from the chair. "I gotta pee. Walk with me to the restroom, Sergeant."

Floyd nearly jogged to keep pace. "We've got a deputy shot and in the hospital. I have search warrants for the shack where our deputy was shot, and for the home and car of the shooter."

"Alleged shooter, Sergeant. They're innocent until convicted." They rounded a corner and almost crashed into two lawyers using the hall to negotiate an out-of-court settlement for an injury case.

The judge dodged the attorneys nimbly and Floyd tried to keep pace. "Whatever. We're looking for drugs, drug paraphernalia, processing equipment, and records." He flashed the two pieces of paper in front of the judge as she pushed open the brown door designated, "Ladies."

Judge Albertson plucked the papers from Floyd's hand and disappeared. After about a minute, a disembodied voice came from deep inside the room. "You've already been in the shack, Sergeant?"

Floyd looked around helplessly, then directed his voice to the door hinge. "Yes. The door was unlocked and open when we arrived. We weren't sure where the assailant was, so we looked for him inside. We left the building undisturbed when we determined he wasn't there." A woman walked by the rest room and gave Floyd a disgusted look.

"This says you saw drugs inside. Did you remove them?"

"No. I just saw one capsule on the floor and immediately left."

There was a long pause, then the sound of running water. Judge Albertson emerged, reading the documents as she walked out. She looked up at Floyd. "I think you had probable cause to continue the search. You don't need a warrant."

Floyd smiled. "Not all jurists are as open-minded as you are. I wanted to walk on the safe side."

Judge Albertson brushed a wayward lock of blonde hair back from her forehead. "I'm okay with these. Give me your pen."

Floyd pulled a ballpoint from his pocket and clicked it before handing it to her. Holding the documents against the wall, the judge signed them and handed the papers and pen back to Floyd. "Give one copy to my clerk for the files." The judge paused and lowered her voice. "You said you had a deputy down. Who?"

Floyd looked around furtively and leaned close. "We haven't notified her family yet. It's C.J. Jensen."

The judge closed her eyes. "Shit. She's only been with you a couple months. It's getting so violent out there and everyone works without backup most of the time." She shook her head in dismay.

Floyd slipped the pen back in his pocket. "The assailant used C.J.'s gun and left it at the scene. We'll process it, but I'm sure we'll have fingerprints. He also fired at a teen who was with C.J. but missed."

The judge nodded and started to take a step, then stopped. "How bad is Deputy Jensen?"

Floyd waited for two lawyers to pass. "She's got a gunshot wound to her upper leg. Lost some blood. Had hypothermia."

"Hypothermia? It's not that cold out." The judge tried to read Floyd's face.

"The kid who assaulted...allegedly assaulted her, removed her sweatshirt, and handcuffed her to a car. She was unconscious in that position for three hours before I found her."

Judge Albertson's face flushed with anger. "Sexual assault too?"

"We don't know yet, but her pants were around her hips."

The judge opened her mouth to comment but thought better of it. She nodded at the warrants. "Go do your job...so I can do mine."

* * *

John Sepanen was standing at the nurse's station in the St. Luke's Hospital emergency room in Duluth. He was on the phone with the Carlton County Sheriff's Department when a surgeon walked down the hall. "That's right, Michael Holm. His daughter's name is Charlene Jensen. She's one of my deputies. We don't know her condition yet, but here comes the doctor now. Have Holm call my cell. I'll be here until I hear from them."

Sepanen looked drawn and tired. The doctor nodded toward a consultation room on the edge of the waiting area. He held the door for the sheriff.

"Your deputy was very lucky. The bullet plowed through the quadriceps...the big muscles on the top of her thigh and missed the major blood vessels and knee. She'll be sore for a while, but I don't expect any permanent damage other than a nasty scar." He pulled a chair back from the table and straddled it, leaning his arms on the back. "Her body temperature was down about five degrees, but we got her warmed up."

Sepanen looked visibly relieved. "Sexual assault?"

The doctor shook his head. "There wasn't one. I also checked the injury on her back. It looks like she was stabbed with a stick. There were a few splinters in the wound, but it wasn't deep enough to puncture her lung. I put a stitch in it."

Sepanen gave a sigh of relief. "Is she conscious?"

The doctor stood. "She's in the recovery room and should be lucid in a few minutes. We'll move her to a surgical room as soon as she's awake."

* * *

Floyd was waiting in his car with search warrants when Deputies Kerm Rajacich and Sandy Maki pulled up. The three deputies walked to the shack where they met Pam and the trooper. Together, they spent an hour walking shoulder to shoulder in a grid, marking the evidence they found.

They were taking pictures of the gun, syringes, plastic bags, and spent cartridges when a stylishly dressed, middle-aged woman walked up the driveway. "Are you the cops who are looking for the realtor?" The red wool coat, leather shoes, and white silk scarf seemed out of place in the rustic setting.

Floyd offered his hand. "Floyd Swenson, from the Pine County Sheriff's Department."

The woman's face was heavily made-up with crow's feet showed at the corners of her eyes. Floyd guessed she was pushing fifty, although her stylish clothes wouldn't lead him to that conclusion.

"Peggy Warner, from Peggy Warner Realty." She shook his hand gently. "I understand you want to get into the cabin." She looked at the shack.

"Actually, we're going to search the shack. We have a search warrant, but we'd like to talk to the owner."

Peggy walked toward the structure as they spoke. "We've had a lot of problems with this property. Someone keeps taking down my signs." She reached over the door frame for the key, then realized the door was unlocked.

She sighed. "Half the time it's unlocked when I get here." She pushed the door open and stepped back.

"You could change the lock." Floyd peered past her into the darkness.

"When I change the locks, they break the door. There's nothing here to steal except the stink." She sniffed and wrinkled her nose.

"Do you know who's been breaking into the cabin?"

"I assume they're kids. Sometimes they leave a few beer cans or a booze bottle. They party here and leave." She stepped into the shack only as far as the light shone through the door.

Floyd pulled a flashlight from his belt. He cast the beam around the single room. "Who's the owner?"

Peggy covered her nose and mouth with her hand, obviously offended by the smell. "The property is owned by a family trust. The owner died a year or so ago. The widow directed me to sell the land and building."

Floyd shone the beam of the light on the small kitchen vanity. "We think the vandals stashed some drugs under the sink." He walked across the room and opened the cupboard door. "Is there a well under here?"

When he looked back, Floyd saw that the realtor had taken out a small handkerchief and was holding it over her nose and mouth. Pam and Sandy were standing next to her. "There's a shallow well pit that was dug by hand when the cabin was built. The hand pump on the sink used to work and the sink drains outside the wall. The original owner built this as a deer hunting camp in the fifties and that's about all it's ever been. There are forty acres with the cabin," Peggy said, her voice muffled by the thin fabric.

Floyd knelt and pulled the ring on the trap door. With difficulty, it pulled loose from the surrounding floor. He lifted the square of plywood from under the cabinet, setting it next to him. He then stuck his head under the sink and shone the flashlight down the well.

"It's deeper and bigger than I would have guessed. It's about fifteen feet deep and a yard wide. The walls are stacked stone. I see broken glass in water at the bottom." His voice echoed against the stone pit walls. He eased back out. "I need a bigger flashlight."

As Floyd got up from the floor, Sandy walked over, pulling his five-cell flashlight from a belt loop. He knelt down and stuck his head under the sink. "Lots of cobwebs. Looks like broken gallon jugs in the bottom. Smells bad." He backed out and sat looking at the others for a second. He shook his head and unbuckled his uniform belt. "There are hand-holds built into the walls. Looks like I'll have to climb down to retrieve the evidence."

They watched Sandy back under the sink and lower his feet into the well pit. He slowly disappeared down the hole. Floyd lay on his belly, shining Sandy's flashlight down the narrow pit. They heard crunching glass and sloshing water when he reached the bottom.

"Man, it stinks down here." More glass crunched. "There are some brown chemical bottles down here and some glass test tubes, like we used in the chemistry lab. Can you pass down a bucket or something to put the stuff in?"

Tom Thompson turned toward the door. "I'll get something."

Floyd relayed the news. "Can you see anything else, like pill bottles or bags of powder?"

"No, the chemical smell is so strong I've got to come up and breathe." Floyd backed out and soon Sandy followed. His uniform pants and shirt were smeared with dirt, mold, and dampness. His pants were wet to mid-calf. A cobweb hung from his hair.

Watching Sandy brush the cobweb away, Floyd asked, "Do you think we need a hazardous materials team?"

Sandy stood up and brushed off his knees. "I'm no chemist, but I think the smell is more offensive than toxic." He pushed his hand into his pants pocket pulling out a fistful of white and red capsules. "I'll bet this is mostly what they were trying to ditch. A bunch of the pills stuck to stones jutting out. I imagine the rest dissolved in the water."

Tom Thompson returned with a canvas gym bag, nylon rope, and a pair of leather gloves. "I couldn't find a bucket, but this should do." He handed the items to Sandy. "I figure you'd need the gloves to handle the glass."

Five minutes later, Sandy was down the hole again. The crunching of broken glass was heard from under the cabinet. Soon there was the sound of a splash.

"Oops. Dropped a bottle…aw shit, all the caps fell in the water and they're dissolving."

Floyd felt a tug at the rope and pulled the gym bag up and out from the cabinet. He spread the contents on the floor. Several brown chemical bottles were intact, their liquid contents swirling when they were handled. Other items were just shards of lab glassware. All of the contents were wet and reeked of chemicals.

Sandy's voice echoed up from the hole. "The stink is getting to me. I'm coming up."

Floyd stepped away from the cabinet to give Sandy room to crawl out.

"AARRRGGHHH!" The scream sounded unearthly as it echoed in the hole. It was followed by a splash. "GET ME OUTTA HERE!"

A moment later Sandy's head appeared under the cabinet and his fingers clawed at the wooden floor as he pulled himself from under the sink. As soon as he was free of the cabinet, he staggered from the shack. The others were close behind. His face was ashen. He bent over with hands on his knees, gulping breaths of air.

"What's wrong? Did the chemicals get you?" Floyd asked. "Do you need an ambulance?"

Sandy's eyes were closed as he continued to struggle for air. He wavered for a second and then fell to his knees, retching violently. The others watched anxiously as he wiped the spittle from his mouth with a shaking hand.

"I pulled a stone loose and saw a stick poking out from behind the stone. When I grabbed the stick to pull myself out…there was a hand attached to it."

* * *

Tony Oresek and Eddie Paulson found the remote shack by following landmarks Floyd relayed to them via cell phone. Peggy Warner's pink Cadillac looked decidedly out of place among the various official vehicles, most with light bars flashing. Tony and Eddie unloaded a gurney and rolled it up the rutted driveway.

Eddie nodded to Floyd as they passed. "I checked with the nurses in the emergency room before we left, and C.J. is stabilized. She's been moved to a surgical floor."

Floyd nodded. "Thanks."

A generator hummed behind the shack and two halogen lights, provided by the Pine City Fire Department rescue crew, lit the inside of the building like daylight. Peggy Warner sat with Pam in her cruiser at the top of the driveway. Pam was recording the history of the property's ownership from Peggy. They watched the medical examiner and gurney disappear into the shack.

Pam summarized what she had learned from Peggy. "So, the bottom line is that the shack was built just after World War II, and it's changed hands every three to five years since."

"That's right," Peggy responded. "I represented the last three sales for the estates of deceased owners. The most recent owner was Art Johnson from Brooklyn Park. I joked with my husband that the property must be unlucky because every owner died a few years after the purchase." Peggy didn't seem very upset about the history. Because Pam seemed disturbed by her callousness, Peggy added, "None of them were young people."

"Do you know about any of the owners before the most recent sales that you handled?" Pam folded up her notebook.

The realtor shook her head, making her hair bounce and exposing the gray roots. "I heard from the first wife who said her uncle had owned it before they bought the property from him. She said something about a widowed aunt." Peggy shrugged. "But I don't know who the owners were. It's on the property abstract in my office."

Pam shoved the notebook into her pocket. "Email a copy of the abstract to me. I want to track down the previous ownership."

Peggy considered Pam's interest in tracing the past owners. "Do you think the body's been there for years or decades?"

Pam and the realtor stepped out of the cruiser. "We'll have to wait for the medical examiner to make that determination." Pam paused, "Maybe there's more than one body down there."

Peggy Warner's face turned white, and she closed her eyes. "I need to go to church and light some prayer candles."

* * *

Eddie donned a protective suit and climbed into a nylon safety harness. He pulled a chemical respirator over his head, tightened the straps, and pulled on heavy rubber gloves. He was easing back down the hole when Pam reached the shack. A fireman was holding a rope attached to Eddie's harness. Next to him on the floor were an arm and a leg lying on the rubberized body bag. The body parts had a patina of white that Floyd assumed to be mold. Mysteriously, there was very little sign of tissue decomposition or smell of decay. The limbs reminded him of the embalmed body of a veteran they'd exhumed from a cemetery.

Tony Oresek hovered over the remains and made notes as he poked and prodded with his latex-gloved fingers. The sound of water dripping inside the well pit was the only sound inside the cabin.

The fireman reached to grab something under the cabinet. His head disappeared and he grunted while lifting out a torso. He dragged it free of the cabinet and untied the rope before rolling it over onto the body bag. Floyd stared at the small breasts, the color of Ivory soap. A second fireman let out a moan and ran for the door.

After a few minutes, the fireman on the rope pulled up a second leg and arm, then he stepped back. Finally, a mass of wet, tangled hair appeared under the cabinet, where it seemed to levitate. The fireman reached out and passed it to the ME.

From under the cabinet came Eddie's muffled voice. "That's it. Only one."

He struggled out of the hole, pulling off the rubber gloves and respirator. "All the body parts were hidden behind the wall of the well. I suspect they were buried outside the shack, next to the well pit. When Sandy pulled the stone loose, it exposed the dismembered corpse."

Eddie stood, water dripping from his Tyvek suit. The ME picked up the skull and gently swept the hair back, exposing a lopsided face with an eye bulging from the left socket. Oresek rotated the head in his gloved hands, viewing it from every angle. The room was silent as he studied the object. A third fireman smothered his gagging and ran for the door. Oresek finally set the girl's head on the body bag, realizing the remaining people were staring at him expectantly. He stood, stripped off his latex gloves, and dropped them onto the body bag. He removed his glasses and placed them into his pocket. "You can load her up."

Floyd pushed next to Tony as Eddie zipped the bag shut. "Tony, talk to me."

Tony and Floyd stayed behind as the remaining people followed the bag and gurney. "Teen girl. Looks like a gunshot wound to the head. I'd guess she's been dead for a year or so, but there's so little decomposition it's hard to tell. It's very cold in the well and decomposition has been slow. Kind of like storing meat in a root cellar. Still, I'd expect more deterioration. She's amazingly well preserved. It's almost like she's been embalmed."

Tony weighed his thoughts and added. "The mold is the key. A body has to be in the ground quite a while to accumulate a layer of mold. I've only seen mold like that when we've done a cemetery exhumation." He hesitated, then asked, "Have you had any grave robbers lately?"

Floyd shook his head. "Not that I'm aware of. Besides, I can't remember a teen who died from a gunshot to the head."

Tony shrugged. "The body might not have been stolen locally." He thought for another moment and asked, "Are the kids who are hanging out here into witchcraft or necrophilia? There are some pretty sick people out there."

Floyd shrugged. "Looks like the body parts weren't severed cleanly."

"Hatchet or ax. It takes less of a hole in the ground to dispose of body parts than a whole body. Less work. Quicker."

"Suicide?" Floyd asked.

Tony shook his head. "The entry wound is in the neck, then exits through the skull. Let me complete the post-mortem exam before the sheriff gives a statement to the media."

* * *

Glenda Planck walked into Juan Santiago's hospital room and was surprised to find his parents there. In her experience, juvenile offenders generally didn't have a family support network to keep them out of trouble. Juan's father was watching television and his mother was working on embroidery. Glenda hesitated for a second.

Ray Santiago looked across the room and was surprised to see someone as strikingly attractive and well dressed as Glenda staring at him. He muted the television with the remote control. "Can I help you?"

Glenda put on her best business smile and offered her hand. "Hello. I'm Glenda Planck."

Her smile was infectious, and Ray Santiago couldn't help smiling back, even though Glenda evoked a level of discomfort. "Are you in the right room?" He stood and shook her hand.

Glenda moved to Juan's bedside and flashed a smile at the boy's mother before focusing on the patient. "Hi, Juan. How are you doing?"

Juan stared at her and nodded. "I'm okay."

329

Glenda reached into her briefcase and handed Ray one of her business cards. "One of Juan's friends asked me to be his attorney."

Ray Santiago turned dark. "You're an ambulance chaser?"

"Not at all. I have a prosperous practice and am offering my services to Juan at no charge to you. My fees are being covered by Mr. White." She turned to Juan. "You know Mr. White."

Juan looked pained and he pushed the button for another shot of morphine. He drifted off without responding.

Ray Santiago read Glenda Planck's card for the third time. "I'm sorry, but I don't know Mr. White. Why would he pay a lawyer to represent Juan?"

Glenda hesitated. It would have been so easy if the parents hadn't been around. Now she was negotiating her representation when she should have been reassuring Juan that he would be fine as long as he kept his mouth shut. She'd lost control with Juan's mother and father present.

"Maybe I should come back later." Glenda turned to leave.

"Wait." Ray Santiago was at her side. "You didn't answer my question."

Glenda sighed and looked at her watch. She had to drive back to her Minneapolis condo, shower, change clothes, and be on the way to the Guthrie Theater. She didn't have time to dance around Mr. White's interest in providing her legal assistance with Juan's father, a blue-collar Neanderthal.

"Look, Mr. Santiago, Juan is in big trouble. My client would like to help him out. Juan will get top quality legal defense instead of a public defender who is juggling three hundred cases."

Ray Santiago was skeptical. "What's in it for your client?"

Glenda considered her words carefully. "He's a benevolent man."

Ray Santiago considered the answer. "Is he the one who owned the drugs that caused Juan's arrest? Is that why he's so benevolent? If you do a good job of defending Juan, Mr. White isn't associated with Juan's arrest. Is that what this is about?"

Glenda saw little benefit in arguing. "I think I'm in the wrong room. Excuse me."

Ray Santiago was not the Neanderthal Glenda Planck thought him to be. He grabbed her elbow and led her into the hallway. "Let me explain something to you, Ms. Planck. Juan made a mistake, but be assured, his mother and I care deeply about him, and we will look after his legal defense. I work two jobs and his mother works one just to pay tuition for Juan's sister at the University and to keep our little farm together. It looks like all that work has kept me from taking care of what's really important. It won't happen again. We're with

Juan through this mess, and we don't need his drug dealing friends to help."

Glenda pulled her elbow away from Santiago and gave him a smile that was half grimace as she glanced at her watch again. "It's no skin off my nose. I just hope you won't be disappointed with the outcome. Don't lose my card. Mr. White's money will buy a first-class legal defense." She turned and marched down the hall toward the elevator.

Ray called after her. "Tell Mr. White we don't want his help."

* * *

Glenda drove out of the hospital parking lot and activated her hands-free cell phone. "Call Mr. White."

The phone rang twice before a male voice answered. "Yes."

"Tell your employer the client in the hospital has refused my services."

"I'll make sure he gets the message."

Glenda turned toward downtown Minneapolis where she lived in a river-view condo. She wondered what Mr. White would do about her message. She suspected she'd learn about his response in the news. Whatever happened, her conscience was clear, and her standing with the bar association wasn't in jeopardy.

* * *

Floyd drove to Cloquet on his way home from the hospital. He glanced at the sign advertising the only Frank Lloyd Wright designed gas station in the world. The building's huge glass windows looked out over a city park on the edge of the St. Louis River.

He drove to a plant that made wooden matches. The factory was a long, two-story brick building with a mountain of pine logs stacked outside. The visitor parking area was located near a single-story annex with large windows. Floyd parked his cruiser in the empty lot and walked to the visitor door. He pressed a buzzer and waited. It was nearly eleven p.m. by the time a security guard responded to the buzzer. He tapped his watch and pointed to a sign with the lobby hours.

Floyd held his badge to the window and the guard opened the door. "Is there a problem?"

"I need to talk to one of your workers, Christine Tomlinson."

The guard drew a deep breath. "I can't pull someone off the production floor. You'll have to wait for the shift change at eleven."

The guard directed Floyd to a seat in the lobby and he picked up a copy of *Outdoor Life* magazine. A door creaked down the hall, preceding the arrival of Christine Tomlinson.

Floyd stood, as a lean woman with tired eyes and graying hair covered in a bouffant hair net walked into the room. She was obviously distressed at the sight of Floyd's uniform.

"I heard there was a deputy sheriff here to see me." She clutched her purse with both hands. "Has something happened to Laura?"

Floyd smiled and shook his head. "Laura's fine." He directed her to a chair across from where he'd been seated. "But I need to talk to you about Laura. She had a close call this morning."

Christine Tomlinson fished a cigarette from her purse and lit it with a match. She shook the match and looked for an ashtray. "Damn, I hate the no-smoking laws." She waved her hands in the air to disperse the smoke. "You don't mind, do you? I haven't had a cigarette since my break at seven and I need one now. Tell me about Laura."

"She was with my deputy this morning, and they were assaulted by a gunman."

Christine's eyes grew wide. "Someone held them up?"

Floyd shook his head. "No. They surprised one of Laura's friends at a hunting shack they use as a hangout. Laura's friend shot and wounded my deputy. Your daughter is uninjured."

Christine Tomlinson got a sudden shot of adrenaline. Her eyes darted from Floyd to the window, and she crossed her legs. Her foot bobbed nervously. "But you said that Laura's okay. How about the deputy?"

"She'll be okay, but I need to know more about Laura's friends. Tell me about Tammi Wagner."

Christine waved her hand at the smoke she exhaled. "I don't know Laura's friends. I work rotating shifts, so I don't see them when they come around. I'm either asleep or gone most of the time Laura is home. The divorce has been tough on both of us, but this is the only job I could find with benefits."

When Floyd didn't respond, she shrugged. "I don't remember Tammi. There have been a couple of guys, but they're all pretty strange. I told Laura she could do better than them, but she has a problem with self-confidence. I think she's flattered that they pay attention to her."

Floyd took out a notebook and scribbled some notes. "Did you know they're into alcohol and drugs?"

Christine shook her head. "I smelled marijuana smoke on Laura's clothes. But, hey, I did a little weed when I was young. We all did."

Floyd turned solemn. "We recovered over a kilogram of methamphetamine from one of her friends." When the chemical name didn't register with Christine Tomlinson he added, "It's called meth, crystal meth or angel dust. We submitted the pills for chemical analysis." The woman nodded recognition and Floyd went on. "We also found a dead body at their hangout."

Christine dropped her cigarette and ground it out with her toe. "A human body?" She immediately lit another cigarette.

Floyd nodded. "I don't think Laura knows anything about the death, but she knows about the drugs. Because she's a minor and she's cooperating with our investigation, she'll get special treatment in the courts. Her friends were in possession of dealer quantities of controlled substances."

Tears welled in Christine's eyes as she struggled to find a place to stub out her cigarette. She finally gave up and ground it out on the tile floor beside the other butt. She fished a tissue from her purse and wiped her eyes. "Where's Laura now?"

Floyd folded his notebook and put it away. It was obvious that Christine Tomlinson had no idea what Laura was into. "We have her in protective custody. You'll be able to see her tomorrow."

Christine dabbed at her eyes and blew her nose into the tissue. "One more casualty of the divorce. God, if I'd only known what a mess this was going to be... Who would have thought that taking a job with rotating shifts would be so tough? I thought I could trust her." Christine composed herself. "Can I see her tonight?"

Floyd shook his head. "Not tonight. But I'll ask her to call your home tomorrow."

Chapter 20

Floyd woke from a nightmare. In the dream, he'd been cradling C.J. as life ebbed from her body. When C.J.'s breathing stopped, he'd looked down and saw it was Mary, not C.J., who was dead in his arms. Drenched in sweat, he threw back the covers and thought about calling the hospital to check on both C.J. and Mary. Deciding it was just a stupid dream, he took a scalding shower. With the water pounding on his back, he thought again about holding C.J.'s cold body against him to keep her warm. He stepped out of the shower and turned the thermostat up until he heard the furnace start.

When the phone rang, he ran with a towel around his waist to the extension in the bedroom.

"Hi, Floyd, I thought I'd drive up this morning and visit." The chipper voice of Mary's sister lightened his spirit.

"Hi, Trish. She'd be happy to see you. She was still groggy last night." He omitted that he'd also spent an hour with C.J. who was lucid and unhappy about being held in the hospital overnight.

"Emily said the surgery went well." The apprehension in Trish's voice begged for reassurance.

"Yes, it all looks pretty non-threatening."

"Well, I think I'll head out in about an hour. Will I see you at the house?"

Floyd looked at the clock. "I'll meet you at the hospital."

"Floyd," there was a long pause, "are you investigating the girl they found in the well? The news said she was found near Hinckley."

Floyd took a deep breath and let it out. "I suppose that made the news in the Cities. Yeah, I'm helping with the investigation."

"It sounds so…so gruesome. I kind of hate to think about you dealing with all that stuff. I heard you had a deputy who got shot, too. Sometimes I'm afraid to listen to the news."

A picture of C.J. handcuffed to her car ran through his mind. "Me too, Trish."

He hung up the phone, his mood melancholy. The lingering smell of chemicals on yesterday's clothes reminded him of the previous day. Cradling C.J. to his chest had smeared her blood and vomit on his shirt, pants, and jacket, those smells mingled with the chemical odors from the shack. Floyd found clean clothes in the drawer and threw all the soiled clothing into the washer. The activity helped divert his thoughts.

He fed mixed the last leftovers from the refrigerator with puppy chow. She wolfed the food down while he petted her and picked off three more wood ticks.

"You know, if you stay around here much longer, I'll have to buy puppy chow." The puppy ignored him. "And name you."

Floyd stopped in Moose Lake for breakfast. Sarah Jacobson brought a cup before he was seated. She poured fresh coffee from a carafe and then sat down across from him. "I hear you nearly lost a deputy yesterday."

Floyd sipped the coffee and nodded. He had lost his ability to express any emotion. "Yup." He also didn't need to feed the local gossip grapevine.

"One of the guys from the sheriff's department said you saved her life by warming her up with your body until the ambulance arrived." When Floyd didn't answer, Sarah reached across the table and patted his hand. "You're quite a guy." She got up and pulled out a guest check. "The usual, with the egg over easy?"

Floyd nodded. Sarah stepped to the next booth and handed the morning paper to him. "Somebody left one behind."

The front page of *the Duluth News-Tribune* featured a picture of emergency vehicles lined up on a township road with the headline, "Pine County deputy wounded." He read through the article with detachment, like someone else had lived the events years ago. After mentioning C.J.'s shooting, the writer focused on the unidentified female body recovered at the site of the attack.

Before he finished the article, Sarah was back with the "mini-cake" special and fresh coffee. She placed a container of warm maple syrup on the table and topped off his coffee.

"Anything else?"

Floyd shook his head. "No. But thanks."

Sarah slid into the booth again and leaned on her elbows as Floyd smeared the butter on his one, huge pancake. A waitress at Art's for over a decade, Sarah knew Floyd well.

"You're awfully quiet today."

"Yup." He poured syrup over the butter and cut a piece of pancake.

Unsatisfied with his answer, Sarah pushed on. "I thought you'd be happier that your deputy pulled through. Isn't she doing well? The paper said she was in good condition."

Floyd sighed. "She went into a bad situation without back up. That's all." He ate a bite of egg and hoped that Sarah would leave.

Sarah shook her head. "There's more. What is it?"

Floyd stared at her through his eyebrows as he chewed. "I'd rather not talk about it right now, Sarah."

Sarah persisted. "You gotta. It'll eat you up if you don't."

He set the fork on the plate and wiped his mouth with a paper napkin. "Mary had cancer surgery. It looks promising, but she won't talk to the oncologist about follow-up treatments."

Sarah looked crushed. "Is she still in the hospital? I'd like to send her a card."

"She'll probably get released soon. That's where I'm going now." He pushed the plate away.

Sarah pushed the plate back. "You'll need your strength. I'll leave you alone."

Chapter 21

There was a group of people in front of the Duluth hospital when Floyd turned into the parking ramp. Four news vans, their satellite dishes aimed at the heavens, blocked the sidewalk. Taking his parking slip, he saw the sheriff in the midst of a press conference. He turned on the radio and scanned until he found a station carrying it live.

"...Deputy Jensen is expected to recover fully and return to regular patrol duties with the department." Floyd switched off the radio and pulled into a spot reserved for police vehicles.

Instead of going to Mary's room immediately, Floyd decided to visit C.J. He stopped at the nurse's station to make sure she was seeing visitors. The perky receptionist told him there were already visitors in the room.

Floyd peeked into the room and saw Travis Conrad, Pam's husband, talking to a couple standing by the window. It struck him that he was about the same age as C.J.'s father.

"Floyd, come in here. C.J.'s mother and father are here from Carlton." Travis waved him into the room.

Floyd shook hands with Peggy and Mike Holm before greeting C.J. She tried to smile but her face was bruised and swollen. Color had returned to her hands and neck, a welcome change from her ghostly white appearance when Floyd had cradled her in his arms. Her wrists were bandaged where the handcuffs had cut into her skin, her other injuries hidden under the sheets. Floyd noted that the room was filled with flowers.

Mike Holm was subdued, and both parents looked tired. C.J.'s father seemed especially drained. "We drove up last night, after we found a neighbor to milk the cows." Looking at his daughter he said, "Peggy and I needed to see with our own eyes that Charlene was okay."

Eddie Paulson, wearing blue scrubs, slipped into the room and stood by the door. Floyd nodded to him, but the others didn't notice him in the corner.

C.J. held up her arms toward Floyd and flexed her fingers. "See. I'm okay. Everyone is worried but I'm fine."

Peggy Holm shook her head. "You need to rest." She turned to Floyd. "We've been trying to talk her into coming home where I can take care of her."

C.J. grimaced. "I'm okay, Mom. I don't need to be nursed back to health." She shifted her focus to Floyd. "I guess I owe you big-time for the rescue."

Floyd nodded toward the corner. "You owe Eddie. If he hadn't been persistent enough to track me down, you'd probably still be out there."

C.J. and her parents looked at Eddie, who turned crimson. No one had mentioned his role in C.J.'s rescue to them. He held up his hands and stuttered. "N…n…no. She was late and I called. I'm no hero."

Floyd shifted the conversation. "It looks like a greenhouse in here. Who are all the flowers from?" He moved to a vase of long-stemmed yellow roses and read the card. "Dinner's on me next time." It was signed by Eddie. Floyd looked across the room at Eddie, who shrugged and looked embarrassed.

C.J. chimed in. "There are some from the sheriff's department, and the Hinckley firemen." She pointed to a table across the room. "Those are from the sheriff. The daisies are from you and Mary. Sandy and Barb sent the azalea. And I can't even remember who all the others are from." She reveled in the attention despite her pain and brush with death.

Floyd gave a polite wave. "Well, I've got to visit Mary. She's downstairs. It's nice meeting you, Mr. and Mrs. Holm."

C.J.'s expression turned sad. "I'd heard Mary had surgery. Is she doing okay?"

Floyd looked at Eddie, who shook his head, indicating that he hadn't told C.J. anything.

"She's recovering from the lumpectomy. Everything looks promising."

C.J. beckoned Floyd to her bedside. "I want to give you a hug."

Floyd hesitated, but C.J.'s parents moved aside. He moved to the bedside and leaned over. C.J. gave him a gentle squeeze. Her warmth was a contrast to the chill of her body the day before.

She whispered in his ear while she clutched him. "Thanks. I heard about the hug you gave me yesterday." She hesitated. "Keep my job open. I'll be back."

He whispered in her ear. "We're counting on your return."

C.J. put her hand up. "Wait? Who's taking care of Bailey?"

"Pam brought Bailey home with her," Travis said.

C.J. smiled at Travis. "Bailey's never been around an infant. I hope it went well."

Travis snorted and told them about Bailey's antics as Floyd left the room and punched a number into his phone.

Floyd waited for the dispatcher to answer the non-emergency lines as he walked down the hall. "Is Pam there?"

"Hang on, I'll page her."

Pam answered on the first ring. "Deputy Conrad."

"I heard you took Bailey home last night."

"What? No, good morning, how are you?"

Floyd stopped at the elevator and stepped aside. "Sorry. I'm a little preoccupied."

"Bailey is laying on my feet. She spent the night with us, howled every time Luke woke up and underfoot any time we were dealing with the baby." Pam paused. "How is C.J.?"

"She's resisting her mother's attempts to take her home and be nursed back to health."

"I can't imagine letting my mother care for me. How are her wounds? Is she in a lot of pain? Did Travis bring flowers?"

"The gunshot wound is healing nicely. Her face is bruised and swollen. I don't know what drugs she's on, but she seems to be in good spirits. Travis delivered flowers from you two, and Eddie slipped in just before I left. He'd sent a bouquet of roses with a card saying the next dinner was on him."

Pam made a choking sound.

"Are you okay?"

She blew out a breath. "We didn't have any dog food, so Travis fed Bailey fried eggs for breakfast. They seem to be causing a lot of gas."

Floyd chuckled. "The sheriff commented about Bailey's farts yesterday."

"Oh, wow. They're ten times worse today. I've got to hang up and take her outside before someone comes in to search for a dead body."

"Anything new on…"

"Not now. I've got a Bailey emergency!"

* * *

The array of flowers in C.J.'s room made Floyd aware of how barren and depressing Mary's room was the last time he'd been there. He took the elevator to the lobby and bought an arrangement of cut flowers from the hospital gift shop.

"Good morning. I brought you some flowers." He was surprised to see four other arrangements had shown up since he was last in Mary's room. "Who sent you all these others?"

Color had returned to Mary's face, and she was much more alert than she'd been the previous day. The tubes had been removed from her nose and someone had brushed her hair.

"You brought flowers? That's very nice."

He set the flowers on a table and hung his jacket over the back of a chair.

"Barb Watson stopped by this morning with a cyclamen from the shop. The sheriff sent the daisies. And my sisters sent the arrangement of colored daisies. A guy named Eddie Paulson showed up this morning with the carnations on the windowsill. He was awfully nice, although I don't think I've met him before."

Floyd smiled and thought of Eddie's role in the surgical suite. "You probably don't remember, but you've met him."

Mary shook her head. "I'd remember a guy with a ponytail who looks like Willie Nelson."

Floyd laughed. He sat next to Mary's hospital bed detailing the happenings of the previous day for her. He tried to make small talk, but the story about C.J.'s rescue was the only thing that seemed to interest her. Discussions of Mary's own condition were off limits.

"How's C.J. doing?"

"Very well. She's really sore and will need therapy to get back into shape. If any more flowers show up, they'll have to open an annex to her room."

Mary smiled but it quickly faded. "I heard about the body in the well on this morning's news; is it the girl who disappeared a while back? What was her name, Wagner?"

"It may be. It'll be tough to identify whoever it was. The medical examiner is trying to find her dentist. He says that since the advent of fluoride toothpaste these young kids have so few cavities it gets…"

Mary put up her hand. "Boundaries. I do not want to know the gory details."

Floyd stopped mid-sentence. "Have you seen the doctor?"

"He was in early this morning."

"When can you come home?"

"He says tomorrow." Mary looked back at Floyd. "He thinks he got everything."

Floyd felt his stomach tighten. "And?"

"We'll discuss that with the oncologist after I'm discharged."

Floyd sat on the edge of Mary's bed. "We have other things to discuss too."

Mary's look turned to concern. "What? Is something happening at the department?"

Floyd took Mary's hand. "I know a judge who'll marry us any time I ask."

Mary shifted in the bed and pushed a button to release an extra dose of painkiller. "I want what Pam and Travis had."

Floyd reflected on Pam's wedding in her little family church with two dozen friends and relatives. "I'll call the minister and see what's possible."

"Okay."

"Trish is on her way. She should be here soon."

Mary nodded, then closed her eyes as the morphine hit. Floyd kissed her gently, let go of her hand, and stepped out of the room while she slept.

* * *

After his visit to Mary's room, Floyd walked to the morgue. He expected the ME would perform the autopsy on the girl's remains before noon.

Tony Oresek and shook Floyd's hand. "Eddie says Mary's surgery went well. I spoke to the surgeon, and he was pleased with the procedure and prognosis."

"Are medical examiners exempt from HIPAA laws?"

Oresek smiled. "It was a consultation with a fellow practitioner."

Floyd put on a smock while Oresek pulled on a pair of surgical gloves and protective goggles.

Eddie walked to a desk in the corner and opened a computer file. "We checked dental records and confirmed that our Jane Doe from the well is Tammi Wagner. We pulled tissue samples before you got here. The body is full of chemicals. I found the same mixture we found in Ted Palmquist's liver."

Tony opened the torso with a Y incision. Cutting tissue samples from the liver and kidneys, he handed them to Eddie. The ME stepped back. "There's no liver damage, unlike Ted Palmquist. In his case, the chemicals were concentrated in his enlarged liver. The hydrocarbons are dispersed through all this girl's tissues, like she was stewed in them." He closed the skin flaps over the abdomen.

He turned to the x-rays of Tammi's skull displayed on a wall-mounted computer monitor. "The bullet that killed her went all the way through her skull. If you can find the scene of her murder, you may be able to recover it."

Tony returned to the exam table and inserted a plastic rod into the entry wound in the girl's skull. He rotated the head and looked at the relation of the rod to the surface of the skull with clinical detachment. "Given the angle the bullet entered and traversed the skull, I've got to rule her death a murder. She was incapable of holding a gun at that angle and pulling the trigger." He simulated the position of the gun with his finger and tried to put it to his head. "Can't do it."

"What can you tell me about the gun and bullet?"

The ME pulled a lighted magnifying glass over the skull. "The entry wound is nine or ten millimeters in diameter. The massive tissue damage is more consistent with something much more powerful than a 9 mm or .38 caliber bullet." Oresek stepped back. Do you have a specific gun in mind?"

Floyd pulled out his cell phone, dialed Pam, then switched to speakerphone. "I'm with the ME and we're looking at the wound that killed Tammi Wagner. Tell me about the gun you and C.J. recovered after the chase."

"Hang on while I pull up C.J.'s report. I remember it was a chrome-plated revolver."

She paused. "Here it is. It was a .357 magnum Colt Python."

Floyd looked at Oresek who nodded. "Thanks."

"Wait! Was it the murder weapon?"

"That caliber would be consistent with the wounds. The bullet passed completely through the skull, so we don't have a slug for ballistic comparison."

Floyd ended the call and removed the smock. "Is there anything else I should know?"

Oresek looked at the torso. "You should check the shack and surrounding area for a hatchet or ax. You might be able to lift some fingerprints off the weapon used to dismember her."

* * *

Floyd answered a radio call as he drove south from Duluth.

"You've got a meeting with the sheriff in 45 minutes."

Floyd looked at his watch. He was passing Barnum, just about an hour away. "I'll be there as soon as I can." He'd barely hung up the mic when the Minnesota State Patrol dispatcher announced a pursuit. A follow-up announcement gave the license number of a green Pontiac Firebird. A trooper announced that the pursuit had just turned onto I-35 northbound at Hinckley, requesting assistance from any available agencies.

Floyd switched on his lights and sirens and accelerated as he approached the northern Pine County line. Announcing his location, he listened for updated information about the chase and the location of other responding officers. Knowing the pursuit was nearing him from the opposite direction, he turned under a bridge and switched off his lights, the concrete bridge pillars shielding him from the approaching chase. He removed stop sticks from his trunk and prepared to throw them in front of the rapidly approaching Firebird. With the car only yards away, he threw the sticks in front of the vehicle, then yanked the attached rope to get them off the road before the pursuing trooper passed. Tossing the sticks in the ditch, Floyd jumped into his cruiser, and joined the pursuit, now nearly a mile ahead of him.

Strips of shredded tire littered the highway after a little more than a quarter mile, followed by the marks of steel wheels on the concrete surface. The trooper slowed and Floyd moved in alongside him to block traffic approaching from behind. The Firebird was swinging from side to side as its steel rims hit imperfections in the highway surface. Sparks flew into the air every time the steering wheel moved. A front tire rim dropped into an expansion joint, locking the steering and causing the rear of the car to skid sideways. Sparks sprayed momentarily before the car's sideways momentum threw it into a roll. Rust, dust, car parts, and chipped concrete flew into the air as the car flipped repeatedly before flying into a marshy ditch.

The trooper braked onto the shoulder and threw open his door, rushing toward the car with his pistol drawn. Floyd blocked the right lane with his car and announced, "The chase ended at mile marker two-oh-two. Please dispatch Willow River fire and rescue, and an ambulance."

With his gun now holstered, the trooper looked into the driver's window of the upside-down car. Steam rose from the watery ditch where the engine was partially submerged.

Floyd stopped at the edge of the ditch. "I called for rescue and an ambulance."

Nodding without looking up, the trooper reached into the car, then backed away as a bloody arm came out of the broken window, followed by a bloody head and torso. Brady Werther crawled out, then rolled onto his back on the grass, letting out a moan. A siren wailed as the first fire truck left the garage, four miles away. It was followed a minute later by a second siren. An ambulance approached from Moose Lake, following another trooper.

* * *

After repeatedly refusing transport, Brady's head was bandaged, and the trooper helped Floyd handcuff and load the boy into the backseat of the county cruiser.

When Floyd got to the courthouse, he turned Brady over to the jailer and waved at the dispatcher as he went through the sheriff's department security door. He located Pam in Sheriff Sepanen's office with Bailey at her feet, looking content.

Floyd walked through the door and sat in a chair next to the dog, patting her head. "What's up?"

The sheriff got up from his chair and closed the door. "What the hell happened out there? We listened to the radio chatter in the dispatcher's cube, waiting for the crash, and hoping it wouldn't involve you or the need for a coroner."

Floyd replayed the chase for them, describing Brady Werther's condition as shaken, but uninjured, the speeds having topped the hundred-mile-an-hour mark early in the chase.

Bailey, sensing the stress in Floyd's voice, got up and waddled to him with her tail slapping his chair. Her "basset chirping" demanded attention. He reached down and scratched the dog's head.

Pam put her hand on Floyd's arm. "You're okay?"

"I'm fine. All I did was deploy stop sticks and follow the trooper until the chase ended."

The sheriff shook his head. "We're lucky no one was killed."

Floyd leaned forward. "In all the excitement, you probably forgot that I just sat through Tammi Wagner's autopsy. Tony Oresek says a single high-velocity expanding bullet struck her head and killed her."

Pam closed her eyes and let out a breath. "I wonder who pulled the trigger?"

Floyd looked at his watch. "The jailer should have Brady processed by now. Let's lean on him to see what he knows about the gun Juan Santiago threw out during the earlier chase." Floyd got up and walked toward the door. He realized neither the sheriff, nor Pam were following him. "What's wrong?"

Standing behind his desk, Sepanen pointed a finger at Floyd's chest. "I don't want another episode like the one with Dylan Johnson. You won't touch him. Understood?"

Floyd took a deep breath. "Yeah, I let Dylan get under my skin. It won't happen again."

Pam held Bailey's leash, trying to prevent her from racing out of the office. "Brady shot and brutalized C.J. We all want to beat him to death, but that can't happen."

The sheriff nodded in agreement. "I want your word you won't touch him."

Floyd glared at the sheriff. "Okay. I won't touch him."

The sheriff looked at Pam. "Make sure Brady's car gets towed to the impound lot."

Pam nodded. "I'll get a search warrant to go through the trunk and interior, too."

Floyd paused at the door. "Did you get pictures of the tire tread impression at the hunting shack?"

Pam pulled out her cell phone. "They're right here."

"Retrieve pieces of Brady's tires that were shredded after he hit the stop sticks and compare them to the pictures from the shack. Then let me know if they match."

Floyd nodded toward the door. "John, you can be my chaperone when I question Brady. I read the boy his Miranda rights when I brought him in."

The sheriff got up and looked at Bailey, whose eyes were perpetually sad. Her tail started spinning circles. "Take the damn dog with you to the impound lot, Pam. Maybe she'll run out of gas outside."

* * *

Brady Werther sat quietly in the interview room with his feet on the floor, his hands cuffed on his lap, and a row of tape sutures across the left side of his forehead.

He looked up when Floyd and the sheriff entered the room.

Floyd sat down in the chair closest to Brady and leaned his elbows on the table after checking to make sure the red recording light was blinking on the ceiling-mounted camera. The boy's eyes flickered with recognition, then he looked down at his hands. The sheriff stood with his arms crossed and his back against the door.

"Brady, we found Tammi Wagner's body." Floyd expected a response but got none. He went on, hoping to shock the teen. "Did her eye pop out immediately when you shot her or after you chopped off her head?"

Brady's head shot up and his eyes raced between the two cops. They betrayed nothing. He shifted in his chair and mumbled, "She committed suicide?" He looked down at his hands.

Floyd leaned back. "No Brady. The medical examiner says the angle was wrong. She couldn't have shot herself. Besides, suicide victims don't dismember themselves with an ax. I think you shot her, cut her up, and buried her by the well." His voice grew sharper as he spoke.

Brady stared at his hands. "I didn't do it."

Floyd slapped his hand on the table, startling the prisoner. "Bullshit, Brady. You knew where the body was buried. You knew she'd been shot in the head. You did it and you buried the body."

Brady threw a nervous look at Floyd who started pacing the small room. "It was her dad's gun. You can check. He probably killed her."

Floyd shook his head. "It was stolen from his apartment. Did you steal it?"

Brady suddenly realized Floyd knew everything. His voice lost its surly edge as he shook his head. "No. Tammi brought it. She pulled it out and started to wave it around after she got a bad hit of meth. She pointed it at us...I was scared."

Floyd leaned close to Brady's face. "Did you take it away from her? Did you shoot her? Did you run away?"

Brady's response was almost inaudible. "No."

"What happened, Brady? Tell me." Floyd sat down in the chair and leaned close. "I want to hear the story in your own words."

Brady's voice cracked as he pleaded. "I didn't do it. She was waving the gun around. Everyone got scared. Dylan wrestled with her. I don't remember what happened after that. I ran for the door, then the gun went off."

Floyd was close, his nose inches from Brady. "Dylan said you did it."

Brady's eyes were riveted on Floyd, waiting for him to give a sign that he was kidding. "Dylan's a liar. She was on a bad trip. She freaked and pulled out the gun. Dylan tried to take it away from her and that's the last I saw. I was out of the fort before the gun went off."

Floyd let the words die out. "What were you on, Brady? Meth? Acid? Crack?"

Brady shook his head. "We never did crack. Just tabs of acid and meth we made ourselves. It was bad meth, but it was cheap. There was a lot of pressure…"

"Pressure to take some…even if you didn't like it?"

Brady nodded dumbly. "Most of us did acid that night. Dylan badgered Tammi into trying some meth he'd made himself. She got paranoid and went crazy after he told her she was the first to try the new batch. She had the gun in her backpack and pulled it out. Dylan wrestled it away and made fun of her. He said she was so stupid she couldn't even shoot the gun. She pulled away from Dylan and covered her face, but Dylan kept taunting her." Brady started to sob. "She cowered and started to scream. Dylan laughed and pulled the hammer back, waving it around and prodding her with it. She was begging." Brady was obviously overcome.

"And he shot her." Floyd went on.

Brady nodded, unable to get the words out.

"Who cut her body up and buried her?" Floyd leaned back and looked at the sheriff, who winked at him.

"We all did...Ted, Dylan and me. Dylan made us. We were so paranoid and scared that Dylan said he'd kill us if we didn't help." Brady's words came in spurts.

"Where'd the meth recipe and chemicals come from?"

"Dylan got the recipe off the internet, and we stole the chemicals from school. We tried a bunch of different reactions. Taco was the chemist. He tried a lot of different combinations before we finally got one that worked. Then Dylan sent us all out buying up Sudafed and cold tablets all over the county. He and Taco cooked it when Taco's parents were working." Brady broke into sobs. He didn't mention the guy in the Cities who eventually became the source of good meth.

Floyd waited, hoping Brady would go on, but Brady stared at his hands.

There was a knock on the door, and the sheriff stepped aside. Pam walked in and gave Floyd a thumb's up sign.

"Brady, tell me about yesterday at the hunting shack."

Brady looked up nervously, first at Floyd, then at Pam, as if he was making sure she wasn't the deputy he'd assaulted. "I don't know what you're talking about."

"Laura drove out with one of my deputies and surprised you in the shack."

Brady shook his head. "I was in school."

Pam set two pictures of tire treads on the table, fresh off the printer. "Your tires match the impressions we took at the shack, and Laura said you shot at her and assaulted Deputy Jensen."

Brady's mouth opened, but no words came.

Floyd pushed the photos aside and leaned close to Brady. "Deputy Jensen is in the hospital. She's injured, but I'm sure she'll identify you as her attacker. Leaving her handcuffed to her car half naked with a gunshot wound is attempted murder. So is shooting at Laura Tomlinson as she ran away."

"I wasn't really aiming at her."

Floyd glanced at Pam and the sheriff. They had an admission that he was there and had fired C.J.'s weapon. His fingerprints were undoubtedly on the pistol.

"I'm under eighteen," he mumbled.

Floyd gave his most stern look. "Brady, this isn't a speeding ticket where you'd get a fine and a slap on the wrist. You're going to be tried as an adult. You shot at Laura and the deputy and left. You didn't know if you'd hit Laura and you tried to rape Deputy Jensen before you left her bleeding and handcuffed to the car."

Brady squirmed. "I didn't rape her. I only…" He froze and looked at Pam, who took a step toward the table, but was restrained by the sheriff.

Floyd got up and walked over to Sepanen. "Is Dylan in custody?"

The sheriff shook his head. "A lawyer from the Cities posted bail. They both disappeared." He knocked on the door, signaling the jailer. "I'll get the county attorney down with someone to transcribe this interview. Bakken can explain Brady's situation and maybe offer a reduced plea in return for a signed statement about Dylan and Tammi's murder."

Brady looked up. "I'm not signing anything."

Pam took a deep breath and let it out slowly, then glanced at the camera's blinking light. "You don't have to sign anything, but I'm sure the jury will enjoy watching this taped interview and your admissions of guilt."

"I didn't admit anything."

Floyd got up. "I'll let you and the county attorney watch the tape together and then you can decide how deep you've stepped in it."

Brady glanced at the camera, then tried to remember what he'd said as Floyd, Pam, and the sheriff left the room.

Sepanen slapped Floyd on the shoulder in the hallway. "You haven't lost your touch."

"It was Pam showing up with the tire impressions at the right moment that broke the floodgates. Even when he gets a lawyer, they're going to watch that tape and the lawyer will advise him to take a plea agreement in return for throwing Dylan under the bus."

They stopped in the bullpen where Bailey was tied to a leg of Pam's desk. The dog, mostly muscle and ears, had dragged the desk five feet across the floor. Pam knelt and stroked the dog's head. "Bailey, it's too bad you're not a hungry tiger. I'd throw you into the interview room and let you shred that piece of shit."

The sheriff shook his head. "We'd be slapped with a police brutality case if you put that dog in a closed room with a suspect. She'd gas him to death."

On cue, a fart ripped out of Bailey's behind. She jumped, surprised by the sound.

Floyd laughed and turned his head. "I've got to go."

"No!" Pam pleaded. "I can't take her home again. Travis will kill me if she's there when he gets home. You take her, Floyd."

Floyd never slowed on his dash to the exit. "Maybe the sheriff wants a dog for a night."

The sheriff stuck his head out of his office. "Bullshit, that damn dog is not coming home with me."

Chapter 22

The ringing phone rousted Floyd from a night of restless sleep. "The doctor just came through and said I could go home." Mary's voice was stronger and had conviction.

Floyd shook the cobwebs from his head. The clock showed that it was seven-fifteen. "Wow. It'll take me a couple of hours to get showered and drive to Duluth. I'll be there around nine-thirty."

"I guess that'll be okay. I'll give Emily and Trish a call to let them know. Emily thought she might come up again today. I'll tell her to come to the house instead."

"Sounds good. I'll see you in a bit."

Floyd hurried through his shower, then collected a washer load of towels. With the machine loaded, he let the puppy back into the house, fed her puppy chow, and washed a pile of dirty dishes accumulated in the sink. He was rinsing the last bowl when the phone rang. Stumbling over the puppy, Floyd wiped his hands and dashed to answer the call. The puppy yelped when he tripped on her, then cowered under the table, whimpering.

"Hello." His voice sounded disgusted as he tried to coax the puppy out from her hiding spot.

Emily's voice greeted him. "What did you just do to the dog?"

Floyd left the puppy in her hiding spot. "She got underfoot when I reached for the phone. She'll be okay." He watched the puppy peek at him from under the table.

"Mary wants me to come up after lunch. It might be better if I came up earlier and brought lunch. Are you okay with that?"

Floyd watched the puppy edge out from under the table and ease up to his bare foot. She licked his foot tentatively, then went into the living room and curled up on a crumpled blanket. "Sure, bring lunch. I haven't made any plans yet."

"I checked with my boss. I can take a few days of vacation to stay with Mary."

Floyd hesitated. "I have a lot of comp time. You don't need to use vacation for that." He wasn't interested in having Emily around the house but felt uncomfortable telling her that. He'd hoped to have Mary to himself.

"Floyd, you have a murder investigation to run." There was a long pause and Emily added, "I'm having a really hard time dealing with this. I need to be there. I need to hold Mary's hand and make sure she's really well. Is that okay with you? I mean, I don't want to intrude, but…"

Floyd took a deep breath. "Sure. That would be nice. With C.J. in the hospital, the sheriff probably wants me on the road."

* * *

Christine Tomlinson met her daughter in a courthouse interview room. Laura had spent the night at a foster home and looked rested but uneasy.

"Hi, Mom."

Christine rushed across the room and enveloped Laura in a hug. "I've been so worried about you."

Laura squirmed out of the hug and self-consciously looked toward the female jailer who'd driven her from the foster home to the courthouse. "I'm okay."

Laura's face was scrubbed pink and was without the makeup she typically used to shade her eyes and make her face look pale. She wore new jeans and a men's plaid shirt with the sleeves rolled up. Christine looked at Laura's outfit in amazement. "Where did you get those clothes? They look great on you." It had been almost eighteen months since her daughter had entered her "black phase," not wearing anything that wasn't black.

"My other shirt got torn up in the woods yesterday. The deputy took me to a foster home and the lady there bought this stuff for me." Laura pulled at the fabric of the shirt. "I think it's...grotesque." She sat in the chair farthest from her mother.

Christine pulled the other chair close to Laura's side and sat. She brushed a lock of freshly shampooed hair from Laura's face. "I heard that you had an exciting day yesterday."

Laura shrugged.

"You saw a deputy get shot. That must've been scary."

Laura looked up at her mother and shook her head. She crossed her arms and stared at her lap.

"How bad was it, honey?" Christine quietly watched the tears form, then run down the girl's cheeks. When Laura started to sob, Christine pulled the girl into her arms, hugging her close. "It'll be okay."

Laura shook her head. "Dylan's going to kill me." Laura choked out the words between sobs.

Christine pushed Laura back and looked into her teary eyes. "Why would Dylan want to hurt you?"

Laura wiped the tears from her cheeks with the sleeve of the shirt. "Because I showed the cops where the fort is. He'll be royally pissed."

Christine looked lost. "What's the fort?"

"It's where we went to get high. It's out in the country. I think it was somebody's old hunting shack. It was supposed to be a secret."

Christine asked. "Is that where you went with the deputy?"

Laura nodded. "Brady was there, and he shot the deputy." A rush of realization ran over Laura. "They told me she was okay. Is she really?"

Christine nodded. "Yeah. She's in the hospital. The newspaper says she's recovering."

Laura started to sob again and fell into Christine's arms.

"What's the matter, honey?"

"I'm so dead. I showed the cops the fort and saw Brady shoot the deputy. Dylan has to kill me."

Christine closed her eyes and hugged Laura close. "It'll be okay. We'll move away from here, and they won't find you. Maybe we can live in Texas." She held Laura away and forced a smile. "Would you like to live in Texas?"

The girl studied her mother's face. "Really? You'd quit your job and move to Texas?"

"Of course, I will. You're the most important thing in the world to me."

* * *

It was ten-thirty when Glenda Planck slid out from between her satin sheets and slipped her naked body into a fluffy terry cloth robe. She wandered to her gourmet kitchen where she ground freshly roasted coffee beans and poured boiling water into the French press. While the coffee steeped, she opened the living room drapes and surveyed the gloomy landscape from her condo window. A male couple walking a dog passed by three stories below.

Glenda prided herself at being beyond the petty homophobia that engulfed the religious zealots who populated much of Minnesota. She felt entirely at ease in this upscale neighborhood known for its artistic residents.

She opened the hallway door and retrieved the "Strib," as the locals called the *Minneapolis Star Tribune*. She was sipping coffee when she flipped to the second section and saw the front-page article detailing the assault on a female Pine County deputy sheriff and recovery of an unidentified female body from a remote hunting shack.

"Holy shit!" Seeing Brady Werther mentioned as the assault suspect, Glenda ran for the bedroom to retrieve her smartphone. She called Mr. White's phone number and left a message. While waiting for the return call, she scanned the article, then read the entire text a second time. Brady Werther, Tyler Espe, Juan Santiago, and Dylan Johnson were in deep trouble. The article was circumspect about the details, but it revealed enough to make it clear this wasn't going to be resolved by her clients pleading guilty to minor drug possession charges.

The phone startled Glenda. "Hello."

"You left me a message." Mr. White's voice was thick with sleep.

"Have you seen the morning *Strib*?"

"Not yet. Why?"

"Get a copy. Open it to the front page of the local section and call me back."

Mr. White was annoyed. "Just tell me what I need to know."

"We have a problem. Get a paper, read it, then call me back."

Glenda was toweling off after her shower when the phone rang. She wrapped the towel around her chest and picked up the phone. "Glenda."

"I read it." There was a pause. "Does this mesh with what you found out yesterday?"

Glenda sat down on the bed and carefully weighed her words on the outside chance someone had tapped her phone. "There's a lot of new information since I spoke to my clients. I only spoke with one client in jail. I called the other two and left messages that weren't returned. I talked to the injured client. He had…visitors who weren't interested in having me act as his counsel. They were quite agitated and directed me to cease my efforts on his behalf. I got the impression that they were…" she paused to search for the right phrase, "they were too self-righteous to consider an arrangement with your interests. I suspect they'd strike a plea bargain that would negatively affect parties with other interests in the case."

Mr. White summarized Glenda's words. "My interests might be at risk?"

Glenda took a deep breath. "I'd prefer to discuss this in person rather than over the phone. Would you consider a meeting at my office?"

"Out of the question," was his curt reply. "We will not have personal contact. Period." He paused. "I can't risk face-to-face encounters."

Glenda tipped her head back and carefully chose her words. "My clients up north are barely more than juveniles, and they continue to act like juveniles. They're unable to appreciate the value of your sponsorship, and apparently have no vision beyond the moment they're in." Glenda let the words sink in. "I hate to lose clients, but speaking as your lawyer, you should sever your ties to them and distance yourself."

Mr. White waited to respond so long that Glenda asked, "Are you still there?"

"Yeah. I'm just thinking." The line was silent for several more moments. "You're sure these clients are involved in the newspaper article. No chance it's a coincidence?"

"It's them."

Mr. White sighed. "I've appreciated your assistance over the last couple years. Any chance you'd be interested in moving to another city?"

Glenda smiled. "You're not enough of my business for that to be a viable offer. But I appreciate the compliment."

"Good luck, Ms. Planck. A courier will deliver a payment tomorrow. I assume this discussion and any future questions about me are covered by attorney-client privilege."

"They are."

* * *

Mary was dressed when Floyd arrived at the hospital. The flowers were gathered into boxes and the room had already taken on an air of emptiness. Mary was sitting in the bedside chair reading a magazine.

"It looks like you're anxious to get out of here."

Mary looked up and forced a smile. "It's time." She pushed herself to the edge of the chair. The color drained from her face as Floyd helped her stand.

"You still look pretty pale." She sat on the bed as a nurse walked into the room.

"I've got your discharge orders." The nurse handed a yellow sheet to Mary. "You need to read through these directions. If you develop a fever or start having any bloody discharges you need to contact..."

It was eleven o'clock when Mary stepped into the pickup. Floyd loaded the flowers into the back seat. She was shivering and turned the heat control lever all the way to the top when Floyd got behind the wheel.

Floyd pulled away from the curb. "You're still chilled?"

Mary let out a deep breath. "A little. I think it's the pain."

"Emily said she'd bring lunch. I don't know what she has planned, but she promised to pick up something."

Mary sat quietly. "I'm not very hungry."

"Emily is taking a couple of days of vacation. She's got my cell phone number so we can stay in touch." He paused. "I thought I'd stay home but she was pretty emphatic that she needs to be around and make sure you're really okay."

Mary nodded. "Emily and I will be fine. I won't be much company. All I seem to do is sleep." They rode silently for a few moments. "Don't they need you for the murder investigation?"

"With C.J. out, they'll be short-handed." Floyd thought for a while then added. "On the other hand, if I won the lottery tomorrow someone would take over the investigation. Life would go on at the Pine County Sheriff's Department. I've got about a decade of vacation and comp time built up. How would you feel about taking a trip? We could go someplace warm for a couple of weeks."

Mary looked at Floyd with surprise. "I didn't know you had any interest in traveling. I thought you were excited about fishing. A two-week trip would be right over the opening weekend of the fishing season."

Floyd shrugged. "Priorities change. There'll be lots of fishing openers."

"Maybe a trip would be nice. I've heard that Sedona, Arizona is beautiful. Is it warm there?"

"It's south. It's got to be warmer than northern Minnesota."

* * *

Floyd considered his options. With Mary back home he was distracted from anything work related. Mary's sisters were stepping up to help with the household chores. Trish would be dropping by every few days with a casserole, and Emily had taken a week of vacation to provide Mary with around-the-clock care. With that assurance, Emily shooed Floyd out of the house, handing him a travel coffee cup and telling him to take his anxiety out on the sheriff's department.

He sipped the coffee until it was cold and bitter. He dumped the dregs in the driveway of a gas station and bought a fresh hot refill.

Pam looked up from papers on her desk when Floyd walked in. "Mary doesn't need you at home?"

"Her sister is here for a week. She threw me out." Hearing Floyd, Bailey pushed past Pam's legs and walked across the room. Floyd set his cup aside and bent down to pet the dog. "Is there anything new on Ted Palmquist's death?"

Pam shuffled papers and pulled out several sheets. "I printed the results from the well water testing and here is the property abstract you asked the realtor to email. Laurie Lone Eagle wants to talk to you, and there's a note from Bert Mlankoch, who also asked for you. Harold Wagner wants to talk to C.J."

Floyd picked up the pile of notes. "So, what are you going to do? Sit on your butt and watch me work?"

Pam rolled her eyes. "I'm trying to find Dylan Johnson who seems to have disappeared after his lawyer bailed him out. I think we should talk to him about the body at the hunting shack."

Floyd gave a sly smile. "I suspect he wouldn't like to talk about that at all. I'm sure his lawyer wouldn't like Dylan to talk about the body, or anything else."

The dispatcher paged Floyd and he picked up the nearest phone. "Swenson."

The voice of Tom Parrish, the Assistant Pine County Attorney greeted him. "Ray Santiago called the sheriff from the hospital. Juan wants to talk about the drugs and Tammi Wagner. I'm driving down with a public defender and the sheriff wants you to come along."

Floyd closed his eyes and contemplated the offer. "I don't suppose this is an offer. The sheriff told you I was coming along?"

"That was my interpretation of the conversation. If you're not interested, you can send someone else, or I can go by myself. Either way, it's okay with me."

Floyd took a deep breath. "It's not that I don't like you, Tom. I think professional insulation between the sheriff's department and the county attorney is appropriate." He struggled to couch his words in politically acceptable lies. Floyd's distaste for attorneys, in general, was well known.

Parrish chuckled. "Let's cut the bullshit, I'm not going to invite you to my Christmas party, but you're a good cop. The sheriff wants you along for the questioning. I don't care if you don't want to travel together, or if you just tell me to buzz off. My obligation has been satisfied by informing you of my plans."

Floyd smiled. "I appreciate your candor. Who's the public defender?"

"I called the office this morning. They haven't appointed anyone yet. As soon as I get a name, I'll try to grab that person and we'll run to Robbinsdale."

"Juan isn't represented by the same attorney who sprang Dylan Johnson?"

Parrish chuckled. "She showed up in Juan's hospital room, and Ray Santiago told her to pound sand. Evidently there was quite a discussion about who she represented and why he would want to pay for an attorney to represent Juan."

"Do you have any idea who she really represents?"

"Not really. I think it's interesting that this female barracuda shows up in Pine County and starts throwing around her charm and money with Dylan Johnson, then she drives to the hospital and offers to represent Santiago. There are some big bucks involved here. We haven't even scratched the surface of this operation if all we snare are Dylan Johnson, Juan Santiago, Brady Werther, and Tyler Espe."

Floyd thought for a second. "Tell you what, I'm going to make a few phone calls. Call my cell phone when you decide what time you're going to meet in Robbinsdale. I may leave before that to follow up on some other things, but I'll meet you at Juan Santiago's room."

Parrish chuckled again. "Nothing personal, but I'd hoped you'd have an excuse so we wouldn't have to spend half the day together driving back and forth to the Cities."

Floyd walked to his desk with Bailey on his heels and dialed Laurie Lone Eagle's number at the Bureau of Criminal Apprehension. Bailey crawled under his desk, curled up, and immediately passed gas. Pam was laughing as Laurie answered the call.

"Hi Floyd. Are you calling from a bar? I hear a woman laughing."

"I'm at my desk. That's Pam Conrad laughing about the dog that just crawled under my desk."

"When did you get a police dog?"

"It's a basset hound that belongs to C.J. Jensen. She's in the hospital and Pam's watching Bailey."

"You left a message for me to call."

"Pam updated me earlier. The body you found at the hunting shack was Tammi Wagner. There weren't many details in the *St. Paul Dispatch*, other than unidentified remains had been recovered. I assume the scene was pretty gruesome and her body badly decomposed. Pam said you had someone in custody, but he was released before you found the body."

"The kid who shot her was in jail, but a lawyer from the Cities got him released before we knew about Tammi's death."

"That's bad timing." Laurie paused as she weighed her words before broaching the next topic. The words ran out in a rush. "Pam also told me about Mary. I'm so sorry."

Floyd pushed a pencil across the desk. "Thanks. It's going to be a little tough for a while."

"Floyd, if there's anything that I can do...."

"I appreciate your concern." He struggled to control his voice and had to pause before completing his thought. "We're meeting with the oncologist this week to review options. At this point, it looks promising."

Laurie jumped in to change the topic. "Is there anything I can do to help with the Wagner murder investigation?"

"You are a glutton for punishment, Laurie. Glenda Planck was the lawyer from the Cities who represented Dylan Johnson. She showed up out of the blue, got him sprung within hours, and paid for his bail with a personal check. I'd like to know why and who paid the bill."

"Phew! That could be tough considering attorney-client privilege. She's not likely to volunteer the info, and it'll be tough to crack without her cooperation. I might be able to check who she's represented in the Ramsey, Hennepin, and Carver County courts. Maybe there's some thread to tie her to Dylan. I can't make any guarantees."

After ending Laurie's call, Floyd punched in the numbers to Bert Mlankoch's medical office. The receptionist put him on hold.

Mlankoch was breathless when he answered the phone. "Floyd, caught me between hospital rounds and my first appointment." Floyd could hear papers shuffling while he waited for the doctor to continue.

"Ah, here it is," Mlankoch said. "After you told me about Ted Palmquist's autopsy results, I did some checking. I've diagnosed a couple leukemia cases in the past few years. I spoke with the state epidemiologist's office and shared the information and my concerns about a possible localized leukemia outbreak with them. They checked the Pine County death records against the entire state and found northern Pine County is suffering a significantly higher rate of leukemia deaths. When I looked at my patient records, I have had a few cases, and they've all been east of Hinckley."

Floyd pulled out the report with the chemical analysis of the well water. "We tested the well at the hunting shack where Ted Palmquist had been hanging out and came up with a bunch of chemicals." He read the list to Mlankoch. "Any chance these would be linked to an unusual incidence of leukemia?"

"Absolutely! Benzene, toluene, and other aromatics are notorious carcinogens. I told the epidemiologist we might have a radon or groundwater problem."

Floyd scribbled a note he attached to the analytical report. "Thanks for the lead, Bert. I'll follow up on this."

* * *

Floyd relayed the information about the leukemia outbreak to Laurie Lone Eagle's voicemail and rousted the snoring basset from his feet. Bailey reluctantly left her spot under his desk and walked to Pam. Bailey pushed her feet aside and curled up under the desk. The dog punctuated her displeasure with a release of gas.

Pam recoiled from the smell. "That stink is enough to gag a maggot."

Floyd laughed as he walked out of the bullpen and left the courthouse. Having not heard from the county attorney, he decided to drive to Robbinsdale and eat lunch on the way.

The morning traffic on I-35 was sparse. The truckers were extremely wary of the brown police car, all driving slightly slower than the speed limit as he passed. By the time he crossed the Chisago County line, Floyd was leading a convoy of semi-trucks and cars, all uninterested in passing him. Deciding to relieve the freeway congestion, he turned off at the Harris exit and drove downtown. He took the open parking spot in front of the Kaffe Stuga restaurant and sat in a corner booth where his back was against a wall, and he could watch the customers entering and leaving.

A matronly waitress brought a mug and a pot of coffee. "Are you having anything more than coffee?"

Floyd smiled as she poured. "Is it too early for lunch?"

The waitress shrugged. "People order lunch at ten in the morning and others order breakfast at three in the afternoon. Doesn't make any difference to me or the kitchen." She appraised Floyd for a second. "Should I leave another cup?"

Floyd shook his head. "I'm alone." He looked past her at the pies cooling on the counter. "Have you got a slice of blueberry pie?"

She nodded her head. "You want ice cream on it?"

"Sure."

As she sliced the pie and scooped the ice cream, Floyd listened to the conversations around him. The restaurant wasn't particularly busy, people leaving at the same pace as new patrons arrived. The waitress returned with his pie and a fork. "Is it unusually quiet today?"

She looked around the small dining room. "Not really. Things pick up a little at noon, but most mornings are quiet."

"I'm driving to the Cities, and it just seems life is so frantic there. This seems peaceful."

The waitress checked the patrons, then sat across from him in the booth. "You eat your pie and let me tell you something. I used to live and work in Cottage Grove. That's down on the south edge of the Cities. The new houses they built kept getting bigger. The speed on the freeway kept getting faster. The customers in the restaurant were getting ruder, and the tips got smaller. I moved up here and it was as if I'd moved to a different world. The pay isn't as good, but houses are cheaper, the people are polite, and the pace isn't insane. I like it a lot."

She paused and watched Floyd eat pie. "Cops like you always come in pairs. That's why I asked if I should leave another cup."

Floyd smiled. "I've got an appointment down in the Cities, so I'm alone today."

A pickup parked in front of the café and the guy who climbed out looked like he'd been working on a greasy engine. The waitress got up and patted Floyd's shoulder. "I like having cops stop in. They don't make trouble, they pay their bill, and they tip better than the retirees." She took Floyd's empty plate. "I'll be right back to refill your coffee."

Floyd contemplated the previous few days and the way his life had been turned upside down. It had been terrible to even consider the prospect of life without Mary. Yet, that could be what faced him if she refused further treatment.

C.J.'s assault had also rattled him, and he shivered even thinking about it. With Laura Tomlinson and C.J. as witnesses, they had a solid case against Brady Werther…if the county attorney didn't plea bargain it down to some insignificant charge.

The big mystery was where all the drugs had come from. C.J.'s research had shown the kids had all the chemicals needed to turn decongestants into methamphetamine. But Dylan, Tyler, Juan and Brady weren't the chemists needed to make and package meth, and there had been drugs besides meth thrown out of Santiago's pickup and in the shack. Glenda Planck showing up out of nowhere had to be the link. The question was if they could use her to get to the other players?

The cell phone chirped in Floyd's pocket. He fumbled with it, then punched too many buttons. The call rolled over to voicemail, and he waited a minute for the message icon to appear. "This is Parrish, we're meeting Santiago at two o'clock in Robbinsdale."

Floyd checked his watch. It was barely ten-fifty. He was only an hour from Robbinsdale. The coffee was good, and the café was quiet. He held up his coffee cup and the waitress returned to his booth with a refill in seconds.

She topped off the cup. "How was the pie?"

"It was so good I want another piece. No ice cream this time."

"The sour cream raisin pie is just coming out of the oven. Can you wait for it to cool for a couple minutes?"

Floyd's eyes lit up. "For sour cream raisin pie, I'll wait."

* * *

The door to Juan Santiago's hospital room was open, and the bed nearest the door was empty. Floyd knocked gently on the door frame. The drapes were pulled around the bed farthest from the door and murmured voices came from behind the fabric.

Ray Santiago peeked around the edge. He squinted at Floyd for a second, then recognition registered on his face. He nodded toward the door and led Floyd into the hallway.

Ray was about the same size as Floyd, with a lot of muscle on his upper body from years of hard labor. He seemed smaller and older than he had in the hospital a few days earlier. The stress was taking its toll on him.

Ray stared at the floor. "Listen, Sergeant Swenson, I'm not much of a talker, but I've got a few things I need to get off my chest." Ray looked into the room at the drape shrouding his son's bed. "I was pretty upset at the hospital the other night. I've got a clearer view of a lot of things now and I owe some people apologies." He offered his hand. "I mouthed off and I was wrong. Sorry."

Ray's hand was huge with calluses as hard as horn. Floyd shook it and nodded his head. "I've got some family stuff of my own going on, and sometimes it's hard to stay objective."

Ray took a step toward the room, but Floyd stopped him. "The county attorney is coming to talk about a plea agreement, but I've got a different issue. A stunning blonde attorney showed up in Pine City and bailed Dylan Johnson out of jail. I understand she showed up here too. Do you have any idea who she really represents?"

Ray shook his head. "It's something with the drugs. You can bet on it. I talked to Juan, and he'd never heard of her before she showed up that night. He doesn't know too much about the drug business. He knew there was some link in the Cities, but he doesn't have any names or anything. Dylan and Brady made those contacts. From what I understand, Juan was buying cold medicines that somebody else was cooking into drugs. I guess they were selling a little around town and making a few bucks to party on, then something happened that brought in more and better drugs." Ray paused. "As much as it pains me to say it, Juan was a kid who got dragged in over his head. He's not the brains of the outfit. Juan's just a dumb kid who made some really stupid choices."

Floyd was impressed with Ray's frank assessment of Juan's situation. "I assume you heard about Tammi Wagner."

Ray nodded. "We've talked about it. Juan is willing to make a statement about what happened the night Tammi died. He wasn't there, but the others told him."

Ray escorted Floyd down the hall, farther away from Juan's room. "There were a bunch of them at that shack out east of Hinckley that night. Juan says Tammi had sex with the guys a couple times last fall because she wanted to be in the group. According to Juan, she was really interested in Ted, but Dylan had pressed himself on her a couple of times and she told Juan she wasn't going to go along with it anymore. That night they were experimenting with something Dylan had brewed up and Tammi had a bad reaction to it. When Dylan made a pass at her, she pulled out a gun. Dylan took it away from her. Things got out of hand and Dylan shot her when she got really crazy."

They walked to the empty family waiting area, and Ray fell into a chair. He ran his meaty hand over his face. "What a mess. I know Harold Wagner. How can I look him in the face again after this?"

Santiago stared at the floor for a few seconds and added, "My wife thinks we're at fault too. I figured that keeping food on the table and a roof over our heads was about as much as I was responsible for. Hell, that's all my dad ever provided for us. Now everyone says I need to talk to Juan and see what's on his mind. I don't know what to say to him. I talk to him like a kid, but he's not. I want to beat him within an inch of his life, but my wife says you'd throw me in jail. I feel like throwing him out of the house, and his mother says we need to help him through this." Santiago ran his hand through his short-cropped graying hair. "I'm so confused."

Footsteps clicked down the hall and Floyd looked out the door. Tom Parrish and a younger man, dressed in a cheap suit, were standing at the entrance.

Floyd stood and nodded toward the two men. "I think the lawyers are here."

Floyd and Tom Parrish sat in the waiting room while the public defender met with Juan and Ray Santiago. Floyd repeated Ray's story about Tammi's death. "Of course, it's all second-hand hearsay at this point. I assume the public defender will have some version of this and will agree to let Juan give a statement in return for some immunity. The one thing you have as leverage is that Juan wants to clear his conscience."

Tom Parrish took notes and set the legal pad aside when Floyd finished. "You're right. I can't use your statement because all you have is hearsay. But it's good to know what I can expect out of the negotiation." Parrish crossed his legs and straightened the crease in his suit pants. "How's Deputy Jensen doing?"

"Better. She plans to return to duty as soon as the doctors will let her. She'll have a nasty scar on her thigh from the bullet wound."

Parrish nodded. "I interviewed her. She's one of the most polished deputies you've got. She'll do well on the witness stand when she testifies against Brady Werther. I hope you can keep her around."

"I hope this incident hasn't scarred her psyche. Some cops never recover from being shot. It gets inside their head, and they can't function."

* * *

Floyd arrived home a little after six. The smell of garlic and basil greeted him as he walked into the kitchen. The puppy flew against his legs, and he struggled to keep her from getting pinched as he closed the door.

Emily was washing dishes. "I've got lasagna in the oven, and I'll put the garlic bread in now. We'll eat as soon as you get cleaned up."

Floyd hung his jacket behind the door and slipped off his shoes. "Where's Mary?"

"She's resting in the bedroom. We've had a busy day. We took out all the old pictures and put names on the backs. Then we mounted them in albums."

Floyd walked to the bedroom and knocked gently on the door before entering. Mary was lying on the bed, her eyes opened when he stepped into the room. He removed his holster and set the gun on the top shelf of the closet.

"Emily has lasagna ready as soon as I clean up."

Mary pushed herself up on one elbow. "I'm not very hungry, but I guess I'll come out and be sociable anyway." She eased her legs over the edge of the bed gingerly. "How was your day?"

Floyd walked into the bathroom and washed his hands. "It went okay. I met with Ray and Juan Santiago. They worked out a plea agreement with the county attorney's office. Juan supplied lots of information about Tammi Wagner's death and the drugs we found during the investigation."

Floyd wiped his hands and met Mary at the bedroom door. He pecked her on the cheek. "I hear you had a busy day too. Did it go well, or did you wear yourself out?"

"It went okay," she replied. "I'm pretty tired, but I'm not too sore."

"You went through old pictures. Were you feeling nostalgic?"

Mary shrugged. "It was something to do."

Floyd pulled her close and held her in a hug. "I had pie down in Harris. I got kind of nostalgic too."

"About what?"

"Life in a small town. My job. Us."

"What about us?"

"I want there to be time for us, as much time as we can get. I want to hear what the oncologist has to say, then I'd like you to think about how we can get the most out of our time together."

Mary took a breath and bit her bottom lip. "And if he says there isn't much to be done?"

Floyd pulled her close. "Let's be positive. There are years ahead of us. He'll explain how to make the most of them."

"Okay."

Chapter 23

Laura Tomlinson was watching television and contemplating the prospect of moving to Texas. She'd never been farther south than Minneapolis, so the idea of a move to Texas was exciting. The sheriff's department and the school agreed she was at risk as long as Dylan was free. She was hidden in a foster home and was excused from school until Dylan was in custody.

When the doorbell rang, Laura jumped up to answer it. She was totally surprised when Dylan grabbed her arm and pulled her through the door and down the steps. "C'mon, big mouth. We're going to a funeral."

Laura struggled briefly, but Dylan punched her, and she fell against the pickup fender in shock. He pulled her to the driver's door and pushed her whimpering form across the seat. In less than a minute, they were out of the driveway and racing down the street.

Laura slithered into a heap on the floorboards and cried. "How did you find me?"

Dylan sneered. "Like I said, you're a big mouth. You sent Courtney Harstad a Snapchat telling her where the cops were hiding you. Within an hour it was all over the school."

* * *

Harold Wagner didn't answer his phone. Floyd stepped into the ready room and picked up a newspaper. The obituary said Tammi's funeral started at one in Pine City. He looked at his watch and decided to drive to the service.

The funeral home was empty except for a small gathering in the corner. The casket was closed, and Floyd found himself staring at it. The ghastly sights from the hunting shack played through his head.

He was jarred to reality by the funeral director's voice. "Sergeant Swenson, are you here for the ceremony?"

Floyd looked around the room. "Yes, yes. Is Mr. Wagner here?"

The funeral director pointed out a balding man standing in the corner, talking to two women. The man appeared subdued, but not overcome with grief. He was wearing a light blue sport coat with brown pants. The ill-fitting outfit looked like it might've come from a thrift store.

Floyd made his way across the room. "Excuse me, Mr. Wagner?"

Wagner looked away from his conversation with the women. "Yes?"

Floyd offered his hand. "I'm Floyd Swenson. You left a message for C.J. Jensen, but she's on medical leave. Is there anything that I can do for you?"

Harold Wagner shook his head. "No. I just wanted to make sure Deputy Jensen was okay, and to thank her." He excused himself to the women. He and Floyd stepped away from the rest of the people. "Deputy Jensen seemed like a nice, caring person and I think she's the only one who's tried to find Tammi. I appreciated her effort."

Floyd felt embarrassed that the department hadn't made a more vigorous investigation of Tammi's disappearance at the time it was first reported. It wouldn't have saved Tammi's life, but he wondered if they could have prevented Ted Palmquist's death. His mind moved back to Wagner's comments about his injured deputy "C.J. is a special person. We're lucky to have her."

In the background an organ started to play, and the few people present drifted to the rows of chairs. The service was short, and afterwards a short caravan followed the hearse to the cemetery with Floyd's cruiser following. After a short graveside service, the crowd dispersed as the funeral director's people readied the casket for interment.

Floyd was the last person in line. He shook Harold Wagner's hand. Walking across the cemetery to his car, Floyd tried to decide what to do next. Motion caught his eye as someone slipped behind a tree in the farthest corner of the cemetery. Floyd noted the spot and quickly walked to his cruiser. He started the engine, but instead of driving to the cemetery gate he cramped the wheel and sped toward the tree where he'd seen the motion.

A yellow Ford pickup emerged from behind a lilac hedge, racing for the back gate. Two people were visible inside the cab. Floyd thought he recognized Dylan Johnson as the driver. He steered the cruiser down a narrow, intersecting cemetery driveway to block the pickup's path.

Floyd switched his radio to the state-wide frequency. "Pine County is in pursuit of a yellow Ford pickup with a homicide suspect. South of Pine City near the cemetery."

Floyd turned when he got to the gate and accelerated until he caught up to the pickup. He clipped the pickup's bumper as it made the corner. Dylan glared at Floyd in the rear-view mirror. Laura Tomlinson was huddled against the passenger door. She looked at Floyd through the rear window with terror on her face.

The pickup raced down the gravel road behind the cemetery. Laura kept looking out the back window and appeared to be alternately kicking and beating Dylan. Dylan occasionally swung a fist at Laura, causing her to cower against the passenger door.

Floyd accelerated hard in the pickup's dust plume. He quickly closed the gap between the vehicles. He knew his car could outmaneuver Dylan's pickup, and Floyd was certain his driving skills would have Dylan off the road within a few miles.

The pickup slowed as it approached Highway 61 and Floyd assessed the risk of chasing it through downtown Pine City. He thought about Laura's fear that Dylan was going to kill her and Juan Santiago's allegation that Dylan was the person who shot Tammi Wagner in the head.

Floyd accelerated hard and pulled alongside the pickup, surprising Dylan by suddenly appearing at his shoulder. Dylan jerked the steering wheel, throwing the pickup against the police car. Floyd steered hard into the pickup, forcing it into a picket fence. Dylan careened off the fence and turned onto old Highway 61, toward downtown Pine City.

As the pickup swerved back and forth through traffic, Floyd saw Laura thrown against the passenger door and then she disappeared from view. Crossing the river, the highway was now empty except for their two vehicles.

"I'm now northbound on Highway 61. Confirm Dylan Johnson as the driver. He has a hostage." Floyd dropped the mic on the floor as swerved to miss a car pulling onto the highway from a crossroad.

The dispatcher's voice crackled over the radio. "I've got Deputy Maki behind you and a state trooper coming from the north on I-35. He's blocking the road before the interstate entrance ramp."

Floyd's cell phone trilled as he passed the Beroun freeway exit. Concentrating on the pickup, the phone's ring annoyed him. He pulled it off his belt and dropped it onto the seat as he passed the county garbage transfer station. The state trooper was parked broadside across the road ahead of the pickup, partially blocking the two-lane roadway. Floyd eased off the gas and the pickup slowed while Dylan considered his options.

The pickup swerved hard to the right, just missing the trooper's car, but running over stop sticks deployed to deflate his tires. Laura popped into view, pulling on the steering wheel. The pickup bounced over the gravel shoulder, crashing into the ditch. The two occupants pitched forward violently as the pickup slammed into a tree.

Steam rose from the hood as a cloud of dust enveloped the pickup. Both heads had disappeared from sight by the time the dust cleared.

Floyd followed the pickup, locked the brakes and skidded to a stop on the shoulder, blocking the back of the pickup. Jim Lahti, the state trooper, was out of his cruiser and running past Floyd. He held his gun next to his leg, ready for a confrontation.

The driver's door of the pickup creaked open, and Dylan stumbled from the cab. He wobbled and stared numbly at Jim Lahti who froze halfway down the ditch. Dylan's face was a mass of blood. His nose had been flattened and he had deep cuts under his eyes and on his forehead. Blood dripped from his chin. He staggered to the bed of the pickup and rested against it. He turned toward the trooper with a pistol in his hand.

"Drop the gun!" Lahti raised his weapon and looked frantically for some cover to hide behind. He backed slowly until he was behind the fender of Floyd's cruiser. He crouched and yelled again, "Drop the gun!"

Floyd circled behind his car, approaching the passenger side of the pickup. He ducked behind the pickup and drew his pistol. He popped up, aimed his weapon across the pickup bed, and yelled, "Drop the gun!"

The occupants of cars stopped by the trooper's roadblock scrambled for cover.

Dylan was unaware of Floyd until he heard the command. He spun toward Floyd's voice, wiping at the blood in his eyes and trying to clear his vision. "You're the sonofabitch who tried to break my finger!" Dylan raised the gun with both his hands and rested it on the pickup bed.

Floyd spoke softly, but with evident threat. "Drop the gun, Dylan. If you point it at me, I'll shoot."

Dylan hesitated. "Fuck you. You're going to shoot me anyway."

Jim Lahti, the state trooper, trotted toward the pickup, his gun held against his leg. "Drop the gun and we'll get you medical help. You're injured."

Lahti's voice distracted Dylan for a moment. He wiped his free hand across his face, then hesitated, staring at the blood. More sirens wailed nearby.

Though obviously impaired, Dylan pointed his gun ominously toward Floyd, his hand wavering from loss of blood or a concussion.

"Put it down Dylan. Don't make it worse."

Dylan turned toward Floyd, who ducked for cover behind the fender. "WHAM!" The pickup shuddered as the .357 magnum hollow-point slammed into the fender well left of Floyd, punching a thumb-sized hole in the metal. The noise reverberated and echoed off the trees.

Dylan reeled from the recoil of the big magnum. When he recovered control of the heavy gun, he struggled to pull the hammer back and bring the weapon around for another shot.

"Drop the gun. You need an ambulance." Lahti pleaded, as Floyd took a furtive peek over the pickup bed. Dylan's head was hanging down and he wobbled dangerously. After a second, Dylan lifted his head and swung the gun toward Floyd.

The trooper aligned Dylan's torso in his sights. and shouted another warning. Seeing the muzzle swing toward Floyd, and aware of the dozen people now stranded in their cars behind his roadblock, Lahti fired three shots.

Dylan slumped. The gun fell to the ground as he slid down the pickup fender.

Jim Lahti raced across the ditch and kicked the gun aside. He knelt beside Dylan. "He's still alive." Blood ran from three holes in the boy's chest and foamy blood gurgled in his mouth.

Speaking to the mic on his shoulder, Lahti said, "This is the state patrol calling for an ambulance at I-35 and Highway 23 intersection. We have a shooting victim."

Wailing sirens grew closer as Floyd opened the pickup cab. Laura was crammed under the dashboard. Her eyes were open, but she was dazed and bloody. "Are you okay?"

The girl moaned. There was a huge gash on her forehead and her lower lip was sliced and hanging. "Stay still, we've got an ambulance on the way."

When Floyd stepped out of the truck, Lahti had a first-aid kit open and was putting on a pair of latex gloves. He looked up at Floyd. "I don't like the look of the frothing blood in the kid's mouth. I think he's got a punctured lung." On cue, Dylan coughed spraying pink foam.

Pam's cruiser screeched to a stop next to Floyd's car. She raced to Floyd's side. "Why didn't you answer your phone?" She was breathless as she looked at the grisly scene.

Floyd looked at Pam with befuddlement. "Call? I…was…" Floyd pointed numbly at the pickup. "Laura's hurt bad. We need an ambulance." A second sheriff's car squealed to a stop, followed by another state trooper who sped to the scene from I-35.

"Emily called dispatch. Mary's in the emergency room. C'mon." Pam grabbed Floyd and dragged him into her cruiser. She started the engine and floored the gas pedal. The tires screamed as they accelerated toward the Sandstone hospital. "Mary's having trouble breathing. An ambulance took her to hospital."

* * *

Pam drove Floyd to the hospital with her car's siren screaming. She parked in an ambulance stall and left the lights flashing as they ran inside.

The emergency room desk was empty, so they rushed back to the exam rooms. Pam hung back while Floyd knocked gently on the only closed door. After a few seconds, a nurse emerged from the room.

"It appears Mary has an embolism." Annette Larson, the nursing supervisor, was apparently filling in for a nurse who was on break. Having dealt with a variety of emergencies at the hospital for over two years, Pam and Floyd both knew Annette and trusted her. She was often the first person to deal with emergencies, covering until the on-call doctor arrived. Her face was somber, and she looked tired. She pushed back a lock of blonde hair that had slipped loose.

Through the partially open door they heard Bert Mlankoch. He spoke to Mary, who was lying on the exam table, while Bert read a strip of EKG tracing. Emily was standing at Mary's side and holding her hand. Mary looked past them all and gave Floyd a weak smile. Mary's breathing was labored.

Floyd smiled at Mary and then looked back to Annette. "What's an embolism?"

Annette looked back over her shoulder. "It's a clot that breaks loose and blocks a blood vessel." She kept her voice just above a whisper.

Floyd nodded. "Like a stroke."

Annette nodded. "Right. Usually, a stroke is when the clot blocks a blood vessel in the brain. This one is in Mary's lung. It's a pulmonary embolism. They're very dangerous and very painful." She stepped aside and motioned for Pam and Floyd to come into the exam room.

Floyd moved to Emily's side and patted Mary's hand. "Are you in pain?"

Mary shook her head. "They gave me something for pain. I can't catch my breath." A small green tube ran under her nose, supplementing her oxygen.

Floyd looked up at Dr. Mlankoch. "What do we do?"

Mlankoch set the EKG trace aside and answered, "Annette called for a helicopter, and I spoke to the pulmonary specialist at North Memorial a few minutes ago. He suggested a clot-dissolving medication and it's already attacking the embolism. There's not much else to do here except give her oxygen and monitor her vital signs until the helicopter arrives." He patted Mary's shoulder.

Floyd leaned down and kissed Mary softly on the forehead. She gave him a pained smile. "I get to ride in a helicopter," she whispered.

The ambulance roared up outside, and they heard the clatter of the gurney being extracted from the back. Pam peeked out of the door as two paramedics pushed Laura Tomlinson down the hall. "Move the cop car out of the ambulance bay! There's another ambulance en route." they yelled down the hallway.

Pam rushed out the door, keys in hand. Floyd left the exam room and followed the paramedics in the hall. "How is Laura?" One paramedic was pushing the gurney while the second held an IV bag high.

Floyd caught a glimpse of the girl's face as they passed. Her eyes were shut and her face a mass of bruises and dark blood. The torn lip looked terrible, and it jiggled as the gurney bounced as the paramedics wheeled past. "Not good."

Floyd, Emily, and Pam sat in visitor's chairs and listened to the clattering gurneys, panicked EMTs, and hushed conversations down the hallway.

The commotion continued until the sound of a helicopter drowned out the voices. Dr. Mlankoch rushed into the waiting room and pulled Floyd aside. "We are putting Dylan on this helicopter. Mary's stable and can wait."

Floyd glared at him. "Dylan is a dope dealing murderer. You want to put him ahead of Mary?"

"Mary's stable, Floyd. It might mean the difference between life and death for Dylan."

"What about Laura?"

"Her injuries are superficial. She's going to Duluth in an ambulance. She needs a plastic surgeon more than anything else."

Floyd rejoined Pam and Emily in the waiting area. Pam overheard the triage discussion with the doctor and her nod to Floyd signaled her understanding of the changing plan. Emily was agitated. "What's going on, Floyd? Why isn't the helicopter taking Mary?"

"Mary's stable, and a guy with severe injuries needs the helicopter right now."

"What? Aren't you going to stop them?" Emily was on her feet and Floyd grabbed her arm.

"I don't like it either, but the doctor has to assess who's in greater danger. There's another helicopter on the way."

Emily's face turned red but held her tongue until she sat down. "If something happens to Mary…"

Bert Mlankoch stepped into the waiting room. "The other helicopter just passed over Rush City and will be here in five minutes. We've got the girl stabilized and she'll be on the way to Duluth in a minute."

Emily was on her feet and in the doctor's face. "If something happens to my sister…"

Floyd and Pam stood and guided Emily to the far corner of the visitor's area as the doctor returned to his patients. Floyd took a deep breath. "Doc Mlankoch said the drugs are dissolving Mary's clot. She's out of danger and there was a gunshot victim who needed to be transported first."

"Do you trust him?" Emily asked.

Pam put her hand on Emily's arm. "Yes. If Mary was in danger, she would've been on the first helicopter."

The second helicopter roared outside the hospital, its rotor wash causing dust devils which raced past the waiting room windows. Within a minute, the second air crew pushed a gurney down the hallway and Annette waved them into Mary's room.

Floyd followed them into Mary's room. "Can I ride along?"

A jump-suited male nurse quickly assessed the situation. "I'm afraid we don't have space for passengers. But the nurse radioed us and said she's stabilized. There shouldn't be any problem with you driving down to meet us."

The helicopter crew lifted Mary from the bed to the gurney and strapped her down. As they transferred the IV bag, Floyd reached over and touched Mary's hand. Her eyes flickered. She squeezed his hand and whispered. "It's getting better."

Floyd released her hand and followed the flight crew to the door, watching them load Mary into the back of the helicopter. They lifted off amid swirling dust.

Pam nodded toward the parking lot. "C'mon, you two are getting a police escort to the hospital."

Emily dug in her purse for her cell phone. "Wait! We've got to call Trish to let her know what's going on. Which hospital are they taking Mary to, is it North Memorial?"

A heavyset woman, with tear-streaked cheeks elbowed past Emily and Floyd. Following her was deputy Kerm Rajacich. They watched the woman speak with Annette Larson.

Rajacich stopped by Pam, Emily, and Floyd at the door. "That's Wanda Dreyer, Dylan Johnson's mother."

They watched the exchange between the nurse and Dylan's mother, then Dreyer joined the group of deputies.

"I can't deal with this," the woman sobbed. "First I lost Art, and now Dylan's been in a terrible accident."

The deputies exchanged a look of revelation. "You're Art Johnson's wife?" Floyd asked.

The woman blew her nose into a bandana. "Yes."

"Did your husband own the hunting shack where Tammi Wagner's body was found?"

"Yes," the woman replied. "He bought it a few years ago so he and Dylan would have a place to deer hunt. It's all such a mess. If it weren't for my brother taking Dylan under his wing I couldn't have coped."

A BMW raced up to the entrance and a twenty-something man ran to the lobby. Wanda Dreyer looked up with relief. She reached for him and buried her face into his shoulder.

"Chuck," Wanda sobbed, "they put Dylan in a helicopter and took him to Robbinsdale."

The man was starkly thin and wore blue jeans and a black leather vest over a white t-shirt. "I'm sure he'll be okay, Wanda." He gave the uniformed officers a glare. "Despite being hounded by these cops."

Chuck Dreyer guided his sister through the door and into the BMW. Floyd, Emily and Rajacich followed. As Emily climbed into the back seat of Pam's cruiser, Floyd leaned close to Kerm Rajacich.

"Run a check on Chuck Dreyer," Floyd said. "Dylan's mother says he's been a replacement for Dylan's father, but I don't like his looks." As an afterthought, Floyd added, "Check his phone records to see if he's spoken with a lawyer named Glenda Planck."

* * *

When Floyd, Pam, and Emily arrived at North Memorial, Mary had already been seen by a pulmonologist and was getting additional clot-busting drugs. Floyd spoke with the head nurse while Pam and Emily went to Mary's room.

"Mary, how are you?"

Mary opened her eyes and nodded to Emily. "It's a lot better. I can breathe again." Floyd came in behind them and patted Mary's shoulder. She added, "The doctor says Emily's quick call to 911 really saved me a lot of problems. The pulmonologist said the Sandstone clot treatment saved me from permanent lung damage."

Emily fidgeted with her purse clasp, then looked at Floyd. "Mary's shortness of breath scared the hell out of me. She tried to talk me into driving her to the clinic, but I insisted on calling the ambulance. It's nice to know I did the right thing."

Mary looked very tired. "Why don't you guys leave and let me sleep."

After saying goodbye, Emily and Pam went to the family waiting area while Floyd spoke to someone at the nurse station.

Emily dropped into an overstuffed chair and announced, "I'm exhausted."

Floyd joined them and sat across from Emily and rubbed his face with his hands. "It's been a long day." He turned to Pam. "I talked to the emergency room. Dylan Johnson didn't make it. The flight crew was giving him CPR when they arrived, and they couldn't get his heart started again."

Emily gasped. "Oh my! I didn't want him to get the helicopter before Mary. I feel terrible."

Trish stepped into the waiting room as Emily broke into tears. Fear gripped her as she rushed to Floyd and asked, "Is Mary okay?"

"She's doing well. We just heard that a suspect we were chasing didn't fare as well."

Trish sat in one of the vinyl-covered chairs in the waiting room. "So, what's up? Emily just said you were on the way, and I should meet you here. The visitor's desk didn't even know Mary was in the hospital when I first arrived."

Emily blurted out, "Mary had an embolism, but she's doing okay." She stood and took her sister by the hand. "She's sleepy, but we can stick our heads in to check on her."

* * *

Pam delivered Floyd home with Emily and Trish rotating hospital shifts watching Mary. The puppy tugged at its leash and yelped as Pam pulled in the driveway. Pam shut off the engine and reached for the door handle. "I'm fine, Pam. Go home to your husband and baby. I'll call Trish and let her know I'm home."

"Nope, I told the sheriff I'd stay with you until everything was under control. I'm walking you to the door."

Floyd reached down, unhooking the puppy from the leash as she tugged at his pants cuff. Floyd picked her up, letting her lick his face and nip at his ear lobe while Pam watched.

"Crap!" Pam said, putting her hand on Floyd's arm. "Bailey's still tied to my desk in Pine City! I've got to run."

Pam looked back before pulling onto the road. Floyd was sitting on the steps with his hands over his face, the puppy tugging at his elbow. Tears ran between his fingers. She hesitated but decided not to intrude on his moment of relief.

* * *

John Sepanen cornered the county attorney Tom Parrish in the courthouse hallway. "Any loose ends we need to tie up on the Tammi Wagner murder and the drug charges?"

Parrish shook his head, "No. I'm sorry we plea bargained away the cases against Juan Santiago and Laura Tomlinson in an effort to prosecute Dylan Johnson for the Wagner murder. It seemed like the thing to do when Dylan was alive. Now that Dylan's dead, we're left with only Tyler Espe and

Brady Werther, who were obviously lesser characters in this whole mess. We have a solid drug case against Brady, and we've got him for assaulting C.J. Jensen. I'm sure he'll plead guilty to the assault if we drop the drug charges. I can't imagine a lawyer wanting to stand in front of a jury and explain that his client didn't shoot a deputy when we have both the deputy and an eyewitness who will identify him and testify that he shot her."

Sepanen pulled out a cigar and rolled it in his fingers while he thought. He stuffed it into his mouth and clenched the end in his teeth. "Who hired the lawyer that sprang Dylan Johnson, and put up the bail money?"

Parrish shook his head. "We can ask, but the attorney doesn't have to tell us."

Sepanen sighed. "Looks like someone got away with something."

Parrish cracked a smile. "The system has holes."

Sepanen shook his head. "You should have that carved on your headstone."

Chapter 24

Gravel crunched in the driveway as Floyd removed the hay covering Mary's rose bushes. He grabbed the puppy and held her to his chest while a gray car with a state logo parked next to his pickup. Laurie Lone Eagle stepped out of the car and Floyd set the puppy down. The puppy raced round Laurie's ankles with unending energy after a week on her puppy chow diet.

"Who's your new friend?" Laurie, almost a foot shorter than Floyd, wore her hair cut into a professional, short style that accentuated her round face and Native American features. Floyd removed his gardening gloves and walked to Laurie, greeting his friend and former associate with a hug.

Nipping at their feet as they hugged, the pup circled around before giving up and making a puddle in the grass at the driveway's edge. They watched and smiled. "She just showed up one day. Nobody ever came to claim her. So…"

"How's Mary doing?" Laurie asked.

Floyd kicked at a rock in the driveway with his toe. "She's doing really well. Mary's sisters are taking turns staying with us. I get in the way."

"Is she on chemo or radiation?"

"She had a blood clot scare, but that's resolved and isn't a long-term concern. We're talking to the oncologist again this week. He wants a PET scan to see if the cancer's spread anywhere before he decides how to proceed."

"I'm glad she's following up and moving ahead with a plan." Laurie jammed her hands into her pants pockets and leaned against the fender of her car. "I may have an answer about the polluted well at the hunting shack. The Army ammunition plant generated thousands of gallons of waste solvents during World War II. Lots of it was dumped onto the ground or sealed in steel drums that were buried on the arsenal property. It's rumored waste was dumped in several other places too, but the records only show outgoing loads, but not the destinations. The Pollution Control Agency has received numerous anecdotal reports of drum dumping on leased lands in northern Minnesota for decades. They've discounted a lot of the tips as hearsay generated by anti-government groups. There are also rumors about radioactive waste dumps and wolves that glow in the dark.

"The PCA found a Hinckley guy whose father owned a disposal business and dump site up until the late 1950's. Things were pretty loose back then, and his records are terrible. He took a lot of the Army waste and buried hundreds of barrels without knowing they contained toluene, trichloroethane, and benzene. The same thing happened in Arden Hills and all the barrels are now leaking and polluting wells in Arden Hills and North Oaks. I checked the property abstract you faxed to me. The waste disposal guy owned the property where the hunting shack is located before he subdivided the land into forty-acre hunting parcels."

Floyd grimaced. "So, the kids were drinking water out of a polluted well. What happens now?"

"The PCA is lining up a backhoe and an assessment team as we speak. If all the buried drums are now leaking, we may be talking about thousands of gallons of carcinogens in the ground and water table. It'll probably be a superfund clean-up site."

Floyd shook his head. "We live such a sheltered existence here. Is this going to poison all the wells in the county?"

Laurie shrugged. "It depends on how fast the aquifer is moving and which direction it flows. Based on the cancer reporting collected by the state epidemiologist, it appears the plume of contamination is spreading slowly south. The PCA toxicologist says the concentration of carcinogens in the water will remain low because the chemicals are only minimally soluble in water. But the tissue samples from Tammi Wagner's body were sky high. I talked to a guy at the EPA, and he says the fatty tissues in Tammi's body stripped the solvents out of the ground and concentrated them in her body."

"Like she was embalmed." Floyd nodded. "I s'pose that's why there was so little decomposition of the body."

"Exactly," Laurie replied. "The shack is on the edge of the dump site and the soil around it is loaded with chemicals. Tammi's body didn't decompose in the contaminated soil."

"Why didn't all the stoners get leukemia, like Ted Palmquist?"

"Ted got the biggest dose of chemicals because he was a brittle diabetic. He was probably thirsty all the time and drank a lot of water from the contaminated well. Just being near the chemicals isn't enough to cause leukemia. You have to either eat, drink or inhale the carcinogens to get enough in your body to cause problems."

Floyd looked impressed. "Good detective work, Inspector Lone Eagle. How about the previous owners, did they all really die?" They watched the puppy attack an unopened dandelion flower.

Laurie nodded. "The state epidemiologist confirmed that at least half of the previous owners of the subdivided hunting land died from leukemia. That's the most common disease associated with benzene and toluene exposure. He says ingesting those aromatic hydrocarbons is often deadly. You can bet that there will be a hell of a lawsuit out of this. Of course, everyone who coordinated the disposal back in the 40's is dead as is the guy who accepted and buried the barrels. I'm sure the lawyers will find someone to sue."

Floyd gave a phony laugh. "Great. That does me a lot of good."

Laurie changed the subject. "What happened to the kids who killed Tammi Wagner?"

Floyd shook his head. "Juan Santiago's public defender negotiated a plea. Juan agreed to testify in return for having the felony charges dropped. He corroborated the story about Dylan shooting Tammi and the whole scheme with the methamphetamine. The kids got the recipe for synthesizing meth on the internet. They stole the chemicals and lab equipment from the school but didn't know enough about the chemistry to actually make the right stuff. Juan said Dylan found some guy in the Cities who could do the chemistry if they supplied the materials. Together they had quite an operation running.

"Juan set Dylan up as the fall guy. Then Dylan died. Tyler Espe will probably get off with some minor drug charges. Brady Werther is in the worst situation with drug and assault charges pending. He's screaming that he can implicate their partner in the Cities, but all he had is a disconnected phone number and a fictitious name Dylan gave him. We have the DEA following various leads, but they all come to dead ends. So, it looks like Brady takes the fall."

Laurie's eyes sparkled and her lips curled into a smirk. "Do you remember asking Pam Conrad to check on Wanda Dreyer's brother?" Laurie asked, nonchalantly. "It turns out that Chuck Dreyer lives in a really big house in Minneapolis, with fancy cars and no visible means of support. I called the DEA and asked about him. After about four phone calls my director got a call saying the DEA has been tracking him as a suspect in a major methamphetamine ring for a few months and warned my boss to have me back off."

Floyd blew out a resigned sigh.

Laurie rolled her eyes. "I had a discussion with the director and explained your case. He made a call to the U.S. attorney and dangled the bait of Dreyer's involvement in a homicide case. After that discussion and armed with the information from your case and the DEA, I got a search warrant and pulled all the phone records for

Dreyer's house and cell phone. His home phone and primary cell phone were clean, but his second cell phone made and received several calls to Glenda Planck. It also had incoming and outgoing calls to Tyler Espe's house. We went to the Minneapolis drug task force and discussed your cases and our suspicions. They were setting up surveillance when they saw him loading suitcases into the trunk of his car. He had his passport and a one-way first-class ticket in his pocket for Mazatlán."

Floyd stared in amazement. "So, he hired the lawyer to represent the kids?"

"It fits. Uncle Chuck takes troubled Dylan under his wing and sets him up in the family business."

"Too many coincidences for it not to be true. I assume it will be hard to prove."

"The DEA and Minneapolis Police are searching. I guess we'll see what they can uncover." Changing topics Laurie asked, "What happened to Laura Tomlinson?"

"Because of Laura's cooperation and her injuries in the car accident, the county attorney doesn't plan to press charges. She's a first-time juvenile offender, so even if she'd been convicted, she wouldn't have been imprisoned. Last I heard, her mother had their house up for sale and they are moving somewhere warm."

"C.J.'s recovering?"

Floyd chuckled. "C.J.'s mother moved into her apartment and is taking care of her. C.J. called the sheriff and asked if there was *anything* she could do at the office."

"You said a dispatcher screwed up. Is that how C.J. ended up handcuffed to her car for several hours? What happened to the dispatcher?"

"The sheriff fired her. The union filed a grievance to get her reinstated with back pay but I don't see that happening. She spent hours on her phone playing games, and she blew off Eddie Paulson's call reporting C.J. missing. The county attorney says we have sufficient evidence of incompetence and dereliction of duty to make the firing stick."

"What led all these teens to this mess anyway?" Laurie asked. "I mean, beer has been the drug of choice up here for years."

Floyd stared at the puppy as she chewed on one of his old boots. "All of these teens lived in dysfunctional families and the drugs were cheap and readily available to them." Floyd paused. "All the carcinogens came from the Army?"

"My EPA contact called them a toxic legacy from the second world war. They're cleaning chemicals that were drummed up and buried in dumps. Over time, the sealed drums broke open or rusted through and the chemicals leached into the water table."

Floyd sighed. "Maybe I'm just old and tired, or maybe I'm just looking at the worst side of everything, but it really stinks that someone thought dumping their toxic chemicals in a swamp was a good idea."

"It was a different time, and the war effort took precedence over everything." Laurie glanced at her watch. "I've got to run. Let me know if there is anything I can do."

Floyd smiled. "Make the world a safer place."

Laurie hugged him and stepped back. "The tone of your voice makes me think you're saying goodbye. Have you submitted your retirement papers?"

Floyd shrugged and turned away.

* * *

Pam was in the upstairs nursery changing Luke when she heard a knock on the front door. She knew Travis was downstairs unloading boxes, so she let him answer the door. Hearing Floyd's voice, she walked downstairs with the baby. Floyd and Mary were standing in the living room amid empty boxes and packing material. Travis was clearing the couch and a chair when Pam walked in.

Mary approached Pam and put her arms out. "Can I hold Luke?"

"Of course!" Pam carefully passed the infant to Mary who cooed and brushed his cheek with her finger.

Floyd and Travis sat on the couch, talking quietly. When Pam looked their way, Floyd stood and handed her a bag. Inside was an Easter basket, topped with a giant chocolate rabbit. "Mary said little Luke wouldn't be interested in a chocolate bunny, but I figured his mom might take care of it for him."

Pam wrapped him in a hug. "Thank you!" She was distracted by Mary clearing her throat. "What?"

Floyd sat and folded his hands. "Last week was Palm Sunday. The sermon was about renewal and new beginnings. Mary and I walked out to the cemetery, to Ginny's grave, and we had a talk." Floyd paused, trying to form the words. "I'm retiring."

Pam sat next to him in disbelief. "But…"

He put up his hand. "It's past time for me to move on." He looked up at Mary. "I went to the cemetery and told Ginny that Mary and I were getting married and…I wasn't struck by lightning, so I guess that's a sign from Ginny that it's okay."

Pam hugged him. "But we need you. I need you."

"I'm only a phone call away, and you know how much I enjoy a cup of coffee."

"That's not the same."

"It's time for you to step up. You're ready for a bigger role."

"When are you going to tell the sheriff?"

"We stopped at the office on the way here. He shook my hand and we talked about how I thought things might work when I'm gone. We agreed that you're not physically ready to go on patrol. Instead of pushing papers around, like you were supposed to when you came back from maternity leave; he's making you a full-time investigator."

"What? Who's going to…"

"C.J. has proven herself. She's going to be the new patrol sergeant. John's going to hire a rookie to replace you."

Pam was shaken. "I'm not ready to be an investigator!"

"You've been ready longer than I've been willing to admit. I've been blocking your growth by not stepping aside. It's your time."

Pam looked at Travis who was smiling like he'd known what Floyd was going to say.

Luke started to cry. "I think he wants his mommy." Mary handed the baby to Pam. "If we hang around any longer, I'm afraid Travis will expect us to help move furniture."

Travis and Pam watched their visitors walk down the sidewalk from their front window. Tears streamed down Pam's face and Travis had his arm over her shoulder. "I'm not ready for this. I'm a newlywed with a baby and…"

Travis pulled her close. "You've never been better prepared for anything in your life."

Pam looked at Luke, squirming in her arms. "I'll miss Floyd and his politically incorrect comments."

"Like he said, he's only a phone call away. You're going to need his guidance and counsel more than ever before."

Handing off Luke, Pam reached for a box of tissues with tears streaming down her face. "This is going to be a mess. Floyd's leaving, I've got new responsibilities, Luke needs his mommy, and I break into tears about twice a day."

Travis pulled her close. "You're stronger than you realize. You'll get through this."

The knock on the door interrupted them. Travis opened it to a woman trying to control a basset hound. Her grip on the leash slipped and the hound raced across the living room to Pam.

Travis was ready to lunge after the dog, but Pam put her hand down. "Bailey, you came to visit!"

Travis put out his hand to the woman. "How are you, C.J.?"

"I'm good. I hope this isn't a bad time."

He stepped back and gestured for C.J. to come in. "Pam said Bailey has added an element of humor to the office."

Pam petted Bailey, then gently lowered Luke so Bailey could sniff him, her tail wagging happily. Luke grabbed a floppy ear and Bailey endured the pulling with her tail wagging.

Travis watched Pam, Luke, and the dog. He leaned close to C.J. and said, "You look like you lost a boxing match, and I detected a bit of a limp. How's your recovery?"

"My bruises are turning from blue to yellow and green. The good news is that the bullet scar is healing nicely. The bad news is that I'll never work as a bikini model again."

Ignoring C.J.'s attempted humor, Travis said, "Hurts like hell to get shot."

C.J. turned to Travis and studied his face. "You've been shot?"

Travis focused on Pam, Luke and the dog while he answered. "One of my many stops in scenic Iraq was a field hospital." He turned to C.J. "Not all the scars are physical. I hope you've got a good therapist to help you cope with the PTSD."

"The sheriff gave me a number to call. I haven't..."

"Make the call. I spent a lot of hours talking to an Army psychiatrist. It helped me get my head straight."

Nodding, C.J. watched Bailey struggle and finally get onto the couch. The dog nestled under Pam's arm, then turned and planted her butt against Pam's hip, immediately passing gas. Pam laughed and waved, trying to disperse the smell.

Travis turned when he sensed another presence at the door. Eddie Paulson put out his hand. "I'm C.J.'s home care aide."

Travis cocked his head. "That's quite a career change from the medical examiner's office."

"I took some vacation to help C.J. while she recovered."

C.J. sat next to Bailey and put her arms out. "Can I hold Luke?"

Pam passed the baby over the dog and C.J. accepted him gently. Bailey watched, not sure why her owner was handling the baby, but not interfering.

"Eddie's staying with you?" Pam whispered.

C.J. never looked up from the baby but nodded slightly. "My mom went home yesterday, and Eddie demanded that I let him care for me."

"That was sweet."

"He sleeps on the couch but rushes in every time he hears me roll over, moan, or snort."

Pam looked skeptical. "Eddie's sleeping on your couch?"

"I've got a king-sized bed and I told him to sleep with me," C.J. whispered, "but he's afraid he'll roll over and hurt me."

Pam watched Eddie and Travis talking in hushed tones. She imagined they were comparing their military credentials. "Eddie's an absolute gentleman. He won't touch you unless you initiate the contact."

Blushing, C.J. said, "Eddie said he didn't want to mess up our friendship by doing something stupid. He's probably right. I'm still grieving and, well, I'm probably not ready to move on." She hesitated, then leaned across the dog and passed Luke back to Pam. "But I miss the companionship and intimacy. I'd forgotten how special simple things are, like having a discussion over a meal."

Pam accepted Luke back and made sure the men weren't listening. "I waited a long time to find Travis. Even then, I didn't rush to the altar. I knew Travis was my best friend before I pressured him into proposing to me."

"You did what?"

Bailey punctuated C.J.'s question by passing gas.

Luke squirmed when the smell hit his nose. Pam laughed and stood. "Let's brew coffee. I'll tell you about the Prince Charming proposal."

Eddie watched the women walk to the kitchen with Bailey at their heels.

Reading Eddie's expression, Travis said, "You're in love with C.J."

Eddie continued to watch the kitchen. "Am I that transparent?"

"I have that look when I watch Pam walk away."

Staring at the floor, Eddie shook his head. "I'm too old, too wounded, and too cynical to be in a relationship. I'll be her friend as long as she lets me, but we'll never be more than that. She's still grieving, and I understand that process takes time."

Travis took a deep breath and blew it out. "You're a kind, patient friend. That's rare."

Eddie looked at him. "That's what C.J. needs right now."

Travis nodded toward the kitchen. "I smell coffee. Let's have a cup."

"Pam said something to C.J. about a Prince Charming proposal."

Travis laughed and steered Eddie toward the kitchen. "Pam had her dream proposal scripted. I was ordered to show up with a ring and take her out for dinner. She said if I couldn't do that, I should leave her apartment key in the dish by the door and never look back. I couldn't find a jeweler anywhere, so I called Floyd..."

The End

Dean Hovey is the award-winning and best-selling author of three mystery series. He uses his scientific background, travel, and life experience to create engaging characters, gripping storylines, and memorable locations. One reviewer said Dean creates characters he'd like to invite over for a beer and discussion.

Dean and his wife split their year between northern Minnesota and Arizona.